Passion
Becomes Her

Also by Shirlee Busbee

Scandal Becomes Her

Seduction Becomes Her

Surrender Becomes Her

Passion Becomes Her

SHIRLEE BUSBEE

ZEBRA BOOKS
KENSINGTON PUBLISHING CORP.
www.kensingtonbooks.com

ZEBRA BOOKS are published by

Kensington Publishing Corp.
119 West 40th Street
New York, NY 10018

All Kensington titles, imprints, and distributed lines are available at special quantity discounts for bulk purchases for sales promotion, premiums, fund-raising, educational, or institutional use.

Special book excerpts or customized printings can also be created to fit specific needs. For details, write or phone the office of the Kensington Special Sales Manager: Kensington Publishing Corp., 119 West 40th Street, New York, NY 10018. Attn. Special Sales Department. Phone: 1-800-221-2647.

Zebra and the Z logo Reg. U.S. Pat. & TM Off.

ISBN-13: 978-1-4201-0541-4
ISBN-10: 1-4201-0541-8

First Zebra Trade Paperback Printing: July 2010
10 9 8 7 6 5 4 3 2 1

Printed in the United States of America

For JULIE MABIE, friend, confidante and fellow
AMERICAN Shetland Pony lover!

And

MIMI WOOLEM, for all of the above, but particularly
the ability to, ah, stir the pot!

And

To HOWARD, for all the things you are to me.

Chapter 1

From his place of concealment near the Marquis of Ormsby's palatial London town house in Grosvenor Square, Asher Cordell watched the comings and goings of the multitude of handsome carriages that thronged the road in front of the brilliantly lit house. Any member of the *ton* still in town at the end of June, and fortunate enough to receive an invitation to Lord Ormsby's annual masked ball, was here tonight. Instituted over two decades ago, in time the Ormsby Masked Ball had come to signal the end of the Season, and after tonight most of the gentry would scatter far and wide across the breadth of England to spend the remainder of the summer at their country estates.

By London standards the hour was still early, approaching midnight, and Asher decided that he had wasted enough time determining that everything was going precisely as it should. Tonight's task wasn't difficult. It was a simple robbery—child's play for him. He'd already done two dry runs and could, he felt confident, find his way over the rear wall, through the spacious gardens, and into Lord Ormsby's library blindfolded. The previous evening, during the final practice run, standing in the middle of Ormsby's darkened library, he'd fleetingly considered stealing the famous Ormsby diamond necklace then and there, but decided against it. Changing plans on whim, he'd discovered, could cause fatal complications.

In the shadows of his hiding place, Asher grimaced. Christ. Could it ever! Last spring's events at Sherbrook Hall had certainly proven that fact and he wondered if the outcome would have been different if he'd held to his original plan. He sighed. Probably not. Collard had been up to no good and there was no telling how it would have ended. Bad enough that Collard had murdered that unpleasant wretch Whitley. Bad enough that he'd shot and killed Collard, even if it had been to save his own neck.

He shook off the memory and concentrated on the task before him. This would be his last theft, he reminded himself; the last time he took such risks. After tonight, he would retire to Kent and spend his days overseeing his own holdings, becoming finally the respectable, wealthy gentleman farmer everyone already thought he was.

Eager to put the past behind him, he was on the point of slipping around to the back of the house when he recognized the latest vehicle to halt before Lord Ormsby's doors. The coach was not in the first stare of fashion and was pulled by four rather unimpressive bay horses, but the moment the vehicle lumbered into position, as if royalty had arrived, the milling contingent of meticulously groomed gentlemen lingering on the steps leaped to attention.

Asher grinned. Who would have ever guessed that eighteen-year-old Thalia Kirkwood would take London by storm? Odes, poems praising her fair beauty were forever being written about her these past few months. Thanks to her, flower stalls all across London did a bustling business, the scented, colorful blossoms purchased by eager swains finding their way to the modest house just off Cavendish Square that her father, the retiring Mr. Kirkwood, had taken for the Season. It was rumored that at least one duel had been fought over the fair Thalia and gossip claimed that since May her father had turned down offers from at least a half dozen lovesick, imminently suitable gentleman—a few with the prospect of a title in the offing. To the dismay and long faces of many young bucks tonight, the current betting in the gentlemen's clubs was that before the family returned to Kent at the end of the week, Thalia's engagement to the Earl of Caswell would be announced.

It might be a masked ball, but there was little effort at disguise and there was no mistaking Thalia's tall, voluptuous form as she regally mounted the steps to the house, the upswept silvery fair hair gleaming in the torchlight. Her velvet cloak was sapphire blue, a perfect foil for her blond beauty, the color deepening, he knew, the icy blue of her brilliant eyes. The gentlemen swarmed around her, like bees to a fragrant bud, the servants bowing and scraping as they opened the heavy front doors.

Almost lost in the pandemonium surrounding Thalia's progress was the descent from the coach of her widowed older sister, Juliana. Though her husband had been dead for four years, it still gave Asher a start to think of Juliana as a widow. His lips twitched as he watched her gather up the folds of her pale green gown. He'd always considered her, at twenty-eight, only five years younger than himself, in much the same light as he did his two younger sisters, and thinking of Juliana even being *married* had been a challenge for him. He shook his head. Damn shame her husband, the younger son of a baronet with extensive lands in Hampshire, had died of lung congestion only three years into the marriage. There had been no children, but Juliana had been well provided for and shortly after her husband's death she had purchased a charming estate not five miles down the road from the home she had grown up in. With their mother long dead, upon Juliana's return to Kent, she had fallen back into her previous role of surrogate mother to Thalia. Since Mr. Kirkwood abhorred the constant round of soirees and balls so necessary for a young lady's successful Season, Juliana stepped into the role of chaperone for her younger sister's London Season. The notion of Juliana being anyone's chaperone was pure folly as far as Asher was concerned, recalling some of her youthful escapades. He decided that if anyone needed a chaperone, it was the elder sister, not the youngest.

Eyes narrowed, he watched as Juliana, a pair of elegant gentlemen on either side of her, followed her sister up the steps. Her cloak was in a soft shade of lavender and, as tall as Thalia, she carried herself with much the same grace as her younger sister. There was a glimpse of sable hair as Juliana passed by the torches on either side of the door and then she was gone.

Annoyed for allowing Thalia and Juliana's arrival to distract him, Asher shook himself and focused on the task at hand. After a last look around the area, he worked his way to the alley that ran behind the handsome homes that faced the square. His dark clothing making him nearly invisible, like a shadow he flowed along the wall at the rear of the houses. Arriving at the section of the wall he wanted, he made a careful survey and, seeing nothing to alarm him, he swung up and over the stone wall and silently dropped down onto the other side. Several feet beyond the place where he stood was the trades-men and servants' entrance to the house and in the faint light of the small flickering torch above the doorway, he saw that the area was deserted.

Excellent, he thought, as he did a slow scan of the grounds. It was unlikely there would be any trysts by the staff tonight—from past experience he knew that every servant, even those hired just for tonight, would be far too busy seeing to the needs of the aristocratic guests to have any time for dallying.

He easily found the doors to the library and within two minutes of having breached the rear walls was standing inside Lord Ormsby's library. He stood motionless a moment, his gaze moving slowly around the room. A faint sliver of light show-ing beneath the door that opened onto one of the hallways of the interior of the house broke the utter blackness. Dark shapes loomed up here and there but, already familiar with the layout, he quickly crossed the room to where Ormsby's ornate desk sat in front of a pair of long windows.

He'd discovered Ormsby's hiding place the first night he'd broken in to the house, although "broken in" didn't quite describe simply pushing open the door to the library and strolling inside. He'd also learned during his observations of the routine of the Ormsby household, except for the front door and the gates at the rear of the building, that there was nothing to halt anyone with thievery in mind. The house was a sitting goose, ripe for plucking. He grinned. Which made his job so much easier. Sliding out the bottom drawer on the right side of the desk, his skillful fingers made short work of finding and opening the secret drawer. Something resembling a sneer crossed his lean features. Did Ormsby really think that a clever thief wouldn't discover the drawer and its contents?

Asher needed no light to find the famed Ormsby diamond necklace; the size of the diamonds and the heavy weight of the necklace told him the minute he touched it. He'd never actually seen the real necklace; in fact, except for the occasions the current marquis had shown it off to his various acquaintances, it had not been seen in public for nearly fifty years, not since Ormsby's mother had died. But Asher had once seen the necklace in the portrait of Lady Mary, wife of the first Marquis of Ormsby, which hung in the grand gallery at Ormsby Place.

Though he'd made note of the necklace—after all, it was rather famous—he hadn't thought to steal it . . . at the time. Like a dutiful guest he had studied the painting, his keen eye making note of the size and brilliance of the stones even in a mere portrait. No, he hadn't thought to steal it then and he wouldn't be here tonight taking it from the secret drawer and carefully slipping into the specially sewn pocket of his jacket, if Ormsby hadn't . . .

His mouth tightened. He didn't as a rule steal from people he knew, nor was he inclined to hold grudges, especially against neighbors, even vain, arrogant, obnoxious neighbors, but in Ormsby's case he was willing to make an exception. Bastard shouldn't have shot my grandmother's favorite old dog, he thought grimly.

Petty to steal a priceless family heirloom because of the death of a dog? Asher shrugged. Perhaps. But it would be a long time before he forgot his grandmother's grief-stricken features when the body of her elderly spaniel, her companion and friend of many years, was dumped at her feet by one of the Ormsby grooms.

With all the arrogance of his master, the groom had said, "Milord sends his apologies. He saw the beast on the road and thinking it was the dog that has been killing the hens lately, shot him before he realized it was your old Captain."

Standing beside his grandmother, Asher's hands had clenched into fists and he fought back the urge to seek out and throttle Lord Ormsby for his cruelty to an old woman. In his heart he knew that the killing of Captain had been deliberate—not two days previously, to the marquis's open fury, his grandmother had turned down Ormsby's latest offer to buy several hundred acres of her land that adjoined his estate. Ormsby had simply killed the dog in petty retaliation. Another example, Asher thought tightly, of Ormsby striking out when displeased and to those weaker than himself.

When the groom rode away, Asher had helped his grandmother into the house. He had then quietly made arrangements for Captain to be buried near her favorite rosebush, a place the old woman and the old dog often sat for hours enjoying the garden and the soft play of light over the trees and shrubs. Watching the dirt fall into the dog's grave, he swore that Ormsby would pay *something* for his grandmother's sorrow. The great lord of the district wasn't going to walk away unscathed this time.

It had taken Asher a while to come up with an appropriate plan to ensure that Ormsby felt, perhaps for the first time in his arrogant life, the pain of loss that he often inflicted upon the common folk of the neighborhood. Killing him was out of the question—even Asher wasn't prepared to kill a man over a dog and an old woman's grief—but there had to be a way to pierce that smug composure. . . . He smiled in the darkness. The idea, when it came to him, had been perfect: Ormsby loved nothing more than himself and his possessions, so what better way to make him suffer, than to steal his most famous possession, the Ormsby diamond necklace?

What the devil he was going to do with the damned thing now that it rested in his pocket escaped him. He didn't need the money and selling it was out of the question. The necklace was too famous and the hue and cry once its theft was discovered would make it unlikely that any of his usual contacts would touch it. He could break it up into individual diamonds and have those reset if the whim took him, but he balked at the idea of such wanton destruction. If the portrait was anything to go by, it was a beautiful and uniquely designed piece of jewelry and he had an inherent dislike of destroying something so lovely. His lips twisted. Unless he wished to have his neck stretched on the gallows or face deportation to some godforsaken continent on the other side of the world, he'd have to hide the necklace somewhere it would never be discovered.

Asher slid the drawer shut. He'd bury the bloody thing in the ground if need be and plant a rosebush over it; for him it was enough to know that Ormsby's pride would have suffered a grievous wound. Bastard. Shouldn't have shot my grandmother's dog.

The opening of the door rooted him to the spot. He caught the merest glimpse of a woman's form in the light from the hallway before she shut the door behind her.

Without a moment's hesitation, he took a half dozen quick steps backward and melted into the heavy velvet folds of the drapes that hung at the sides of one of the long windows of the library. His back pressed hard against the wall next to the window where the drapes were gathered, he reached for the small pistol he carried inside his vest, but decided against it and his hand fell by his side. Escaping unseen was his plan and that didn't include firing his pistol; using the pistol would be his last resort. His thoughts scrambling, he listened intently as the female intruder walked swiftly in his direction. Had she seen him? No. He'd been too careful and he knew that no one had seen him slipping into the library. When she opened the door? No. He'd been on the other side of the room, concealed in the darkness well beyond the brief flash of light that had heralded her entrance; she could not have seen him. So why was she here? There was something furtive about her movements and he noted the fact that she had made no attempt to light a candle. What was she up to? Something occurred to him and he closed his eyes in a silent prayer. Please. Not a lovers' rendezvous.

A moment later, there was a faint ray of light beneath the curtains and, peeking through the drapes, Asher saw that his intruder had lit a tiny candle. Her back was to him and he stared bemused as she hurriedly explored the desk, obviously looking for something. He leaned his head back against the wall. Someone else thinking to steal the Ormsby necklace?

Intrigued, Asher watched as she hastily fumbled through first one drawer, then another. Under other circumstances he might have been amused at the situation, but with the Ormsby necklace burning like a fire red brand against his thigh, he rather wished that if she wanted the blasted necklace, she'd beaten him to it. For a second he wondered what would happen if he stepped from the drapes and gifted her with the necklace. Except as a way to inflict some humility in Ormsby, the necklace meant nothing to him. He considered the idea. No. The silly wench would probably scream at the sight of him and all hell would break loose.

Resigned to waiting for the woman to leave, he had just leaned his head back against the windowpane, when he heard her gasp. He jerked forward to see the cause of her alarm. The door was opening again.

As he had done, she flitted backward to hide amongst the drapes. Instinct more than design had Asher catching her around the waist and pulling her snugly against him at the same instant his other hand clamped over her mouth. Into her ear he hissed, "I mean you no harm—and for God's sake, don't scream or struggle."

The slight form in his arms stiffened and a curt nod was his answer, but Asher kept his arm locked tightly around her and his hand firmly over her mouth. Women were simply too damned unpredictable.

The latest arrival stood for a long moment in the doorway, the light from the large candelabrum he carried flooding the room with a soft glow.

"Hiding, my dear?" drawled the new arrival. When only silence met his words, he added impatiently, "Come now, I know that you are here. Did you really think that I wouldn't see you slip away? That I wasn't expecting you to try something?"

Asher's teeth ground together at the first sound of that rich, mellow voice. *Ormsby!* Bloody hell! If Ormsby discovered him here in the library, he'd have to shoot the bastard, after all. As for the woman . . . Christ! Could this last, simple job get any more complicated?

Loosening his grip on the woman's waist and praying that she wasn't going to cause him trouble the moment he removed his arm, he started again to reach for his pistol. The sound of another male voice froze his actions.

"Ormsby! I say, old fellow, what are you doing wandering around back here? Aren't you supposed to be dancing with the fair Thalia soon?"

Asher nearly groaned aloud. Killing Ormsby was one thing, but a second man as well? His only choice was the tall window behind him and he hoped to God that he sustained no real injury from leaping through it. But if he survived the window and if he could reach the back wall and disappear into the darkness . . . A faint, reckless grin flashed across his face. He might salvage tonight after all.

"Ah, thank you, Kingsley," drawled Ormsby, "for reminding me. I forgot."

"Forgot!" exclaimed Kingsley. "Forget a dance with the

loveliest chit to grace London in decades? My dear man, you alarm me."

His voice bored, Ormsby replied, "I think you forget that I have watched her grow up. Remember if you will that the Kirkwoods are my neighbors. I am well acquainted with the family."

"That reminds me of something, been meaning to ask you for weeks—how the deuce could you let such a pretty piece slip through your fingers? I would have thought you'd have sewn her up before she ever stepped foot in London." Kingsley chuckled. "Losing your touch, old fellow? Her engagement to young Caswell will be announced any day now."

"Really? I wouldn't place my final wager just yet, if I were you."

"You know something the rest of us don't?"

"There is, my friend, if you will recall, many a slip between the cup and the lip. Miss Kirkwood is not yet Caswell's bride."

"You mean to snatch her out from underneath his nose?" Kingsley gasped. "The gossip says that it is a love match— even someone of your wealth and title can't compete with love. So how do you propose to change the tide?"

Ormsby laughed, although there was little humor in it. "I play my cards close to my vest but I would warn you not to buy a betrothal gift for the pair just yet," he said. "Now come along, let us rejoin my guests. I have left them too long."

Asher watched as the light retreated and Ormsby ushered Kingsley toward the door. But Kingsley seemed in no hurry. "But why did you leave in the first place? Ain't like you to wander off."

An ugly edge to his voice, Ormsby said, "I had my reasons. Believe me I had my reasons."

"Yes, but—"

The door shut and from inside the library there was only the faint murmur of voices as the two men moved down the hall.

Deciding not to wait around to see who else would pay the library a visit, the door had hardly shut before Asher shoved the young woman out from behind the drapes and began urging her toward the French doors that opened onto the gardens. He didn't have a precise plan; his one thought was to escape the grounds as fast as he could. The woman was a problem. He couldn't just let her go. Or could he?

He considered the idea. She'd certainly been quiet as a rock while Ormsby had been in the library. Clearly she hadn't wanted to be discovered either. He didn't know her reasons for sneaking into the library or for going through Ormsby's papers, but he knew one thing: she'd been up to no good. And if she'd been up to no good, then she had ample reason not to raise the alarm. Dare he risk it?

His hand still over her mouth and griping her arm firmly, he pulled her outside. Pushing her ahead of him, they walked through the gardens, Asher not stopping until the back wall loomed up before them and the faint light from the torch over the servants' entrance pierced the darkness. He still hadn't made up his mind what to do, but taking everything into account, especially the fact that she had made no attempt to escape from him, it was possible that she might actually keep her mouth shut and not raise the alarm.

He glanced at the wall, still considering. Even if she screamed, he'd be up, over and away before anyone reached this deserted part of the grounds.

His lips pressed against her ear, he asked, "If I let you go, do you swear not to scream?"

She nodded vigorously and against his better judgment, he removed his hand.

The moment his hand dropped, she spun around to face him and breathed, *"Asher?"*

His heart stopped. Christ! *Juliana.*

Hands on her hips, she demanded, "Asher Cordell, what were you doing in Lord Ormsby's library? I nearly died when you grabbed me."

"I think the question should be," he said quickly, "what were *you* doing there?"

"That is none of your business!" she answered sharply. "I am an invited guest to Lord Ormsby's home—you are not."

"And how do you know that? I am quite respectable— Eton, respectable family and all that. He could have invited me."

Juliana snorted. "Don't try to bamboozle me! He can't abide you and you know it."

"I know," Asher said mournfully. "His dislike is a terrible burden for me." He looked hopeful. "Do you think there is something I could do to make him think better of me?"

She strangled back a laugh. "No! At this late stage there is nothing you could do to change his mind," she said bluntly. Shaking an admonishing finger at him, she added, "Perhaps if you hadn't turned the pigs loose in his newly planted field or hadn't stolen his best bull and put the animal with Squire Ripley's heifers he wouldn't think you so ripe for the gallows." She sent him a severe glance. "And we won't even talk about the disgraceful way you act around him. Asher, you actually yawned in his face at the Woodruff's ball in January! What were you thinking?"

"That he's a bore?" When she narrowed her eyes at him, he added hastily, "Juliana, I was thirteen when I turned the pigs loose, and you know it was an accident—how could I know the gate would shatter when that old sow charged it?" She sniffed.

"And I wasn't much older when the incident with the bull occurred." He grinned reminiscently. Juliana merely stared at him. "All right, I confess," he said, "I was a holy terror but you must admit that squire's calves the next year were some of the finest raised in the district."

"The squire may think you a fine fellow, but that act certainly did not endear you to Ormsby in the least," she muttered. Puzzled, she studied him in the dim light. "Why do you go out of your way to annoy him?"

Asher shrugged. "Mayhap if he showed a little consideration of others I wouldn't be so inclined to treat him so, ah, impolitely." The necklace searing his thigh, very aware of the passing time and the chance of discovery, he added, "And enjoyable though this little interlude has been, don't you think you ought to rejoin the guests?"

"After you tell me what you were doing skulking about in Ormsby's library," she said firmly.

Despite the tension coiling in his body, Asher leaned negligently against a small tree near the wall. Smiling at her, he said, "Of course. Right after you tell me why you were there."

She threw him a fulminating look. "You are the most infuriating, insufferable creature I have ever known in my life!"

He straightened up from his languid pose and bowed deeply before her. Smiling impudently at her, he murmured, "One does so try to please."

Her bosom swelled with indignation. "I've a good mind to tell Ormsby that you were in his library!" she threatened, knowing full well she'd face wild lions before she'd betray Asher—even if he was the most insolent and maddening man she'd ever met.

Amusement fled and an expression she had never seen before flashed in his eyes. In all the years she had known him, which had been nearly all her life, Asher had charmed her, shocked her, irritated her and infuriated her beyond reason but he'd never made her feel frightened before. Unconsciously she stepped backward and nervously measured the distance to the house.

Cursing himself, Asher wiped his expression clear of all sign of the violence that he feared had become an integral part of him. Forcing a smile, he flicked a gentle finger along her cheek. "Let us cry *pax*, Juliana, and go our separate ways and keep our secrets. Agreed?"

He didn't like it that she flinched when he touched her, but he kept the same easy smile on his lips and resumed his casual pose against the tree while he waited for her answer.

In the shadowy light, she sent him a searching look, then nodded. Without another word, she turned on her heels and marched back to the library's French doors.

Asher followed a few steps behind her. As she stepped into the library she glanced back at him. Her thoughts jumbled, she tried to think of something to say, but nothing came to mind.

She almost jumped out of her skin when he touched her on the shoulder. "Run along," he said softly. "I'll wait here until I know you're in the hallway."

Annoyed, but unable to think of anything else to do, Juliana did just that. Cautiously opening the door to the main hallway, she peeked out and, seeing it deserted, stepped quickly into the hall. Shutting the library door behind her, she hurried toward the ballroom.

Asher waited until he was certain she wasn't coming back and then walked across the room. At the desk, it took him only a moment to find and reopen the secret drawer and replace the Ormsby necklace. It was a bitter moment. He'd planned this for weeks and now it was all for naught. But he had no choice—Juliana knew he had been here and when the outcry, and there would surely be one, over the theft of the necklace arose, she would know that he had stolen it. Easing into the garden, he grimaced. And she was such an honest little thing, most likely she'd feel honor bound to tell Ormsby of his presence in the library or nag him to death until he returned the thing. Easier to return it now and wait for a better time.

Despite the outcome, Asher was lighthearted as he scaled the back wall and disappeared into the darkness. He was a great planner. And there would be another opportunity.

Arriving at his rooms near Fitzroy Square, he began to pack. He'd come to town this time without a valet and had traveled light. All of his belongings fit into the one valise and, buckling it shut, he looked around to see if he'd forgotten anything. He hadn't.

Tomorrow would find him riding back to Kent and the people he held dear. He'd had some reservations that he could settle down to the uneventful life of a gentleman farmer, but tonight's events insured that there would still be a little excitement to be gleaned. The Ormsby necklace was still out there and sooner or later he'd find a way to snatch it right from under Ormsby's nose. And Juliana . . . what the devil had she been searching for? He grinned. Finding out her secret might make life very interesting indeed. . . .

Chapter 2

Juliana sped down the hall, the terror of discovery by Ormsby making her heart beat so hard and fast she felt sick. Her roiling stomach eased only slightly when she made it undetected to the grand gold and cream ballroom and in seconds was lost in the beautifully gowned and groomed crowd that swirled around the edges of the huge room.

Smiling and replying she knew not what to those guests who spoke to her, she made her way to where she had left her sister standing with her friend, Miss Ann Tilley, and Miss Tilley's mother, a pleasant matron, noted for her easygoing manner. As she had known would be the case, several admiring gentlemen now surrounded Thalia, each one vying for her attention. A quick glance around revealed that Ormsby was nowhere to be seen in the crowded room. As the minutes passed and Ormsby did not appear, Juliana took a relieved breath. A young man from the group clustered around Thalia noticed her and asked politely if she would like some lemonade. She shook her head no and watched amused as he immediately rejoined the crush around Thalia and Miss Tilley. Widows of no great fortune or beauty held little appeal for the majority of the gentlemen here tonight—even if the widow's sister was the reigning queen of the Season.

Juliana's heart gradually slowed to normal, but she could

not completely put away the events of the evening. It had been stressful enough almost getting caught by Ormsby in the library, and finding Asher lurking behind the draperies had nearly undone her. It would be a long time before she forgot those strong hands holding her prisoner or the feel of his hard body pressed against her back. A warm tingle raced down her spine as she remembered the sensation of all those powerful muscles tensing and bunching between their bodies as they'd stood locked together behind the drapes. She'd known that Asher was lean and fit, she just hadn't, until tonight, known precisely *how* lean and fit.

Thalia sent her a questioning look, intruding into her thoughts, and Juliana gave a slight shake of her head. Silently she mouthed, "Later."

Thalia turned away and began to effortlessly charm the nearest male. Ordinarily Caswell would have been standing at Thalia's side, keeping encroaching males at bay, but he had been unable to attend tonight's event. Only last evening as he had walked home from his club, he'd been set upon by footpads and suffered a terrible beating. When he came to call this morning at the Kirkwood residence, his handsome face had been a mass of bruising and from the careful way he moved, Juliana knew that he was in pain from other less obvious injuries. Both sisters had been horrified by his condition and he had spent several minutes reassuring them that, while unsightly and painful, he would recover fully.

Smiling crookedly, he had added, "But I doubt that I want to show my face at Ormsby's tonight."

Both sisters understood completely—he did look ghastly. Thalia had immediately announced that she wouldn't attend the ball either.

His gray eyes gentle, he had said, "My dear, go. Let London see the enchanting Miss Kirkwood one last time. Go for me." He had raised Thalia's hand to his lips. "When next you return to the city, it will be as my bride."

Thalia sent him a tremulous smile, and stammered, "You d-d-don't m-m-mind the delay in announcing our engagement?"

He had shaken his head. "I don't understand why your father wishes to delay it, but it is enough that he has given me permission to make my addresses and that you have made me the happiest of men by agreeing to marry me." He had pressed a kiss upon her fingers and murmured, "The announcement can be made at any time, sweetheart. The important thing is that we are to be married and that by this winter we shall be man and wife."

Choking back a sudden rush of tears, Thalia had cried, "Oh, my love, I hope so. I do so hope so." She had thrown Juliana an anguished look and raced from the room.

Perplexed by her actions, Caswell had asked anxiously, "Is something amiss? Did I do or say something to distress her?"

Juliana had smiled reassuringly at him. "No, no, of course not. I am sure it is just nerves."

And my sister's nerves certainly aren't going to be helped by my failure tonight either, Juliana thought miserably. That wretched Ormsby! She still couldn't believe that he'd nearly caught her. She'd been so careful. But apparently, not careful enough, and he'd come into the library disrupting her search for the one thing that stood in her sister's path to happiness.

Somehow the two sisters managed to get through the remainder of the ball and the only unpleasant moment came when it had been time to bid their host good night. The smirk on Ormsby's face when they had stood before him politely taking their leave made Juliana's hand itch to slap his cheek. Hard.

Poor Thalia could not even look him in the face and her voice had been barely above a whisper when she had spoken to him. He had held her hand longer than polite and murmured, "Ah, but our parting is not for long, is it, my dear? I'm sure I shall see you in Kent often this summer. After all, we are neighbors and you know how dear you and your family are to my heart. You could even say that we are quite intimate, yes?"

His words struck her like a blow and Thalia stood stricken in front of him like a beautiful blue-eyed bird mesmerized by a snake.

Her teeth clenched so tight she thought they might shatter, Juliana moved up quickly and unobtrusively gave her sister a nudge toward the door. Smiling coolly into Ormsby's eyes, she said, "It was a wonderful ball. We enjoyed ourselves immensely."

His lips thinned at her interruption, but the marquis contented himself with a polite nod. "Thank you," he said. A mocking note in his voice, he added, "I trust you found the evening everything you hoped it would be?"

Thinking of the interlude with Asher, she managed a real smile and murmured, "Oh, yes, it was even more than I expected."

Which was almost the truth, she thought to herself as she followed her sister down the steps and into their waiting carriage. Asher's presence had indeed been more than she had expected and for the first time since she had fled the library, she wondered about his being in the library. What had he been up to?

There was no time for further speculation about the vexing Mr. Asher Cordell because the instant the carriage door shut behind her, Thalia leaned forward and questioned anxiously, "You found *nothing*?"

Aware of the coachman and grooms just beyond the partitions that enclosed the coach, she answered softly, "No. We will talk of it later." She cast a warning glance toward the front of the coach and relaxed when Thalia, catching her meaning, sighed and leaned back against the worn velvet seat across from her.

Arriving at the rented house, they disembarked, and seeing Thalia's pale, strained features as they went inside, Juliana said quietly, "There is no need for you to see Father tonight.

Go upstairs and let your maid attend you. After I have seen him, I will come visit you and tell you all." She made a face. "Such as it is."

Grateful not to face the reproachful and disappointed looks of their father, Thalia nodded. She gave the waiting butler her cloak, pressed a kiss on her sister's cheek and ascended to the upper floor.

Juliana smiled at Potts, the butler her father had hired for the Season. "My father?"

Potts returned her smile and said, "I believe he is awaiting your return, Mrs. Greeley. You will find him in the study."

Thanking him, she walked down the hall to the small, comfortable study. Entering the room, she found her father sitting in one of the large overstuffed black leather chairs that were arranged in front of the gray-veined marble fireplace. The light from several candelabra cast a pleasing glow around the room, but Juliana missed the cheery crackle and dancing flames of a fire.

Her father glanced up quickly at her entrance, hope flaring in his eyes. She shook her head. "I'm sorry, Father," she said, walking toward him. "I found nothing."

Her heart ached as she watched the hope die out of his gaze. He stared at his snifter of half-finished brandy standing on the table next to his chair and said heavily, "Well, you said it was unlikely that he'd keep it where it could be easily stolen."

She took a seat in the matching chair next to his and said, "We still have time. Caswell seems content to wait to make the announcement."

"But for how long? We cannot fob him off much longer or we will accomplish the very thing Ormsby is trying to do: end any possibility of a marriage between Caswell and your sister."

"I think you misjudge the depth of emotion that Caswell feels for Thalia. He is deeply in love, as is she, and I'm certain that he would wait indefinitely for her."

"I hope to God you are right." He looked at her sadly. "What was she thinking? What prompted her to be so indiscreet? I cannot believe that a daughter of mine could act so imprudently!" He buried his head in his hands. "If only she had told us about the letters sooner. At least before I gave Caswell permission to court her and she accepted his proposal. I can hardly tell the earl now that I have changed my mind or that Thalia didn't mean to accept his offer of marriage. What a ghastly tangle."

Juliana sighed. "I know she should have told us sooner, but she never expected that Ormsby would continue to pursue her once we came to London. I certainly didn't. I assumed once she'd refused him that he'd retire gracefully from the ranks. Of course we didn't know about the letters then." Thoughtfully, she added, "I don't think anyone was more shocked than Thalia when Ormsby actually proposed. Remember—she was only seventeen, barely out of the schoolroom when she fancied herself in love with him and wrote those letters. What she felt for Ormsby last summer was simply infatuation: her heart wasn't truly touched. Those letters, while imprudent, were merely the youthful scribblings of an innocent young woman who thought she was in love with an exciting older man." Her jaw clenched. "If anyone is to blame it is Ormsby. If you will recall he never asked your permission to court her, never once gave a hint what he was about. He presented himself in the guise of our neighbor and friend and laid siege to her behind our backs. Certainly, she should have refused to meet him clandestinely, definitely she should never have written him such passionate letters, but you know very well that *he* was the one encouraging her improper behavior." Her lips tightened. "You'll never convince me that he didn't know precisely what he was doing."

"Youthful scribblings!" exclaimed Mr. Kirkwood. "Is that what you think Caswell will believe if Ormsby lays those letters before him?"

It was on the tip of her tongue to suggest that they pull

Ormsby's fangs and allow him to do precisely that. She believed that Caswell loved Thalia enough to realize that those letters, those damnably indiscreet letters, consisted of nothing more than the mawkish sentimentality of a naive girl who had fallen for the practiced charm of an older man. The problem was that while Thalia had recovered her senses almost immediately, Ormsby had not. Worse, he had made it unpleasantly clear that he intended to marry her. Juliana grimaced. Despite her own dislike of the man, on the face of it, a match between the marquis and Thalia wouldn't have been a bad thing. Ormsby was wealthy and titled and it wasn't uncommon for older men to have much younger brides.

"If Thalia hadn't fallen in love with Caswell, would you have countenanced a match with Ormsby?" Juliana asked abruptly.

"Good heavens, Juliana, he is nearly my age!" he declared angrily. "And he's a dissolute rake in the bargain. A dirty dish like Ormsby would certainly have never been on my list of prospective husbands for either one of my daughters, let alone my youngest!" He shook his head. "I bear much of the blame for what has happened. I should never have allowed him to visit the house as I did. I knew his reputation, but I just never thought—" He took a deep breath and muttered, "But to answer your question, if your sister had wanted him . . . if she had loved him . . ." He sighed deeply. "I suppose I would have eventually given my permission for them to marry." Curiosity in his gaze, he glanced at her. "Why do you ask?"

She made a wry face. "Just that it would have made life so much simpler for us if she *had* fallen in love with him."

"Never say you'd be happy to see an innocent like Thalia married to a libertine like Ormsby!"

Juliana shook her head. "I'd move heaven and earth to keep it from happening," she said vehemently. "He is everything you say—a rake and a libertine. No. I would never want to see Thalia married to someone like Ormsby."

"But what are our choices?" Mr. Kirkwood asked. "Ormsby

holds all the cards. If I do not send Caswell packing and give her hand to Ormsby he swears he will give the letters to Caswell or make them public. Either way your sister's happiness will be ruined. *She* will be ruined if those letters get out."

Juliana's gaze dropped from the desperation in his. Her father's words were true and unless they could lay their hands on those incriminating letters, Thalia's future looked bleak. If Caswell rejected her because of the letters, Thalia's heart would be broken and there would be gossip aplenty. The engagement had not been made public, but everyone was expecting an announcement any day and speculation amongst the *ton* would run rampant if Caswell and Thalia suddenly went their separate ways. Even if Caswell loved Thalia as much as Juliana believed he did and married her anyway, Thalia still would not be safe. Thwarted, with Thalia lost to him and married to another, Ormsby was quite capable of making the letters public out of spite, and the public consumption of those very private letters would make Thalia the object of stares and whispers. Rank would not save her; many society hostesses would not allow the new Countess of Caswell to step foot in their homes.

Thalia would never marry Ormsby—of that Juliana was certain—but he could still ruin her. Her hands formed into fists. That blasted Ormsby, she thought furiously, he was vicious enough to go ahead and publish the letters just to punish Thalia for refusing him. The bitter fact remained; as long as Ormsby held the letters, Thalia's future was in his hands.

"What are we to do?" Mr. Kirkwood asked again, breaking into Juliana's thoughts.

With more confidence than she felt, she said, "What we are going to do is get the letters back!"

"But how?" her father cried, staring at her as if she'd gone mad.

Juliana stood up and shook out the folds of her gown. "I have no idea," she answered, "but I am sure I shall think of something." Hiding her own reservations, she smiled at him and said bracingly, "We can do nothing at present and for now I suggest that we do just as we planned and return home at the end of the week. Don't forget, Mrs. Tilley, her daughter, and the Crawleys and their daughter are coming to visit us at Kirkwood. Once we arrive home, we shall be busy preparing for our houseguests. Caswell and his friends, Mr. Bronson and Lord Hartley, might even arrive ahead of the others. Before long your poor little house will be bursting at the seams."

"But—" he started to object.

Determinedly she overrode him. "There is nothing we can do about the letters at the moment and I know it is not easy, but if we go around with hangdog faces or suddenly change all of our plans, everyone will know that something is very wrong." She took a deep breath. "Caswell will simply have to curb his impatience to let the world know that he and Thalia are to be married. And if he presses to make the announcement, we shall just have to fob him off as best we can." Her eyes hardened. "I'm sure that before too long I shall find a way to get those foolishly written letters of Thalia's away from Ormsby."

Bending over, she kissed him on his forehead. "Don't worry, Father, I shall see to it."

"Thank you," he said low. Gruffly, he added, "I know that I shouldn't lay this on your shoulders and that if I were any kind of a man, I'd call Ormsby out."

"Don't you dare!" she cried, alarmed, the image of her father lying dead on the dueling field flashing before her eyes.

He smiled wearily. "I shan't. I know from Ormsby's reputation that it would be certain death for me." His face hard and determined, he added fiercely, "I would gladly face death if I knew that it would save either one of you." His eyes, the same whiskey brown as his eldest daughter's, met hers. "You do know that, don't you? That I would do anything in my power to protect you?"

She sent him a shaky smile. "Yes, I do, but I don't think allowing yourself to be slaughtered by Ormsby will help us very much." Relieved that he wasn't seriously thinking of challenging Ormsby, she said in a calmer voice, "Leave it to me. I shall bring us about, you'll see."

From under her lashes she noted that this trip to London and the anxiety over Thalia's future had taxed his frail constitution and added new lines, new grooves to his thin, austere features. A shy, retiring man, used to the quiet, routine life in the country, he was out of his element here in the bustle and noise of the city. His whole world revolved around his two daughters and his home, Kirkwood, and Juliana knew that he suffered greatly from his inability to remove the threat to Thalia's happiness.

When his wife and their mother had been alive, Mrs. Kirkwood had coddled and protected her tall, unassuming husband and doted on her two daughters. They'd been, Juliana thought mistily, a happy family. It had been Mrs. Juliet Kirkwood who had cheerfully run the household and made most of the decisions that affected their lives. Content to leave everything in his wife's capable hands, Mr. Kirkwood had lost himself in his library and his letters or puttered around the estate, admiring and encouraging the changes his energetic wife had wrought.

To everyone's shock, it had been the lively, robust *Mrs.* Kirkwood and not Mr. Kirkwood who had died from a lung infection that had swept through the neighborhood when Juliana had been seventeen and Thalia barely eight. Her death devastated everyone, but especially Mr. Kirkwood, and he wandered through the house and grounds like a dazed person for months afterward as if unable to comprehend the enormity of the tragedy that had struck.

He had never, Juliana knew, recovered from her mother's death. None of them had, she realized with a pang. She missed her mother unbearably and to this day she still expected the door to fly open and her mother, flushed and smiling from some victory in the garden or over the testy Kirkwood bailiff to come rushing into the room full of her exploits. Now more than ever, Juliana wished for her mother's calm, sure hand on the reins of their lives. Mother would have known how to handle Ormsby, she thought. Mother wouldn't have tolerated his threats, she would have boxed his ears and sent him away with his head in his hands. Guilt smote her. Her mother wouldn't have allowed this situation to happen in the first place. Her mother would have known instantly what Ormsby was about and neighbor or no, marquis or not, she'd have put a sharp stop to his sniffing around Thalia. It is my fault, Juliana admitted painfully. I should have taught Thalia better. Warned her of the dangers. Watched her more carefully. Mother would have and Mother would have also found a way to best Ormsby. Determination flooded through her. And so shall I, she vowed. So shall I!

Juliana's chin lifted and she said again, "I shall find a way to bring us about safely—never you fear. Thalia *will* marry her earl and we *will* beat Ormsby at his own game."

A smile on his fine mouth, Mr. Kirkwood said softly, "You sound just like your mother. She was always so certain she could overcome whatever odds lay in front of her."

Swallowing the lump that rose in her throat, Juliana brushed another kiss across his forehead and declared, "Well, then we shall just have to follow in Mother's footsteps, won't we? She wouldn't have let Ormsby best her and neither shall we!"

Wearier than she realized, Juliana walked up the stairs to the upper floor. She dreaded the coming conversation with Thalia. Not because Thalia would reproach her or blame her for tonight's failure but because that unbelievably lovely face would crumple, those lovely icy blue eyes would fill with tears and she would collapse in a convulsive mass of guilt-ridden sobbing that would rip out Juliana's heart. No one blamed herself more than Thalia for the situation they were in or suffered more greatly. The child is beating herself to death over this and it has to stop, Juliana decided firmly as she paused before the door to her sister's room.

There was no denying that Thalia had been at fault and Juliana didn't try to pretend otherwise. While it was indeed Thalia's fault, Juliana had repeatedly attempted to make Thalia see that it wasn't *entirely* her fault. And that the majority of the fault lay squarely at Ormsby's feet. Even if he intended to marry her, Juliana concluded, he should have never gone about it the way he had. Her eyes narrowed. The sneaky cur knew that Father would never have allowed Thalia to make an alliance before she had even had her first Season and so he had set about cutting the ground from beneath their feet in a most underhanded manner.

Anger burned in her breast when she remembered Sunday evening and Ormsby's awful visit. When he'd laid the first one of Thalia's letters before her father and confessed all, he'd been so complacent, so smug, so confident he would leave the room as Thalia's husband-to-be. He'd been certain that his threat of making the letters public would assure the acceptance of his suit. And it might have, if things had not gone so far with Caswell. If Thalia hadn't been madly in the love with the earl and if her father hadn't already given his approval of the match, it was very likely, with Thalia's letter in front of him, that Mr. Kirkwood would have acceded to the marquis's demand for Thalia's hand.

Juliana smiled fiercely. Things hadn't gone as Ormsby had planned though. Her father had been aghast, but he had coolly told the marquis that his conduct had been reprehensible and that under no condition would he countenance the match. Once Ormsby had snarled his determination to wed Thalia by fair means or foul and stormed from the house, the appalled, tearful interview that followed between Mr. Kirkwood and his two daughters had been most painful. Presently, the relationship between Mr. Kirkwood and his youngest daughter remained just as strained and uncomfortable as it had been that night—he wounded and disappointed and Thalia consumed with guilt and remorse and Juliana unable to help either one of them.

We are all caught in a most damnable coil, Juliana admitted as she opened the door to Thalia's bedroom.

Her sister leaped to her feet from the chair she had been sitting in when Juliana entered. "F-f-father? Is he still very angry with me?" Her beautiful form hidden beneath a voluminous and virginal nightgown of delicate white cambric, Thalia looked very young and frightened as she stood before Juliana.

Juliana smiled and shook her head. "No, pet, he is not angry with you. He never was. He is angry at the situation."

"It is all my fault. My fault. I don't deserve to marry Piers! Oh, I wish I had never been born!"

Flinging herself on the bed, Thalia dissolved into a shaking bundle of misery and sobs. Sinking down onto the bed beside her, Juliana gently rubbed her back, waiting for the worst of the storm to pass.

Eventually, Thalia raised tear-drowned eyes to look at her and asked dully, "Oh, Juliana, what are we to do? I cannot marry Ormsby! I hate him. I know I thought I loved him, but I don't. He's beastly!" A fearful expression crossed her face. "Father won't make me, will he?"

"Don't be silly! Father has no intention of allowing Ormsby to get his way." She pushed back a tumbled lock of glorious silvery fair hair from Thalia's forehead. "And when has Father ever made you do anything you didn't want to do, hmmm?"

Thalia forced a smile. "I know that I am spoiled, but I truly never meant to cause so much trouble." She looked away. "It was so exciting at the time. I knew it was wrong, but I felt grown-up, adult for the first time. No one had ever paid attention to me the way he did. It isn't that I didn't feel loved by you and Father or that you neglected me or anything dreadful like that, but Father is always buried in his books and you are forever rushing about that sometimes I felt like a shadow watching everyone else's life. Lord Ormsby was interested only in *me.*" A note of pleading in her voice, she asked, "Do you understand?"

Her every word was a knife blade in Juliana's heart. Yes, she did understand. They *had* been involved with their own lives and neither she or her father had realized that Thalia, newly emerged from the schoolroom and eager to try her own wings, had felt isolated and ignored. Ormsby, Juliana thought bitterly, had taken full advantage of the situation.

"I do understand, pet, and I blame myself for this whole affair," Juliana admitted. "If only I'd—"

"Oh, Juliana, do not! I beg you. It is not your fault. You have been everything that is wonderful. It is my fault! *All* my fault." Thalia buried her face in the bedclothes and began to sob again. "It would serve me right if I had to marry Ormsby. I am wicked. Wicked!"

"What you are," said Juliana calmly, "is a dead bore. All these dramatics and tears. I tell you I don't believe I've ever seen such a Tragedy-Miss—not even on the stage. Wait! Perhaps that's what you can do—run away and go on the stage."

Thalia gulped back a half laugh and sat up. "Thank you," she said, wiping at the tears on her cheeks. "You always make me see how silly I am being. What are we to do?" she asked again, echoing her father.

"We are," Juliana said, rising to her feet, "going to best Ormsby. He has your letters someplace. I intend to find them."

Awe on her face, Thalia said, "Oh, Juliana, can you?"

"Of course I can!" Juliana declared roundly. "Now, into bed with you. We cannot have Piers coming to see his lovely bride-to-be and finding her with swollen eyes and a red nose. Good heavens! Unthinkable that the gorgeous Miss Kirkwood would suffer from such common complaints."

Thalia giggled. "It is a good thing he did not see me when I had the mumps. Remember how swollen I was?"

Juliana shuddered theatrically. "Horrible. He'd most likely have run screaming from the house."

"Thank you," Thalia said again, her blue eyes soft and full of affection. "There is not a wiser or kinder sister in the whole world than you."

Her own face reflecting her love for her sister, Juliana bent down and pressed a fleeting kiss on Thalia's forehead. "You are a good, sweet young woman and greatly loved. Remember that as you go to sleep."

Leaving her sister, Juliana entered her own bedroom. She managed a smile for her maid, Abby, and prattled lightly about the night's events as Abby helped her undress and slipped a soft gown over her head. It was only when Abby had departed and Juliana was alone in her room that she allowed the smile to fade and her shoulders to droop.

Lying in the bed in the dark, the weight of responsibility for making things right for Thalia and her father crushed down on her. What a terrible coil they were in and it was clearly up to her to set matters right. She must get those letters back from Ormsby! Thalia and her father's happiness depended upon it.

If only she had been able to search Ormsby's desk tonight and find the letters. But Ormsby, devil that he was, had followed her and ruined any hope of that! Of course, if Asher hadn't been lurking behind the curtains, once his friend, Lord Kingsley, had distracted Ormsby, she'd have been able to complete her search before returning to the ballroom.

She frowned, thinking about the implication of Asher's presence tonight. What had he been up to? She didn't for a moment believe that he had been invited to the ball, yet he had been hiding in Ormsby's library. . . . Was Ormsby blackmailing Asher?

Juliana sat up in bed, oblivious to the rumble of London traffic as she considered the events in the library. Asher had been up to no good tonight, that much was obvious. Why else had he been hiding behind the drapes? Why else had he covered her mouth and kept their presence a secret? He could have pretended they had stolen away for a private moment, but he had not. Her eyes narrowed. Asher hadn't wanted to be found any more than she had . . . which meant he had something to hide.

Knowing Asher, it was perfectly possible that Ormsby was aware of something disgraceful that Asher would not have appreciated becoming public. Asher Cordell had always been a mysterious figure in the neighborhood, appearing and disappearing at will, with no explanation of why or where he had been. The source of his fortune, rumored to be sizable, was also a mystery. His grandmother, dear Mrs. Manley, had made the occasional, vague reference to "investments," but little else. Juliana wrinkled her nose. No one would be rude enough to inquire too deeply anyway. Except Ormsby . . .

Could Ormsby have discovered something disreputable about Asher? And was Asher trying to get it back? Hmmm. If Asher was going to be poking about in Ormsby's things, looking for whatever it was that had brought him to the library tonight, might he be willing to help her in the quest to get Thalia's letters back?

A dreadful thought crossed her mind. But if Asher were successful, would she be exchanging one blackmailer for another? She shook her head. No. Infuriating though he might be, Juliana was convinced that Asher would not stoop to blackmail. She almost giggled. Besides, *he* didn't want to marry Thalia. And if he was going to be snooping about Ormsby, he could very well snoop for her.

Optimistic for the first time since Ormsby's visit on Sunday night, Juliana lay back down again. As sleep crept over her a nebulous plan formed in her head. She would talk to Asher. Asher would help her.

Chapter 3

Driving through the gently undulating Kent countryside the scant distance that separated his estate from his grandmother's, Asher was almost happy. It was good to be home, good to be amongst familiar things, places and people. Determined to put his past behind him, he was looking forward to becoming what he had always appeared to be in the neighborhood, a well-to-do gentleman landowner.

He had arrived back from London yesterday afternoon and had spent today conferring with the small staff that kept his comfortable home running smoothly and his bailiff, who made certain that the various farms and properties were producing as they should; tonight he was dining with his grandmother.

A muffled sound from the blanket-covered basket on the seat beside Asher made him grin. Some weeks ago he'd spoken with the farmer who leased one of his grandmother's farms and he'd made a slight detour to Farmer Medley's this evening to pick up the small occupant of the basket. His grin faded. His grandmother had mourned Captain's death long enough. It was time she had something to distract her.

Reaching an offshoot marked by two towering oaks on either side of it, he turned the pair of blacks pulling his blue and gold curricle off the main road and drove down the driveway that led to his grandmother's estate, Burnham. Asher had never met his great-grandfather, but he knew that when Sir Hilary Burnham died over forty years ago, with no male relative to inherit, the title had died with him. Which was just as well, Asher thought, because if there had been a male heir, his grandmother wouldn't be living there now.

The tile-roofed house, when it appeared at the end of the meandering driveway, was charming. Adorned with a pair of picturesque gables in front, the house was two storied; a small lake adrift with white and yellow water lilies and edged with drooping beech and spreading ash trees nestled at one side of the house. Ivy clung here and there to the aged yellow brick and the wide latticed windows glinted in the gold and scarlet rays of fading sunlight. It was not a large house but it had amply suited the needs of the various Burnhams who had lived there over the centuries. Certainly, his grandmother loved it and Asher felt great affection for the place himself. Which he supposed wasn't a bad thing since his grandmother had made it clear to the family that she intended to leave the estate to him, her eldest grandson.

Stopping his horses in front of the house, he handed the reins to the grinning stable boy who ran up. "Hullo, young Pelton," Asher said, reaching for the basket. "Father well these days?"

"Indeed, sir, he is. Mrs. Manley's draught banished my pa's congestion just as if it had never been." Young Pelton wrinkled his nose. "Smelled terrible though."

Basket in hand, Asher laughed and leaped lightly from the curricle. "My grandmother's concoctions *always* smell terrible, but they work."

"I beg your pardon," said his grandmother in a teasing voice from behind him, "but my peppermint tea does not smell terrible at all."

Asher turned and something warm and light moved within him. His grandmother, Ann Manley, was seventy-five years old and even with her silver hair and softly wrinkled pink and white complexion, she looked and carried herself like a woman a decade younger. The top of her head barely reached Asher's broad shoulders and her form was slim; her eyes were the same deep cobalt blue of his own and in her younger days, her hair had been as gold as the summer sunshine.

Walking to where she waited on the wide path that led to the heavy oak front door, he dropped a kiss on her scented temple. "Of course, you're right. I could never disagree with such a lovely lady."

She laughed and swatted him playfully on the cheek. "And you are a far too practiced flirt for a woman to take anything you say seriously." Her eyes fell on the basket he carried on his arm, noting that the old blue blanket was moving about wildly. "Now what have we here?"

Grinning, Asher presented her the basket. "Go ahead," he said when she stared at the gyrations made by the blanket, "lift it up."

She did and her expression melted into one of pure delight at the sight of a tail-wiggling spaniel puppy in the basket. While the puppy and his grandmother stared bemused at each other, Asher said quickly, "He's a boy. Eight weeks old yesterday. The pick of Farmer Medley's latest litter."

"Oh, Asher!" Taking the tricolored puppy with the floppy ears and big eyes from the basket, she held him to her breast and laughed when the puppy promptly washed her chin with his tongue. Stroking the puppy, she asked, "Medley's line?"

Asher nodded. Quietly, he said, "The same as Captain. Medley said that this little fellow traces several times all the way back to Captain's dam." To his dismay, his grandmother's eyes filled with tears and she choked back a sob. "I thought it would please you," he muttered, bewildered.

Half smiling, half crying, she clutched the puppy tighter and said, "Oh, he does. He does!" She kissed Asher's chin and added, "I'm crying because I'm happy. I would love any puppy you gave me, but one that is related, even distantly, to my dear old Captain is more than I could have dreamed."

"I hoped he would lighten your heart." He ran a gentle

hand over the puppy's head. "He won't be Captain, but I think he will grow up to be a good, loyal companion to you—just as Captain was."

Dinner was delightful. They'd eaten alfresco next to the small lake with the stubby legged puppy gamboling at their feet and exploring his new home. As dusk deepened into lavender shades, Asher's grandmother's hand resting on his arm, the basket dangling from her other hand, they strolled around the lake, watching the antics of the puppy. As they wandered, they considered various names for the new pet. Asher was all for continuing the military theme but Mrs. Manley smiled faintly and declared that this time she wanted a rather more romantic name. Grinning down at her, a brow quirked, Asher teased, "What—Romeo?"

She laughed. Noting that the puppy was beginning to lag, she bent down and picked him up. After giving him a brief cuddle, she placed the puppy in the basket, where he curled up and promptly fell asleep. Smiling at the puppy, she said, "Nothing quite that romantic. I was thinking of something along the lines of Jupiter or Zeus."

Doubtfully, Asher eyed the roly-poly black and tan and white bundle nestled in the basket. "Somehow he doesn't look very Zeus-like."

"Well, not at the moment," his grandmother agreed. "But you must agree that he is a very handsome fellow even now. When he is grown, I am sure that he will be the handsomest dog in the neighborhood."

"If you feel that way, why not name him Apollo?"

She beamed at him. "What an excellent idea!" Looking down at the puppy, she murmured, "Welcome to Burnham, Apollo." Sleeping deeply, Apollo did not seem to be impressed with his new name.

Asher was content when he drove away from Burnham an hour later. His grandmother was enchanted with her new companion and he didn't doubt that despite the basket he currently occupied, before too many hours passed, Apollo was going to end up in bed with his new owner. Captain had slept at the foot of her bed and he didn't expect that Apollo would suffer a lesser fate.

A family of wealthy farmers had owned his own estate, Fox Hollow, for several generations and while not overly impressive or large, the house was quite handsome. Like Burnham, "comfortable" was the word that came to Asher's mind as he drove past the sprawling brick and half-timbered house with its two wide bays that flanked the iron-hinged double front doors. There were over a thousand acres of rolling fertile land and forest that came with the estate, but its main appeal to Asher had been that it adjoined Burnham. When the surviving widow had approached his grandmother about the prospect of adding it to Burnham, Mrs. Manley had suggested that Asher buy it for himself. Smiling at him, she said, "That way you will have your own place and won't feel like you're standing around waiting for me to die." The very thought of her death sent a pang through him, and while he had never once felt that he was standing around waiting for her die, her advice was sound and he had bought Fox Hollow for himself five years ago.

Asher smiled faintly. Ormsby had been eyeing Fox Hollow for himself and had already offered the widow a bit over half of what it was worth when Mrs. Dempster approached Mrs. Manley seeking a fairer price. Fox Hollow had been worth every penny Mrs. Dempster was asking and Asher had been more than happy to pay the widow's price. His smile faded. Which only gave Ormsby another reason to dislike him. He shrugged. Bastard should have made Mrs. Dempster a fair offer.

Leaving his horses in the hands of his stable master, Asher ambled back through the darkness toward the house, feeling oddly at loose ends. For nearly as long as he could remember there had always been a new goal, a new scheme to consider and implement, but those days were behind him now. Except for the theft of the Ormsby diamonds, Asher was determined to leave behind that part of his life that did not bear too close an inspection. He had been very lucky that his part in any of the various schemes in which he'd partaken had never been discovered. He'd known that as long as he continued to dare fate, it would be only a matter of time before disaster struck. After last year's near thing, he'd been damned lucky that he hadn't found himself heading for the gallows at Newgate. That blasted Collard!

Asher's lips thinned. Over the years, he may have sailed close to the wind or worse, but he hadn't left any bodies behind until Collard had killed the luckless Whitley last spring. It was one thing to trick a fellow or, he admitted with a grimace, steal from him, but murder? It had ever been his policy to get over the heavy ground as light as possible and the events in Devonshire the previous year had shaken him and had made him rethink his way of life.

It wasn't, he argued as he walked up to the front door, as if the desperate need that had once driven him to take such dangerous risks existed any longer. Burnham was safe these days and his grandmother no longer lived in fear that she would lose her home. She had, he thought grimly, nearly beggared herself seeing to it that he and his half brothers had been educated at Eton. He hadn't known at the time that she had risked Burnham itself, quietly adding debt she could ill afford to see that her grandsons were educated in a manner befitting their birth. When he discovered her sacrifice he had been appalled and had immediately taken steps to stop the drain on her pocket. And if his methods had been desperate and fraught with danger and beyond the pale, he hadn't cared. His grandmother would not lose Burnham.

He shook himself, pushing away the bad memories. Presently, Burnham was secure and his younger half siblings were secure in their futures and no longer had call upon his purse. His two sisters, with respectable dowries discreetly provided by Asher, had made excellent matches. John, almost twenty-five and the half brother closest to him in age, was running the family estate, Apple Hill. Robert, next in age at nearly twenty-four, had his commission and horses, at no small cost to Asher, in an elite Cavalry unit, currently serving in Portugal.

As for his stepfather, retired Lieutenant Colonel Denning . . . Asher's mouth thinned. Despite an inclination to the contrary, he'd had no choice but to save his stepfather's estate if the girls, at the time only twelve and ten, were to have a roof over their heads. And, he added grimly, if John was to have anything left to use one day to support a family of his own. Asher shook his head. Already struggling to shore up his grandmother's finances, he had nearly buckled when he'd discovered what "Colonel," as his stepfather preferred to be called, had been up to.

It had been nearly a decade ago that the colonel had damn near lost everything, including Apple Hill, at the gaming table and Asher had scrambled frantically to keep the family from certain ruin. He'd been ruthless in his quest to pay off the colonel's debts before it was too late and his methods, he admitted with only a slight twinge of guilt, had been definitely illegal. But, he reminded himself, those days were now in the past and it was time he stopped worrying about the family and concentrated on living his own life. Still, he admitted, as he opened one of the double doors, it felt peculiar not having some ruse or scheme rattling around in his head, and the growing notion that respectability might prove exceedingly boring nagged at him.

Stepping into the oak-paneled foyer, he was greeted by Hannum, his butler. Hannum wasn't a proper butler, but since he had assumed all the duties of a butler and was married to the housekeeper, both of whom Asher had inherited when he had bought the house, Asher couldn't think of him as anything less. To his amusement, both of them treated him with a friendly familiarity that would have raised eyebrows in a more conventional household than his own.

His staff, originally consisting of Hannum and his wife,

had grown over the years to encompass several more servants all related in some fashion to the Hannums. These days, his stable master, Liggett, was the husband of the Hannums' eldest daughter, Margaret. Margaret herself also worked for him, since Mrs. Hannum had mentioned a few years ago that another pair of hands around the house would certainly be welcome and she knew just the person for the job. Asher was confident that the fellow and his helper who worked the gardens and the extra stable boys were also related in some way to the Hannums. He grinned. He didn't mind. The Hannums were honest, hardworking and didn't get under his feet.

His grin widened as he took in his butler. Built on an oak-like frame, in his youth Hannum had been a fairly successful pugilist, as his broken nose and missing teeth attested. The first sight of those rough, battered features had been known to give visitors pause—which suited Asher just fine. Flashing a grin that revealed gaps in his teeth, Hannum asked, "And was Mrs. Manley happy with the little dog?"

Handing Hannum his gloves, Asher replied, "Very. She has named him Apollo."

"Oho! Now that's a fine name."

"What name?" demanded Mrs. Hannum. Salt and pepper hair neatly contained in a muslin cap, she was wiping her hands on a big white apron as she appeared from the nether reaches of the house. "The puppy? Was your grandmum pleased with him?"

Asher nodded. "Indeed, she was. I suspect that even as we speak, the newly named Apollo is making himself quite comfortable in bed with her."

"Apollo, hmmm? Yes, that should do nicely." She shook her head, her blue eyes somber. "Such a shame what happened to her old Captain."

"Yes, it was," Asher agreed softly. "But I think that Apollo will keep her busy and brighten her days."

Leaving the Hannums to their tasks, Asher wandered toward the back of the house to his study. "Study" was rather a grand word for a room that had probably first seen light as a storage room adjacent to the house. These days, with painted white plaster walls and some tall windows that overlooked a section of the gardens at the rear of the house and a fine woolen rug in shades of green and russet on the brick floor, Asher found it more than adequate for his needs. On wintry days, the brick fireplace that had been installed at some point long before he owned the place kept the room warm and cozy. A few bookcases lined the walls and the furniture scattered about was worn and comfortable. Heavy woven drapes in green and gold that could be drawn closed to shut out the cold of winter edged the windows.

After lighting a couple of candles to dispel the increasing darkness, Asher stood in the middle of the room, staring at nothing in particular. Restless and unable to settle, he wandered around the room, his fingers running lightly over the array of bottles of liquor and glasses on a long oak sideboard against one wall. He scanned the bookcases, even took out a book or two, but the thought of delving into Bacon's *Essays* or plowing through a volume of Caesar's *Commentaries on the Gallic War* did not appeal to him.

Approaching his desk, a massive, battered thing, chosen more for its size than any beauty it might have once had, Asher tossed aside a few papers lying there, looking at them but not really seeing them. Eventually he returned to the sideboard and poured himself a snifter of brandy.

Casting himself down into an overstuffed, diamond tufted russet leather chair, he threw one leg over the wide arm and sat sipping his brandy. His gaze moved around the room as he considered his future.

At the moment, day after day of complete and utter boredom stretched before him. Yet . . . this was where he wanted to be. The quiet, the tranquility and sedateness of country life had been what he had yearned for all the years he had trod that reckless, dangerous path. He *was* happy to be home, happy not to be looking over his shoulder, happy not to be risking his life and reputation. His jaw clenched. Or leaving his family open to shame and humiliation if he'd been caught in any one of a number of less than honest undertakings. He'd worked hard, he admitted ruefully, to be bored.

His problem, he finally decided, was that he didn't know what to do with himself. He had never thought much about the future, or rather much about *his* future. He'd been too busy making certain that everyone else's future was secure to worry about his own. He grimaced. That wasn't precisely true—witness the investments in shipping and coal and tin mines that he had made, as well as his purchase of Fox Hollow. Obviously he had given some thought to his own future, too.

The problem was that he really didn't see himself as a farmer, even a gentleman farmer. Besides, he had a perfectly good bailiff who did an excellent job of running the farms. He grinned. And Wetherly would not take kindly to any interference from his employer. Wetherly was perfectly content to report to him and listen gravely to any suggestions he made, might even implement one or two of those suggestions, but in the end, they both knew that it was Wetherly whose skillful guidance and keen oversight made Fox Hollow profitable. As for Asher's other investments . . . well, again, he had a perfectly good man of business, Mr. Elmore, and no more than Wetherly would Elmore appreciate having him coming into the London office and constantly peering over his shoulder. Asher was not, however, an indolent employer— he understood and knew precisely what was going on in his affairs at all times.

Finishing off his brandy, he got up and poured himself another one. Snifter in hand, he wandered around the study for several more moments, stopping here and there, staring blankly at nothing before moving on. He halted before the windows that overlooked the gardens. By now it was dark outside and he could see nothing beyond his reflection in the glass as he sipped his brandy.

A taller than average man with black hair stared back at him. Beneath the dark blue jacket his form was muscular, his shoulders broad, his thick, unruly hair worn perhaps a trifle longer than was fashionable, kissing the back of his neck, waving near his temples. The features that met his gaze were considered by most to be handsome. The black brows below the wide forehead were strongly marked, the nose arrogantly masculine and the mouth wide, with a bottom lip fuller than the narrower upper one. He looked a perfect gentleman, but even now, he thought, staring at his image in the window, the deep-set cobalt blue eyes were watchful and full of shadows, secrets. . . .

Asher snorted and turned away. Next he'd be talking to himself.

Reseating himself, he considered the problem. So if he wasn't going to immerse himself in farming and he wasn't going to lose himself in the day-to-day business of watching his investments, what the hell was he going to do? He certainly had no intention of becoming a dilettante or a dandy or even one of those bored men about town one was forever running into in London.

There weren't, he concluded, many occupations for a man in his position. He supposed he could raise horses. . . . He considered it. He liked horses. He had a good eye and currently had a stable full of fine animals. He had the land. But he didn't see himself spending the rest of his life pouring over pedigrees and constantly searching for that magical "nick" that would enable him to consistently produce horses clamored for by the fashionable. Breeding dogs didn't appeal either. He'd leave that to knowledgeable men like Medley. The same applied to sheep and cattle. And horticulture was never going to be his forte—he could only correctly identify a half dozen of the hundreds of plants that grew in his garden.

Christ! he thought irritably. I need a hobby. Or a wife.

He jerked. A wife? By God, that was rich! What the devil would he do with a wife?

An arrested expression on his face, he stared around at the empty room. What would it be like to have a wife, he wondered? To look over at the chair next to his and see a woman, a pretty woman, sewing or reading? Would she look up and smile affectionately at him? Would he feel that same powerful sense of belonging, of protectiveness he felt toward his grandmother, his siblings? There was a slight stirring between his legs. And what would it be like to know that when he slid into bed at night, that there would be a warm, willing body waiting for him? And what of children?

An odd feeling, half fright, half delight, raced through him. He'd never thought of himself as a father. It was possible, he admitted, that he'd be a decent one. Something dark and dangerous moved across his features. He sure as hell would make certain that they were taken care of and not leave their fate up to the turn of a card as his stepfather had done.

But did he really want a wife? Could he adapt to having someone else to care for? To be responsible for?

The prospect of taking a wife did not leave him, even as he ascended the stairs that night and climbed into bed. His lonely bed, he admitted ruefully.

Having a woman share his bed had never been a problem for him, but a mistress, or a passing fancy, was not quite the same as a wife. A wife was forever. A wife would live in his home. Would bear his children. A smile flitted across his mouth. And have to meet with Mrs. Manley's approval.

A yawn took him. Finding a wife would be a daunting task and one that he wasn't likely to accomplish tonight. He'd sleep on it.

During the next week as he settled into the rhythm of living once again at Fox Hollow, Asher discovered he wasn't quite as bored as he had feared and the notion of finding a wife faded from his mind. To his pleasure, after all his reservations, he found himself adapting very well to taking each day as it came. He realized that a week wasn't such a long time, and he reminded himself that over the years he had often been at home sometimes for months on end and had not grown bored. Considering the situation, he suspected that it would merely take him time to grow used to the fact that he wouldn't be spending the days and weeks consumed with the planning it took for him to make certain nothing was left to chance prior to embarking on another risky scheme. Best of all, he thought, he wouldn't be away from Fox Hollow and his grandmother for months on end. Life at Fox Hollow, he reminded himself, was precisely what he wanted. He enjoyed consulting with Hannum and Mrs. Hannum about the running of the house every morning, conversing with his stable man, riding over the estate and seeing and approving the changes and improvements implemented by Mr. Wetherly. He visited with a few of his nearest neighbors, Squire Ripley just down the road from him, and Mr. Woodruff, a wealthy landowner whose broad acres abutted his on the south, and spent an agreeable time discussing crops, orchards, the cattle, swine and the like.

Coming home on Monday afternoon, Asher was surprised to find a delicately scented note waiting for him on the green marble table in the foyer. He stared at it a thoughtful moment, studying his name written on the front of the envelope in bold flowing script before picking it up. Not from his grandmother or one of his sisters—he knew their handwriting intimately. Was it an invitation, perhaps, from one of the ladies in the neighborhood? Most likely. Or something more sinister? Living as he had, the threat of blackmail was never far from his mind and though he had always been careful in the extreme, there was always the possibility that someone from his past had seen something, or heard something that might prove profitable . . . for them. For a while, he thought with a tiger's smile. But only for a while.

Leaving his gloves and whip on the table, he carried the envelope back to his study, where he settled into a chair. In one quick movement, he ripped the envelope open. Without reading the contents, his gaze skipped instantly to the bottom of the page. Juliana?

He made a face. Too busy settling into life at Fox Hollow, he'd pushed the night in Ormsby's library in London to the back of his head but he suspected that it was about to come back and bite him in the rear.

A swift perusal of the note brought a frown to his forehead. Juliana wanted to meet with him? Secretly? What the deuce was the little devil about?

Surely she wasn't trying her hand at blackmail? He dismissed that idea as silly. She had no need to stoop to such measures and though his presence in the library was suspicious, it didn't prove anything. A speculative gleam in his eyes, he stared down at the note in his hands. He hadn't given her presence in the library any thought since that night, but now he wondered, why *had* Juliana been there?

His gaze skimmed over the note again. A faint smile curved the corners of his lips. Apparently, he would find out tonight at midnight at their clandestine meeting at the old gatehouse. Ah, he did so love intrigue, and it appeared that Juliana was about to provide the one thing that was missing from his life.

Chapter 4

Her heart thudding painfully in her chest, Juliana slid from her mount and scurried through the black night to the old derelict gatehouse. The small stone gatehouse had been abandoned several generations ago when the road that had originally led to Kirkwood had been changed to skirt the creek that routinely overflowed and flooded the driveway.

Seen in sunlight, the creek burbling in the background, the tumbling ruin presented a picturesque sight, the stones faded to a soft rosy gray, the wooden shutters hanging drunkenly beside the two windows and the slate roof mossy and green. Roses still twined near the doorway and huge old lavender plants sprawled over the winding path that led to where the front door had been.

But tonight, with a waning moon overhead, there was nothing picturesque about the place to Juliana's mind. She shivered and hesitated beside her horse, the air seeming to thicken and swirl around her, the creek moaning dolorously in the background. Before her the gatehouse itself was a hulking shape and she wondered, not for the first time, why she had chosen this time and this place to meet Asher.

You chose this place, she reminded herself wryly, because you couldn't think of anywhere else. She eyed it in the gloom. It's only the gatehouse. There's nothing sinister about it.

Telling herself not to be a ninnyhammer, she took a determined step forward, and nearly jumped out of her skin when an owl hooted nearby. Annoyed with her reaction, she gripped her purple cloak tighter around her and, her jaw set, strode forward.

Her cloak brushed against the heavy, old lavender plants and the calming scent of lavender floated in the air. It's only the old gatehouse, she reminded herself again as she continued down the path toward the house. And Asher will be here. There is nothing to be frightened of.

The gaping hole where the door had once hung appeared before her and her step faltered. The scent of damp mildew and dirt drifted to her and she could swear she heard something scurry away. Her fingers tightened on her cloak. Good heavens! Who knew what was inside the place? Mice, no doubt, the logical part of her brain answered. A few rats, perhaps. Surely nothing else . . . nothing dangerous. But she remained rooted to the spot, staring at the shadowy doorway, unable to move forward, the thought of confronting a beady eyed stoat or an angry badger foremost in her mind. As she hesitated there, she heard a noise, just the faintest whisper of sound, and instinctively, she took a step back. She was not normally a coward, but nothing, she realized, short of divine intervention, was going to get her to enter the gatehouse tonight.

"Rather unpleasant place for a meeting, don't you agree?" Asher drawled as he loomed up in the doorway before her.

Despite her best intentions, Juliana shrieked and leaped back several feet.

"My point exactly," Asher said, stepping out into the faintest gleam of moonlight. "Why the devil did you choose this place and why do we have to meet at midnight?"

Gathering her ruffled wits about her, Juliana snapped, "I couldn't think of anywhere else and I didn't want to cause suspicion."

One of Asher's brows flew upward and he glanced around. "And you think if someone sees us here together at this time of night that it *won't* raise suspicion?"

"If there was anybody around to see us, of course, it would raise suspicions, but I chose this place precisely because no one would see us," she said from between clenched teeth.

He studied her for a moment in the faint moonlight. From the set of her jaw and her rigid stance, it was obvious that she wished she were anywhere else but here. Yet this meeting and the time and place had been of her choosing. He frowned as something occurred to him, something that should have occurred to him the moment he read her note. Not only was this an odd place to meet, but this sort of behavior was out of character for Juliana. Except for a few escapades when they had been children, Juliana had always trod the path expected of her and had never shown any desire to stray off the straight and narrow. Unlike him, she had never caused her parents a moment's worry and had always done the right, correct thing. A paragon of virtue, that was the Juliana he knew. What the deuce, he wondered, was so important that, should they be discovered, she would face gossip and the loss of her reputation?

He glanced around again. Ordinarily, he would have agreed that the gatehouse was the perfect site for a secret meeting. It was well hidden, forgotten by most people, and it was highly unlikely that even a poacher would stumble across them. Still, it wasn't a place he would have chosen to meet a respectable young woman like Juliana. He half smiled. Nor would Juliana if she had actually been inside the gatehouse.

"Don't you dare laugh at me, Asher Cordell," Juliana said fiercely, catching sight of his smile. "I wouldn't have asked for you to meet me if it wasn't important."

Asher shook his head. "I wasn't laughing at you," he said. "Merely the circumstances."

He reached for her and Juliana started violently at the

touch of his hand on her arm. "Easy now," he said quietly, just as he would to calm a frightened mare. "I mean you no harm." Holding her firmly, he said, "I don't doubt that whatever brings you here is important, but this is no place for us to have any sort of meeting. You're frightened half out of your wits and you're going to be jumping and screaming at shadows and not concentrating on the matter at hand."

"You're right," she admitted miserably. "But I couldn't think of another place." Stiffly, she added, "I am not in the habit of meeting gentlemen in such an unseemly fashion."

"No, I'm sure you're not," he agreed. Turning her, he half dragged, half walked her to her horse. Tossing her up into the saddle, he said, "I'll just be a moment. My horse is hidden behind the gatehouse."

"Oh! I wondered. . . ." She stopped, gave him an uncertain smile. "I'm sorry I'm acting so strangely. It is just that—"

He waited and when she said nothing more, just giving him an embarrassed shake of her head, he slipped away in the darkness. A moment later, he reappeared astride a big, black gelding. Giving her a reassuring smile, he said, "Follow me. I know a quiet place where we can talk."

Despite her unease with the situation, Juliana followed him without argument as he guided his horse into the forest. She frowned when she realized that they were riding farther and farther away from Kirkwood. How on earth would she ever find her way home?

As if sensing her unease, Asher stopped and when she came alongside him, he said, "Don't worry. I'll make certain that you find your way back home."

She half smiled and nodded. "Where are we going?" she asked.

"There's a poacher's hut just a bit ahead. It's equally as unlikely for anyone to be around, but I know from observation that it is cleaner and more comfortable than the gatehouse." He grinned at her. "It even has a pair of stools."

"How do you know?"

"Because, my sweet, I checked it out before I rode to the gatehouse."

She frowned. "Why did you do that?"

"Because it is not my habit to meet beautiful young women in mice- and rat-infested buildings."

"Oh," she said stupidly, her mind busy with the astonishing idea that *Asher* thought she was beautiful. Before she could stop herself, she blurted, "Do you really think I'm beautiful?"

"Fishing for compliments?" he teased.

In the darkness, she blushed. "No. Oh, no," she replied hurriedly. "I was just surprised to hear you say it. No one has ever called me beautiful before—Thalia's the beauty in the family."

He snorted and kicked his horse into motion. "In some people's opinion," he muttered under his breath.

Several minutes later, Asher pulled his horse to a stop in front of a small building nestled in a grove of trees and indicated that she should do the same. He had not lied when he had called it a hut, Juliana thought, studying the bare outlines of the place. She was positive the linen closet at Kirkwood was bigger.

"Wait here," he said as he dismounted.

Entering the windowless hut, Asher quickly lit the candle he had brought with him. In his earlier reconnoiter he'd made certain that the faint light from the candle could not be seen outside the hut and, using several drops of dripping wax as a base, he stuck the candle in the middle of a small, battered table. He glanced around again. The table, two rough wooden stools and an old pile of rushes in one corner made up the furnishings. He grimaced. Not what Juliana was used to, but the best he could do considering the time frame.

Juliana saw the briefest gleam of light when Asher opened the door to rejoin her. In a few minutes she'd be inside that little hut with him. She bit her lip, suddenly assailed by doubts.

She couldn't pretend that the adult Asher Cordell wasn't a very different kettle of fish from the impatient, sometimes kind, sometimes mocking boy she had known in her childhood. And don't forget how insufferably superior he could be, she reminded herself with a scowl, as certain youthful memories crossed her mind.

Preoccupied with her thoughts, at Asher's light touch on her hand, she jumped, causing her horse to move restively.

"I'm sorry," Asher said at her side. "I didn't mean to startle you."

She gave him an uncertain smile and allowed him to help her from her horse. His hands were firm around her waist as he lifted her down and though her heart kicked a little in her breast, his touch was politely impersonal. As it should be, she told herself firmly. This was not a dalliance and she was a silly goose to think that Asher, Asher who had pushed her into the creek when she had been eight and he an imperious thirteen, would ever look upon her as anything less than a nuisance. It was Thalia's future that was at stake. Thinking of Thalia and why she was here, Juliana stiffened her spine and marched into the hut.

It was even smaller inside than she had imagined and again she was reminded of the linen closet at Kirkwood. Grateful for the candlelight, she pushed back the hood of her cloak and took a few steps further into the hut.

Reaching the table, she turned and looked back at Asher, her heart doing another one of those uncomfortable kicks, as he stood there, his broad shoulders resting against the door, his arms folded across his chest. The expression on his face reminded her forcibly of the same look he'd worn the time her pony had bucked her off and she had sat on the ground bawling. There had been kindness, resignation and impatience in that look and it seemed that in nearly two decades, nothing had changed between them.

His voice revealing his irritation, he said, "Now, perhaps you'll tell me what is so important that we have to meet at this hour and in such secrecy." His eyes narrowed. "You haven't been gambling have you? Gotten yourself in the River Tick?"

Affronted, she glared at him. "Of course not! I know that some society ladies wager far more than they should, but I am not among them."

He shrugged. "Then why this meeting?"

Her gaze dropped from his and she stared down at the scarred top of the table. All the reasons why this had been a rash idea flashed across her brain, but she pushed them away. In the time since she had written the note to him nothing had changed and whether or not it was foolish or reckless, she had no choice but to forge ahead as best she could.

She took a deep breath, marshaling her thoughts. It seemed incredible to think that just over a week ago she and Asher had nearly been discovered in Ormsby's library in London. Even distracted by all the packing and closing up of the London house prior to their departure for Kent, the problem of Thalia's letters had been foremost in her mind. Probably the worst of it had been the trip from London to Kirkwood with the three of them locked within the confines of the small traveling coach. Thalia, her lovely face frozen in a mask of despair, had spent the journey stifling back tears, while Mr. Kirkwood sighed heavily from time to time and stared moodily out the coach window. Knowing it would be useless, Juliana hadn't even made a pretense at conversation and had passed the hours trying to figure a way out of their dilemma—a way that didn't involve Thalia being disgraced or married against her will to that wretched Ormsby. By the time they finally reached Kirkwood late Friday afternoon, despite some rather wild schemes, she had concluded that her original solution was still the only way: she had to get the letters out of Ormsby's hands.

There had been one stroke of luck, she admitted ruefully, although Thalia probably didn't consider coming down with measles lucky. Granted her own first response had been one of utter horror when Thalia had woken up Saturday morning covered in spots! But Juliana, taking this latest setback in stride, had quickly come to view it as a blessing. Thalia's condition made any notion of a house party out of the question and gave the family a perfect excuse to warn prospective guests away and postpone any party until the first week of August. Even an-almost-fiancé could be kept at bay and Juliana had been smiling when she had penned the note to Caswell explaining the situation. Thalia was mortified that she had fallen victim to such a childish complaint, but like Juliana she had come to view it as a reprieve. Thalia wouldn't be able to see her beloved until all signs of spots had disappeared and she had recovered her looks, but that also meant that she didn't have to face Ormsby either. And, Juliana thought grimly, Thalia's illness gave them some maneuvering room and some time in which to steal those wretched letters. Which brought her to this meeting with Asher.

She wouldn't have considered enlisting Asher's aid, if it hadn't been for their odd meeting in Ormsby's library. No more than she had he wanted to be discovered, which meant he had no business being there and that his reasons for lurking behind the drapes had been less than noble. He'd been up to something. She'd dismissed the idea out of hand that Ormsby had invited him to the ball. Ormsby loathed Asher. But even if Ormsby had invited him to the ball, what had Asher been doing in that darkened library?

Her breath caught as a likely notion occurred to her. Sympathy in her eyes, she blurted out, "Is Ormsby blackmailing you, too?"

Asher stiffened and he straightened from his position against the door. So *that's* why Juliana had been in Ormsby's library. The bastard had something he was holding over her head and she had been searching for it. A wave of cold rage surged through him and, the cobalt blue eyes darkening dangerously, he demanded, "Is Ormsby blackmailing you?"

His voice was like a whiplash and Juliana flinched. Asher muttered something ugly under his breath and in one swift stride was at her side. Catching her arms in his iron grip, he half snarled, "What the devil have you gotten yourself into?"

A little alarmed by his reaction, Juliana struggled to escape him, but his hands only clamped down harder on her arms.

"Be still!" he ordered, ignoring her struggles. "Now tell me, what does that scoundrel Ormsby hold over your head?"

The expression on his face reminded her of the one she'd glimpsed that night in Ormsby's gardens in London and a thrill of fright raced through her. His face had been in shadows that night, but here in this little hut the flickering candlelight revealed the stark menace in his features.

With huge eyes she stared at the dark, lean face above her, searching for any sign of the boy she had known. It was not there. This was a dangerous man, a hard man, a man, she realized with a sickening thud of her heart, not to be trifled with. Dear God! Why had she ever thought he would help her?

Several terrifying thoughts occurred to her. She was alone with him in the dead of night, alone with a stone-eyed stranger who held her helpless, his fingers biting painfully into her flesh. Escaping him was impossible. Her breath hitched and something else occurred to her. No one knew that she was meeting him. No one, including herself, knew where she was. Good heavens! If he was of a mind, he could murder her and no one would ever find her body.

Her thoughts chased themselves across her expressive face and, seeing the fear in her eyes, Asher's hold on her arms gentled and the look that had made her so afraid of him vanished. His voice softer, kinder, he said, "I won't hurt you. I would never hurt you. I'm sorry if I frightened you." He grimaced. "You know how I feel about Ormsby and the idea that you might be in his clutches . . ." Smiling wryly, he added, "I'm afraid that I let my temper rule there for a moment. Forgive me?"

She nodded uncertainly, her fright ebbing. Asher's contempt and dislike of Ormsby was well known and she should have been aware, she admitted, that the violence she had sensed in him, the violence she had seen on his face, had been directed solely at Ormsby.

His touch unbearably tender, he cupped her cheek. The dark blue eyes warm, he murmured, "Never be afraid of me. I might want to run Ormsby through or lose my temper because of him, but always remember that my anger is directed at him. Never you." His voice deepened. "Always know that no matter how much or how often you may enrage me, I would never, *ever* harm you."

Breathless, her rosy mouth half parted, she stared up at him. This, she thought giddily, was the darkly charming, utterly mesmerizing Asher who sometimes drifted through her forbidden dreams, arousing her, making her writhe and twist with longing.

Asher meant only to comfort her, but as he looked down at her, comfort became the last thing on his mind. He'd always thought that Thalia's blond and pink beauty was overrated and that Juliana, with her sable hair and whiskey brown eyes, was the true beauty in the family. Staring at her tonight, he was even more convinced that his opinion was right. She was tall like Thalia, her bosom and hips shapely, but she didn't have the almost-too-voluptuous curves of her younger sister. To his mind Thalia was cool perfection with her icy blue eyes and alabaster complexion, but Juliana . . . Juliana's dark hair and brilliant eyes coupled with skin the color and texture of a ripe peach made him think of hot, tropical nights. Nights where she was naked in his arms and exotic scents filled the air. His gaze locked on the generously curved mouth just below his, Asher felt his body tighten, felt the swelling, lengthening between his thighs. He wanted her. Badly. Tilting her face to his liking, his lips came down on hers and for a moment, for him, the world spun away and he lost himself in her sweet warmth.

She was soft and yielding under his mouth and one arm slid around her, pulling her next to him. He groaned at the sensation of her breasts crushed against his chest and heedlessly he deepened the kiss, his tongue thrusting into her mouth. Her shy response delighted him and his tongue explored at will, seeking, demanding more.

The thought of repulsing him, resisting him, never crossed Juliana's mind. Part of her knew this was dangerous, knew that she should push him aside, but she'd never felt this way in her life, never known such a wanton, primitive desire. Not even her husband's lovemaking had brought her to this fevered pitch nor aroused this urgent yearning to feel Asher's naked body pressed to hers, to luxuriate in the long, slow slide of his big body merging with hers. As the seconds passed and their mouths feasted on the other's, her nipples peaked and her arms closed around his neck, her tongue twining with his. Her cloak fell unheeded to the floor.

A delicious shudder racked her when his hand clenched her buttocks through her delicate gown and he pulled her closer to him, forcing her into intimate contact with the swollen rod of flesh between his legs. She was damp, burning to get closer to him, and she tilted her hips, rocking against him, seeking succor from the sweet ache that throbbed low in her belly.

Certain he would die if he did not have her, his lips never leaving hers, his tongue claiming her mouth as he intended to claim her body, Asher tipped her back onto the table. He moved immediately between her legs, his hands making short work of pushing her skirts out of the way. His fingers found her core and a soft growl of satisfaction came from him when he discovered her damp and hot and ready for him. He lifted his mouth from hers and tore at the opening in his breeches. His rigid member sprang free and wedging himself between her thighs, he looked down at her, a sumptuous banquet laid out for his taking. Their eyes met and in that moment reality exploded viciously through Asher.

Christ! This wasn't some strumpet he'd paid for. This was *Juliana!* And worse, he was seconds away from taking her like a rutting boar!

Cursing, Asher yanked down her skirts and jerked her up

from the table. Spinning away from her, with painful haste, he stuffed himself back into his breeches. His breathing hard and labored, his fists clenched at his sides, he closed his eyes and willed himself sane. By sheer force of will he beat back the howling desire that raged within him, throttled the almost overwhelming urge to turn and finish what they had started.

Stunned by the sudden turn of events, it took Juliana a moment to realize that she had come within seconds of making love with Asher Cordell on a table in a poacher's hut! Shame, embarrassment and horror flooded through her. Merciful heavens! What had come over her? What had she been thinking? Or not thinking, the practical side of her brain questioned slyly.

With a trembling hand, she brushed back a tangle of sable curls. Tears of shame and rage at her promiscuous behavior filled her eyes and threatened to spill down her cheeks. She had acted like a common whore. Regret and despair clawed through her. What must Asher think of her? Biting her lip to keep from sobbing, as much from anger at herself as shame, she brushed down the skirts of her gown. And how was she to approach him and ask for help in saving Thalia after this?

Wishing she could just die, Juliana took a deep breath and swung around to face Asher.

Though he was conscious of his aching member pressing against the front of his breeches, Asher had himself under control. When Juliana turned to face him, he said stiffly, "I never meant for that to happen and I cannot express how unforgivable it was of me to take advantage of you that way. I shall speak to your father in the morning."

Juliana blinked at him. "What? What does my father have to do with this?"

"Good God, Juliana! I just took shameless liberties with you and you have to know that there is only one outcome for us." His cool composure rather battered, he said reluctantly, "I hadn't planned to marry so soon, but the notion of marriage had crossed my mind recently and after what just happened between us . . ." He ran an agitated hand through his black hair. "I certainly never considered you as a prospective wife and I'm aware that I am the last man you would wish to marry but we shall just have to make the best of it and manage to rub along together." Without much conviction, he added, "It shouldn't be too bad. We're not children anymore. I won't put many demands on you and for the most part we shall each have our own lives. I am not without the means to support you and I promise you, though this isn't what either one of us wanted, that I will treat you well." When she simply stared goggled-eyed at him, he threw her a harassed look and muttered, "I know we haven't always gotten along with each other. I'm sure that you'd often have liked to box my ears—in fact, I think you did once." He half smiled at her. "I *know* there have been times that I thought you the most infuriating creature it had ever been my misfortune to know, but under the circumstances, putting our feelings for each other aside, the only honorable thing for me to do is to offer you marriage. As I said, I'll speak to your father tomorrow . . . this morning."

If Asher had slapped her Juliana couldn't have been more astonished or angry. Still stunned by what had happened, or *almost* happened between them, the marriage offer hit her like a blow from an oak club. Not knowing what to expect, it never would have occurred to her that Asher would offer her marriage and the fact that he was ineptly and insultingly trying to do just that left her reeling. Marriage? To Asher? She didn't know whether it would be a fate worse than death . . . or a dream come true. Miserably, she pushed that thought away. Only a lovesick pea goose would ever consider marriage to Asher a dream and she was *not* in love with him. He was a beast. And right now she hated him. It was obvious, too, she thought bitterly, that the last thing he wanted to do was marry and that *she* certainly had not been on any list of his possible brides. He didn't want to marry her, did he? Well, she wasn't about to marry *him!*

Drawing herself up, she glared at him and said icily, "First of all, there is no need for you to speak to my father. I think you forget that I am well beyond the age where I need my father's permission for anything. You also forget that I have been married before. I am, I would remind you, a widow. For a number of years I have had command of my own home and fortune." Her voice scathing, she spat, "I have no need of anything from you—not your name or your fortune."

Asher stared at her a long time. She was magnificent, he thought idly, with her bosom heaving, her cheeks flushed rosy and her eyes glittering with temper. The remnants of his earlier desire still nagging him, if he wasn't certain that she'd plant him a facer, he'd have grabbed her and kissed her and finished what they'd started. And the consequences be damned.

Her rejection of his offer of marriage didn't come as any surprise, though. Juliana had always possessed a contrary streak, but he wasn't certain how he felt about having his first proposal thrown back in his face. Surely, he wasn't *disappointed?*

Picking his way with care and taking his cue from her, he said, "Very well. If you don't wish to marry me, since as you've pointed out, it is your decision to make, I shall withdraw my offer."

Ignoring the twist in her heart, her initial burst of anger disappearing, she mumbled, "Thank you."

"And what occurred between us?" Asher asked with a cocked brow. "Do we pretend that it never happened and forget about it?"

"Of course!"

He shrugged. If she wanted to play it that way, so be it, but it was going to be a hell of a long time before he forgot what her mouth tasted like and how that temptingly curved body felt pressed next to his. He didn't think he'd ever wanted a woman as badly as he wanted her. He wasn't used to being denied and remembering how close they'd come to joining, he felt pressure build in his groin.

Suppressing a curse, he turned away from her and said, "Now that we have that out of the way, you want to tell me why we're here? And what Ormsby has to do with it?"

More to give herself time than anything else, Juliana reached down and picked up her cloak where it had fallen to the floor. Her eyes on her cloak, she folded it neatly over her arm and said, "You were in Ormsby's library to rob him, weren't you?"

"Perhaps. Why do you want to know?" He swung back to face her and his gaze narrowed. "You were there to rob him yourself, weren't you?"

She swallowed and nodded. This was the moment she'd dreaded. It had seemed so logical when she had first considered the idea, but now that she was faced with telling another person how foolish Thalia had been, she hesitated. Did she trust Asher enough? Would she be exchanging one blackmailer for another?

No, she decided firmly. She had proven embarrassingly incompetent when it came to sneaking about undetected and attempting theft. A shudder went through her as she remembered that moment of sheer terror when Ormsby had almost caught her in his library. She had had every right to be in Ormsby's house and even with that advantage, she hadn't been successful. Uninvited, Asher had managed to find his way into Ormsby's London house, which she admitted, showed a certain amount of skill. Skills she didn't possess. He was male, too, which also gave him an advantage that she didn't have.

For her to make another attempt to find and steal Thalia's letters, unless she was foolhardy enough to break into his home, she'd have to wait for Ormsby to invite her to his country house and hope that an opportunity presented itself, but Asher . . . Asher obviously didn't suffer from those constraints. He'd already broken into Ormsby's London residence—why would he balk at breaking into another house owned by Ormsby?

His voice gentle, Asher broke into her thoughts. "Is he blackmailing you?"

She shook her head. "No."

Pushing her down onto one of the wooden stools, Asher took the one across from her and said, "Tell me."

She stared into his dark face for several seconds, studying him. It was her sister's future she was risking. Did she dare? Could she trust him?

Her gaze dropped and, twisting her hands in her lap, she realized she had no choice, that she'd known the moment she'd written him that she'd have to trust him. "Suppose Ormsby did have something," she hedged, "say some indiscreet letters that he was using to blackmail someone with, could you steal them from him?"

"Of course."

Her head jerked up. "You sound very confident."

"I got into his London town house, didn't I?"

"Asher, getting into his house would be the least of your worries," she replied tartly. "How will you find the letters? How will you know where to look? He could hide them anywhere."

He pulled on his ear. "Most people are creatures of habit. Ormsby probably has one particular hiding place that he keeps . . . things that are valuable to him. I'm not saying I could find the letters my first time into the house, but it wouldn't take me long. There are only so many places someone like Ormsby would hide certain things."

When she didn't say anything, he leaned forward, caught one of her twisting hands between his, and said quietly, "I can help you, if you'll let me. Tell me."

And so she did.

Chapter 5

Asher didn't say a word for several minutes after Juliana finished speaking, but his expression said more than enough.

Juliana stood it as long as she could and then a little angrily, she said, "I know it was wrong of Thalia, but you have to remember how young she is, was."

"Your sister," he finally said in tones of great disgust, "would deserve it if she found herself married to Ormsby. Of all the addle-brained—"

The martial light in Juliana's eye made him think better of what he had been going to say. He held up a hand and muttered, *"Pax!"* When Juliana gave him a curt nod, he asked, "Do you know how many letters we're talking about?"

"Yes. Three."

"And how long do we have to get them back?"

Juliana bit her lip. "I've been able to postpone the house party until the end of the first week of August—a month from now. Caswell will no doubt be angling to see Thalia before then, but with Thalia not feeling well"—she half smiled—"and covered in spots, I don't think we have to worry about him for at least two weeks, perhaps even three. I believe the same would apply to Ormsby, although he will be harder to keep at bay, since his motives are entirely different than Caswell's."

"Not so very different," Asher said dryly. "They both want to marry Thalia."

Juliana sighed. "Yes, I suppose you're right. The difference is that while Caswell would accept a rebuff from Thalia and retire with a broken heart, Ormsby has no intention of having his suit rejected. He means to marry her by fair means or foul." She watched him anxiously. "You do understand that Thalia and Caswell are truly in love? And that Thalia can barely stand to be in the same room with Ormsby? She was foolish in what she did, but no one expected Ormsby to continue to press his suit after my father told him that Thalia did not want to marry him. What sort of man wishes to marry a woman who cannot abide him?" Not expecting an answer, she concluded angrily, "No gentleman would act as Ormsby has."

"I certainly won't argue with you there. My mother loathed him and referred to him often as a blackguard and a scoundrel." He flashed a smile. "From what you've told me tonight, it would appear that Mother was right."

Curiously, she asked, "Is that why you dislike him so? Because of your mother?"

He started to deny it, but then he said slowly, "That's probably the beginning of it. She never had a good word to say about him, so even as a very young child, my opinion of him was never high. As I grew older and I ran afoul of him a few times, I was quite capable of loathing him on principle—with no help from my mother."

Juliana frowned slightly. "I wonder why your mother held him in such low esteem? Ormsby has always been friendly with your stepfather and most people in the neighborhood hold him in respect, if not affection. Ormsby has often dined at Kirkwood and until recently my father considered him a friend. I've always thought him a bit cold and arrogant, but I would never have expected him to act as he has. Father is shocked and disillusioned." Her lips drooped. "By Thalia as much as Ormsby. It is a dreadful situation."

"Not as dreadful as it would be, my girl," Asher mocked, a faint smile on his mouth, "if I wasn't around to pluck your chestnuts from the fire."

She sent him a look. "And how do you intend to do that?"

His smile faded and he stared off into space. "I don't yet know precisely how I will get the letters back, but I will." His eyes met hers and, taking her hand in his, he said softly, "I swear to you that I will get Thalia's letters back."

There wasn't much to be said after that and shortly they were riding through the forest heading toward Kirkwood. Once the stables and outbuildings of the home place came into view, Asher halted his horse at the edge of the forest and said, "You go on. I'll watch from here." He studied the main house, not far from the stables. Spying a light in one of the upper windows, he asked, "Where the light is? Is that your bedroom window?"

"Yes. I left a candle burning when I left."

"Good. Once you dowse your candle, I'll know you're safely inside. Now run along."

Ignoring the mixed feelings of amusement and insult at his cavalier dismissal, she warned, "Remember, no one must know what we are about." She hesitated, then asked, "How will we manage to see each other without causing speculation?"

He grinned at her, his teeth a brief gleam of white in the darkness. "I suspect that my grandmother is going to be coming to see you often to help nurse Thalia. I shall, of course, be a dutiful grandson and accompany her."

Juliana shook her head, a rueful smile crossing her face. "I should have known you'd already have a plan. Even as a boy you were always planning."

"Only fools," he said harshly, "rush in blindly. Having a plan tends to limit the damage."

The note in his voice troubled her and she cast him a look, but the darkness hid his expression—not that his face would tell her anything even if she could see it. She realized that he hid much of himself behind what she was coming to believe was a deliberate facade of mockery and indifference. One thing she was sure of: if anyone could save Thalia from Ormsby's designs, it was Asher.

From his position in the forest, Asher watched as Juliana rode to the stable and disappeared into the long, low building. He cursed the opaque gloom that allowed him to see only eerie shadows, but the steel band of tension coiling in his gut lessened when he spied the dark shape that left the barn a few minutes later and hurried to the Kirkwood mansion. Waiting for her to reach her bedroom, he wasn't aware of how taut he held himself until her window went dark and he felt a sense of ease.

With Juliana safely in her room, he sat there in the darkness, considering what he had learned. His physical reaction to Juliana, something to be studied later, he forcibly pushed to the back of his brain and focused his powerful intellect on Ormsby and the finding of Thalia's letters. His thoughts drifted to Ormsby's reasons for pursuing a woman who had made it clear she wanted nothing to do with him. That Ormsby might be in love with Thalia he rejected immediately. If Ormsby loved her, he'd want her to be happy and Asher couldn't see any happiness coming to either one of them if Ormsby claimed Thalia as his bride. His lips thinned. Especially if that same bride was in love with another man. Christ! What was Ormsby thinking?

His horse moved restively under him and, deciding he wasn't going to solve the problem or come to any solutions immediately, he was on the point of turning his horse around when movement near the Kirkwood stables caught his attention. A large, dark shape was moving swiftly away from the stables and heading down the driveway toward the main road. Frowning, he watched from the concealing forest as a horse and rider sped by. Now why, he wondered, was someone riding away from Kirkwood at this time of night?

He glanced in the direction of Juliana's windows in the main house, but beyond the vague, dark outline of the house, he could see nothing. Could the rider be Juliana? His gaze narrowed. Had she waited long enough for him to leave and was she now on her way to another rendezvous? A rendezvous, perhaps, with Ormsby? Was everything she had told him tonight a lie? Part of a scheme concocted by Ormsby to spring some sort of trap on him? Instinct told him, no . . . but he wasn't taking any chances.

Urging his horse out of the forest and onto the road, he raced after the departing rider. As the miles passed, the rider ahead of him held the horse at a hard gallop, never once slackening the pace or looking at the road behind him. Which was as well, Asher thought with a grim smile. At this time of night, the road was deserted, with respectable folk tucked in their beds, and beyond a few broad curves and a slight dip or two, the road offered little chance of concealment. Without losing the rider ahead, he kept a careful distance between them, the sound of his own horse's passage covered by the pounding hooves of the other horse, but Asher knew that one quick glance backward by the rider and the jig would be up.

Long before the horseman slowed and turned the horse from the main road, Asher had guessed the destination. Ormsby Place. He halted his horse and stared at the massive, ornate gateway that graced the main entrance to Ormsby Place.

His face set, he stared at the faint outline of the gateway in the darkness. Could it be Juliana ahead of him? Was she even now meeting with Ormsby? Something implacable crossed his face. Would she be coming from his arms and crawling into bed with the marquis? Laughing at how cleverly she had embroiled him in their scheme? He brushed those ugly images aside and kicked his horse forward. He didn't believe Juliana capable of such deceit, but there was only one way to find out.

Familiar with the layout of the area from previous visits,

Asher directed his horse from the road and cut through the huge swath of parkland that surrounded Ormsby Place. The woodland not only hid him from the other rider, but the soft ground muffled the sound of his horse's hooves as they galloped through the night. He slowed the animal as Ormsby Place rose up in the distance ahead of him. Stopping again, he listened intently, pleased when he heard the thud of hoofbeats only a short distance in front of him. Following the sound, he kept pace, but once the rider swerved away from the grand circular driveway in front of the house, and rode in the direction of stables, he increased the speed, arriving ahead of his quarry.

Leaving his horse tied at the edge of the parkland, Asher slipped through the night, keeping low and running toward the sprawling stable area. He reached the first of several stables and pressed himself up against the side of the building just as the horse and rider came trotting up. Edging around to the corner he watched as the rider halted the horse and leaped out of the saddle. Not Juliana, he thought cheerfully. This person was definitely male if the height and lanky build was anything to go by; Asher sensed that he was young. So who? And why?

The man opened one of the wide double doors of the stable and disappeared inside, shutting the door behind him. Asher waited a second, carefully scanning the area, listening intently. Sensing no danger, he glided around to the front of building. At the double doors, he slowed checking for any opening that might give him a glimpse inside. Finding none, he wasted another moment, pressing his ear to the stout wooden doors. Only the faint sound of horses moving around in their stalls came to him. He hadn't expected to be able to see anything—even if there had been a slit or a knothole, it was pitch black inside the stable. He looked at the doors for a long minute, then dismissed any notion of opening them. There was no use alerting his quarry to his presence.

Leaving the doors behind, he crossed to the opposite corner of the building and glanced down the side. Nothing but shadows met his eye and he stopped in place, thinking of his next move. From his position he could see the front area and a slight tilt of his head allowed him to look down the other side of the stables. His head resting back against the boards, he considered what he knew of the Ormsby stables.

Not often, but upon occasion, either with his stepfather or his grandmother, he'd been a guest at Ormsby Place and more than once, the marquis had proudly shown off some of his much-sought-after blooded stock. Asher's mouth twitched. He didn't fault the man for having an eye for a good horse or for knowing how to breed for one and if he could admire Ormsby for anything it would be for his undeniable talent for breeding some outstanding horses. He owned one himself.

But it wasn't horses that Asher was thinking about tonight. He was trying to recall the exact layout of the building he leaned against. He remembered that a wide alleyway ran down the center with several spacious stalls opening onto it. There was a grain room, a tack room, an office, and if he remembered correctly, a large room on this side at the far end where the head groom slept. Since his quarry had not reappeared and it was unlikely there was anybody else inside . . . Whoever he had followed, he concluded, had to have come to see the person asleep at the other end of the stable.

Asher froze as the muffled noise of something falling or being tipped over and the startled snort of several horses came from inside the building. Someone cursed loudly and a second later a small light bloomed near the end of the long building, the light shining out from the window into the darkness. There were more curses, two voices now, and neither sounded very happy to Asher. After a last glance around the area in front of the stables, Asher slid around the corner and swiftly covered the area that separated him from the source of the light.

He ducked down as he ran past a row of windows and

stopped just before he reached the last window in the building where the light flickered. His back pressed against the wall, he crept nearer the window.

The night was warm and the window was open and the voices of the two men inside carried easily outside.

"What the hell are you doing here this time of night?" snarled a voice Asher didn't recognize.

"You told me if I saw anything queer at Kirkwood I was to let you know straightaway. Said there'd be money for me," whined the other man. Asher didn't recognize the second voice either.

There was another curse and the first man said, "Damn your eyes! I didn't mean at bleeding three o'clock in the morning!"

More whining and grumblings were exchanged.

"This had better be bloody good," warned the first man. "I ain't paying for some cock and bull story."

The whining man mumbled something and then reported the odd behavior of Kirkwood's oldest daughter.

"And you didn't follow her when she left?" demanded the first man. "Find out where she went? Who she met?"

The whining-voiced man must have shaken his head no, because there was a blistering string of curses from the first man.

"I tried, I tell you," protested Whiney-voice. "But I was fair betwattled when I spied her sneaking into the stables and saddling her own horse at that time of night. She kept glancing around, nervous-like. It was plain as the nose on your face that she didn't want anyone to see what she was doing. Never would have thought a respectable lady like Mrs. Greeley would be slipping about like a common bit of muslin. By the time I had me wits gathered and a horse saddled, she'd disappeared."

"How long was she gone? Or are you going to tell me you went to sleep and don't know when she returned?"

"No, I didn't go asleep. I ain't that much of a fool, despite what you may think!" Whiney said indignantly. "I dunno for sure how long she was gone, not having a timepiece and all, but I expect that it was only an hour or two. Once she came back and put her horse away, I slipped to the front of the barn and watched as she ran to the house. Then I lit out for here."

There was silence for several minutes. From his position outside the window, Asher guessed that the Ormsby man was considering Whiner's information.

"You told me to let you know soonest I could if I saw anything strange. Ain't this the sort of thing you're after?" asked Whiney after a bit. "It ought to be worth something."

The Ormsby man muttered something that Asher didn't catch. He heard the sound of a drawer opening and some coins clinking together. A moment later, Whiney exclaimed, "Bloody hell! That's all I get for my troubles!"

"For now," growled the other man. "All you told me was that Mrs. Greeley took a midnight ride. Can't see that it was worth much."

The whiner protested, but the Ormsby man waved him away. "I've paid you more than that bit of nonsense is worth and if you wasn't me brother, I wouldn't give you that much. Now go on back to Kirkwood before you are missed."

"You always was a stingy fellow," complained Whiney.

The other man gave a hard laugh. "And you always were a fool! Sometimes I think Ma played Pa false to saddle me with a looby like you."

"Seeing as how you don't think much of what I brought you," Whiney said, "don't think I'll be doing you any more favors."

"I told you: bring me something useful and there's money in it for you." He paused and added, "If you'd followed her and knew where she went . . . now that would have been worth something."

They spoke for a few minutes more, the Ormsby man gradually coaxing the whiner out of his sullen attitude.

From his position outside the window, wanting to identify

the men, especially the one from Kirkwood, Asher considered risking a glance inside the room, but dismissed it. It would be his luck, he thought sourly, that both men would be staring right out the window, straight at him. Consoling himself with the knowledge that the two men were brothers and that finding out which one of the stable boys at Kirkwood had a brother who was the head groom at Ormsby should be simple enough to do.

Business concluded, the two men in the stables parted, the Ormsby man saying, "Now remember, keep your eyes open."

Muttering, the whiner exited the room and a second later the candle went out. Asher remained where he was and only when he heard the noises that indicated the Ormsby man was most likely settling back into bed, did he move.

Silently he slid along the side of the building toward the front of the stable. Hearing the stable door open and close, he picked up his speed and was at the corner of the building and able to watch the Kirkwood servant ride away into the darkness. When the sound of the horse's hooves disappeared into the distance, Asher hurried to where he had left his own mount tethered.

Riding back through the quiet night toward Fox Hollow, Asher was thoughtful. Tonight had been . . . interesting. Under different circumstances, Ormsby's determination to marry Thalia might have amused him, but the use of her letters to force a marriage between them put the situation in a whole different light. He grinned. He'd have stolen the letters from Ormsby for the sheer delight in doing so, but saving Thalia from Ormsby's clutches added a touch of nobility to the task. If Juliana was correct, Thalia was in love with Caswell, and what could be nobler than seeing two lovers united?

And then there was Juliana . . . His loins tightened uncomfortably as the memory of her soft body, the taste of her mouth beneath his, rolled over him. Christ! He had reacted like a green boy with his first woman. He had fallen on her like a ravening wolf on a spring lamb and almost taken her on that battered table in a bloody poacher's hut. Even now with some distance from the event, his reaction to her appalled him. She was damn near like a sister to him, he thought incredulously, and he had been moments away from mounting her as if she were a trollop in a waterfront tavern.

Though there were five years between them, from the time he was around eleven years old and his stepfather had lost a leg in some nameless battle and returned to Apple Hill, they'd grown up together. He shook his head remembering those carefree childhood days. The times she had tattled on him and his brothers and he'd seethed to box her ears! He'd viewed her in those early years as one of the most irritating members of the female species that it had ever been his misfortune to know. But he'd had affection for her, too, and when he thought of her at all, it had been with the same fondness he bestowed upon his younger sisters. Yet that had changed in an instant tonight and he doubted he'd ever be able to go back to thinking of her with anything that remotely resembled brotherly affection.

The stark fact was that he had wanted her in the most basic way a man could want a woman. And he had wanted her, he reminded himself uneasily, more than he could remember wanting any woman.

Even after Fox Hollow came into view and he dismounted and took care of his horse, his thoughts were on Juliana and the passionate interlude in the poacher's hut. His own reaction, he half understood—he was male and it had been several months since he'd had a woman. As he entered the house and walked upstairs to his rooms on the second floor, it was Juliana's reaction to his blunt advances that preoccupied him. So why hadn't she boxed his ears and rung a peal over him? The Juliana he had known certainly would have. He grinned. With relish—and then lectured him on the impropriety of his actions.

Not bothering to light a candle, Asher stripped off his clothes and slid into bed. Settling beneath the sheets and light coverlet, his hands behind his head, he stared into the darkness, still reviewing those combustible moments in the poacher's hut. It gratified him that Juliana had not repulsed him, but he wondered why she had not. Did her response bespeak a woman who was willing game for any man . . . or had her sweet generosity been for him alone? He rather liked the idea that her reaction might have been simply because he was the man kissing her.

Thinking of those heated kisses, he was fascinated that his often vexing childhood companion had revealed, if only for those moments, a distinctly amorous proclivity. Who would have ever suspected, he wondered, that underneath those damned muslin skirts and hiding behind that prim and proper exterior existed such a passionate creature? More importantly, could he coax that decidedly sensual being out of hiding again? His grin widened. Oh, yes, he rather thought he could.

It would have been pleasant to drift to sleep thinking of Juliana, but knowing he could put it off no longer, he shoved the enticing paradox of the eminently respectable Mrs. Greeley aside and concentrated on the rest of the night's events.

One thing was obvious: Ormsby had a spy at Kirkwood. But why? Ormsby held the upper hand: he had the letters. Did he fear that despite the threat of scandal Thalia would throw caution to the winds and try to run away with Caswell anyway? Asher frowned and briefly considered the possibility that the head groom's meeting tonight with his brother had nothing to do with Ormsby or Thalia, but he dismissed it. What would be the purpose? No. Ormsby had to be behind it. And going on that assumption, from what he'd overheard tonight, it would appear that Ormsby had enlisted the help of his head groom, but hadn't been very specific about what sort of information he wanted from the Kirkwood stable boy.

Asher didn't doubt that the head groom would report Juliana's midnight ride to the marquis, but beyond, perhaps, arousing Ormsby's curiosity, Asher didn't see that it would do any harm. He would warn Juliana, though, of the spy in her stables.

As for the spy in the Kirkwood stables, Asher concluded that identifying him would be enough for now. No use alerting Ormsby that his agent had been unmasked and give him an opportunity to plant another one somewhere else on the estate. Once the stable boy was identified, they'd be able to circumvent his learning anything useful. An unpleasant smile curved Asher's lips. And, if necessary, allow them to feed Ormsby whatever half lies they wanted.

The stealing of the letters held the least interest for Asher. He'd taken on harder jobs than this before and been paid damned well for it, too, he admitted. For a moment the rein on his thoughts sprang free and he lost himself thinking of ways to extract a suitable and oh so satisfying price from Juliana for his efforts on her behalf. Money was not involved.

A yawn took him. He could solve nothing tonight and dawn was only hours away. He yawned again. First thing in the morning, he had to ride over to his grandmother's and warn her that she was going to go visit poor little Thalia Kirkwood this afternoon. His pulse gave a jump. And he would see the delightfully proper Mrs. Greeley. A smile on his lips, he slept.

Juliana did not sleep so well. For the first time since she had temporarily moved back into her father's home to help with Thalia's debut, she resented being here. She had her own charming house not too many miles down the road and tonight she missed its familiarity and comforts terribly. Not that Kirkwood wasn't a pleasant house; it just wasn't *her* house.

After the meeting with Asher tonight, her nerves were jangled and she desperately wanted the comfort of her own things around her, needed to walk through the cozy rooms she had created and find her equilibrium. From the instant Ormsby had called upon her father and the existence of

Thalia's indiscreet, foolish letters had been revealed, life had seemed to spin out of control. And Juliana needed control.

For so much of her life, most things had been beyond her control. She had been a dutiful daughter, submitting gracefully to her father's kindly rule, never once struggling against the edicts of society that gave him complete sway over her future. When it came to marriage, it had never occurred to her not to marry a man her father and the polite world thought suitable. It hadn't, she thought, half hysterically, even occurred to her *not* to marry. Marriage was what was *expected* of a young lady of her class and the alternatives, governess, spinster aunt or household drudge, did not appeal. And so just shy of her twenty-first birthday she had married. A very nice, respectable man with a modest fortune.

Wandering around her former rooms at Kirkwood, she wondered, not for the first time, if she had ever loved William Greeley. She hadn't *disliked* him and he had been a pleasant enough man, but . . . No, she hadn't loved him. She'd been genuinely fond of him, enjoyed his company and had been content to be his wife. She had exchanged her father's rule for her husband's and without complaint had adapted to her new circumstances. Marriage gave her a trifle more freedom—a wife wasn't as constrained as a single woman—but it would never have occurred to her to thwart society and kick over the traces. Settled into her husband's home on his father's estate in Hampshire, she'd hoped for children, they both had, and in time that might have happened if he hadn't died of consumption barely a month prior to their third anniversary.

Finding herself widowed at twenty-four had been a shock and her world had turned upside down. For the first time in her life there was no male figure to be deferred to, no one to exert the gentle despotism under which she had lived, and for a few months she drifted aimlessly, much like a ship without a rudder. Of course, her father and her father-in-law gave her sage advice on what she should do and where she should live and she listened to them politely, but a part of her was even then vaguely aware that they could not *compel* her to follow their advice.

Her in-laws had wanted her to continue to live in the pleasant house she had shared with their youngest son, but after only a few months, Juliana found herself longing more and more for the familiar lands of her birth. Lonely, missing her husband, she yearned to be near her sister: she wanted, she realized, to return to Kent. The marriage settlements she received from her husband had been generous and she woke up one morning with the invigorating knowledge that she could do precisely as she pleased with no one to gainsay her. If she wanted to move nearer her sister she could, and with only a little pang she had kissed her in-laws good-bye and moved back to Kirkwood.

Her father, assuming she had come home to stay, had been astonished when a few weeks later, she mentioned that she wanted to buy a charming little estate hardly more than five miles away from Kirkwood. He counseled against it, happy to have his eldest daughter once again seeing to Thalia and taking the burdens of running the household off his shoulders, allowing him to lose himself in his books. Surprising herself as much as him, she demurred and promptly purchased Rosevale—a half-timbered, two-story house, and the three hundred rich, fertile acres that went with it.

Turning a deaf ear to those who suggested that she was far too young and pretty to live on her own, she set about turning Rosevale into *her* home. She conceded to convention on one point though, installing her dear old nursemaid, Mrs. Rivers, in the house to still any wagging tongues. It was sufficient to satisfy her father and since Mrs. Rivers was a cheerful and sensible lady who was far too grateful to live in ease and comfort beyond her means to ever raise any objections to anything Juliana suggested, the two women were very pleased with the arrangement. Her small staff, cook, housekeeper, maid, gardener and stable man, insured that everything ran smoothly and she had settled down happily to live a tranquil life in the country. She wanted for nothing. Her father and sister were nearby. She had her own home, her own fortune, and could and did arrange her life as she chose. It had proven to be exhilarating.

When she offered to help her father with Thalia's London debut, Juliana thought of it as a pleasant, enjoyable diversion. Originally, she would be gone from Rosevale for a few months while the family was in London, and once they came back to Kent, she would return to her own snug little home, except for times such as the house party, when her presence would be needed at Kirkwood.

Her lips drooped. It seemed so simple, she thought unhappily, before Ormsby had destroyed everyone's plans and set her feet on the perilous path she now trod. For someone as respectable and conventional as Juliana, the notion that she would creep into Ormsby's London study with theft on her mind had been inconceivable. But that was before, she reminded herself, Ormsby had threatened to destroy Thalia's chance for happiness.

From the moment she had opened the door to Ormsby's study and slid into that dark room, she'd known that she was on shifting, dangerous ground, every step she took fraught with disaster. And nothing had changed since then. If anything, she may have made things worse, enlisting someone else, allowing someone else to know how foolish her sister had been. . . .

The memory of lying on that horrible old table, her skirts up around her waist, her body hot and yearning, eager for Asher's possession, burned across her mind and she flushed. Good God! *She,* not Thalia, had been seconds away from being thoroughly compromised and ruined!

She buried her face in her hands, humiliated and ashamed. Her sister's very future was at stake and she had acted like a common trollop. What had she been thinking? Certainly not of Thalia, she admitted wretchedly, and Thalia had to be her first and *only* priority.

Juliana took a deep, calming breath. What happened tonight had been an aberration, a moment out of time, a moment not to be repeated. She couldn't explain it, she wasn't even certain how it had happened—she only knew that once Asher had touched her and taken her into his arms, the world had simply vanished and there was only Asher kissing her, touching her, arousing her beyond anything she had ever imagined. In those wild, frantic seconds, she forgot everything except how wonderful his mouth felt on hers, how hungry, how *demanding* her body had been for his possession. Nothing had mattered then. Not Thalia, not respectability, not even danger. Just thinking of those never-to-be-sufficiently-regretted moments, desire, uncontrollable and urgent, flooded through her and to her horror her nipples peaked and an aching heat flared between her thighs. Her fists clenched at her sides and she willed the feelings away. What was wrong with her? Even with her husband she'd never experienced such powerful sensations, yet Asher . . . She swallowed painfully. With Asher she had forgotten every scruple, every precept she had ever known. And it must not happen again. It must *not,* she reminded herself desperately, because only folly . . . and heartache awaited her down that path.

Chapter 6

A sher's first chore the next morning had been to write his grandmother a note, telling her of Thalia's measles and with the warning that he would be driving over this afternoon to take her to call upon the Kirkwood household to offer assistance. Once the note was on its way to Burnham, he enjoyed a breakfast of tender scones just from the oven, coddled eggs and rare sirloin, washing down the whole with a tankard of ale.

Retiring to his office, he looked over some papers his farm manager had left earlier on his desk for his perusal, but his mind had been on last night's events and his thoughts drifted.

He had no doubts that he could find and recover Thalia's letters in the time frame that Juliana had given him. Finding the letters would be the trickiest part, but in the course of his less-than-respectable career, he had discovered that most people were predictable, even more so when it came to concealing items of importance. He'd known a few individuals who did not follow the normal pattern of behavior and had caused him some unpleasant surprises, but those people were the exception, not the rule.

Now that the marquis had quitted London, assumptions aside, it was almost a certainty that Thalia's three letters were hidden somewhere within his palatial home. The *most* likely place the marquis would have put them was in the safe in his study. Like many other people Asher could name, Ormsby thought his safe was cleverly hidden behind a huge landscape by Gainsborough that hung on the wall opposite the marble fireplace. Asher shook his head. First place any experienced thief would look. He grinned. He'd found Ormsby's safe and examined it years ago when the idea of stealing the Ormsby diamonds had originally occurred to him; that knowledge would prove useful now. Breaking into the house wouldn't present much of a challenge; the room was on the east side of the sprawling mansion and faced a small garden. From the study a pair of French doors opened onto it and would allow him easy access. Even better, Ormsby wouldn't be expecting a thief brazen enough to break in to the house when everyone in the neighborhood knew the marquis to be in residence.

Asher wasn't ignoring the dangers or being overconfident. He trusted his skills, honed during numerous situations like this one, but he was also aware that the slightest miscalculation or misstep could bring disaster down on him. His lips twisted. And leave him in the gaol and his grandmother and the rest of his family unable to show their faces in public because of his disgrace. No. Getting caught wasn't in his plans.

He stood up and walked to the window and stared out. Breaking into Ormsby's house and opening the safe was a simple enough task for a man of his talents. It could get dicey, however, if Ormsby had installed a new safe within the past few years or if the letters were *not* in the safe. He considered the idea for several minutes, then shrugged. A new safe might present difficulties, but none that a clever thief couldn't overcome. If the letters weren't in the safe, he'd have to reconsider the situation. Even if the letters were not in the safe, all might not be lost—it was possible that Ormsby was arrogant enough to keep them lying around in his desk, never thinking that a thief would dare rob the Marquis of Ormsby in his own home. Asher smiled. He couldn't help it. He was going to enjoy filching those letters from Ormsby . . . and watching Juliana's face light up when he laid them in her hands.

*　*　*

After writing a few letters and telling Hannum he'd be gone for the day, Asher strolled down to the stables. In a matter of minutes he was tooling down the road in his curricle, pulled again by his favorite pair of blacks.

Arriving at Burnham he found his grandmother waiting for him in the front parlor. Of the puppy there was no sign and after greeting his grandmother, he inquired after the missing Apollo.

"Don't you worry about him," she said with a twinkle in her eyes. "He is presently visiting with Cook for the sole purpose of convincing her that the nice ham bone she was saving for some soup would be much better served if she gave it to him." She laughed. "He learned immediately how easily a pitiful glance from those big brown eyes of his elicits the most delicious tidbits from Cook. And I am no better—as you probably guessed he has joined me in bed." She beamed at him. "Oh, Asher! I do so enjoy having a dog with me again." She shook her head. "But I fear that he is already spoiled beyond redemption."

She kissed him on the cheek and said, "Thank you, my dear. I did not know how dull my days were until Apollo arrived. He is just the tonic I needed."

Together they walked into the foyer where Mrs. Manley's butler, Dudley, was waiting with her parasol and gloves and a small reed basket packed with two jars of her favorite restorative jellies. Once she was settled in the curricle, the basket snug against her side, Asher leaped nimbly into the vehicle and, lifting the reins, set the horses trotting smartly down the driveway.

Reaching the main road, he kept the horses at the same pace and, glancing over at his grandmother, caught her watching him with a speculative gaze. Smiling, he demanded, "What? Why are you looking at me like that?"

"Did you know," she began conversationally, her eyes now on the road ahead, "that I have always had a fondness for the

Kirkwood girls, Juliana especially?" She obviously didn't expect a reply, because she rattled on. "And of course, Thalia is a charming girl and a great beauty, but I didn't realize that she was to your taste."

Asher's hands on the reins jerked and he shot his grandmother an incredulous look. "You think this is about *Thalia?*" he demanded.

"What else can I think when my favorite grandson, who has never paid the least heed to any of the young ladies in the neighborhood, suddenly asks me to accompany him to the reigning beauty's home?" she asked reasonably.

"This has nothing to do with Thalia," he muttered. "It seemed a neighborly thing to do." He cleared his throat. "And it was Juliana I was thinking of, more than Thalia. I'm sure that Juliana would enjoy a break from the sick room and nursing the invalid."

She sent him a bright look. "Ah, I am to keep Thalia occupied while you and Juliana share a few minutes alone?"

He grinned at her. "Do you mind?"

She shook her head and grinned back at him. "I suspected it was something like that, but I wanted to be certain. And I must say, I am relieved."

"Relieved? Why?"

"I know she is a beauty, but Thalia would never be my first choice for a granddaughter-in-law."

He shuddered. "Good God, no!"

"But Juliana will do very nicely, I think," she said, and patted him on the arm.

Asher yanked his horses to a stop in the middle of the road. Ignoring the plunging and rearing of the horses at such cow-handed handling, he turned to stare at his grandmother. "You're matchmaking," he accused, his expression outraged.

His grandmother laughed. "Oh, Asher, if you could see your face!" Her eyes tender, she caressed his cheek. "At this moment, you look so much like your grandfather and mother that it takes my breath away."

"That's a dashed silly thing to say. Mother was a beauty and I ain't," he said loftily, "beetle-browed and beaky nosed like the portrait of him in the gallery at Burnham!"

She laughed. "Oh, I agree—that awful portrait! Believe me, my dear, he looked nothing like that."

"And furthermore," he growled, reverting back to the original subject, "I have no intention of marrying Juliana Greeley. I am merely trying to be *polite*."

She looked back at him. "Are you so sure?"

Setting his horses in motion once more, his eyes firmly ahead, he said, "Of course I am! Marriage is the last thing I . . ." The words died in his throat. Hadn't he been thinking of marriage just the other night? Hadn't he gone to his bed, considering the notion? The memory of Juliana spread out like a feast for a starving man on the poacher's table scorched through his mind and it didn't take much imagination from him to place her in his bed at Fox Hollow. As his wife.

He glanced over at his grandmother and found her watching him with a knowing smile. "Stop it," he said, half laughing. "You're manipulating me."

She shook her head. "No. Simply trying to make you see what is right in front of you."

"You've done so," he admitted wryly. "Now let it rest. When and *if* I decide to marry *anybody*, let me do my own courting."

"Just as long as you court the right woman."

Mr. Kirkwood was pleased that they had come to call, but Asher could see the signs of strain on the man's face and to his eye, Juliana's father seemed even more distracted than usual. While others might not notice it, knowing the circumstances it was obvious that the threat Ormsby presented to his youngest daughter's happiness was preying on his mind. Though he hid it well, there was to Asher's eye a forced manner about Mr. Kirkwood's welcome, and after a brief visit with the pair of them, Mr. Kirkwood rang for a servant to fetch Juliana. Everything went just as Asher had planned. In a matter of minutes Mr. Kirkwood had retreated to his library, Mrs. Manley was upstairs entertaining the invalid, and Asher had whisked Juliana away for a stroll through the gardens.

It was a warm day and they did not hurry down the various winding paths, Juliana eventually leading him to a shady arbor covered with twining yellow and white roses. Seating herself on one of the stone benches inside, after arranging the skirts of her green sprigged muslin gown, she looked over expectantly at Asher.

It had been years since they had spent any time in each other's company and the Asher of today was far different from the boy she had known in her childhood. Surreptitiously she eyed him. He sat down next to her, his shoulders resting against the back of the bench, his legs stretched out in front of him and crossed at the ankles. Her gaze wandered to his tousled black hair, worn a trifle longer than the fashion of the day, but she decided that the careless style suited his lean, almost swarthy features. The dark blue coat fit his muscular body superbly, his cravat was neatly tied and the nankeen breeches clearly defined his strong legs. His black boots were spotless.

Not unaware of her examination, the cobalt eyes gleaming with laughter, he teased, "Do I pass inspection?"

Juliana flushed, embarrassed to be caught staring. Stiffly, she said, "I apologize."

"Don't. Stare as much as you like . . . provided I can take the same liberties."

"Oh, cease!" she said impatiently. "I am not in the mood to bandy words with you." She glanced at him. "Have you made any plans to get back Thalia's letters?"

Asher shrugged. "Certainly. I'll take a couple nights to reconnoiter and then if all looks well, I'll strike. Assuming they are where I think they are, you'll have Thalia's letters back before too many more days pass."

"I pray God you are right," she declared fervently. "The whole affair is wearing everyone down. Thalia is so fretful and I know that not all of it is because of her illness. She feels so guilty and ashamed and is afraid of what the future may hold." Juliana sighed and stared down at her hands folded in her lap. "And poor Papa is beside himself with worry. He, too, is full of guilt and because of his inability to save her is nearly as ashamed as Thalia. It is dreadful."

Asher's warm hand covered hers. "And what of you?" he asked softly, astounded at how badly he wanted to shoulder her problems and slay the dragons that threatened her peace of mind.

Juliana deftly removed her hand from beneath his and half laughed, half cried, "Oh, I am, as usual, being the rock of the family. I cannot give way to despair because if *I* do they will both feel that all is lost."

"Your father is a grown man. Your sister is no child and this situation is of her making. Don't you think it's time that they both stopped relying on you for rescue and stood up and took care of their own problems?" he asked sharply.

"How dare you!" she exclaimed, glaring at him. "I came to you for help, not for criticism of my family!"

Conscious of the misstep, Asher threw up his hands and said, "I apologize. I spoke without thought and did not mean to find fault." He smiled crookedly at her. "Forgive me? Please?"

When he looked at her in just that fashion, with that uneven smile curving his mouth and the dark blue eyes warm and caressing, Juliana feared that she would forgive him just about anything. Angry with herself, she muttered, "Of course. You have promised to help and I do not want to be at daggers drawing with you. I have troubles enough without adding to them."

Looking down at his crossed ankles, Asher said wryly, "After what I discovered last night, I'm afraid that you have more troubles than you realize."

"What do you mean?" she demanded, her eyes wide with alarm.

Bluntly he told her of the events that had occurred after they had parted. For several seconds after he finished speaking, there was silence in the arbor.

"Good God!" she finally burst out. "Ormsby has placed a spy in our midst? Why? He has the letters."

"I suspect he's taking no chances that the prize slips away from him."

"But as long as he has the letters—"

"The letters only have as much power as you are willing to give them," Asher said. "Suppose Thalia takes it in her head to throw caution to the winds and elope with Caswell?" Juliana started to protest such an idea, but Asher held up his hand, silencing her. "Think about it for a moment. The instant Thalia becomes his wife, the power shifts to Caswell. Once Caswell and Thalia are married, it's true that Ormsby could still make the letters public, but that wouldn't reflect well on him, now would it? Society might look askance at your sister, but Ormsby's role in the whole affair, especially an attempt to ruin a young bride married to a well-liked gentleman of the *ton*, would make him look the scoundrel he is. Ormsby wouldn't risk that happening." When Juliana looked thoughtful, he added, "Don't forget, Caswell is reputed to be both an excellent swordsman and marksman—do you think that Ormsby would be willing to die on the dueling field?"

"And don't *you* forget that Ormsby's reputation on the dueling field isn't to be lightly dismissed," Juliana said almost absently. Asher's words made a great deal of good sense and she wondered why none of them had ever considered the cost to Ormsby if he went ahead with his threats. Because, she thought bitterly, we were only thinking of the price we would pay—and Ormsby was counting on that. Something occurred to her and she gasped. Looking at Asher, she said, "Ormsby has planted a spy to warn him when Caswell arrives—especially if he arrives clandestinely. He's hoping to prevent Thalia and Caswell from eloping!"

Asher nodded. "That's my conclusion." He grinned at her.

"Ormsby isn't as confident as he pretends. He may hold the letters, but he doesn't hold Thalia."

Frowning, Juliana stared ahead. "There's no question of an elopement at this time—not with Thalia covered in spots." She bit her lip. "And I don't know that Caswell would agree to an elopement . . . not without knowing why it is so imperative. And once he knows the reason behind it . . ." She grimaced. "Instead of eloping with her, he's just as likely to walk away and break Thalia's heart or challenge Ormsby to a duel. Neither outcome is particularly appealing."

He looked curiously at her. "You don't think Caswell loves her enough to overlook the letters?"

She shrugged. "I don't know. I believe that he is devoted to her and truly loves her, and what she did isn't so very bad, but Ormsby will make it out to be so much worse." She made a face. "No gentleman wants to marry a woman who may have already played him false."

"Hmmm, I wonder if it went that far," Asher mused aloud.

Juliana shot him a fierce look. "Thalia may be a little goose, but she would never have allowed Ormsby to seduce her!" she said hotly. "She may have met him secretly, at his instigation, I might remind you, and she wrote some foolish letters but that is *all*."

Asher kept his thought to himself and murmured, "Then we have nothing to worry about. I shall get your sister's letters back for you." He glanced at her. "From what I told you about him, do you have any idea who the man is that I followed to Ormsby's last night?"

"Yes," she said glumly. "Just before we left for London this spring, Papa hired a new stable man. We hadn't yet learned of Ormsby's perfidious nature and at that time, when Papa mentioned that he was looking for someone, Ormsby suggested Willie Dockery for the job. Willie's brother, Melvin, is now his head stable man and has worked for Ormsby since he was a boy; Ormsby spoke very highly of Melvin. All of our other servants have been with us for years. It can only be

Willie." Her lips tightened. "He shall be gone from the place before the hour passes."

"I would advise you not to send him packing." When she looked at him surprised, he added, "You know this fellow's identity and where he is, which means you can use him to your own ends." He cocked a brow. "There have been no complaints from your head stable man about him?"

"None that I know of, but that doesn't matter—I want him gone."

"If you abruptly fire Willie," Asher said quietly, "it will arouse Ormsby's suspicions and might cause him to take some sort of action we won't like."

Her shoulders slumped. "Of course, you're right. I hadn't considered that." Her expression troubled, she asked, "So what are we to do? Let that snake continue to nest in the stable?"

He grinned at her. "At least we know where the snake is."

She shuddered theatrically. "Wonderful."

After Asher and his grandmother bid Juliana and her father good-bye, they drove away from Kirkwood. Asher thought that the meeting with Juliana had gone well and he was pleased that he now knew the identity of the stable man he had followed last night. He wasn't certain how to make use of that information just yet, but he was confident he would think of something.

"You look rather satisfied with yourself," his grandmother said, breaking into his thoughts.

"I just spent an enjoyable half hour with a charming woman. Why shouldn't I be satisfied?" He lifted a brow. "And your visit with the lovely Thalia?"

"Well, the poor thing isn't so lovely at the moment. The spots really are dreadful and she is just covered with them." She frowned. "She was pitifully happy to see me and so grateful for the jam, but I'm a trifle worried about her. I know she is not comfortable and no doubt mortified at her condition but she seemed . . . too fretful and too cast down for my liking. I fear something is preying on her mind." Her frown grew. "And now that I think of it, Kirkwood seemed unusually distracted—even for him." She threw Asher a considering glance. "Is there something that you are not telling me?"

"Why, no," he said, looking innocent. When she continued to stare at him, he added hastily, "Grandmother, I hardly know the young lady and haven't exchanged a word with her in years. As for Kirkwood, I have not met the man more than a half dozen times in my life. What could I know?"

She watched him for another, very long minute and then shrugged. "Of course, you couldn't know anything." Her eyes on the road once again, she asked abruptly, "Have you seen John or your stepfather since you've been home?"

He frowned. "No. I had planned to ride over to Apple Hill later in the week. I thought perhaps Friday. Why?"

She looked uncomfortable. "You know I try not to meddle, but I am worried about the situation at Apple Hill."

When she said nothing more, Asher prompted, "And?"

His grandmother sighed. "Not to tell tales out of school," she began reluctantly, "but John came to see me a few days before you returned home." She glanced at Asher. "I've always tried never to betray anyone's trust, but I think in this case you should be aware of what is going on." Looking down at her hands, she said, "Though John pretended that all was well, a blind man could see that he was beside himself with worry. He didn't want to tell me, but I finally got it out of him: Denning is insisting that John break the entail you had set up and that they sell that lower two hundred acres to Ormsby." Bleakly, she added, "I fear that Denning has gotten himself into deep water again."

His expression grim, Asher said, "I'll ride over tomorrow morning and find out for myself what is going on."

She laid a hand on his arm. "Your feelings for him aside, please remember that John and his other children do love him."

"I'm not going to throttle him if that's what you suspect,

but I am not going to allow him to ruin John's future either." Exasperation evident in his voice, he said, "That's why I set up the entail the way I did the last time I pulled Denning from the River Tick. It was to ensure that he couldn't gamble away any more of John's inheritance."

She patted him lightly on the arm. "I know. And though you don't speak of it, I'm aware that it was you who provided the handsome dowry for the girls and paid for their London Season and for Robert's commission in the Cavalry." She looked away and sighed heavily. "I was so pleased when Denning first came courting your mother. I thought they would make a good match. His family was well known locally, I knew that one day he would inherit a fine estate and he was so very handsome and dashing in his uniform in those days." She smiled ruefully. "I think I was almost as smitten as your mother but of course, we didn't know about the gambling then." She looked up at his rigid profile. "But he was kind to you, you can't deny that."

Keeping his gaze on his horses, Asher muttered, "I never denied that, in his fashion, he was good to me. I realize he could have treated me very differently and I respected him for the way he never once made me feel like a stepchild." His voice hardened. "What I cannot forgive is the way he cared nothing for the future of his wife and children." He glanced down at her. "You better than anyone know that there were times that Mother struggled to keep us decently clothed and fed because of his gambling debts. You risked Burnham to keep us afloat and if it hadn't been for you, it would have gone very hard for us. Certainly, I and my brothers could not have attended Eton if it had not been for you." His expression bleak, he added, "You damn near beggared yourself because Denning could not and would not stay away from the gaming tables." Coldly he went on, "It is the way he risked his family that I cannot forgive. And you'll never convince me that it wasn't worry and strain as much as anything that caused Mother's death."

"She died in childbirth. . . . It happens," Mrs. Manley said softly, her eyes sad.

He threw her a hard look. "Following the drum behind him all over Europe and bearing five children in less than seven years certainly didn't help either. You don't know what it was like. I do. I may have been a child but I remember some of those Army camps and the rough conditions—rougher than they needed to be because Denning was always short of money for the things that would have made Mother's lot easier." His voice grim, he said, "Even when Mother was pregnant with Elizabeth and he finally sent us all home to Apple Hill it wasn't because he was thinking of her or any of us. It was *convenient* for him for us not to be underfoot. Having a wife and a pack of children interfered with the picture of a handsome, dashing Cavalry officer he presented to the world. Besides, with us out of sight, he didn't have to face the fact that every time he lost money, he was taking food from our mouths."

"I know. I know it was bad."

"*Bad?*" he burst out. "You knew how she struggled at Apple Hill just to keep us clothed and with a roof that didn't leak over our heads. I know you were slipping her money even then and she was humiliated for having to take it from you. And Lieutenant Colonel Denning? He came home just long enough to pat us children on the head, remark how big we were growing and get her pregnant again before riding gaily off to rejoin his squadron. That last pregnancy killed her—and the baby she tried to birth." Thickly he said, "But did the colonel come home to see to his motherless children? No. He left it up to you to see to our welfare. It was because you swooped down and removed us to Burnham that we didn't grow up like a pack of savages. I sometimes think fate extracted a suitable revenge when he lost a leg at Villers-en-Cauchies and had to retire."

His nostrils white and pinched, Asher fought to control his anger and bitterness. Most of the time, he managed to keep his feelings about his stepfather at bay, but sometimes . . . He took a deep breath and growled, "At least I was eighteen when he returned and did not have to share a roof with him or I'm afraid I'd have done him a violence."

There was little Mrs. Manley could say. Asher spoke the truth. Denning had been a wretched provider and she knew full well how Jane had struggled to maintain her little family with a scant degree of comfort. Shaking her head, she thought back to that horrible time when Jane had died. She had planned to be at Apple Hill for the birth of Jane's sixth child, but she had been away visiting friends, when several weeks before she should have, Jane had suddenly gone into labor. By the time a servant had arrived with an urgent message and she had hastened to her daughter's side, it had been too late. After an agonizing labor, the baby, a boy, had been stillborn and within a few hours, Jane just slipped away.

She didn't hold it against Asher for feeling the way he did. She despised the retired lieutenant colonel as much as her eldest and best beloved grandson did. Like Asher, she blamed Denning for Jane's death—and for nearly causing her grand-children to be cast penniless and homeless onto the street. Though she had taken them to live at Burnham, while Denning continued his military career—and profligate ways—if Asher hadn't found the means to add to the support of the family, heaven knew what would have happened to all of them. Denning would have lost Apple Hill and if not for Asher, I might have lost Burnham, she admitted with a shiver.

She knew that some of the money her grandson had provided over the years had come from gambling. He had saved the family from ruin, she thought ironically, by participating in the very vice he railed against his stepfather for and she suspected he resented Denning for that, too. But unlike his stepfather, Asher never gambled while in his cups and he had a keen eye and a clever brain and, undeniably, the devil's own luck.

"You have a right to feel as you do about him," she said.

"And I don't blame you. Just don't let your feelings for him ruin your relationship with your brothers and sisters."

"I haven't yet," he replied grimly.

There was nothing else to be said and, forcing a smile, Mrs. Manley inquired, "Are you planning on keeping an old woman company and dining with me this evening?"

His expression softened and he teased, "Of course. I must see how Apollo is fitting in."

"And it would have nothing to do with Cook's light hand with pastry, now would it?"

He laughed. "Well, that is an inducement, but actually it is your charming presence that draws me to your table."

Having pushed aside the bad memories, Asher was smiling when his horses turned down the driveway that led to Burnham. After tossing his reins to the stable boy who ran up when they pulled to a stop in front of the house, he leaped down and went around to the other side to help his grandmother out of the vehicle.

Together they strolled into the house. They were walking across the foyer when Dudley popped out from the nether reaches of the house.

Smiling at them, he said, "I thought I heard a vehicle drive up." Taking Mrs. Manley's parasol and gloves, he said, "While you were gone, Madame, a missive arrived. I placed it on the table just inside the door of the front parlor for you."

"Thank you." Lifting a brow, she asked, "And Apollo?"

Dudley grinned. "He has been quite content since Cook relented and gave him the ham bone. He has spent the afternoon under the kitchen table gnawing happily."

Asher and Mrs. Manley smiled and walked into the front parlor where Mrs. Manley picked up her note. Recognizing the handwriting, she gave an exclamation of pleasure.

Asher, who was wandering around the restful blue and cream room, looked over his shoulder and asked, "Good news?"

"Well, I hope so," Mrs. Manley replied as she opened the envelope and began to read.

A moment later, beaming at Asher, she said, "It is indeed good news. My dear friend, Barbara Sherbrook, will be arriving a week from Friday, or Saturday depending on how swiftly she is willing to let her nephew, Lord Thorne, push the horses." She chuckled. "She will never travel a step without a male escort. Lord Thorne will escort her for a visit and then her son, Marcus, will arrive to escort her home to Sherbrook Hall." She clapped her hands together in delight. "We write often, but seldom get to see each other. I am so looking forward to the visit. It will be wonderful to catch up with each other and hear all the news about her son, Marcus, and his bride." She looked thoughtful. "Although," she murmured, "I don't know that 'bride' is correct any longer—they married last spring. Barbara had practically given up that he would ever marry and provide her with grandchildren." She looked sly. "We old ladies do so love to see the next generation and right now, my dear friend is over the moon—Marcus and Isabel are expecting their first child soon."

Feeling as if he'd just had a poleax shoved where it had no business being, Asher froze. "Er, Sherbrook?" he croaked. "I don't believe I've heard that name before."

"Well, perhaps not but I've known Barbara for a very long time—our fathers were good friends. Barbara and I have been dear, *dear* friends for decades." She smiled affectionately at him. "I don't believe you've met any of the family yet but I'm certain that when you do you'll find the Sherbrook family most enjoyable." Tapping her lip with the note, she added, "I thought it was quite romantic that after all these years Marcus and Isabel married. He had been Isabel's guardian before she married her first husband—poor fellow, he died in India, but Barbara had always thought that Marcus and Isabel were made for each other. It seems she was right."

Chapter 7

Asher decided that he was a much better actor than he realized. After that first paralyzing moment, he was able to say with commendable calm, "I look forward to meeting your friend and eventually her son and his wife. Mrs. Sherbrook, and I believe you said Lord Thorne, will arrive on . . . Friday a week, wasn't that the date?"

At his grandmother's nod, he continued, "Then I shall make certain that I am available for that date." Staring at his grandmother's pleased expression, he wondered sourly if there was some way he could come down with the measles in the meantime. Or smallpox. The plague would be even better. Anything that would prevent him from coming face to face with Marcus Sherbrook when he arrived to escort his mother home.

All through the evening, he managed to maintain an outward appearance of normalcy, but inwardly his brain was racing and he was cursing this turn of bad luck. He would swear on his mother's grave that until this afternoon, he'd never heard his grandmother mention the Sherbrook name. It was possible that she had upon occasion spoken of her friend "Barbara." In fact now that he thought of it, he vaguely remembered her talking about someone named Barbara from time to time, but he'd never paid any heed. Why would he? His grandmother knew many people and had many friends that he had never met and had only heard of in passing. It was unfortunate, he thought wryly, that she had never disclosed Barbara's surname to him. But would it have made any difference to the events of last spring? He grimaced. Probably not. Once he had determined to gain possession of the memorandum that Whitley had stolen from the Horse Guards, knowing that his grandmother was a friend of Marcus Sherbrook's mother would not have deterred him from his ultimate goal.

Taking leave of his grandmother a few hours later, driving through the deepening twilight toward Fox Hollow, the knowledge that in little over a week, he would come face to face with the man whose wife he had abducted ate at him like acid. Never mind that he had also broken into Marcus's safe and extracted a very important memorandum. A memorandum he had later sold to the Duke of Roxbury.

Approaching the stables at Fox Hollow, he wondered if he could have done things any differently. But he already knew that answer. Yes, once he had learned that Marcus possessed the memorandum, all he'd have had to do was drop a note telling Sherbrook where the memo was hidden, then ridden away, knowing the memorandum would be returned to its proper place. He could have called off the whole affair then and there. He could have aborted the kidnapping of Isabel Sherbrook and all the rest of it. But did I? he asked himself bitterly. No. I was fixated on winning and once I set the plan into motion I was too bloody determined to get the document myself . . . and get paid damn near a king's ransom for its return, don't forget that.

Walking toward the house, he made no excuses for himself and, faced with the same set of circumstances, he knew that he would do the same thing again. Still it didn't sit well that he had inadvertently involved a friend of his grandmother's. In the past he had done things that he was not proud of, but he always kept the dark side of his life from ever impinging upon the very family he risked everything to keep safe.

Tossing his gloves onto the table in the oak-paneled foyer,

he walked to his study. After pouring some brandy, snifter in hand, he wandered around the room, restless and uneasy.

Finally throwing himself down in his favorite black leather chair, he sipped his brandy and considered if meeting Marcus Sherbrook would prove his downfall and bring shame and dishonor on the family—his greatest fear. He didn't think so. Sherbrook had never actually seen him and as for his wife . . . He had abducted Isabel Sherbrook but he had spent scant time in her company and beyond his voice the few times he'd spoken to her during her captivity, she would have no way of identifying him. Besides, why would either one of the Sherbrooks connect the grandson of Barbara Sherbrook's dear friend to the events of last spring? Still he didn't like it. He had an ear for voices himself and having once heard a voice, never forgot it.

He frowned. But how likely was it that Isabel Sherbrook would recognize anything about him? He had not spoken more than half a dozen sentences to her last year. She might *think* his voice sounded familiar, but he suspected it was highly improbable that she'd connect him with the man who had abducted her and briefly held her prisoner over a year ago.

Feeling a trifle more confident, he finished off his brandy. Rising to his feet, he walked over to the sideboard and set down the empty snifter.

He wasted several more minutes wandering around the study, before deciding that sleep was out of the question. Discarding several ways to pass the time, he finally hit upon the notion of a night ride and a brief reconnoiter of the grounds surrounding Ormsby Place. It would certainly not come amiss—it had been a number of years since he had visited at Ormsby Place and there would be nothing wrong with double checking that there was not some new impediment to what he hoped would be an easy theft. In fact, it would be wise to survey the house and area with fresh eyes before he made any definite plans.

His mind made up, Asher returned to the stables and, waving aside the groom's offer to help, he saddled a long-legged blood bay gelding. Moments later he was cantering away into the darkness.

The ride to Ormsby Place was without incident and shortly he was guiding his horse through the same forest he had traveled just the previous night. From the concealment of the forest, he studied the stables and, finding the area dark and quiet, moved on toward the grand house.

Leaving his horse tied to a small sapling, well away from any inhabitants or accidental discovery, Asher made his way toward the house where his lordship lived in a palatial manner. Approaching the towering three-storied plaster and stone house from the west, he slipped around to the opposite side of one of the two wings that jutted out from the main portion of the house.

It was fortunate, he thought, as he flowed silently around the house, that the gardens that surrounded the building were extensive, with several paths leading off in all directions to secluded corners. He rather thought that a small army could hide amongst the shrubbery, trees and vine-covered nooks and crannies that abounded throughout the area. Having worked his way around to the east wing of the house, he stepped inside a white lattice-worked gazebo that overlooked a small ornamental pond and considered the tall, sprawling building that lay just beyond the pond. A wide expanse of lawn dotted with a few handsome oaks and artistically planted trees and shrubs lay between him and the house, but from here he had a clear view. Crossing the small courtyard that adjoined the study would be the only time that he'd be fully exposed and since he didn't intend to linger, he didn't think it would give him any trouble.

There was little light from the moon and the house was a huge dark shape in the distance. From the black windows that faced him, it was apparent that this wing of the house was not being used tonight. As he recalled, the marquis's suite of rooms was on the second floor in the west wing. The central part of the house held most of the living areas and at this time of night, Ormsby was most likely somewhere in that central section. The first floor of the east wing comprised the ballroom, the music room, a small salon and the library and study, with more bedrooms on the second floor. He assumed either the nursery, or attics or servant quarters filled the third floor—he'd never explored that far. His gaze moved carefully over the dark expanse before him, considering the dangers. There was no gleam of light anywhere, so it was fairly safe to assume that Ormsby was not in his study tonight . . . at least not at the moment.

Leaving the gazebo, Asher glided across the lawn, using the trees and shrubs to cloak his movements. Swiftly crossing the small courtyard, he tried the handle of the French doors and smiled when the knob turned in his hand. He'd been counting on the custom of seldom locking doors in the country.

Slipping inside the spacious room, he waited a moment for his eyes to adjust to the utter blackness that met him and then brought forth the small candle he carried in the pocket of his jacket. A flick of flint and a tiny light burst into being.

Shielding the flickering candle flame with his body, he glanced around the shadow-filled room. Nothing seemed to have changed since the last time he had been in the study. The furniture and arrangement looked the same; the Gainsborough still hung on the wall in front of him, hiding, he hoped, the same original safe. Drifting across the room, he stopped in front of the huge painting, undecided of his next move.

He hadn't come here tonight to steal the letters, but since he had gotten this far undetected the urge was strong. Frowning, he thought about it for several seconds, weighing the chances for success. If the letters were in the safe, he'd have them in his hands in a matter of moments. . . . But first he'd have to remove the painting, open the safe, search for the letters, and assuming they were there, remove them, then replace everything as it had been, all of which would take time, not a great deal of time, but time he might not have. He saw no point in advertising that a robbery had taken place and intended when he left the room for there to be no sign that anything was amiss—or that anyone had been there. But not knowing where Ormsby was in the house and conscious that, at this hour, the marquis could take it into his head to wander into the study at any moment, Asher decided that beyond a peek behind the painting, he would do no more.

Shifting the painting slightly, he winced at the low grating noise it made when it slipped a little in his grip and scraped against the wall. After waiting a tense second, he angled his head and, using the light from his small candle, took a quick look behind the painting. The safe was still there and it looked to be the same one he'd seen years ago. The urge to strike now, to take down the painting and open the safe and look for Thalia's letters was nearly overpowering, but he fought it back. Since the near debacle last spring, he was almost superstitious about changing plans on a whim and while the impulse was there, he reminded himself that he'd come to *look* tonight, nothing more.

He stiffened, the hair on the back of his neck rising. There was something . . . some change in the air current, some faint sound. . . . There was nothing to alarm him, but instinct warned him that he dare not linger and Asher listened to his instincts. Not questioning his actions, with lightning speed, he replaced the painting as it had been and darted out the French door, barely taking time to quietly shut the door behind him.

Not wanting the scent of a just-snuffed flame to taint the air in the room, once outside, he only stopped long enough to thoroughly pinch out the light of his small candle before sprinting to one of the big oaks that dotted the lawn. Concealed behind the big tree, he dropped the now-dead candle in his pocket and risked a look at the house, his pulse jumping at the spray of light that bloomed into being behind the windows and French doors of the room he had just so precipitously vacated. Christ! That had been a narrow escape and he blessed his instincts, knowing that he had escaped detection by a hairsbreadth.

He watched for several minutes as someone traveled slowly around the room, the candlelight marking the movement. It was no small gleam of light that Asher saw shining out from the study; whoever it was carried a large candelabrum, making it almost a certainty that it was the marquis who was wandering around in the room and not a nosy servant. Asher froze when a tall man, recognizable in light from the blazing candelabrum he held in one hand, stopped in front of the French doors and looked outside. Ormsby.

For an unbearable moment, the marquis stood there staring into the night, almost as if he sensed that Asher was staring back at him. Ormsby turned, as if speaking to someone else. Returning to his original position, Ormsby opened the French doors and strolled outside. With narrowed eyes, Asher watched him wander around the small courtyard, the candelabrum he carried casting a golden glow wherever it fell. What the bloody hell was the man doing? Asher wondered.

The unpleasant thought occurred to Asher that, just as his instincts had warned him, the marquis might very well possess the same instincts. Was Ormsby merely enjoying the night air? Or was he suspicious? Had he sensed an intruder?

Whatever the marquis's reasons for this nighttime amble, after a few excruciatingly long minutes, he returned to the study, but not before Asher caught sight of Ormsby's companion, who came to the door and inquired acidly if the marquis was going to stay out there all night. Asher recognized the voice instantly and there was no mistaking that brawny build or the peg leg. Denning!

Contempt billowed up through Asher at the sight of his stepfather standing in the middle of the opened French door. There was no doubt in his mind that the colonel and the marquis had been gambling when Ormsby had decided to pay a visit to the study. Even if his grandmother had not warned him, Denning's presence here tonight would have given Asher a clear indication that the colonel had allowed the lure of the card table to overcome his scruples . . . what few scruples his stepfather possessed, Asher thought grimly.

Apparently satisfied that there was no one lurking about, Ormsby returned to the house and rejoined Denning. He shut the French door behind him and Asher watched as the two men passed from his view. A second later the study went dark.

Only when he was certain that the marquis was not coming back did Asher move, and then on fleet feet he covered the distance that separated him from his horse. It had been a near thing and he wanted to put as much distance as possible between himself and Ormsby Place. It might have been only an accident, a coincidence that had brought Ormsby to the study tonight, but Asher had a healthy wariness of coincidence. Whatever had brought the marquis to the study, he now had new respect for Ormsby's instincts and the next time he entered the marquis's study he'd make damn certain Ormsby was away from the house. As for his stepfather . . . Denning's presence at Ormsby's tonight made a trip to Apple Hill tomorrow even more imperative than it had been.

Untying his horse and swinging into the saddle, he headed home. Denning's presence tonight at Ormsby's troubled him, but he was not going to dwell on it. There would be time enough tomorrow to face that complication and he concentrated on the near discovery by Ormsby aware that, regrettably, until Denning had appeared, he'd enjoyed that little game of cat and mouse with the marquis. Especially, he admitted with a wicked grin, escaping unscathed.

Asher was not grinning the next morning as his horse, a black today, trotted toward Apple Hill. It was a tricky situation he faced.

He would have no trouble nailing his stepfather's hide to the barn, but his brother presented a problem. In a month or less, John would turn five and twenty and was no longer the green boy he'd been when Asher had last pulled the colonel from the River Tick and set up the entail to keep the remainder of Apple Hill safe from Denning's compulsive gambling. Asher knew that things would be different this time and that he'd have to walk softly. A grown man now, John wouldn't take kindly to his older brother riding in and running roughshod over him—even if, Asher thought wryly, it was for his own good. No, he'd have to proceed cautiously and be certain he did not offend or wound his brother's pride. Or rouse John's protective instincts for his father.

His mouth grim, he turned his horse down the long meandering drive that led to Apple Hill. While most of his affection for his stepfather had died long ago, Asher knew that his half siblings loved their father. Why wouldn't they? he thought wearily. Denning's habits may have destroyed the love and respect *he'd* held for the man, but he had never let his brothers and sisters know how close their father had brought them all to ruin and they had great affection for the colonel.

John may have suspected there was more to it than met the eye when Asher insisted, none too gently, on the entail, but he was certain that none of the others guessed that the money that gave them their glowing opportunities had come from him. Oh, they knew that their older half brother had been generous and that Asher had *helped* place their feet firmly on the path to comfortable futures, but none of them had any idea of the full extent of his involvement. That they looked at their father as their benefactor suited him and avoided, he admitted wryly, too many questions about the source of the large sums he expended on them.

His stepfather assumed the money Asher filtered through his hands for the benefit of the family came from gambling, and in truth a large part of it had. Asher had never seen any reason to disabuse him of that notion. Not surprisingly, it had been his stepfather who had first introduced Asher to the world of gambling—he'd not been six years old when Denning had placed a pack of cards and a pair of dice before him and began teaching him the various games of chance. Denning had been amazed at how quickly Asher had taken to the dice and cards and to this day he was prouder of his stepson's quick understanding and phenomenal memory at the gaming tables than any other accomplishment. Addicted to any form of gambling himself, Denning never once questioned Asher's glib explanations of having had a run of luck at the races or in one of the gambling halls in London.

The road rose slightly and when Asher topped a gently rolling expanse, the house came into view—the neat rows of apple trees that had given the estate its name fanning out behind the main dwelling in the distance. Originally, Apple Hill had been a narrow three-storied manor house, but several additions over the centuries had nearly quadrupled the size of the building. The central block with its tall gable was half timbered with the other additions, a pair of two-storied wings on either side consisted of a charming conglomeration of various materials—wood, brick and stone. Yellow roses climbed wildly at the corners of the two wings, their scent drifting in the air; in the spring lilacs bloomed near the front door and presently heavy headed pink and white peonies nodded against the foundation of the main structure, adding to its charm. Despite his bitterness, Asher retained several fond memories of Apple Hill and his youth. His stay here, he reminded himself, as he halted his horse at the side of the house, had not been entirely without joy.

Leaving his horse tied at the side of the house, he followed the brick walkway that led to the front. Stopping at the age-darkened oak door, he raised the black iron knocker and knocked.

A moment passed, then the door opened and there, with a smile on his face, stood Apple Hill's butler, Woodall. A middle-aged, rotund little man with pleasant features and alert brown eyes, Woodall and his father and grandfather before him had all served the Denning family. Woodall had always been a favorite of Asher's and he remembered with pleasure the extra sweets, sugar plums especially, that the butler had slipped him and his half siblings at Christmastime.

"Master Asher! Why, this is a most pleasant surprise!" exclaimed Woodall. "Master John will be delighted to see you."

"And the colonel? Is he in?" Asher asked as he handed Woodall his gloves and hat.

Some of the pleasure in the older man's face faded and he nodded. "Yes, he is, but he is still abed." He coughed delicately. "It was very late when your stepfather returned home last night."

Asher refrained from comment, saying lightly, "Well, perhaps he will be up and I shall see him before I leave this afternoon."

Woodall looked doubtful. "It may be very late when the colonel arises," he warned.

Asher smiled at him. "You forget that I am most familiar with my stepfather's habits. Now lead me on to John."

Shown into the estate office at the rear of one of the wings, Asher wasn't surprised to find his half brother hard at work. At the sight of Asher, a welcoming smile lit up John's face and, laying down his quill, he rose to his feet from behind the messy oak desk where he had been seated. After crossing the distance that separated them, John enthusiastically pumped Asher's hand, exclaiming, "By Jupiter, it is a pleasure to see you! I heard that you were once more at Fox Hollow and had been planning to ride over and visit with you soon."

While they did not resemble each other to a great degree, that the two men were related in some manner was evident in their tall and muscular builds and their coloring and a similar look through the eyes and mouth. All of Jane's children favored her; it was most obvious through the eyes, but they all also had her black hair and olive complexion, her daughters slightly fairer skinned than her sons. Only John and Martha, Jane's eldest daughter, had inherited the exact color of their mother's eyes—a striking green. Since they had different fathers it was natural that Asher possessed certain features that the Denning siblings did not and there was a chiseled elegance about his jaw and nose that the others did not possess.

Indicating a worn, but comfortable leather chair, John said, "Be seated. Shall I ring for Woodall to bring refreshments?"

Smiling, Asher shook his head. After seating himself, he watched as his half brother took the chair across from him. John appeared relaxed and cheerful and Asher could discern no sign of worry about him. Certainly he did not look like a young man on the verge of signing away a portion of his inheritance. Had his grandmother, Asher wondered, been wrong? Misunderstood John's words?

Glancing around the familiar room, with its heavy masculine furniture and haphazard arrangement, Asher's gaze stopped on the paperwork scattered across the top of the desk. Looking at John, his brow lifted and he said idly, "I would have thought that you'd be out inspecting your farms on such a fine day. What keeps you chained inside, pouring over account books?"

John wasn't fooled. He grinned at him and asked, "Grandmother told you about my frantic visit, didn't she?"

Asher shrugged. "I may have heard something that made me think that all might not be well."

"And you've come riding to my rescue once more?" John teased.

Asher frowned at his boot. John wasn't acting like a young man weighted down with trouble, and he wondered again if his grandmother had misunderstood. No. John himself had just alluded to a "frantic" visit and Asher reminded himself that Denning had been at Ormsby's last night.

His gaze still on his polished boots, Asher asked quietly, "Do you need rescuing? You know that I am always at your disposal."

"Now if you'd asked me that question just yesterday morning and made that offer, I'd probably have fallen on your neck with cries of gratitude," John admitted frankly. He flashed Asher an embarrassed smile. "When I spoke to Grandmother,

I feared that I would have to break the entail, but things have worked out splendidly. Father told me yesterday afternoon that he has come about and that he is quite plump in the pocket. He said that I never need fear that he will ever be a drain on Apple Hill again. In fact, he hopes to be able to underwrite a majority of the costs of improvements to some of the farms."

John's words did not lessen the knot of unease in Asher's chest. While Denning may have reassured John in the afternoon, the colonel had been at Ormsby's place last night and more than most, Asher knew how quickly a winner at the gaming table one night could turn into a ruined man the next.

His eyes meeting his brother's, Asher asked bluntly, "Is he gaming again?"

John flushed and he nodded. "Yes. He has been a frequent visitor to Ormsby Place since the marquis has returned to the area and I know that they play deep." John leaned forward and said earnestly, "But, Asher, he assured me yesterday, that even though he may gamble with the marquis, he has the funds to cover any losses."

"For now," Asher said grimly. "What if he starts losing? Did he explain how he would meet his debts? In a manner that does not involve Apple Hill?"

"No," John said slowly, "but he was most positive about never asking me, or anyone else for that matter, to cover his debts again." John grimaced. "I do know that he is still gambling with Ormsby because he informed me late last night that he had invited Ormsby to dine with us Saturday evening. When I objected—knowing they'd be gambling long after I went to bed, he waved me aside, telling me that I needn't worry he'd lose to the marquis. . . ." A puzzled look crossed John's handsome features. "I can't explain it, but he was so confident . . . it was almost as if he knew something that would insure that he always won." John laughed uneasily. "And we both know that isn't possible, but Father . . . Father was adamant that his days of walking away a loser were over."

He frowned. "No, not that he wouldn't lose, but that he'd always have the funds to cover his losses."

Asher didn't like the sound of any of it, especially Ormsby coming to dine at Apple Hill on Saturday. The certainty that the colonel was about to bring them all to the brink of ruin took root within him. "No one," Asher said flatly, "wins every time and sooner or later, he *will* have run through whatever funds he may now possess. Your father is a fool if he thinks he has stumbled upon some magic formula that will keep Lady Luck always at his shoulder."

A defensive note in his voice, John said, "You are too hard on him. I know that you paid off some of his debts when the entail was set up. . . ." A shy smile crossed his face and he added, "And for that I am grateful—I will never forget that you helped save Apple Hill, but you cannot hold that one mistake against him for the rest of his life." At the expression in Asher's eyes, he added hastily, "I'll concede that Father has not always been wise, that he has even been foolish when it comes to gaming, but he has always managed to come about—you can't deny that."

Asher struggled to keep the hot, angry words that crowded his throat from spewing forth. He had not *helped* save Apple Hill—without his intervention the family would have been homeless and penniless. And the colonel had always managed to come about because *he*, not Denning, had come up with the funds. He took a deep breath, choking back the resentment and fury that threatened to strangle him. It had been his choice, he reminded himself, to keep the extent of his stepfather's losses over the years from the family and after all this time, he wasn't about to disillusion his brother about the colonel. What would be the point? he thought wearily. John most likely wouldn't believe him and he'd find himself estranged from a brother he loved.

Though it cost him, Asher managed to say, "Yes, of course, you're right. The colonel has always managed to come about." He forced a smile and murmured, "It would appear that you have events well in hand and do not need for me to meddle in your affairs."

Affection in his voice, John said, "But I do appreciate the notion that you were ready to stand by me."

Asher smiled at him. "Always."

The conversation became general and they spent an agreeable time together, their talk roaming from the latest *on dits* from London provided by Asher, to John's improvements around the farm and his plans for more of the same and eventually onto the doings of the various family members. Despite the over seven-year gap in their ages, the two brothers enjoyed each other's company and the hours passed swiftly.

It was the chiming of the clock on the mantel that made Asher aware of the time. Glancing at the clock, he asked, startled, "Is that correct? Can it be three o'clock already?"

"Indeed it is." John grinned at his brother. "We have been as gossipy as two old ladies over tea."

Asher rose to his feet, saying, "I did not mean to keep you so long. I shall be on my way."

"You don't have to leave," John protested, also rising to his feet. "The hour is late enough. Why don't you stay and dine?"

Before Asher could reply, the door to John's office opened and the colonel, his peg leg tapping on the floor, walked into the room. A wide smile on his lips and a warm light in his blue eyes, Lieutenant Colonel Denning exclaimed, "I couldn't believe my ears when Woodall informed me that you had come to call." Reaching out to shake Asher's hand enthusiastically, he said, "By thunder, boy! It has been ages since you have visited with us. What have you been doing since we saw you last?"

His stepfather always aroused mixed emotions within Asher's breast and today was no different. Only to himself would he admit that underneath all his rage and resentment he harbored the remnants of affection for his stepfather. The colonel had turned sixty-seven in April and despite the signs of dissolute living in his face, he was lean and lithe and he still walked with an upright military bearing, his spine and shoulders ramrod straight. He moved with such elegant precision that one almost forgot that he had lost a leg, only the sound of the wooden stump thumping on the floor bringing it to mind. Denning's sandy hair was liberally threaded with gray giving it a champagne hue that was very attractive against his tanned skin and bright blue eyes. At a younger age, he had been a stunningly handsome man and coupled with an abundance of charm, Asher understood how his mother could have fallen under his spell. Despite the years of heavy drinking, hard living and the loss of his leg, he was still a handsome man, and Asher thought wryly, feeling the old, familiar tug of it, possessed far more charm than was fair.

In Denning's presence, unable to hang on to his mistrust and resentment, Asher smiled and shook the colonel's hand. "It is good to see you again, sir," he said warmly. "I'll admit I have been somewhat remiss in coming to call, but I am settled back at Fox Hollow for good and will do better in the future."

"Excellent! Excellent!" The colonel glanced around the room and, spying the cluttered desk, frowned and looked reprovingly at John. "Never tell me you've been boring your brother with business."

John smiled, shaking his head. "No. I was working when he arrived and we just settled here to catch up with each other. I have been trying to convince him to stay and dine with us."

The colonel looked expectantly at Asher. "Capital idea! Woodall has informed me that goose and turkey pie is on the menu." He smiled affectionately at Asher. "And I do seem to recall that it is one of your favorite dishes. Do say that you will stay and dine with us?"

What could he do but say yes?

Chapter 8

Dinner was most enjoyable and when the three men rose from the table a few hours later, they were in a relaxed, convivial mood. Neither Asher nor John had drunk as deeply as the colonel, but despite the prodigious amount of liquor he had consumed, Denning was clear-eyed and steady as he led the two younger men to his private study in the north wing of the sprawling house.

Like John's office, it was a pleasant, masculine room, the furniture owing more to comfort than style. Faded gold velvet drapes hung at the windows, a carpet woven in age-muted tones of bronze and green lay on the oak floor and several heavy chairs covered in brown mohair were grouped in front of the brick fireplace; small dark wooden tables were placed here and there. Crystal decanters and glassware rested on a mahogany lowboy behind two of the chairs and one wall held a bookcase filled with leather-bound books, their gold, scarlet and blue spines adding a burst of bright color.

Off to one side of the room sat a dainty cherrywood writing desk with a blue tapestry-covered chair and at the sight of it, Asher's breath caught and pain stabbed through him. It was his mother's desk and too well did he remember her sitting at it, in that very chair, staring blindly out the window, for what had seemed like hours to him, before she would bring herself back to the matter at hand. And it was usually, he reminded himself with a tightening of his lips, an unpleasant matter having to do with money.

He had been too young for Jane to share her troubles with him, but he had been a perceptive child and, he thought with little shame, not above reading over her shoulder when she had been too preoccupied with their financial woes to notice him. The old anger he had kept at bay during the evening stirred but before it sprang free, Denning's voice broke into his thoughts.

"I see you recognize your mother's desk," the colonel said, unaware of the black feelings the sight of it engendered within Asher's breast. "I was complaining to Woodall just the other day that I needed a table to write on and he suggested your mother's old desk. Said it was in the attics gathering dust and that I should make good use of it." Denning walked over to the desk and, running his hand over the gleaming surface, he stared down at it. For a moment, he seemed to forget the presence of the other two men and almost to himself, he said huskily, "She deserved a far better man than I could ever be." He took a deep breath. "I wasn't the husband I should have been, but she was the most wonderful thing that ever happened to me." He glanced over at Asher and smiled crookedly. "To this day I find myself listening for her voice . . . her laugh. . . ."

Looking into his stepfather's eyes, Asher realized something profound: as much as Denning had been capable of doing, he *had* loved his wife. Asher studied his stepfather with a new awareness. For the first time, he saw him as a decent man seduced by liquor and helplessly enthralled by the turn of a card, the outcome of a wager, rather than the indifferent, careless creature he had always thought him. Which doesn't change the fact, he reminded himself coolly, that while Denning may have loved Jane and his children, he had loved his liquor and gaming more.

Perhaps Denning read some of what Asher was thinking,

for his gaze fell from Asher's, and glancing down at the desk, Denning said, "I miss her."

John cleared his throat and said quietly, "We all do—even Elizabeth, who cannot even remember her."

Denning roused himself from his reflective mood and said briskly, "Well, now, enough of this maudlin talk!" Forcing a jovial note into his voice, he went on, "It isn't often these days that I have two of my sons at home and I don't intend for this delightful evening to end on such a somber note."

Walking to the lowboy, Denning asked, "What would you like?" He winked at Asher. "I believe that I have some fine brandy here that a friend of mine who lives near the coast shared with me. Just imagine—he found a whole case of it stashed in the corner of one of his stalls."

"Smuggled?" Asher asked dryly.

Denning laughed. "In Kent what else would we have?"

All three men decided upon brandy and once snifters were poured they scattered around the fireplace, Denning and John taking two of the mohair chairs, Asher standing with one arm resting on the wide oak mantel. This time of the year the hearth was swept clean but a neat pile of apple wood faggots was stacked within, ready if needed.

"So what do you intend to do with yourself, now that you are settled at Fox Hollow?" Denning asked.

Asher shrugged. "I haven't decided." Staring into the amber liquor in his snifter, he murmured, "There are not that many acceptable occupations for a gentleman. I suppose I shall be a farmer, like John."

John shook his head, his green eyes dancing. "And do you know anything about farming? What sort of soil you have? Which crops will grow well in this area? When to plant them? Harvest them? Market them?"

Asher half smiled. "You point out the very reasons why I have not yet made up my mind what to do."

"Er, do you *have* to do anything?" Denning asked with a

raised brow. "Surely, the farms that go with your property and your investments can keep you comfortably without having to dig in the dirt? Even John, for all the time he spends on the farms, doesn't have to actually do the work. His tenants do that."

"Now, I protest," teased John, looking at his father. "I've planted my share of new orchards and been out in a cold January morning pruning. You have no objections to my digging in the dirt—why can't Asher get his hands dirty?"

Denning waved his hand. "That wasn't what I meant and you know it." He looked proudly at John. "You have a talent for making things grow and you're a good manager." His mouth softened. "Got that from your mother. But Asher now . . ." Denning glanced across at his tall stepson. "Asher strikes me as a man of action. Surprised you didn't go into the military. You always were adventure mad."

Thinking back to last spring and the sight of Collard's body lying on the ground outside of Sherbrook's stable, Asher said, "I believe that I have had enough adventures to last me a lifetime. No, I think I shall simply watch over my estates and live quietly in the country. I may," he said slowly, "even take a wife and set up my nursery."

John guffawed. "You?" he hooted. "And has your fancy settled upon a likely prospect?"

Asher took a long swallow of brandy. Setting the snifter on the mantel, he grinned and said, "Ah, now that would be telling."

He endured several moments of teasing and probing from his stepfather and brother, but when he would not be drawn, the conversation shifted to other topics. Two more brandies and an hour or so later, he rose from the chair where he had finally settled and said, "I fear the hour is growing late. Agreeable though it has been, I must be on my way."

John yawned and said, "Why don't you stay? Woodall can have a bed made for you."

Asher shook his head. "I'm looking forward to clearing

my head on the ride home. I haven't had this much to drink in an age."

Denning snorted. "Green boys, the pair of you. We haven't even finished the decanter. Why, I remember when . . ."

John groaned and Asher put out his hands. "Please," he said with a smile, "no tales of your Army days and the amount of liquor you and your fellow officers consumed."

Not offended in the least, Denning lurched upright, grinning. "Disrespectful, the pair of you!"

Asher said his good-byes and was on the point of turning to leave, when Denning said, "Wait! Just remembered I found something you should have."

Denning stumped over to the desk and, opening the long drawer in the middle of it, reached in and pulled out a necklace. Asher came to stand at his side. Placing the necklace in Asher's hand, Denning said, "I was cleaning out the desk and I found this at the back of the drawer where your mother must have left it."

Asher stared down at the distinctive gold and ivory chain, an exquisite cameo dangling in the middle of it. Memories of his mother wearing this same piece of jewelry flashed across his brain and his heart felt heavy in his chest. "She always said that my father gave it to her," he muttered.

Denning nodded. "That's true. She told me once when I commented on it, that it was the only thing of his that she had to remember him by." He patted Asher gently on the shoulder. "And you."

Beset by strong emotions, Asher managed to say, "I'm glad you found it. Thank you."

Shutting the drawer, Denning said, "Lucky thing I needed a table to write on, wasn't it? Wouldn't have found it otherwise." He rapped the top of the desk with his knuckles. "Always told Jane that she brought me luck and now that I'm using this little desk of hers, I feel like my luck has come back." An odd smile curved his mouth. "Yes, indeed, my luck has changed and I have your mother to thank for it."

*   *   *

Most of the effects of Denning's smuggled brandy had evaporated from Asher's brain by the time he reached home and, deciding not to wake a sleeping stable boy, he unsaddled his horse and gave the animal a quick rubdown. After throwing a large pitchfork of hay into the horse's manger from the loft above, he departed the stable. Walking through the mild night, the stars glittering diamond-bright in the black sky overhead, he reflected on the evening he had just spent. He had enjoyed himself and wasn't even annoyed or feeling guilty for allowing Denning to charm and disarm him once more.

Perhaps, I've mellowed, he thought as he approached the quiet house. Or more likely, with all the sins that could be laid at my door, I've learned to be more understanding of the demons that can drive a man. He knew it wasn't in him to completely forgive Denning but he had reached a point, he conceded, where the white-hot rage that had once burned so fiercely in his breast had become bearable.

Entering the house, he ascended the staircase and walked down the hall to his rooms. Someone, either Hannum or his valet, Rivers, had left a small candle burning on a bombé chest that sat near his sitting room door and another in the middle of the mantel of the fireplace in anticipation of his late return. In the fitful glow of those meager lights, he shrugged out of his jacket and after taking out his mother's necklace from the pocket, tossed the jacket on a nearby chair. Walking over to the gray stone fireplace, he draped the necklace over one of a pair of tall, pewter candelabra that sat on either end of the wide polished oak mantel, centering the cameo so that it swung free. For a long time, he stood there, staring at the cameo, his thoughts vague and unfocused.

After what seemed an age, he shook himself and, taking one last look at the cameo, turned away and sat down in a chair across from the one that held his jacket and pulled off his boots. Standing up, he took off his cravat and dropped the crumpled linen onto the jacket before moving aimlessly about the room.

As he walked, he absently undid the buttons to his shirt and pulled it free of his breeches. Stopping in midstride, he eyed the barely discernible gray and burgundy velvet-hung bed through the door that divided the sitting room from the bedroom, but sleep did not appeal. Not yet ready for bed, but not experiencing the restlessness that had plagued him the previous night, he wandered around the handsome room, stopping once or twice to gaze out the windows; but met with only the darkness of the night, he moved on.

He finally settled in a black leather overstuffed chair. Settled comfortably in the chair, his long legs stretched out in front of him, he stared at the intricate design of the pale gray and blue carpet under his feet, seeing none of it. His thoughts turned inward, he considered the evening he had just spent.

It was a relief to find that Denning had given up trying to induce John to break the entail. Good news, too, that Denning appeared to have found some way of keeping out of the clutches of the moneylenders should his gaming losses—and Asher didn't doubt for a moment that there *would* be losses—become onerous.

His head resting against the high back of the chair, he stared up at the huge oak timbers of the ceiling's exposed beams. Being with John was always a pleasure, but he could not say the same for his stepfather's company—yet tonight he had enjoyed visiting with the colonel. It had been an enlightening evening, too, the discovery that despite the way he had treated her, Denning had loved his mother taking some of the acid sting out of the bitterness he felt toward him. He would never hold Denning in the same affectionate esteem that his siblings did, but he no longer considered his stepfather as being a man totally without merit.

Asher's gaze traveled to his mother's necklace and his heart clenched with anguish. Even before she had married Denning, his mother had rarely mentioned his father but he knew that his father had been a lieutenant in the Royal Navy and had died before he'd even been born. Lieutenant Cordell had been lost at sea when his ship had gone down off the coast of Cuba in a hurricane shortly after they married and his parents' time together had been pathetically short, mere weeks, he'd been told by his mother. He remembered her fingers caressing the gold and ivory chain, a faraway look in her eyes, as she told him about his father, how handsome he had been, and charming, and clever, and how much she had loved him.

His grandmother hardly ever spoke of his father and from the way her lips thinned when she did, it was obvious that she had disliked him or disapproved of him. Why, he didn't have a clue but it didn't matter very much, since the man was dead and had been for over thirty years. Thinking of his early years growing up at Burnham, doted on by his mother and grandmother, Asher smiled. Those times had been some of the happiest in his life, he admitted, just the three of them, his mother, his grandmother and him. And then Denning had entered the picture. . . .

Asher made a face. There was no pretending that he had not resented Denning when the dashing Cavalry officer had come courting his mother. And after they'd wed, he'd hated being taken away from Burnham and his grandmother and the familiar cozy world they'd all had together. He was quite certain that he'd been a spoiled brat and he hadn't, he conceded with a wry smile, been best pleased to no longer be the center of his mother's world. It was a wonder that Denning hadn't throttled him on the spot.

Upon reflection, Army life had not been so very bad and if it hadn't been for Denning's gambling and the strain and anxiety that addiction caused his mother, he might have enjoyed it. How different, how much happier her life, all of ours would have been if only Denning could have resisted the lure of the gaming table, he thought tiredly.

Which brought him back to tonight. He should have been

overjoyed that Denning appeared to have had a phenomenal run of luck and had once again been able to reverse his fortunes, but that information troubled Asher. Denning had been at Ormsby's last night, gambling. He frowned as something occurred to him. Denning had spoken with John yesterday afternoon so he'd have to have come into funds prior to last night. So perhaps last night had not been the only time Ormsby and Denning had sat down to play deep? Was it from Ormsby that Denning had won a large sum? A small fortune, in fact?

It was possible. The Marquis of Ormsby was the head of the wealthy Beverley family and his pockets were deep—he could lose several fortunes and hardly feel the pinch. Part of Asher, admittedly not a very nice part, applauded the idea of Denning fleecing Ormsby, but it also made him uneasy. If it was Ormsby who had lost to Denning, the marquis was highly unlikely to allow his stepfather to walk away from the table with his pockets full of Beverley gold without making a push to win the money back. It was known that Ormsby did not like to lose and Asher suspected that Denning might find himself clinging to a tiger's tail instead of a fortune . . . a very angry, dangerous tiger at that. Damnation! If Denning has dipped his fingers into Ormsby's pocket, he thought disgustedly, it'd be up to me to get him free. On that discouraging note he sought out his bed.

The next morning when he awoke, the uneasiness of the night before still lingered, but he was able to push it aside. If Ormsby was going to be a problem he'd know it soon enough.

At Kirkwood that same morning, Juliana was staring appalled at her father, having just learned how much of a problem the marquis could be. "You did what?" she asked in faint accents, hardly daring to believe her ears.

Mr. Kirkwood looked uncomfortable. "I invited him to dine tonight," he muttered, his eyes everywhere but on her face.

"How *could* you?" she nearly wailed. "Have you forgotten what he is trying to do?"

Mr. Kirkwood cleared his throat and nervously patted his neatly tied cravat. "I haven't forgotten and I swear to you when I came abreast of him on the road during my morning ride, I intended not even to acknowledge him and to ride on past him." Helplessly he added, "But you know Ormsby. He hailed me as if nothing was wrong.... He was so friendly and pleasant that I could hardly be rude...."

"Why not?" snapped his daughter, her hands on her hips. "I certainly can be!" Her expression exasperated, she added, "Father, you can't expect me to entertain that horrid man. You'll just have to write him a note and tell him you changed your mind—that it's inconvenient. Or I am too overwhelmed with the care of Thalia to worry about guests." She scowled. "Which is the truth."

Looking even more miserable, he mumbled, "You are perfectly right to be angry with me, my dear, and I don't blame you in the least. I know I should have given him the cut direct, but I was so startled when he called out to me that I stopped my horse." Unhappily, he ended, "He was behaving so like the man I thought I knew, that before I even knew what was happening, he had invited himself to dinner tonight."

"Well, you'll just have to uninvite him," retorted his daughter, not giving an inch.

"Ah, er, Juliana, I don't think it would be a good idea to make him angry, do you? After all, he does hold Thalia's fate in his hands. If we provoke him..." When Juliana fixed a hostile gaze on him, his lips tightened and he said, "You don't want me to meet him on the dueling field and short of that, there is little that I can do." Coaxingly he added, "It's possible that he has changed his mind, you know. Perhaps he has come to his senses and means to apologize and give the letters back."

The look on Juliana's face told her father precisely what she thought of that idea, and hastily he went one, "I shouldn't have allowed myself to be manipulated by him, and yes, I do realize that I was manipulated, but I *am* only thinking of your sister." Meeting her gaze steadily, he said, "If being polite, for one night, to a man I loathe, gives us any advantage at all, then I am willing to do it. Are you?"

Her father had a point and despite the revulsion that churned through her at the very notion of sitting down to eat with Ormsby, she nodded reluctantly. The invitation had been given and without making a bad situation worse, she saw no clear way out. "Very well, Ormsby will come to dine tonight." Her eyes narrowed. "But not the intimate little dinner he thinks it will be. I cannot imagine anything more dreadful than the three of us sitting down to dine." Her lips tightened. "Left alone with the creature, I'm likely to pick up my fork and stab him." Picking up her skirts, she brushed past him. "Now if you will excuse me, I have a party to plan."

Juliana stormed up the stairs to her rooms. She loved her father, she truly did, but there were times . . . With everything that was going on, how *could* he have fallen for Ormsby's specious charm? Asher wouldn't have. She bit her lip. That was unfair. Her father couldn't help it that he wanted peace at almost any cost, where Asher . . . She smiled faintly. Asher didn't give a damn—especially about Ormsby.

Reminding herself that there was no use crying over spilt milk, she sat down at a small writing desk and considered her next move. Since safety in numbers seemed the wisest course, she immediately wrote a note to the vicar and his wife, certain they would not be taken aback at receiving an invitation to dine at Kirkwood on such short notice. The vicar and her father were excellent friends and the vicar's wife and her mother had grown up together. In the time before Mrs. Kirkwood's death there had been much socializing between the Kirkwood and Birrel families and to this day the Kirkwood family looked on the Birrels as their oldest friends.

The vicar and Mrs. Birrel had offered their help the instant they had heard of Thalia's attack of the measles and had come to call already twice this week. Each time they had brought their two daughters, nineteen-year-old Serena and seventeen-year-old Margaret, with them and to add to the numbers Juliana included them in the invitation. Since Margaret was one of Thalia's bosom friends, even feeling cross and miserable with all her spots, Thalia had been cheered up immensely by her visits. And it wouldn't be so terrible, Juliana thought cheerfully, if they mentioned, and they would, in front of Ormsby how very ill Thalia was . . . and the stream of letters that arrived almost daily from Caswell full of concern about his beloved. Her cheerfulness faded, replaced by worry about Ormsby's reaction to the news that Caswell and Thalia were in nearly constant contact via the mail. It was a risk, but she saw no way, without some uncomfortable explanations, of stopping the vicar's daughters from mentioning the letters. She sighed, longing for the simple days that had been hers such a short time ago.

Her second note had been to Asher, apprising him of the situation. Within it, she had included an invitation for Mrs. Manley to join them for dinner tonight. Mrs. Manley might be startled at such short notice, especially since she had just been here yesterday, but Juliana was counting on Asher to smooth over any rough spots.

It was only after she had sent one of the Kirkwood servants on his way to deliver the notes that it dawned on her that she had made a serious miscalculation. Relations between Mrs. Manley and Ormsby had never been particularly friendly and the shooting of her dog had not done anything to improve matters. And Asher . . . it was almost a given that Asher, feeling as he did about Ormsby, would go out of his way to annoy or insult the marquis.

She buried her head in her hands. What had she been thinking? She hadn't been, that was the problem; she'd let herself be stampeded into foolish action and now had to suffer the consequences. A pang of sympathy for her father rushed through her. Neither one of us, she admitted glumly, had acted very wisely. She raised her head and stared at the top of her desk. It was possible that Mrs. Manley would decline the invitation, but she realized unhappily that Mrs. Manley's absence tonight might compound her problem. Asher would most certainly accept and she worried that if Mrs. Manley was not there to keep him in check around Ormsby . . . She shut her eyes. She would just have to deal with it. And hope to heaven that she could keep Asher and Ormsby from shooting each other over the soup.

Ignoring the anxiety that balled in her chest and keeping her fingers crossed that the looming disaster would somehow, miraculously, be averted, she concocted a menu and hurried to the kitchen to confer with Cook and tell Hudson, the butler, to prepare for guests tonight. If everyone came, she would be one gentleman shy, but as she walked down the hallway to the kitchen, she decided it would do well enough.

Everyone accepted her hasty invitations, even, she thought with mingled relief and misgiving as she descended the stairs a few hours later, Asher and his grandmother. The Birrels had arrived several minutes ago and Juliana's lips quirked at Ormsby's expression when Hudson announced him and he walked into the room to find the Birrel family scattered comfortably around the front salon. He quickly recovered himself and she suspected that she was the only one who had seen that flash of annoyance cross his face before it was swiftly masked. The knot in her stomach clenched tighter. If the sight of the Birrels annoyed him, she thought wryly, just wait until Asher and Mrs. Manley arrive.

From beneath her lashes she studied Ormsby as her father nervously greeted him. Approaching fifty-two years of age, the marquis was still very attractive in a rakish way, the signs of dissipation on his handsome face vastly appealing to certain members of the opposite sex. He was a tallish, well-built man with pale blue eyes and black hair, and watching his effortless charm as he spoke with her father, she had a glimmer of understanding how Thalia, young and innocent, could have imagined herself in love with him. Her mouth twisted.

And, in spite of the situation, how he had manipulated her father into inviting him to dine.

Her father threw a harassed look over his shoulder, and forcing a polite smile on her face, Juliana drifted up to the marquis and said, "How nice of you to join us this evening." Indicating the vicar and his family, she went on smoothly, "I'm sure that you are well acquainted with the vicar and Mrs. Birrel and that no introductions are needed."

The vicar, a tall man himself, walked over to shake Ormsby's hand and said, "Good evening, my lord. It is good to see you again after all this time. If you're in the neighborhood long enough, perhaps we'll see more of you." Since the marquis tended to keep himself aloof from local affairs, if there was the slightest hint of censure in the vicar's voice, Ormsby ignored it.

"It's good to be home," Ormsby said easily. "London can be so fatiguing."

Her dark hair liberally sprinkled with gray and her body plump and round like a little pigeon, Mrs. Birrel joined them. Her head barely reaching her husband's shoulder and her brown eyes bright and inquisitive, she greeted the marquis. "Do you intend to remain long at Ormsby Place, my lord?"

"I have no idea," Ormsby drawled. "At present I have no other plans other than to avail myself of the pleasures to be found so close to home." His pale blue eyes met Juliana's. "Perhaps I'll even be allowed to visit with the beautiful Miss Thalia when she recovers from her illness."

Juliana's teeth clenched but she kept her smile firmly in place. Mrs. Birrel, oblivious to any undercurrents, signaled her two daughters to join them. The two girls, blushing and faintly in awe of the marquis, were formally introduced to the great man of the neighborhood. The flurry of greetings and introductions completed, once Hudson entered with another servant carrying trays of refreshments and everyone had been served, the group split into two factions.

The gentlemen gathered near the ornately carved walnut-fronted fireplace at the far end of the cream and rose room, while the ladies congregated on the silk-and-tapestry-covered sofa and chairs nearer the double doors that opened onto the main hallway. Since Serena, a slimmer, dusky-haired version of her mother, was looking forward to her wedding in the fall to the youngest son of a baronet in the next county, the conversation was centered on that epic event.

Juliana smiled and nodded and made the occasional comment, but she was tense, her ears pricked for the sounds that would signal the arrival of Asher and his grandmother. At least, she reminded herself, *they* know the marquis will be here. She cast a look over toward the fireplace where the marquis stood talking with the other two men, wondering at his determination to marry Thalia at any cost. He had avoided the snares and traps set for him by the most marriage-minded damsels for decades. Ormsby was the last man anyone would suspect of looking for a bride and certainly not a bride hardly out of the schoolroom. With his title and wealth he could look as high as he wished for a wife, yet his choice had appeared to have settled on a woman young enough to be his daughter, a woman with no fortune to speak of and a member of an obscure country family. Why?

Only half listening to the chatter of the Birrel women, Juliana frowned. Thalia was beautiful, there was no denying that, and she was a sweet, biddable young woman . . . most of the time. But she was no match for a sophisticate like Ormsby. Thalia, with her simple enjoyments and naïveté, was perfect for an easygoing young man like Caswell, but Ormsby? Talk about chalk and cheese! And with Thalia desperately in love with Caswell, if Ormsby managed to force her to marry him, Juliana saw nothing but unhappiness ahead for her sister . . . and Ormsby.

The faint clatter of approaching hoofbeats and the clank and rattle of harness shattered her musings. Juliana swallowed. Those sounds could mean only one thing: Asher and Mrs. Manley had arrived.

Rising gracefully to her feet, the skirts of her pale apricot muslin gown swirling around her feet, she said to the room at large, "I believe that will be the last of our guests." And, dear God, help us all.

Chapter 9

Juliana had been wise to pray for help—the trouble started the moment the double doors opened and Ormsby caught sight of the two guests being ushered into the room by the butler. His face flushed with rage, Ormsby turned on his host and hissed, "You fool! What were you thinking when you were misguided enough to invite *them* to be here tonight?"

Poor Mr. Kirkwood shrank back from the rage in Ormsby's face, at a loss with how to deal with the marquis's attack. Birrel's brows rose and in an astonished tone, he said, "I think you forget yourself, my lord. I would remind you that this is Kirkwood's home—he is certainly entitled to invite whom he pleases. If you do not like the company, I suggest you take your leave . . . politely."

Juliana didn't hear what was said between the three men at the far end of the room, but from the expression on their faces she had a fair idea. Her poor father looked ready to faint, Ormsby was clearly angry and the vicar, while taken aback at Ormsby's words, was proceeding in his usual calm manner. Whatever the vicar said to Ormsby seemed to recall the marquis to his senses and, only vaguely aware of Hudson announcing Mrs. Manley and Asher, she watched as Ormsby struggled to regain control of his temper.

Mrs. Birrel and her daughters, delighted to see the newest arrivals, were completely oblivious to the scene between the gentlemen and for that Juliana was grateful. Walking across the room, she greeted Mrs. Manley and Asher warmly, wondering if they had been aware of Ormsby's reaction to their entrance. From the gleam in his eyes, she realized with a sinking heart that Asher had noted the unpleasant byplay at the other end of the room and correctly interpreted its cause.

Mrs. Manley's lips brushed her cheek as they met and Juliana was both charmed and startled when the woman whispered in her ear, "So brave of you to invite us with Ormsby in the house, my dear. I have no doubt that it'll prove a most entertaining evening."

"You're not upset?" Juliana asked in a low tone, torn between despair and laughter.

Smiling at her, Mrs. Manley shook her head. "Oh, good heavens, no! This is the most exciting thing that has happened in the neighborhood for ages. I wouldn't have missed it for the world." She paused, looking thoughtful. "Of course, we *do* have to keep Asher from killing him at the first opportunity."

Giving Mrs. Manley a sickly smile, Juliana turned to greet Asher. Under her breath, she muttered to him, "I *am* sorry. This wasn't a very good idea—I don't know what I was thinking."

Asher grinned. "Perhaps not, but as my grandmother mentioned on the drive over here tonight—it should be . . . interesting."

By the time she had welcomed Asher and Mrs. Manley and they joined Mrs. Birrel and her daughters, Ormsby had recovered himself sufficiently to greet the latecomers with cool politeness when the two groups merged. To Juliana's relief, Asher seemed to be behaving himself, always keeping a few people between himself and Ormsby and beyond the first careless acknowledgment, adroitly avoiding direct conversation with the marquis.

Feeling as if a keg of black powder with a lit fuse was rolling around in the room, Juliana moved amongst her guests smiling and chatting just as if this evening was nothing out of the ordinary and she wasn't terrified. It helped that Ormsby had no desire to talk to Asher and Mrs. Manley and, like Asher, he did a good job of refraining from direct confrontation. By the time dinner was announced and they filed into the dining room, she was hopeful that they might scrap through the evening without incident.

She had agonized over the seating arrangement. The numbers were uneven, with more ladies than gentlemen, and it had been imperative that Asher and Mrs. Manley be seated nowhere near Ormsby. Which meant she kept Asher and Mrs. Manley at her end of the table and left her father to cope with Ormsby at the other end. The Birrels were placed in between to act as a buffer, with Mrs. Birrel seated next to her father, across from Ormsby. If Mrs. Birrel thought it strange that she and not Mrs. Manley was seated next to her host and that her husband was placed in the middle of the table instead of at Juliana's side, she gave no sign. Feeling that the most danger would come from Asher, Juliana made certain that the vicar and Serena sat between Ormsby and Asher on that side of the table.

From the various compliments made about the food from the guests, she had to assume that it was delicious, but she might as well have been eating sweepings from the stable floor for all the pleasure she took from the meal. Once she glanced up and from the other end of table found Ormsby's eyes on her and the expression in their depths was *not* friendly. It was apparent that the marquis had guessed that it was she and not her father who had invited all of the other guests including Asher and Mrs. Manley. Even though a frisson of fright trickled down her spine, she met his gaze and sent him a dazzling smile. Bastard!

Having watched her push her food around on her plate all through dinner, Mrs. Manley murmured, "My dear, it is not so very awful. We are almost through our meal and no blood has been shed so far."

"The evening isn't over," Juliana said mournfully.

Mrs. Manley smiled. "True, but you can rely on Asher to behave himself—he was *raised* a gentleman, even if at times he doesn't act it."

Juliana glanced at Asher and he flashed her a sunny smile that did nothing to calm the turmoil in her breast. Her anxiety increased as the meal came to an end and she faced the unhappy prospect of leaving the gentlemen alone in the dining room with their port and brandy. With only her father and the vicar to run interference between Asher and Ormsby, could disaster be far behind?

To her great relief and gratitude, when the meal ended and the ladies rose to leave the room for the front parlor, Asher followed suit. Looking down the long table at her father, he said, "I hope you forgive me, sir, if I join the ladies?" He glanced at Mrs. Manley before returning his gaze to Mr. Kirkwood, and added, "I am driving a young pair of horses tonight that are known to be fractious and my grandmother has requested that I keep as clear a head as possible." He grinned. "She says she has no intention of being ditched on the way home."

Mr. Kirkwood smiled. "Even a bit foxed, I doubt that someone with your skill at the reins would allow that to happen. But, yes, certainly, go with the ladies." For different reasons, as much as Juliana, Mr. Kirkwood had been dreading the moment the ladies left the room and eager for the protection afforded by the female contingent, he seized on the opportunity Asher has provided him. He looked at the other two men and suggested, "Unless someone has an objection, shall we all join the ladies?"

"An excellent idea," concurred the vicar, having concluded that for unknown reasons, his role and that of his family tonight was to keep Ormsby from cornering his host. Confident that his friend would explain all to him at the earliest moment, the vicar rose to his feet and threw down his napkin, saying. "I think a cup of coffee with the ladies will do very nicely."

If Ormsby disliked this turn of events, he gave no sign, and with the other gentlemen accompanied the ladies into the front parlor. The ladies had just selected their various seats, when Hudson, followed by a footman, entered the room with a pair of silver trays holding the implements and items necessary for tea and coffee. A plate of dainty lemon biscuits and one of thinly sliced gingerbread had been added for those who might like something else to nibble on as they drank their tea and coffee.

After everyone was served, as Juliana had hoped, the Birrel girls, ably assisted by their mother, chatted on about how ill poor Thalia was and how Lord Caswell's letters cheered her to no end. With misgiving Juliana noted the tightening of Ormsby's mouth at the mention of those letters, and she braced herself for trouble.

His pale blue eyes cold as ice fixed on Mr. Kirkwood, Ormsby murmured, "But what is this? Before I left London I heard that there was no question of an engagement between them. It is my understanding that Caswell had not come up to scratch." A warning smile on his face, he added, "Surely, you are not still thinking that they will make a match of it?"

Mr. Kirkwood was clearly at a loss to answer this bold attack and he threw an agonized glance to his daughter. Juliana's heart sank right down to her toes and she geared herself to confront the marquis. His words had to be refuted at once, because as dear and delightful as they were, unaware of what was going on, it would be impossible for the Birrels to keep this conversation to themselves. And if Caswell were to hear of it . . . She swallowed. He'd hotfoot it to their doorstep and demand an explanation from Thalia, measles or no, ill or not, and Mr. Kirkwood. She didn't see either her sister or her father being able to keep secret the existence of those wretched letters and then, she thought wearily, the cat would truly be thrown amongst the pigeons.

Desperately she sought for a reply that would undo Ormsby's words, yet not cause a terrible scene. Help came from an unexpected quarter.

"Oh, don't be ridiculous," said Mrs. Manley. "Of course, Caswell came up to scratch and everyone knows they're in love. Without a doubt, Caswell and Thalia will marry—most likely before the end of the year." She smiled thinly at Ormsby. "You know, Bertram, you really shouldn't listen to gossip. It is so frequently wrong—usually spread by ignorant and low-minded individuals who have no inkling of the truth. You would be wise to keep that particular bit of scandal broth to yourself."

Ormsby's face darkened and he snapped, "I would remind you, Madame, that I left the schoolroom a long time ago and am not in need of any lectures from you."

For Juliana and his grandmother's sake, Asher had been on his best behavior. Well aware that they had been invited to dinner to lend aid, not create trouble, he hadn't needed the reminder from his grandmother on the way to the Kirkwoods' this evening to mind his tongue—and he'd done a good job of it . . . until now. It was beyond him to allow anyone, but especially Ormsby, to take that tone with his grandmother.

From his position near Mrs. Manley, like a big lazy tiger, Asher straightened. His eyes boring into Ormsby's, he said coolly, "You may have left the schoolroom many years ago, my lord, but it appears that you didn't learn anything before you left. I think you owe my grandmother an apology and Mr. Kirkwood as well." He smiled, showing his excellent teeth. "It isn't very gentlemanly to spread such scurrilous gossip or to speak so impolitely to your elders—especially, a woman of my grandmother's station and years."

Aghast, Juliana stared from one man to the other, the violence and hostility swirling between them an almost palpable thing. Not six feet away, they faced each other, Ormsby's face filled with rage, Asher's expression expectant and watchful.

Asher held himself loosely, his blood tingling with excitement, ready if Ormsby should go so far as to forget himself and launch an attack. It was regretful this confrontation was happening here and now, but Asher welcomed it—he hoped, nay, was praying that Ormsby would come at him.

Juliana glanced wildly from one man to the other, her brain scrambling for a way to salvage this impossible situation and avert bloodshed. Staring at them, it suddenly struck her how much, in this moment fraught with violence, alike they looked. The resemblance wasn't obvious, although they were similar in build, both tall, broad-shouldered, slim-hipped men, Asher the taller by perhaps an inch. Both had black hair and olive complexions, but there was something. . . . She couldn't put her finger on it precisely, but she knew that it was something that wouldn't ordinarily be noticed by anyone, something about the way they held themselves, something about the pugnacious jut of the jaw, the taut line of the mouth. . . .

She shook herself. She was imagining things and now was no time to go wool-gathering. Determined to prevent the situation from deteriorating even more, she leaped to her feet and catapulted between the two men. Standing between them, after flashing each man a stern look, she said firmly, "That's *enough!* I'll not have the pair of you brawling like ignorant savages in my father's house. How dare you subject us to such a scene!"

The others in the room had been transfixed by the astonishing scene unfolding before them, but at Juliana's words, the vicar blinked and said quickly, "Come, come, gentlemen. You are both men of reason." He smiled at Asher. "I am sure that the marquis meant no insult to your grandmother." His mild gaze moved to Ormsby. "And you, my lord, your words were perhaps harsher than they needed to be. Calm yourselves." He coughed delicately into his hand. "I would remind you that there are ladies present . . . some very *young* ladies."

For a tense second the two men remained as they were, poised like a pair of combatants on the battlefield, their eyes locked in a duel. Juliana was on the verge of throwing herself against Asher and dragging him away if necessary, when

Ormsby's gaze dropped. Mortified that he had allowed his temper to get the better of him and that tonight's doings, which did not place him in a flattering light, would spread through the neighborhood and beyond, he sought to rectify the damage.

His face flushed with a combination of fury and embarrassment, he said stiffly, "My apologies to everyone. I am not myself tonight." He bowed to the room in general and muttered, "It has been an . . . enlightening evening. Now if you will excuse me, I must be off." And the next second he had strode from the room.

There was a stunned silence when the door shut behind him, and then Mrs. Manley said to no one in particular, "I must say that was better than any drama I have ever seen in a London theater."

Juliana smothered a half-hysterical giggle, hardly daring to believe that the danger, for the moment, was over. "Riveting," she managed as she took her seat again.

Asher sat down casually on the arm of his grandmother's chair and teased, "Well, of course it was—and you must admit I played my role superbly."

Juliana cast him a dark glance and he grinned at her.

Mrs. Manley tapped him smartly on his wrist with her folded fan and said dryly, "While I appreciate your intervention, I think you forget I've been dealing with the Beverley family for longer than you have been alive. Bertram needed a sharp set-down and I would have enjoyed giving him one." She smiled impishly up at him. "But you did play your role very well, indeed."

The vicar cleared his throat and slid his eyes to his two daughters, who were avidly watching this byplay. Recalled to her duties, Juliana looked to the young ladies and murmured, "If your parents have no objections, perhaps you would like a brief visit with Thalia before you leave tonight? I know she would be delighted to see you."

Serena was clever enough to know that they were being

gotten out of the way so that the adults could speak freely, but she had been raised properly and after receiving Mrs. Birrel's blessings, she made no demure when Hudson arrived to escort them to Thalia's room. She might not be privy to what would be said in the room she had just left, but oh, did she and Margaret have an exciting tale to tell Thalia!

The instant the door shut behind the girls and Hudson, Mr. Kirkwood said, "I do apologize to all of you for tonight's unfortunate scene."

"Oh, fiddle!" said Mrs. Manley. "The Beverleys are noted for their arrogant, overbearing ways and you don't need to apologize for someone else's bad behavior—and Bertram has never cared what people thought of his supercilious manner!" She sniffed. "He is far too arrogant to consider other people. *You* didn't do anything wrong."

"I know it is unchristian of me, but I cannot like Ormsby," chimed in Mrs. Birrel. "I remember his nasty ways as a child and he was just as dreadful then." She looked at Mr. Kirkwood. "Don't you remember, Edmund? He was always bullying you or one of the other boys in the neighborhood or making the girls cry." Her normally smiling countenance anything but, she muttered, "He used to pull your wife's hair and mine, too, and frighten us with bugs and snakes. Juliet even called him a bully to his face when he pushed her into a mud puddle and ruined her new gown. He was an unpleasant boy and he grew up to be a most unpleasant man."

"I didn't know him as a youth, but I tend to agree with you, my dear," said the vicar, adding with a smile, "and I don't care if it is unchristian of me to say so. He treats his tenants badly and despite his wealth and my many requests for help has never lifted a finger to lend any aid to the indigent families in the area."

"That's the Beverley family for you—selfish to the bone," Mrs. Manley said bluntly. "His father, Arthur, was every bit as clutch-fisted and indifferent to anyone's comfort but his own—as is his son. Of course, it is no wonder that Bertram grew up to be just as grasping and haughty as his father." She glanced at Mrs. Birrel for confirmation. "He was what, two, three years old when his mother died?"

Mrs. Birrel nodded. "Poor little mites. I was only a baby then myself, but years later, I remember my mother talking about those two motherless babes being left in the hands of that coldhearted man. There was no kindness in him—he was cold and cruel and not the man to have the care and raising of two young boys. She pitied them greatly."

"And they deserved to be pitied," Mr. Kirkwood agreed softly. "I remember that they both went in fear of him, but it was worse for Vincent. Bertram was wary of his father, but Vincent was absolutely terrified of him. To this day, I can recall him turning white at the very sound of his father's voice."

"Vincent?" Asher asked, joining in the conversation. "That's not a name I've heard before."

"That's because the dear boy died, oh, ages ago—before you were born," Mrs. Manley said. "He was a nice boy— nothing like Bertram." She smiled faintly. "If she'd been a different kind of woman, I'd have suspected that Lady Ormsby had cuckolded her husband, because Vincent was . . ." Her eyes sad, she murmured, "He had such promise."

"Oh, my yes," breathed Mrs. Birrel. "And when he died so tragically . . ."

"What happened to him?" asked Mr. Birrel, unfamiliar with this bit of local lore.

"No one knows for certain," answered Mrs. Manley. "He was found with a broken neck just a short distance from the main gates leading to Ormsby Place. Whether his horse was startled and reared and knocked him into a tree limb and that broke his neck, or for some reason he fell from his horse and landed on the ground wrong, breaking his neck, the physician could not say for certain." She hesitated. "There was some question of robbery raised—a gold ring with the Ormsby crest engraved on it that Vincent always wore was missing. To my knowledge it was never found, but since his purse with several gold coins in it and the diamond and ruby stick-pin he was wearing were still on the body, it didn't seem that a robbery had taken place." She glanced around the room. "I ask you, what self-respecting thief would take only a ring, easily identified, and leave behind the coins and the stickpin? It was a mystery but all the neighborhood really knew was that the marquis's heir was dead at twenty-one."

"What a sad story," murmured Juliana. "I never realized that there had been an older brother. I thought Ormsby was an only child."

"Well, he is certainly selfish enough to have been raised as one," said Mrs. Manley.

Serena and Margaret returned just then and the conversation became general. The hour had grown late and shortly, Mr. Kirkwood and Juliana were standing on the front terrace, bidding their departing guests good night. When it was Asher's turn to thank his hostess, Juliana whispered in his ear, "Meet me at the library French doors in an hour. We must talk."

His gaze met hers and he gave her a quick nod.

Asher wasted little time driving his grandmother home, but he didn't escape without a warning from her. As he pulled the horses to a stop at the front of the house, she touched him on the arm and said, "You must be careful with Ormsby. I know that you would like to do him a harm, but be aware that Ormsby is not an honest or fair fighter. You confronted him tonight, embarrassed him before others, and if he can punish you for it, he will." She looked out into the night, her thoughts far away. "Though they were born and raised here, Libby Birrel and Edmund are too young to remember the gossip that flew around the area after Vincent died. The vicar didn't live here then so he wouldn't have heard anything about it, but I can tell you that there was much discreet speculation among several of the people in the area about whether or not Bertram had had something to do with his brother's death."

Asher frowned. "You mean people thought that Ormsby had *murdered* him?"

She nodded. "Yes. I felt the same way and more than once I heard that suspicion raised by the squire's father, the vicar at that time, as well as Denning's father. Everyone in the neighborhood knew that Bertram was jealous of Vincent, envious that his older brother would inherit the title and all that went with it." She sighed. "We had serious doubts about Vincent's death, but there wasn't anything anyone could prove—it looked like a tragic accident."

"What about their father? What did he think?"

"Arthur Beverley was an arrogant despot, but to be fair, the notion of one child murdering the other is something that just about any parent would dismiss out of hand." She made a face. "Arthur had always favored Bertram and would never allow a criticism to be leveled against him—no matter how well deserved—so he most likely would have furiously brushed the idea aside, if anyone had been brave enough to bring it to his attention." She looked thoughtful. "Arthur made no secret of the fact that he found his heir lacking in the traits he highly desired, traits that Bertram had in abundance. I doubt the man even mourned his eldest son's death. He was too delighted that Bertram would follow him into the title."

"Like father, like son?"

"Precisely. There have always been whispers about the Beverleys—they either got their way or terrible things happened to those unfortunate souls who thwarted their desires. Like what happened to my Captain," she said with a slight catch in her voice. "Only sometimes it wasn't only animals that died, sometimes men and the occasional woman died, too. The Beverley family always felt that they were entitled to the best of anything . . . that it is their *right* to own the fastest horse, the biggest jewel or bed the most beautiful woman." Tiredly, she added, "And they will do whatever it takes to have it."

Asher frowned. "Why haven't you ever mentioned any of this before now?"

Her fingers tightened on his arm. "As long as there was no danger to you, I saw no reason to mutter warnings like some old witch stirring a pot." In the darkness he could feel her eyes on him. "But after tonight, I fear for you. Whether you meant to insult him or not tonight, he will perceive your words as such and seek a way to punish you for your temerity."

"What about you?" he asked grimly. "Won't he go after you, too?"

She sighed. "He could, but I am an old woman and he wouldn't get the same satisfaction from punishing me as he would you." Urgently, she added, "Asher, you must always be on your guard."

His warm hand covered hers. "Grandmother, I'm not afraid of Ormsby."

"You should be," she replied sharply.

"What would you have me do? Run and hide from him?" he asked dryly.

She laughed without humor. "As if you would! All I'm asking is that you take care and watch your back."

Driving slowly toward Fox Hollow, Asher was thoughtful. His grandmother's warning about Ormsby lingered and he found himself paying more attention to the passing country-side, his eyes searching the darkness, his ears straining to hear any sound that might herald a danger.

By the time he reached home and tossed the reins to the waiting stable boy, he was feeling a little silly. What did he expect—that Ormsby was going to leap out from behind a tree and attack him?

Dismissing Ormsby from his mind, he walked to the house and, going upstairs, stripped out of his evening finery, including his gleaming Hessians. He dragged on some buckskin breeches, a comfortable linen shirt, and pulled on a pair of old boots. Seeing no reason to tie another cravat, he left the shirt open at the throat and shrugged into a dark green jacket. With his grandmother's words in the back of his head, he made certain a knife was in his boot and that he carried a pair of pistols beneath his jacket. No use making it easy for Ormsby.

At the stables, he saddled a nice chestnut gelding he'd bought several weeks ago at Tattersall's and moments later, astride his horse, he was trotting down the driveway toward the main road and the meeting with Juliana.

The last of the carriages had hardly pulled away from Kirkwood before her father turned toward Juliana and cried despairingly, "What are we to do? Ormsby was furious. He will never forgive the insult and he will blame me, us for it."

Conscious of Hudson listening in the background, Juliana urged her father down the hall and into his office. Shutting the door behind her, she said with more confidence than she felt, "You exaggerate. Yes, Ormsby was furious, but what happened was his own fault, and I'm sure once he thinks about it, he'll realize that."

Her father stared at her as if she had gone mad. "Have you forgotten that this is *Ormsby* we are talking about? The man who holds your sister's future in his hands?" Walking to his book- and paper-littered desk, he sat down behind it and buried his head in his hands. "We are ruined. He will make the letters public or give them to Caswell." Raising anguished eyes to Juliana's face, he said dejectedly, "Either way, there is no hope of a happy future for Thalia."

There was much truth in what her father said, but Juliana wasn't going to allow bleak despair to overcome her. From the second her father had come home with the news that he had invited Ormsby to dinner tonight, she'd known that something had to be done about the marquis. Her hastily arranged dinner party had been nothing more than a thin wall built of sand to hold back the ocean and unless something was done, and quickly, Ormsby would drown them.

If she could take heart from anything, it was that Ormsby had not had things his own way and that he had been the one to leave with his tail between his legs. For tonight, she reminded herself miserably. He would be back and next time they might not escape unscathed.

She had no words of comfort for her father and, leaving him to his own black thoughts, she mounted the stairs to Thalia's room. Thalia would be anxious to learn what had transpired and, not wanting her to fret, Juliana needed to see her and reassure her that the worst had not happened.

Taking one look at the frightened face turned her way when she entered the big bedroom, she knew she had been right to be worried about Thalia's state.

Sitting bolt upright in the bed, her eyes huge in her pale face, Thalia asked fearfully, "He is not here any longer, is he?"

Forcing a smile, Juliana crossed the room and sank down on one side of the bed. Pushing back a strand of Thalia's lank hair that had fallen across her forehead, she said, "No. The marquis is no longer in the house. You are safe."

Relief made Thalia weak and she sank back against the bank of pillows piled behind her. "I was so frightened! When Serena and Margaret came upstairs and told me what he had said and the set-down Mrs. Manley gave him . . . I was terrified he'd insist upon seeing me himself."

"As if I would allow that to happen," Juliana replied, running a critical eye on her sister's countenance. The fever had broken a few days ago and though Thalia looked pale and wan, the worst of the spots were beginning to fade. She has lost some weight, as much from anxiety as her illness. Her lovely skin was still mottled and her eyes appeared sunken but there was improvement. It would still be a while yet before she left the sick room, but the disease seemed to have run its course.

Thalia's eyes closed and tears leaked down her cheeks from

beneath her long lashes. "This is all my fault. Poor Papa is so angry with me and though you haven't said anything, I know that you are disappointed and ashamed of me. If only I hadn't been so stupid. . . ." She choked on a sob. "I don't deserve to be happy and marry my dear, dear Caswell. I deserve to be married to a beast like Ormsby."

"You most certainly do deserve the man you love and there is no way that I will allow you to be married to that wretched creature," Juliana said fiercely. "You weren't stupid and I am not ashamed of you! I can't pretend that I wasn't angry, and Papa, too, but we love you and forgave you almost as soon as we learned of the letters. He knows, as I do, that you were young and not wise and Ormsby took advantage of you." Running a caressing finger down Thalia's cheek, she said, "There is nothing that you could ever do that would make us stop loving you or ever be ashamed of you."

Thalia's eyes opened and the stark misery in their depths made Juliana's heart ache. In a very small voice, Thalia asked, "Do you think I should send Caswell away and m-m-marry Ormsby? If I did t-t-that, you could go back to your sweet little house and Papa could be at ease again. I-i-it wouldn't matter very much what happened to me. Marriage to Ormsby would be a f-f-fitting punishment for my folly."

"Of all the nonsensical—!" Juliana leaned forward and took one of Thalia's limp hands in hers. "Listen to me, sweetheart," she said softly. "Yes, you were foolish, but if Ormsby had been a man of honor none of this would have happened. I swear to you that we will find a way out of this terrible coil!"

"I don't see how," Thalia said. "As long as Ormsby has my letters . . ." Her voice suspended by tears, Thalia turned her head away, unable to go on.

If Juliana could have grabbed a sword and run Ormsby through at that moment, she would have. She had never in her life felt such helpless fury or longing to inflict massive injury to another living creature as she did right then.

Struggling to maintain a calm exterior, Juliana rose to her feet. Brushing her lips across Thalia's forehead, she said quietly, "It is the illness that has made you lose heart. When you sleep tonight, I want you only to think of Caswell. Leave Ormsby to me."

The small nod Thalia gave her was not encouraging, but Juliana knew that there was nothing more she could do right now. Closing the door softly behind her, she stood for a moment in the hallway, her head leaning back against the door.

She'd been brave for Thalia and her father, but doubts of her ability, even with Asher's help, of bringing them all to a happy ending were threatening to drown her. Her father and her sister were tearing themselves apart and she could not bear to watch them suffer. They, none of them, could go on this way much longer. Something, she thought desperately, *must* be done . . . and soon.

Chapter 10

Juliana was so sunk in gloom that she didn't hear Asher's first discreet tap on the library French doors. A moment or two later she became aware of the increasingly insistent sound of tapping coming from outside.

Recalled to her senses, she leaped to her feet from the green and gold damask sofa where she'd been sitting and rushed to the French doors. Opening them, she dragged him inside the dimly lit room.

She peeked out into the dark garden and, glancing back at Asher, asked anxiously, "Did anyone see you?"

"I doubt it. I was careful."

"And your horse? It will not be discovered and questions raised?"

Asher sighed. "I do know what I'm doing, my pet. I took care that no one saw me and I left my horse safely tied some distance away and walked the rest of the way to the house."

The only candle burning in the library was on the dark green marble mantel of the fireplace, not far from the French doors, and shadows abounded. Because of Mr. Kirkwood's love of books, the library was the grandest room in the entire house. Floor to ceiling oak bookcases had been built along three walls of the room, the expanse of leather-bound books broken only by tall windows draped in pale green velvet on the opposite walls that faced outside: the French doors and fireplace dominated the remaining wall. A pair of large, fine woolen rugs intricately woven in shades of cream, gold, green and rose lay upon the polished parquet floors and handsome sofas and chairs flanked by various tables were scattered about the big room. Even now and full of shadows, it was a room that invited one to linger and browse through Mr. Kirkwood's vast collection of books.

Asher wasn't interested in Mr. Kirkwood's books. . . . Mr. Kirkwood's eldest daughter was an entirely different matter. As happened with more frequency than he was happy about, just the sight of her filled him with the most lascivious thoughts. Recalling those moments in the poacher's hut when he'd kissed her, his blood thrummed urgently in his veins, heat flooded him and the desire to find out if reality compared to memory flared through him.

She looked uncommonly pretty tonight in her apricot gown, the color intensifying the depth of those whiskey-hued eyes and the sable richness of her hair. His gaze lingered on her tempting mouth before dropping to the modestly cut bodice, where just a tantalizing hint of the lush breasts concealed beneath the fabric could be seen. Annoyed, but not surprised, he felt a powerful stirring in his groin and knew that if he didn't focus on the matter at hand, that he'd give in to the impulse to find out exactly how much passion lay behind her demure exterior.

Oblivious to the carnal gleam in Asher's eyes, she bit her lip and asked again, "You're positive no one saw you?"

"No one saw me, Juliana," he said impatiently and, grasping her arm, led her over to the green and gold sofa. After gently pushing her down onto the sofa, he sat down beside her and said, "Now tell me what has you in such a fret."

Her hands twisting in her lap, she said miserably, "Everything!" She glanced over at him, her features distressed. "Tonight was a disaster and it is only by the grace of God that you are not committed to meeting Ormsby on the dueling field at dawn. Ormsby was humiliated and enraged when he stormed out of here and I just know that the beastly man will take punitive action against my family for being the cause of his embarrassment." When Asher would have spoken she held up a hand. "You don't have to tell me that it was my fault—I know that! I should never have invited you and your grandmother to dine when Ormsby was going to be here, but I was at my wit's end. When my father told me that Ormsby had inveigled, and believe me there is no other word for it, an invitation to dine here tonight, I could think of nothing but preventing him from cornering my father. If I hadn't been so enraged at Ormsby's effrontery and so determined to thwart him . . . if only I'd thought a moment or two more, I'd have known better than to have involved you or your grandmother." She looked into the shadowy room. "I should have written to the squire and invited him and his wife and family—*anyone* else but you."

"Well, I guess that puts me in my place." The laughing spark in his eyes at odds with his mournful tone, he added, "And here I thought I was riding to rescue the fair maiden. How could I have been so mistaken?"

She glared at him. "Oh, stop it! I am in no mood to put up with your teasing. I've just spent a dreadful evening, terrified of what nearly happened happening and you make light of it." Her gaze dropped and she muttered, "My poor father is so distraught that I live in terror a fit of apoplexy will carry him off, and he lives in fear of what Ormsby may do next, and Thalia . . ." Her voice broke and she wailed, "Asher, Thalia offered to sacrifice her own happiness and *marry* Ormsby!"

Taking one of her hands in his, he murmured, "You have had a bad time of it, haven't you, sweetheart."

Her fingers clutched his and she said bitterly, "Perhaps, but what happens to me is nothing compared to Thalia's fate if I don't find a way to save her from Ormsby." She took a breath, fighting against the helpless despair that threatened to overtake her. Lifting her head, she met his gaze. "We have to get those letters! This situation cannot be allowed to continue." A note of apology in her voice, she added, "I know that I have involved you in something that is none of your affair and I am truly sorry, but I simply couldn't think of anything else to do. It is outrageous of me to make further demands on you, but something *must* done immediately. If it is not, my father is likely to kill himself with worry and shame that he could not protect Thalia from Ormsby's designs, but my real fear is that Thalia will do something utterly foolish."

"More foolish than writing the letters in the first place?" Asher asked unhelpfully.

She jerked her hand free and her eyes flashed with temper. "I just remembered what an infuriating little boy you were."

He grinned, but conscious of the seriousness of the matter, he said slowly, "Ormsby is dining at my stepfather's"—he glanced at the ormolu clock on the mantel and, noting the hour was after midnight, continued—"less than twenty hours from now. Ormsby will be occupied until the early morning hours and his absence provides an excellent opportunity for me to steal the letters—assuming they are where I think they are. If all goes well, you'll have Thalia's letters in your hands before another twenty-four hours passes."

She took heart from his words, until she stopped to think about the danger he was facing. Until this moment, caught up in her own problems, she hadn't really considered the enormity of what she was asking him to do and guilt rippled through her. He was taking a terrible risk for her, her family, by breaking into Ormsby's house and stealing Thalia's letters—if he found them. If he was discovered, not only would his reputation be ruined and his grandmother destroyed but it suddenly dawned on her that there existed the very real possibility that he could be transported to Australia or even hung as a common thief. The idea of Asher dead or transported, the idea of never seeing him again, of never staring into those mocking midnight blue eyes or hearing that drawling voice again infused her whole body with a kind of terror she had never experienced in her life.

Her face white, her eyes enormous pools of dusky gold, she whispered, "No. No. You must not."

Asher's left brow rose. "I must not what?"

In an agitated voice, she said, "You must not take the risk. If you were to be discovered . . ." She shook her head, the horrifying image of Asher's body swinging from a gibbet flitting through her mind. "No. I never should have asked you to take such a risk." Her gaze dropped from his and she stared blindly into space. "There has to be another way. I have to find another way. I see now that it was a foolish plan and I should never have involved you."

Asher captured her hand, bringing her gaze back to him. A crooked smile on his lips, he said, "You can't stop me."

"But you must not!" she cried, her heart pulsing with fear. "I forbid it! Don't you understand the peril you would be in if you were discovered robbing Ormsby's house? What it would do to your grandmother if you were caught?"

"I won't be caught."

"But you don't know that!"

He wasn't going to argue with her. Whether she wanted him to or not, he was going to break into Ormsby's tonight and, if luck was kind, find her sister's letters and steal them from the marquis. It was going to happen and there was nothing she could say or do to change his mind. Seeing the anxiety on her face, a pang of remorse bit him. How could he explain to her that he was going to take great enjoyment from depriving Ormsby of those letters and that in many ways, his theft had *nothing* to do with her or her family? Hell, he was *grateful* for the chance to ruin Ormsby's plans for Thalia.

Lifting her fingers to his mouth, he kissed them, smiling when she jerked them away from him and primly returned her hand to her lap. "You have to believe me when I say I won't be caught," he said easily, part of him wondering what she'd do if he reached over and kissed that sweet little mouth of hers. "Remember, Ormsby will be away from the house.

With Ormsby away, the servants will have either gone to bed or will be busy with their own affairs. There will be no reason for one of them to wander anywhere near the library, much less into it. I already know where the safe is and I am certain that I can easily open it." When she didn't look convinced, he said, "Juliana, I will not be in Ormsby's library for more than ten minutes . . . and if the letters are there, all your troubles will be over."

"But what if . . . ?"

He put a silencing finger to her mouth, enjoying the feel of her lips beneath his finger. "I'll tell you exactly what will happen," he said. "The marquis will go to Apple Hill to dine tonight. Once I know he is there, I shall ride to Ormsby Place and steal the letters. I will be in and out of the library before anyone knows that I am even on the grounds."

Her eyes searched his. She knew that look of old. He would not be deterred. "You will be careful?" she asked apprehensively, giving in to the inevitable. Her gaze dropped to her hands lying in her lap. "I c-c-could not bear it, if s-s-something happened to you."

Her words came as a pleasant shock and he acknowledged what he'd known for a long time, that there was much about Juliana that pleased him—immensely. He studied her downbent head for a long moment, his eyes following the line of an errant curl that dangled near her cheek before drifting to the enticing swell of her breasts. He didn't want to talk about Ormsby or Thalia's blasted letters, what he wanted to talk about . . . ah, Christ, he thought cynically, as between his legs, his member swelled and in his veins, his blood beat faster, he didn't want to talk at all. He wanted, with a craving that was becoming damn hard to suppress, to take her into his arms and kiss her, to touch the silky skin he knew was underneath all that flowing muslin. He wanted that soft mouth crushed under his and that lovely, lush body arching up against him as he sank deep within her.

As the seconds passed and Asher remained silent, Juliana's

eyes lifted to his and she gasped at the naked desire evident in his face. To her mortification, her nipples instantly hardened into rigid little buds and there was heat and moisture at the junction of her thighs.

The air simmered between them and their eyes locked. He looked very handsome as he sat at the end of the sofa, his shirt opened at the throat, the muscular body poised like a cat ready to pounce. They were alone in the quiet house, her father, the servants all gone to bed. . . . No one knew that Asher was in the house. No one would know if he ravished her, as his expression told her he wanted to and excitement quivered through her at the notion of feeling all that hard masculinity pressed intimately against her bare flesh.

In the years since her husband had died, there had been the occasional gentleman who had indicated more than a passing interest in her, but Juliana had never been the least tempted either to encourage a suit or plunge into a torrid affair with any of them. But Asher . . . Her pulse leaped and she admitted that Asher tempted her as no other man ever had—not even her husband. She knew she should say something to break the thickening silence, but all she could do was stare at the sensual curve of his mouth and think how hot it would feel on hers. I should get up, she thought dazedly, and tell him to leave. I should run. But she did none of those things; she simply stared at him, her breathing quickening, the peaks of her nipples obvious beneath the thin muslin of her gown.

She didn't pretend not to know the danger of this moment, couldn't pretend not to know what would happen if she didn't bring a halt to the carnal awareness that swirled around them. She knew what she should do, knew what she should say, but she could not, not when every fiber of her being screamed for Asher to take her into his arms.

The blood pounding like lava through his body beat back any common sense Asher might have possessed and, not giving a damn about the consequences, aware only that if he didn't kiss her, didn't touch her he'd regret it for as long as he lived, he reached for her. Gripped by an elemental passion, his hands closed around her upper arms and he dragged her against him. He found her mouth, kissing her with barely suppressed violence.

Juliana never thought to deny him. Even when his lips forced hers open and his tongue dipped into her mouth to explore and arouse, she did not deny him. His kiss was too seductive, the stroke of his tongue, the hungry invasion, too sweet to deny. When his arms dropped and he cupped one breast, she shuddered and arched up into his caress.

Blind driving passion exploded between them and Juliana sank back onto the sofa, Asher's big body following hers down. Lying half on her, half beside her, he kissed her a long time, many times, each kiss more frantic, more explicit than the last. His hands moved over her, kneading her breasts, plucking at the hard nipples, heat and hunger burning through him, driving him half mad with need.

Juliana reveled in his touch, her fingers moving through his hair and down to the hard muscles of his back. When his mouth left hers, she moaned in regret, only to jerk with pleasure, when his teeth closed around her nipple. As he suckled her through the fabric of her gown, the feel of that demanding mouth on her breast quickened the growing ache between her legs. She moved restlessly beneath him, her hands clutching his shoulders, touching him wherever she could. Frustrated by the clothes between them, she pushed his jacket back and sighed when her fingers slipped beneath his shirt and found warm, naked male muscles.

The sensation of her hand palming his chest, her fingers tangling in the mat of thick black hair that grew there, tore a groan from him. He wanted more, so much more, and hating every moment his mouth was not on her, he reared back, shrugged out of his jacket and ripped off his shirt. His boots and breeches followed.

He turned back to her and in a voice thick with desire, he said, "And now for you. Let's see if the visions that have been bedeviling me for some time match reality." Even if the idea of stopping had crossed her mind, Juliana wouldn't have been able to prevent him from swiftly, efficiently divesting her of every piece of clothing. Her slippers, her gown and chemise joined his breeches and boots on the floor.

By the time they were both naked, Juliana was slumped down on the sofa and Asher was sitting beside her, his bare hip pressing against hers. Briefly they regarded each other, each aware that they had passed the point of no return. His eyes skimmed down her body and he muttered, "Christ! Reality is far better than my poor imagination. You're lovely." He bent forward and his lips grazed her nipples. "Far lovelier and far more tempting than any woman has a right to be."

She'd known that Asher was lean and muscular, but nothing had prepared her for the impact of all that muscled masculine beauty that had been hidden beneath his clothes. Unable to help herself, her hand drifted over him, marveling at the muscles that bunched and jerked wherever her hand touched, almost purring at the sensation of her fingers sliding through the thick mat of hair that covered his chest.

Asher captured her exploring hand and his face taut with desire, he said roughly, "I have enough sanity left to leave now if you tell me to do so." He moved, his mouth hovering inches above hers and his eyes black with need, and declared bluntly, "But be warned, if I touch you again . . . I will not stop until I have made you mine."

Juliana reached for him, half laughing, half crying, "If you do not make love to me right now, Asher Cordell, I shall hate you for the rest of my life."

With something like a groan and curse, he fell upon her, his mouth taking hers with blatant design. His tongue sank into her mouth like a hot shaft and his chest crushed against her breasts.

Drunk on the feel of his warm, naked body against hers, the thrust of his tongue, the rub of his hair-roughened chest against her nipples, she was flung into a vortex of voluptuous sensation. His scent was in her nostrils, her mouth full of the taste of him and the touch of his body, the slide of his muscled length against her almost more than she could bear. She wanted him. Wanted him in the most basic way. Wanted him as she never wanted another man.

Gripped by the same elemental passion that drove Juliana, Asher gorged himself on her sweetness, his mouth and tongue savoring and sampling everywhere it touched. Needing to find succor from the relentless hunger that clawed through him, his hand slid down her belly, seeking the beckoning softness between her thighs. Her mound was covered with a thick thatch of curls and he toyed there a moment before slipping a finger between the slick folds they guarded. She was wet and hot, the tender flesh as delicate as silk, as burning as fire.

Juliana gasped at that first probing invasion, a wild, aching pleasure spearing up through her. Her hips arched and her hands clenched against his shoulders when he slowly pushed in a second finger and stroked her.

Emotions, sensations crowded through her as those knowing fingers brought her nearly to the edge. She'd never felt this way before, not even in the most intimate moments with her husband, and she was unprepared for the frantic hunger that swamped her. Nothing mattered but that he ease this terrible neediness he had kindled within her.

Asher could wait no longer. His fingers slipped from her and he slid between her thighs. Positioning the broad head of his sex against her, he thrust heavily into her, groaning at the heat and tightness that met his invasion. Lying lodged deep within her, every nerve in his body was focused where they joined together. She was fire and ecstasy beneath him, her lush body soft and silky against him and the magic of their union took him by surprise.

He had made love to many women, but none, and never until Juliana, had ever aroused the emotions that were thudding through him. He'd felt passion, desire and pleasure before but tonight there was some new sentiment raging within him that inflamed all those other emotions, made them stronger, more intense; he was helpless against that power. Dominated by this fierce melding of emotions, his hips flexed and he drove into her again and again. He desperately wanted to prolong the moment, wanted to savor the sensations, but he couldn't think, couldn't breathe, all he could do was *feel* and give in to the primitive goad to seek release.

Juliana gasped at his size and heat as he filled her body. In the years since her husband had died there had been no other man and her husband had been her only lover. Now she discovered in Asher's arms that there were lovers and then there were *lovers*. . . . Asher's lovemaking swamped her, enveloped her, hurling her into an entirely new world of sensual appreciation for this one, simple act. Lost in a haze of sensation, she met his every thrust, waves of pleasure surging through her with every movement he made. Her arms clutched him tight, the rhythmic rubbing of his chest against her breasts erotic and arousing, the demand of his tongue and mouth stoking her need of him and the frantic pounding of his body on hers inciting a wildness within her. In a torment of delight and yearning, she writhed under his onslaught, the arching of her hips, the soft sounds she uttered, inciting him to drive harder, faster into her, until at last, she convulsed around him and the world spun away. Her release was his undoing and Asher trembled in her arms and helplessly he followed her over the edge.

They lay on the sofa, their bodies still joined, their rapid breathing the only sound in the room. Tremors still jerking through him, Asher knew he should move, but he could not and lazily, as if to begin anew he thrust into her, but the power was gone and reluctantly he withdrew from her body. He fumbled through their clothing on the floor and, finding a large linen handkerchief in his coat pocket, he carefully placed it between Juliana's thighs and erased all outward sign of their coupling.

After stuffing the handkerchief in his coat pocket, he dropped a kiss on her belly and murmured, "I'm sorry I have nothing better for you—next time we shall be more prepared."

She had almost sobbed when he had withdrawn from her body, not wanting the moment to end, but it was his words that brought her stunningly back to the present. With passion slaked, the enormity of what she had just done, the realization that she was lying naked on the sofa in her father's library and that she had just made wild, frenetic love to Asher, hit her with the force of an avalanche. Her cheeks flamed and she jerked upright. Good God! What had she done? How could she ever look him in the face again? How could she ever consider advising and guiding her own sister when she had shown just how weak and foolish she herself had been? She bit back a hysterical laugh. Letters? Thalia's letters were nothing compared to what she had done.

Mortified by her lack of morals, humiliated that she had allowed this to happen—and never mind that she had *begged* Asher to make love to her—she scrabbled around in the darkness for her clothing. The heat in her cheeks was only made worse, when wordlessly Asher handed her the chemise for which she had searched. Biting back a moan of despair, she snatched it from him and dragged it on. A moment more of frantic sifting of the tangled garments on the floor and she found her gown and slippers. Grabbing them, she scuttled behind the sofa to finish dressing.

Thoughtfully Asher pulled on his breeches and then his boots. He'd heard the soft noises she'd made and those sounds coupled with the way she hustled into her clothes gave him an inkling to her state of mind and he wasn't certain how to deal with her. That Juliana was inexperienced with dalliance he never doubted, but that she might regret what had just passed between them, or where it would lead them, had never crossed his mind. He frowned as he picked up his shirt and shrugged into it. Blast it all! What sort of a blackguard does she think I am? he thought, irritated. Surely, she knows that I intend to marry her? She must know that tonight would never have happened, that I would never have allowed things to go so far, if I didn't intend to marry her. She can't possibly think that tonight was the start of an affair, or worse, a simple tumble never to be repeated.

Listening to the sounds in the darkness as she hurriedly dressed, he was not encouraged. There was a desperate haste about her movements that did not bode well. Once his shirt was buttoned, he tucked it into his breeches and, after running a hand through his thoroughly tousled hair, he said quietly, "Juliana, we have to talk."

Feeling a trifle more composed now that she was again clothed, but longing to rush from the room and hide and never to show her face to anyone ever again, she said, "What about? You have made your plans to steal Thalia's letters and I don't see the need—"

He was around the sofa and his hands had clamped down hard on her upper arms before she knew what he was about. "I don't want to talk," he said from between clenched teeth, "about Thalia—or her damned letters! I want to talk about us. About what happened between us tonight."

Juliana swallowed and, trying for a sophistication that failed miserably, she said, "Oh, that! It was very pleasant."

"*Pleasant?*" he demanded, outraged. She dismissed what had been for him the most glorious lovemaking he had ever experienced as pleasant? Determined not to let her distract him, he took a deep breath and said more calmly, "This isn't about my performance and believe me, sweetheart, it was a great deal more than pleasant! This is about our marriage."

In the darkness, Juliana gaped at him. "M-m-marriage?" she stammered. Grappling with the knowledge that she had abandoned the principles of her lifetime, trying desperately to make sense of her shocking depravity, the idea of marriage hadn't even entered her mind.

His hold on her arms lessened slightly and he shook her

gently. "Of course, marriage. I will come by this afternoon and talk to your father and we can have the banns called on Sunday by the vicar. In a month, we can be married."

Her emotions whirling, Juliana shoved him away from her. "No," she said breathlessly. "I do not want to marry again."

Nonplussed, Asher stared at her, cursing the darkness that hid her expression from him. He turned her words over in his mind. She hadn't said that she didn't want to marry *him* but that she didn't want to marry again. . . . Carefully, he said, "Let me make certain I understand you. It is not just me you have an objection to, but marriage itself?"

She nodded, then realizing that he couldn't see her, she said, "Yes. That's it exactly. I do not want to marry anybody."

"Ever?"

"Yes. Ever."

"So you're willing to become my mistress, but not my wife?" he asked with a note in his voice that made her uneasy.

She hesitated. No, she didn't want to be his mistress, but having given her a taste of heaven tonight, she suspected unhappily that all he'd have to do would be to crook a finger and she'd fall right into his arms again. And become his mistress. Misery formed in her breast. Juliana didn't think she'd like being his mistress, even if what had occurred between them tonight was the most exciting and gratifying thing that had ever happened to her. She'd been a dutiful daughter, a loyal and obedient wife; she'd conformed to society's rules all her life. . . . She bit her lip. Well, except for trying to get Thalia's letters back and making love with Asher tonight. Except for those things, she was as prim and proper and traditional as, as, as the vicar's wife! The idea of becoming any man's mistress, even one who made her entire body melt with one look, was appalling, but the alternative, becoming his wife, was something she could not face at the moment. Feeling her life spinning out of control, she remained silent, unable to think of a sensible reply.

"No answer?" Asher asked dryly.

"I don't want to be your mistress," she stated firmly.

"Ah, so then we'll marry as soon as I can arrange it."

"No," she said.

That one word hung in the darkness between them. His voice full of simple curiosity, he asked, "Could you tell me why? And don't try to fob me off by saying that we don't suit or that you find me repulsive."

Her lips thinned. "If you were a gentleman, you wouldn't press me."

He laughed mirthlessly. "Sweetheart, I may wear the trappings of a gentleman, but believe me, I am *not* a gentleman. Gentlemen," he said dryly, "do not go around breaking into other people's houses and stealing certain, ah, letters from them."

"That doesn't make you any less than a gentleman," Juliana said fiercely, appalled that he thought less of himself for helping Thalia in the only way that *could* help her. "You are doing it for a noble cause—to save an innocent young woman from a life of despair."

"Let's get one thing straight," he said, stepping next to her. "There's nothing noble about what I'm going to do. And I'm sure as the devil not doing it for Thalia." His hands once again closed around her upper arms and he yanked her next to him. "I'm doing it," he growled, "for you. And that's the *only* reason I'm willing to risk my neck. For you, no one else."

A quiver of delight shot through her, but she quickly suppressed it. His reasons didn't matter, she reminded herself earnestly. What mattered was that he was willing to do it and that Thalia would be saved.

Clearing her throat, she said, "And I thank you. I know it was unreasonable of me to have asked you to undertake such a task in the first place, but I am most grateful."

"Unreasonable," he said tightly, "is not accepting my marriage proposal."

"Um, I don't remember that you actually proposed," Juliana pointed out. "You told me that we would be married."

"Is that what this about? You want me to propose?" The incredulity in his tone almost made her smile.

"No, it—"

"If you say that word one more time, I won't be responsible for my actions," he snarled.

Too aware of that sinful mouth just inches above hers, too aware of the disturbing heat and flutter between her thighs his very nearness caused to think clearly, she remained motionless in his arms. That he was holding on to his temper with an effort hadn't escaped her either and she sought for a way to end this increasingly volatile situation.

Impatiently, he shook her again. "Why won't you marry me? Tell me what you find so objectionable."

"Oh, Asher," she cried softly, "I don't find you objectionable in the least." Her hand cupped his cheek. "If I wanted to marry, you would be the very man I would want as my husband."

He turned his head slightly and his lips brushed her fingers. "Then why are you refusing me?" he asked huskily.

How to explain, she wondered miserably. How to explain that she *liked* her life the way it was. How to make him understand that she was happy in her cottage with Mrs. Rivers, her old nursemaid; she was happy arranging her life as she liked, happy to spend her money and time as she saw fit—with no one to gainsay her.

Having lived under the fist of first her father and then her husband, she relished the freedom she had these days. While neither man had ever been a tyrant, she was always conscious that her fate lay in their hands. In the years since her husband had died, she had learned to treasure her independence, and the idea of giving it all up, of seeing the reins of her life that she now firmly held placed in someone else's grip was almost more than she could bear.

She loved Asher. She admitted it. She had been in love with him a long time—probably since childhood. But she didn't want to marry him, she thought stubbornly. The notion of never seeing him again, or worse of watching him marry another woman, made her heart ache and her resolve waver. She'd never thought she'd face this dilemma and hadn't really examined the choice she would make. Some day would she regret turning him down? Was her independence dearer to her than marriage to the only man she had ever really loved? Could she really turn her back on love?

"Damn it! You *have* to marry me," Asher said forcefully, tired of waiting for her reply. "I'll speak with your father tomorrow."

Juliana stiffened. "I think you forget that I am of age and that my father has no say in whether I marry or whom I marry," she snapped, her temper rising. And then she said the very worst thing she could have. Her chin lifted and, oblivious to the hint of challenge in her voice, she said, "You can't make me marry you."

Scarlet waves actually flashed in front of Asher's eyes. His hands tightened on her arms and he jerked her next to him. A second before his mouth came down hard and hungry on hers, he muttered, "Oh, yes, I can. And I *will.*"

Chapter 11

Cloaked by the night, Asher leaned against the oak tree outside the library at Ormsby Place and studied the towering dark shape in front of him. The hour was approaching midnight and he'd already made his rounds double-checking that the servants had done as he assumed they would and with the master gone, had retired to their own quarters. They had.

Earlier, wanting no surprises, he'd shadowed the marquis on Ormsby's ride to Apple Hill and had waited until Ormsby had disappeared inside the house before he made his next move. Ormsby's horse had been taken to the small stable beyond the main house and once the Apple Hill servant had thrown some hay into the manger and seen that there was water in reach, he'd departed, leaving the horse tied in the stall.

Familiar since childhood with the place, it was easy enough for Asher to slip into the stable and the stall. The horse, a fine chestnut gelding with one white foot, snorted at his intrusion, but he quickly soothed the animal. He'd come prepared for the task at hand and brought forth his tools. Picking up the rear right foot of the horse and waiting until the gelding offered no further objections, he loosened the shoe. With luck it would come off within minutes of leaving Apple Hill. Putting the foot down, he patted the horse gently on the flank and disappeared into the darkness.

Thinking about the loose shoe as he stared at the impressive silhouette of Ormsby Place, he smiled. A thrown shoe wasn't a catastrophe, but it would certainly slow Ormsby's homeward journey. Not that he expected the marquis to return home for several more hours yet—he just wasn't taking any chances. He was impatient to have this job over and done with because once he had those damned letters, he could concentrate on a certain bullheaded, obstinate, utterly desirable young widow.

Just the mere thought of Juliana sent a shaft of lust coursing through him and he wondered how he'd been able to tear himself away from her hardly less than twelve hours previously . . . especially without getting her to agree to marry him. He scowled.

What the devil was wrong with her? he wondered sourly as he watched the house. That she cared for him, perhaps deeply, he had already surmised. Juliana would never have allowed him to make love to her if she wasn't halfway in love with him, and just as importantly, she never would have entrusted him with her sister's problems if she didn't trust him.

So why wouldn't she marry him? She had to know that he was not a drunkard or a gambler. . . . Well, he was a gambler when the need arose, but *she* didn't know that. He owned a fine estate. He wasn't unhandsome. He was clean about his person. He was good to his grandmother, his siblings, kind to dogs and animals. . . . He grinned. By God, he was a paragon of virtue—any woman would have been thrilled to marry him.

So why hadn't Juliana thrown her arms around his neck and given him the answer he wanted . . . and expected. He winced at that last. Mayhap that was the problem? He'd been too confident? Rubbing his jaw, he considered that idea but dismissed it. No, it was something else, but damned if he could figure out what and he sure as hell wasn't going to find any answer in the next few minutes. He had a house to break into and letters to find and steal.

He pushed Juliana from his mind and brought all of his concentration back to the matter at hand. Gliding like a shadow, he slipped across the expanse of lawn and a second later was opening the door to the library.

Stepping inside the big room, he paused and though nothing but darkness met his gaze, he glanced around. Almost like a tiger testing the air, he breathed in the scent of the room and, finding nothing to alarm him, Asher walked straight to the wall where the Gainsborough painting hung. Silently, he removed it from the wall and rested the big painting against the empty fireplace.

Lighting the small candle he'd brought with him, he looked at the safe and grinned. Within moments he had it open and was rifling through the contents. His fingers closed around the Ormsby diamonds and he sighed. He didn't dare steal them tonight—when word of the theft of the diamonds spread, and it would, Juliana would know exactly who had snatched them. Thwarted again, he thought wryly.

He shrugged, left the diamonds where they were and moved onto an oilcloth-wrapped packet. His ears pricked for any sound of trouble, he untied the leather binding and opened the packet. It was filled with several letters and he quickly skimmed through them, looking for Thalia's. As his gaze skipped over the various letters searching for Thalia's, a frown creased his forehead. Thalia wasn't the only one Ormsby was blackmailing. Hmmm.

Thalia's letters, all three of them, he discovered about midway through the stack. Wasting no time, he shut the packet, retied it, slipped it into his pocket and closed the safe. Another moment later, the Gainsborough was carefully hung back in place and he had blown out his candle. A few long strides later, he was out of the library, the door closed snugly behind him. Taking a quick assessing glance around the area and seeing or hearing nothing to alarm him, he sprinted for the concealment of the oak trees. Less than three minutes after that, he was on his horse and riding for Fox Hollow.

*   *   *

In his rooms upstairs at Fox Hollow, Asher stared at the long, oilcloth packet he had laid on the table next to the chair where he sat. He had stripped down to his breeches and shirt and was sipping from a snifter of brandy. Set on the table next to the packet, a large candelabrum, all six candles lit, cast a bright, flickering light over the oilcloth parcel.

Feeling as if he was confronting Pandora's box, Asher put down his snifter and gingerly picked up the packet and after only a moment's hesitation, opened it and began to study the letters and notes it contained. The contents were revealing and his assumption that Thalia wasn't the only person to be bent to Ormsby's will because of indiscreet and foolish scribbling was made apparent.

He didn't read the entire contents of each letter, just enough to confirm his suspicions, but it still took time. Several minutes later, he had two stacks of paper on the table beside him. The shortest contained only Thalia's letters, the other and far larger, the remainder. Thalia's he picked up and, walking over to the small mahogany chest positioned near the door to his bedroom, with a bit of muscle, he lifted the chest, knelt down and ran his fingers over the stretch of wooden floor he had exposed. Feeling the very slight edge he was looking for, he worked at it, until he was able to pry it up. A narrow space beneath the floor was revealed and he placed Thalia's letters in it. He carefully replaced the short section of oak planking and tamped it down to hide its location, then replaced the small chest. Everything in place, he considered the placement of the chest, making certain that no sign that it had been moved was apparent. Satisfied that Thalia's letters were safely hidden until he could give them to Juliana, he turned away and walked back to his chair.

Picking up his snifter, he swallowed some brandy and looked at the remaining stack of letters, thinking of his next move. While all of the letters would be damning and embarrassing to the individuals who had written them, only the scribblings of two of the people troubled him and he again divided the stack into two. The larger stack of letters he would see was returned to the various owners. He would have preferred to use Hannum to deliver the individual letters, but his butler's features were too distinct and Asher was determined that the return be done anonymously. Still Hannum would prove useful in selecting which of the servants from Fox Hollow could be entrusted with the delicate task.

His gaze settled on the other two letters and he sighed. One was from a prominent member of Parliament and the other from a well-known general currently serving at the Horse Guards in London: both verged on treason and Asher knew just the man to take care of the problem. These letters he dared not trust to a servant. He grimaced. He was going to have to undertake their delivery himself and it might prove tricky.

He hoped Roxbury was still in London; there was a good chance that he was. The old duke, with his net of gentlemen spies cast far and wide, was unlikely to travel far from the center of the web. Wellesley's ejection of the French Marshal Soult out of Portugal in May had been encouraging news, but the volatile situation in Spain had not yet been resolved. Asher would have wagered a bit on blunt that living amongst the Spanish guerrillas were more than one of Roxbury's adventure-mad gentlemen and that those same gentlemen would be sending periodic reports to London for Roxbury's perusal. The war between Austria and Napoleon was also not yet settled and Asher had no doubt that again, at least one or two of Roxbury's men, acting as the old duke's eyes and ears, would not be far from the fighting. No, Roxbury would not stray far from London.

Asher considered the problem, finally deciding that seeing the two letters were placed in the duke's hands shouldn't be overly difficult. He smiled faintly. He'd slipped into Roxbury's town house once already; doing it again should be child's play.

A yawn took him. He had several busy days ahead of him

and with the visit from the Sherbrook family darkening his horizon, the trip to London and back would definitely be a hasty one. Especially, he thought ruefully, when I have a decidedly reluctant lady to convince to marry me.

His mind drifted to Juliana and her refusal to marry him. He was still baffled by it, but was undeterred. He grinned. The chit should never have issued that challenge. . . .

Juliana was very aware that she had made a tactical error by flatly refusing to marry Asher. And issuing him a challenge to make her marry him, she admitted wearily, even if it had been unconscious, had only made the prospect more enticing to him. After he had left that night, she fled upstairs terrified someone would see her and guess what she had been about. Abby had left candles burning in the sconces on either side of the door and a warm glow met her as she entered the room. Shutting the door behind her, she leaned back against it, her breathing rapid. She was safe. No one had seen her.

Pushing away from the door, she forced herself to cross the room and stand in front of the cheval glass. One look in the cheval glass revealed that she had been right to be frightened of being seen. Her gown showed clear evidence of having been hastily donned, her hair hung about her face in wild tangles, her lips were red and swollen, her pupils dilated and there was a sultry cast to her face. Seeing her, no one could doubt that they were looking at a woman who had just been well loved. Or, she thought furiously, a doxy just risen from her lover's bed!

Turning away from the damning image, she rushed over to the pitcher and bowl that sat on the small pale green marble-topped table on the far side of the room. Tearing off her gown, she threw it on the floor. Her chemise followed and she kicked off her satin slippers as if they stung her feet. With trembling hands she poured water from the pitcher and snatched up the clean cloth and the bar of flowery scented soap lying next to it. Forbidding herself to think of Asher and what they had done together, she spent the next several minutes washing away all signs of her recent activities. Only when her entire body was scrubbed and sweetly perfumed from the soap did she cease her efforts.

Abby had laid out her white linen nightgown and a pale pink robe on the bed and, picking up the nightgown, she slid into it thankfully, leaving the robe lying there. She brushed her hair into order and, feeling a bit more composed, picked up her gown and chemise and examined them. To her great relief, beyond being rumpled both garments were fine and she laid them on one of the dainty chairs in the room for her maid to attend to in the morning. Asher had taken the handkerchief with him; all the incriminating evidence had been disposed of and she breathed easier.

Juliana blew out the candles by the door and the room was plunged into darkness. Climbing into bed, she clutched a pillow to her chest and curled her body around it. Like a wounded animal she lay there, her thoughts chaotic.

Tonight she had made love with Asher Cordell . . . in her father's library! She, who set herself up as mentor to her younger sister, she, who prided herself on the way she lived and had always comported herself like the proper young woman she had been raised, in a moment of intoxicating passion, had acted with all the morals of a Covent Garden whore! Astonishment mingled with shame churned through her. Astonishment because she could hardly believe she had acted that way and hot shame because she had been unable to resist the temptation Asher presented.

But she didn't regret it, she realized dazedly. Not one second of it. No, she could never regret those wild moments in his arms. Never. Never regret knowing his kiss and the magic of his body moving, possessing hers. She would treasure that joining, treasure the memory, but it could not, must not happen again. In the future, she would guard against any opportunity for him to weaken her will. Becoming his mistress was unthinkable, but she was aware how effortlessly it could happen. The need to know again the glory she had found in his embrace would never go away. She knew that and she could only hope that she was strong enough to resist the temptation to find out if her memories and reality were the same.

His offer of marriage surprised her. The idea of marrying again had never entered her mind and she had been astounded to receive a proposal from him. Her lips twisted. Asher's offer of marriage, she admitted, was the least of tonight's surprises.

Her uninhibited response to his lovemaking was a revelation to her. Where had that eager, passionate woman come from? During the years of her marriage, she had enjoyed, or at least, hadn't found the marriage bed distasteful or a chore. But tonight, with Asher, it was as if the woman who'd lain so passively in William Greeley's bed and the woman who had writhed and moaned beneath Asher Cordell were two different beings. Remembering Asher's urgent lovemaking, the way she had reveled in his touch, his caresses . . . a flush covered her entire body and an insidious aching warmth flooded her.

Groaning in embarrassment, she wrenched her thoughts away from that frantic joining in the library and forced herself to consider his proposal. Would it be so very terrible, she wondered, being married to a man she loved? Married to a man who sent her blood singing in her veins and gave her physical pleasure such as she had never imagined? She bit her lip. It was more than possible that she had been the biggest fool in nature to have refused him out of hand.

But marriage, she thought uneasily, would change everything. Asher would naturally expect her to live in his home at Fox Hollow. Would it be so very bad if she had to give up her own cozy little home? A pang went through her. She loved Rosevale; she had fallen in love with its quaint air the moment she had laid eyes on it and it had been the first and only place that had been truly hers. She would miss the tranquillity of the home she had made there for herself after her husband's death, but in the end, she understood that it was only a house. But Mrs. Rivers, what of her? Would Asher insist she send the old woman away, or would he be content to have her former nursemaid live with them? And her fortune, while not large, was more than adequate for her needs, but would he husband it wisely? Or gamble it away as other men had done to their wives' fortunes? What if her father or her sister needed her? Would he forbid her to go to them?

Those concerns might seem trivial when weighed against marrying the man she loved, but there was no escaping the harsh reality that as her husband Asher would have complete control over her person, as well as any assets she brought to the marriage. As a widow, she had the freedom to spend her money as she saw fit, to live as she saw fit, but once they married, she became little more than his chattel. He could say where they lived, how they lived, who she could see and when. He could beat her if he liked. How much money she would have to spend would be up to his goodwill. He could decide the number of servants in their household and who they were. Except for her widow's jointure, and he'd have to die for her to gain control of those assets, she thought wryly, she would have as much say in her life as a dog did about where it slept and what it ate. Did she trust him enough to risk everything?

She stared blindly into the darkness, thinking of the Asher she knew. Over the years, there had been speculation about his long absences from the area, but his family had always dismissed them as either business or pleasure trips—often abroad. Until that night in Ormsby's library in London, she had not seen him eight or nine times since they had become young adults. He had been often gone from the area and she had married, moved away and become widowed before returning to her father's house.

The course of her own life had been such that their paths had not often crossed and there was much about the adult Asher that she did not know. As a boy, he had been kind, if abrupt and impatient with her at times, but he had never been cruel or a bully. If they married, she didn't fear that he would beat her or mistreat her physically. He didn't appear to be overly fond of the bottle and she'd heard no gossip about late night gaming or the flaunting of one mistress after the other. Which didn't mean he wasn't a drunkard or a gambler or a womanizer, just that he'd kept his vices well hidden, but Juliana didn't believe he was any of those things.

One thing she did know: he loved his family, especially his grandmother, and treated her with great care, respect and affection. Didn't it follow that he would show a wife the same care, respect, the same consideration? A soft smile curved her mouth as she thought about Mrs. Manley's new puppy, Apollo. How many men would have shown such thoughtfulness to an old lady? And she did trust him, she reminded herself. Why else had she gone to him when she needed help with Ormsby?

She sighed and hugged the pillow tighter. Was she a fool to have hesitated? A part of her did indeed think that she was, but a streak of practicality, the part of her that thoroughly enjoyed living her life without the hand of a man on her neck, wasn't convinced. Juliana smothered a yawn and exhaustion swept over her. She tried to concentrate, to stay awake, but sleep won out and her lids closed.

An hour before dawn a rattle woke her. Sitting up, she stared groggily around the room, wondering what had awakened her. Darkness met her gaze and she started to drop back onto the bed, when the rattle came again.

Recognizing the sound as pebbles being thrown against one of her windows, she scooted out of bed and hurried to the window. Having a fair idea of the identity of the person who had awakened her, she threw open the window, leaned out and hissed, "Stop that!"

"I will now that I have your attention," Asher said calmly from below her. "You're a hard woman to wake. I've been casting stones at your window for ten minutes."

In the murky light of predawn, his tall form was barely

discernable below her, and conscious that they could be discovered by anyone, she demanded, "Are you mad? What are you doing here at this hour?"

"Delivering the fruits of my labor, sweet. Meet me at the library door and I shall hand them over to you."

"You recovered Thalia's letters?" she gasped, coming fully awake with a jolt.

"Never say you doubted my abilities to serve my lady," Asher mocked.

Whirling away from the window, Juliana fumbled around in the darkness for a moment, searching for her robe. During the night the garment had fallen from the bed to the floor but finally her seeking fingers found it. She put on the robe and after wrapping it securely around her, darted from the room.

The house was not yet stirring, but as she hurried down the stairs, she knew that shortly the staff would be assembling in the kitchen preparing for the day ahead. If she did not want to arouse questions or be found in a compromising position with Asher she had only a few minutes before the possibility of stumbling across a sleepy servant became a certainty.

Reaching the library, she slid into the room and shut the door behind her. Averting her gaze from the direction of the sofa where she had made love with Asher only hours previously, she ran to the French doors and opened one. Asher stepped into the room.

Before she could say a word, he reached into his jacket and extracted an envelope. "All three letters, my lady. I suggest that you burn them. Thalia didn't write anything particularly scandalous, but I don't think Ormsby will be so careless with them again if he was to recover them from you."

Taking the envelope from him, she clutched it tightly to her chest. "They were where you thought they would be?" she asked breathlessly, hardly daring to believe that she actually held Thalia's letters in her hands.

"*Precisely* where I said they would be." The note of satisfaction in his voice did not escape her.

"And you had no trouble?" she asked worriedly. "No one
saw you? Ormsby suspects nothing?" She hesitated, finally
voicing her real concern. "You are in no danger? No blame
will fall on you when the theft is discovered?"

Asher smiled. "There will be no repercussion for me."
When she still looked anxious, he said gently, "No one saw
me, Juliana. I was in and out of Ormsby's like a shadow, leaving no sign of my presence behind me." He made a face. "However, the instant he discovers that he cannot use Thalia's letters
against her," he warned, "Ormsby will know that his safe
was pilfered." He pulled on his ear. "Ah, I took some other
letters he had mixed in with Thalia's, so while he might suspect that your family is responsible for his loss, he'll have to
at least consider that one of the other unfortunates he was
blackmailing was behind the theft."

In the shadowy gray light, her eyes widened. "He was
blackmailing someone else?"

"Yes. As soon as I return home, I shall be seeing that those
letters are returned, anonymously, to their rightful owners."

Juliana almost burst into tears as relief swept through her.
Thalia was safe! Asher had succeeded and he had saved her
sister from a dire fate. Her voice thick with emotion, she said,
"Oh, Asher, I cannot thank you enough! I cannot tell my father
or Thalia what you have done for us, but know that I will be
forever in your debt and that you have my utmost gratitude."

"I don't want your bloody gratitude," he said sharply.
"What I want is for you to marry me."

"Of course," she said, surprising both of them. She hadn't
come to a conscious decision to marry him, but with her
heart overflowing with gratitude, already in love with him, to
continue to refuse him when he had done so much for her
seemed unfair and cavalier. Tonight could have turned out
very differently; he could have been captured, his future ru-

ined and his family shamed. He had risked his life for her; how could she refuse to risk her own for him? "I am forever in your debt and with all that you have done for me," she murmured, "it is only right that I accept your offer."

Asher stiffened. "You're accepting my proposal because you feel you *owe* it to me?" he asked in a dangerous tone.

Confused, she tried to read his expression in the dimness. "Um, ah, well, not exactly, but it seems only fair, doesn't it?"

"Fair?" he spit the word out as if it poisoned his mouth. "You'll marry me because it's *fair?*"

"What is wrong with you?" she demanded. She'd accepted his proposal. What more did he want? Impatiently, she added, "I've agreed to marry you and yes, it's fair. You didn't want to marry me until after . . . what happened tonight in this very room. Was it fair that you *had* to propose to me?"

"I didn't," he said from between clenched teeth, "*have* to propose to you."

"No, you didn't," she agreed. "But you are an honorable man and after . . . after what happened, the only honorable thing you could have done was to offer me marriage."

"And you refused me," he snapped. "The only thing that has changed in the meantime is the return of Thalia's letters." His voice dripping scorn, he said, "Your acceptance of my proposal is my reward to being a good puppy and fetching for you?"

She slapped him. "How dare you!" she declared hotly, incensed. "You are insulting and insufferable and I wouldn't marry you if you were the last man on earth." Spinning around, she stormed from the room.

His cheek stinging, Asher stood there in the darkness, cursing himself, but mostly the infuriating creature that had just left the room. How did she manage to do it, he wondered savagely, as he slammed out of the library and stalked toward his horse. How did she manage to turn him inside out and upside down? He was the one who had been insulted! She'd agreed to marry him out of a sense of gratitude! Because it was *fair!* If that wasn't insulting, he didn't know what was.

Reaching his horse, he swung up into the saddle and rode to Fox Hollow. His destination reached, he left the horse at the stable and wandered into the house.

Though dawn had barely broken, knowing that he would get no more sleep, he walked into the small breakfast room. Several tempting scents met his nose and he was pleased to see that someone had already placed a steaming pot of coffee on a trivet and that several rashers of bacon and some coddled eggs and kidneys sat next to it.

He had just poured himself a cup of coffee when Hannum bustled into the room with a tray of fresh-from-the-oven hot cross buns. Asher lifted a brow and asked, "And how did you know that I would be breakfasting so early today?"

A huge grin crossed Hannum's battered face. "Mrs. Hannum heard you go out. Said that most likely you'd be hungry when you came back." He looked sly. "The missus says that when a gentleman leaves his bed before dawn that there's usually a woman involved." A twinkle in his eyes, he added, "She's of a mind that no lady appreciates being awakened before the sun is shining and that you'd most likely be sent home with a flea in your ear."

Asher laughed and waved him away. "Leave those here and tell your wife that I am grateful they stopped burning witches. I'd hate to have to replace her."

Chortling to himself, Hannum deposited the tray of buns next to the eggs and departed.

Having eaten breakfast, taking one last cup of coffee with him, Asher walked outside, enjoying the fine summer morning. He had no destination in view, but eventually he found his way to the small but pleasant garden behind his office. Taking a seat on the stone bench that sat in the shade of a great oak tree, he considered events. He could forget about

Thalia and her problems. Juliana had the letters and how she and the family handled telling Ormsby that his threats were useless wasn't any of his business. Unless, of course, he decided, Juliana asked for his help. He grinned and touched his cheek. The lady had a temper and would most likely allow herself to be torn apart by wild animals before asking him to help.

His grin widened. But she had agreed to marry him. . . . He scowled. She had agreed to marry him—for all the wrong reasons. Didn't matter though, he admitted, if she was marrying him because she was grateful; he'd settled for that . . . for now. And it didn't matter that she'd taken it back either. His grin returned. She'd said she'd marry him and he wouldn't allow her to go back on her word. He'd hold her to it and while he saw trouble ahead with his recalcitrant bride-to-be, he was confident that their engagement would be announced within a fortnight.

Ormsby worried him and while he might tell himself that Juliana and her family could handle the man, the possibility that the marquis would harm them filtered across his mind more than once. Instinct prompted him to run interference, but instinct also warned that he'd be wise to wait until he had a better grasp of the lay of the land. Keeping his part in the return of the letters was important, but that wasn't as important to him as protecting Juliana and her family from the wrath of the marquis. If need be he'd step in—whether Juliana liked it or not, but for the time being, he was willing to leave the reins in her hands.

Thoughtfully he studied his boots. The two treasonous letters were currently resting with the others in the hiding place in the floor of his bedroom and he was undecided about his next step. His first inclination, having seen that Thalia's letters were in Juliana's hands, had been to return home, get the letters and leave immediately for London, but he questioned if that was the wisest course. The two letters did not contain anything of an urgent matter, but they did reveal that two gentlemen in high positions of trust did not have Britain's best interests at heart. Roxbury needed to be aware of the vipers lurking undetected in his very pocket. Asher frowned. Would delaying his trip to London for twenty-four hours be a mistake?

There was no telling how soon Ormsby would learn that the letters—*all* of the letters—had been stolen from his safe. And as soon as the marquis discovered the theft he would start looking around for the likeliest culprit. Since none of the letters were connected to him, Asher wasn't particularly concerned that Ormsby's suspicion would fall upon him, although it was possible the marquis would like him for the crime simply because of the bad blood between them. Once the announcement of his engagement to Juliana became public, Ormsby would be taking a harder look at him but by that time all of the letters would have been dispersed to their proper places and Ormsby could be suspicious of him as much as he liked.

The one thing he didn't want to do was unnecessarily bring himself to Ormsby's attention and he suspected that a sudden dash for London so soon after the theft, assuming Ormsby discovered it right away, would do just that. There was another more important reason why he hesitated—he doubted that Juliana and her family would wait long before informing the marquis that his threats no longer had any power over them.

He half smiled, thinking that before too many more hours passed Ormsby would have a most unpleasant surprise. He'd told himself he wouldn't interfere, but damned if he wanted to be in London leaving Juliana and her family vulnerable when Ormsby learned that his fangs had been pulled. Snakes were nasty and playing with them dangerous, he reminded himself somberly. Asher had no qualms about his own abilities to avoid a venomous, possibly deadly strike, but he wasn't convinced that Juliana possessed the same skill.

He stared out across the tranquil view—the tree-dotted gently rolling green hills in the distance—knowing that there really was no choice for him. He'd wait until tomorrow to leave for London because he sure as hell wasn't abandoning Juliana to Ormsby's tender mercies.

Chapter 12

Juliana slammed out of the library and raced up the stairs to her room. Upon reaching her bedroom, she wasted several minutes pacing back and forth recalling precisely why she had always thought Asher Cordell the rudest, most obnoxious, definitely the most insufferable person she had ever known in her life.

She had agreed to marry him, but was he satisfied with that? No! For reasons that escaped her he had taken refuge in high umbrage and acted as if she had insulted him. What was wrong with the man? She snorted. He was a *male*. That explained everything.

It was the crackle of the letters still clutched tightly in her hand that turned her attention from the aggravating Mr. Cordell. *Thalia's letters!* She was actually holding them.

Relief, gratitude and resentment mingling in her breast, she sank down onto the side of her bed. She'd deal with Asher later, that ass-eared cretin—right now there was a more important matter that preoccupied her thoughts. With trembling fingers she shifted through the letters, looking at them only long enough to identity Thalia's spidery handwriting.

There were seven pages in all and while she tried not to read them, the occasional phrase or sentence caught her eye and she flushed—as much from embarrassment at Thalia's childishly romantic outpourings as from the knowledge that she was intruding upon her sister's privacy. From what little she had read, the letters were not particularly damning, but they were indiscreet enough to have been a real threat to Thalia's future happiness if they had fallen into the wrong hands.

Taking a deep breath, Juliana considered her next move. Of course, her father and Thalia had to be told—and the letters destroyed. She wouldn't rest easy until she saw them go up in smoke and only ash remained on the hearth. But after that . . .

She swallowed. After their first explosion of relief and joy, her father and Thalia would want to know how she had gotten the letters. She could never tell them or anyone else, she realized uneasily, how the letters came to be miraculously in her hands. In the end she decided it didn't matter. Her father and Thalia would be so overjoyed that they wouldn't press her for explanations. Which left only the problem of Ormsby himself . . .

Juliana wouldn't have been human if the idea of a confrontation with the powerful and intimidating Marquis of Ormsby didn't give her pause. Ormsby would not be happy to have had his prey snatched right from his very mouth. She smiled without humor. Quite frankly, she didn't give a damn about Ormsby's happiness or lack thereof, but she wondered what the best approach would be. Inform him that they had the letters? Or simply ignore him and proceed with their lives and let him discover for himself why his threats no longer held any power over them?

She made a face. Ultimately, how Ormsby was handled would be up to her father; although he would listen to her ideas, he would make the final decision, so she wasted no more time on speculation.

The golden light of dawn was filling her room, chasing away the shadows, and for a moment Juliana stood there uncertain of her next move. Telling her father and Thalia was paramount but she didn't want to arouse the curiosity of the staff by acting out of the ordinary. She hadn't forgotten about Ormsby's spy in her father's stables and though it would take a while for the servant's grapevine to carry the news of unusual doings in the master's house this morning, Willie Dockery would learn of it before the sun was very high in the sky. Once Willie knew that there had been some odd goings on just after dawn in the Kirkwood household, it would be only a matter of hours before Ormsby was informed. Ormsby might not realize the significance, but Juliana wasn't going to take any chances.

The rattle of the tea tray and the opening of her bedroom door jerked her thoughts to the present. Instinctively she lunged for the bed and stuffed the letters under her pillow.

Finding her mistress already up and standing by the side of the bed, the young housemaid said, "Oh, Mrs. Greeley, I didn't expect you to be already awake this morning. Is everything all right?"

Juliana smiled and, sitting down on the edge of bed, her fingers resting protectively on the pillow, she said airily, "Everything is fine, Flora. It is such a glorious morning that I found myself unable to resist rising early."

Setting down the laden tray on a nearby table, Flora smiled. "Indeed it is!" Smiling at Juliana as she prepared to leave, she asked, "Shall I see to it that water for your bath is put on to heat?"

"Yes. Thank you."

After Flora left the room, Juliana helped herself to a cup of tea and nibbled on a small piece of toast, her gaze fixed on the pillow that hid the letters. She wasn't going to rest easy until they were destroyed, but it seemed that she would have to wait a few hours for that pleasure. And find a better place to hide them for the time being.

She had never been a secretive person and it took her several minutes before she shoved them far under her mattress. Not very imaginative, she thought sourly, but unlikely to be discovered accidentally by one of the servants during the short time they would have to remain there.

The intervening time dragged by interminably for Juliana, but finally, she was bathed and dressed and the hour was late enough that her father and Thalia should be awake and ready to face the day.

Feeling a trifle ridiculous, Juliana retrieved the letters and, folding them carefully, shoved them between her breasts. The lavender-sprigged muslin gown she was wearing had a modest neckline trimmed with lace and after checking her appearance in the cheval glass and making certain that no sign of the letters was discernable, she left the room.

Thalia was still confined to the sick room, and knowing that her father usually stopped in to visit with his youngest daughter before breakfast, Juliana hurried down the hall, hoping she had timed her arrival perfectly.

She had. Entering Thalia's room, she found her sister wearing a simple pale blue muslin gown sitting in a chair near the window that overlooked the back gardens, Mr. Kirkwood occupying the other chair. The scattered remains of the tea tray were spread across the small table between them and both looked up when Juliana entered.

Forcing a smile, Mr. Kirkwood rose to his feet and said, "Good morning, my dear. I trust you slept well. Would you care for a cup of tea? I believe that we have left enough for you."

Juliana shook her head, casting a quick glance over both of them. While her color looked better this morning and the spots were becoming even less noticeable, the purple smudges under Thalia's lovely blue eyes bespoke a restless night. Mr. Kirkwood looked little better. There were worn lines down his cheeks and around his eyes that had not been there previously and he had the appearance of man who had not slept well either. The strain of these past terrible days had taken a toll on all of them. They had all been trying to maintain a facade of normality, but Juliana knew how fragile it was. And that it was no longer necessary.

Unable to suppress her news a second longer, Juliana reached into the neck of her gown and withdrew the letters. Placing them on the table before Thalia, she said, "I want you to make certain, but I believe that these are the letters you wrote to Ormsby."

Thalia gasped and stared at the folded papers as if Juliana had placed a viper on the table. Mr. Kirkwood started and looked at his eldest daughter incredulously.

"Thalia's letters?" he croaked, his gaze moving from the papers to Juliana's face and back again. "But how? Never say that Ormsby has had a change of heart that he *gave* them to you?"

Juliana waved his questions aside and, putting a hand on Thalia's shoulder, said softly, "Look at them. Are they yours?" She already knew the answer but she wanted Thalia to confirm it.

Her fingers visibly shaking, Thalia picked up the small pile and rummaged through it. Astonishment flooding her face, she looked at Juliana and exclaimed, "Oh, yes! These are my foolish, *foolish* letters! But how did this happen? How did you get them from Ormsby?"

"That doesn't matter. All that matters," said Juliana firmly, "is that Ormsby no longer has any power over us. Or won't once these are destroyed."

Under the bemused gaze of Thalia and Mr. Kirkwood, Juliana twitched the letters from Thalia's nerveless fingers and marched to the fireplace in the corner and reached for the flint that lay on the gray marble mantel. Realizing what she was about to do, Thalia and Mr. Kirkwood rushed over to watch as she lit the letters on fire.

Together the three of them stared enthralled as the tiny flame grew and spread over the letters. Shoulder-to-shoulder they huddled around the front of the hearth, watching silently as the paper blackened and curled beneath the onslaught of the flickering orange and yellow flame. There was a collective sigh of relief when all that remained was a tiny heap of ash.

Turning grateful eyes on Juliana, Thalia clasped her hands together against her breast and cried, "You have saved me! Oh, Juliana, do you realize what this means? Now I can marry my beloved Piers!" She glanced at her father, saying in a trembling voice, "And, Papa, you will not be ashamed of me or so angry with me anymore?"

Mr. Kirkwood tenderly folded his youngest daughter into an embrace. "I might have been a little angry in the beginning, but I was *never* ashamed of you." He kissed her on the forehead. "Any anger you sensed was at my own helplessness to rescue you." A teasing glint in his eyes, he added, "How could I stay angry for very long with someone so lovely—even with spots?"

Thalia gave a watery chuckle and glanced at Juliana, standing nearby beaming besottedly at them. Leaving her father's embrace, Thalia hugged Juliana and pressed a kiss on her cheek. "You are a true heroine!" Thalia exclaimed.

Her smile full of love, Juliana looked from one to the other. "Believe me, I am no heroine. I am merely a sister and a daughter, who could not bear for that awful man to cause such pain to those I love." Her voice hardened. "And I cannot wait to see the expression on Ormsby's face when he discovers that the Kirkwoods have outfoxed him."

Mr. Kirkwood laughed and, swinging Juliana into his arms, danced her wildly around the room. "I don't know how you did it, my dear, but by God, this is a miracle! Thalia's right— you are a heroine!"

Juliana would have none of it. "Indeed I am not. I was just . . . lucky," she finished lamely, uncomfortable with taking credit for something she had not done, uncomfortable because she could say nothing of Asher—Asher who was the real hero, Asher who risked his reputation, his life to save Thalia. Remorse filled her. He had rescued Thalia and she had thanked him by sending him away with a slap in the face. Her joy vanished as if it had never been and, guilt eating at her, she stared down at her silk slippers, remembering that angry scene in the library, the horrible words she had thrown at him. Misery swept over her. She was an ungrateful wretch. Just as bad, she'd said she'd marry him and then she'd taken it back. So she was a liar, too. And don't forget a strumpet, she reminded herself bitterly, the memory of their urgent coupling flashing through her. Thalia and her father thought her a heroine, but she was nothing more than an ungrateful, lying strumpet!

It was difficult to keep smiling and pretending she was the happiest creature alive when inside she was consumed with guilt and remorse, but she must have fooled the others because no one commented on her actions.

As their first shock and euphoria faded, Mr. Kirkwood and Thalia were eager to learn how she had recovered the letters. Though still heaping praise on her for being Thalia's savoir, they pestered her repeatedly to tell how she had gotten the letters. Unable to tell the truth, Juliana could only shake her head and brush aside their questions. Incapable of bearing either their misplaced gratefulness or their questions any longer, eventually she said, "It doesn't matter how they came to be in my hands, all that matters is that we have destroyed them and Ormsby cannot hold Thalia's innocent indiscretion over her head any longer." Painfully aware that it was *Asher* who should have been the recipient of all this delight and gratitude, she said almost desperately, "I beg you let it be! We have other more important matters before us . . . such as letting Ormsby know that he has no control over us anymore."

Thalia was perfectly happy to drop the subject of how her letters had been retrieved, but Mr. Kirkwood hesitated, his eyes fixed intently on his eldest daughter's face. "Because of this . . . are you in jeopardy?" he asked softly. "Have you sacrificed yourself to save your sister?"

Juliana was able to smile naturally and say, "No, Papa, I am not in jeopardy and I did not sacrifice myself."

He wasn't quite satisfied, but he was willing to let it drop, especially since Juliana had raised a valid point: Ormsby still had to be faced down. Leaving the subject of the return of the letters, the trio began to speculate on the best way to let Ormsby know that he no longer had the power to enforce his demand that Thalia marry him.

Mr. Kirkwood ended the discussion by saying firmly, "Leave it to me, my dears. I shall invite him to call this afternoon and explain matters to him." He smiled grimly. "I shall take enormous pleasure in giving him that information and ordering him from our home. Enormous pleasure."

"Yes, but there is one other thing you need to do," Juliana said quietly. When her father looked at her, she said, "Ormsby placed a spy in our midst. Willie Dockery is his tool. As soon as you have spoken to Ormsby you need to send Dockery packing."

Mr. Kirkwood was aghast at the news, but after a long thoughtful moment, he took it in stride. "I shall look forward to that task, too."

Leaving Thalia happily planning the letter she would write to Piers, Juliana followed Mr. Kirkwood from the room. In the hallway, she touched her father's arm and asked, "Are you certain you want to see Ormsby alone? I would not mind being at your side."

He glanced down at her, his face full of tenderness. "Yes, I am quite certain that I can handle this alone. As your father, it is my duty to protect you and your sister and I have not done a very good job of it so far, have I?" When Juliana would have protested, he laid a silencing finger against her lips and continued, "I am ashamed that I allowed that monster to intimidate and terrify all of us. I should have challenged him the moment he leveled threats against Thalia instead of acting so craven and hiding myself away, hoping for a miracle—a miracle that you, not I, provided." His gaze inward, he said slowly, "If it had not been for your actions in retrieving Thalia's letters . . . I do not even want to think of how differently this may have turned out." He smiled sadly. "You have been the brave one, the gallant one during this entire ordeal. Won't you please allow me to regain some semblance of manhood by confronting Ormsby myself?"

Put that way, Juliana had no choice but to agree. Her eyes followed him as Mr. Kirkwood walked down the stairs, noting the determined air about him, the firmness of his tread upon the steps. Her father wasn't like Asher but he was a good man, a caring, kind father, and she knew that he had blamed himself for the dreadful state of affairs Thalia's letters had caused, but she hadn't realized until now how much his lack of action shamed him. A faint smile curved her mouth. Sending Ormsby away with a flea in his ear would be just the thing to cheer her father up.

Deciding how to spend the day that stretched in front of him occupied Asher for only a few minutes. The hour was still early, but he knew that his grandmother would be up. A ride to Burnham and the casual mention of a trip to London tomorrow would make the trip seem less spur-of-the-moment. After visiting with his grandmother, he would ride over to Apple Hill and mention the trip there, too, but it would also give him a chance to learn how the evening with Ormsby had gone. He grinned. After that, why he rather thought a visit to Kirkwood would round out the day nicely, but since he could hardly just drop in at Kirkwood, he composed a brief message and requested that Hannum see that it was delivered as soon as was polite this morning.

He glanced down at his jacket, breeches and boots. A bath and a change of clothes were definitely in order.

It was still early when Asher arrived at Burnham and Dudley showed him into the breakfast room. Looking handsome and dapper in a dark blue jacket and dove gray pantaloons, his cravat neatly tied, his Hessian boots glistening, he joined Mrs. Manley in a cup of coffee while he laid out his plans to go to London. His grandmother expressed no surprise when he mentioned that he would be leaving for London tomorrow—her interest lay in his *return*. With Apollo snoozing in her lap, having shared several pieces of bacon with his indulgent mistress, Mrs. Manley fixed her eyes on her grandson and asked, "But you will be back in time to meet my friend Barbara?"

Looking as innocent as he could, Asher exclaimed, "Oh, absolutely! You have my word." And that put paid to any idea that might have crossed his mind about hiding out until after Mrs. Sherbrook and her son had departed.

Her fingers lightly playing with Apollo's silky ears, Mrs. Manley looked at him, and Asher barely prevented himself from squirming like a naughty child caught telling tales. "Very well, then," she said lightly, "I shall expect to see you upon your return."

Escaping from the far-too-penetrating gaze of his grandmother, Asher rode to Apple Hill. Upon arriving at the house, Woodall, after a warm greeting, informed Asher that the colonel was still abed, but that John could be found a few miles down the road, inspecting the hop fields.

Asher found his half brother with no problem, the hop fields—with their neat rows of tall poles and artistically strung twine poking up oddly after the grassy rolling hills and the apple and cherry orchards he'd ridden past—were obvious. Pulling his horse to a halt, he dismounted and tied the animal to an old apple tree that had been left when John had torn out the orchard and began experimenting with growing hops.

From where he had been conversing with one of his workers, John spied him when Asher had ridden up. With a smile on his handsome face John joined him in the shade of the apple tree.

Asher looked at the towering vines and raised a brow. "Hops?"

John laughed. "Yes, hops. There is an increasing demand for them from the breweries and though they are finicky to grow and require a great deal of labor, I earn more than enough money from the crop to make it worth all the trouble." He clapped his brother on the shoulder. "Besides, weren't you the one who said I should not put all my eggs in one basket?"

"So this is all my fault?" Asher asked, indicating the acres and acres of towering, brilliant green vines.

John shook his head. "No. But your lecture on having more than one iron in the fire made me think that having all of my most productive lands in orchards might not be wise. Apple Hill is no longer simply orchards—I have dairy cattle, sheep and hops as well as the apples and cherries." He grinned at Asher. "Far more than just one iron in the fire."

The two brothers chatted idly for several minutes, during which Asher threw out that he would be going to London tomorrow for a few days and eventually worked the conversation around to Ormsby's visit last night to Apple Hill.

John made a face at the introduction of Ormsby's name. Rubbing his chin, his eyes on the rows of climbing hop vines, he said, "You know, I simply do not like the man—he is too arrogant for my taste. Carries his consequence around with him like a bloody second skin—I don't see why father finds his company so agreeable."

"I don't think it's the marquis's company that your father finds so agreeable, so much as the fact that Ormsby is a known gambler and has deep pockets."

"I can't disagree—after dinner, utterly ignoring me I might add, they immediately retired to father's study and began to play piquet. I was polite and watched them play several hands, but since cards don't interest me and it was clear neither would give up his seat for me to play a hand or two, I soon bid them good night and left them to it."

"So you don't know how badly dipped the colonel might be?" Asher asked wearily.

John shook his head. "He wasn't losing when I retired for the night, I can tell you that." John looked troubled. "I can't explain it," he said slowly, "but last night was . . . odd. While he was very polite, I had the distinct impression that Ormsby was at the house because he *had* to be and that he resented every minute of it. Another thing—Ormsby is reputed to be an excellent card player and I am no expert but as I watched them play . . ." He sighed. "It'll sound damn silly, but it was almost as if Ormsby was losing deliberately—letting father win."

Asher didn't like the sound of any of it. Ormsby never went where he didn't want to go, yet John, and Asher trusted his judgment, felt the marquis had been to dine at Apple Hill last night under some sort of duress. Remembering back to his own conversation with his stepfather the other day, his certainty grew that there was something more going on than met the eye. The colonel had been too confident that he couldn't lose and now it appeared, if John was right, that for some reason Ormsby was ensuring that the colonel won. Knowing Ormsby, his pride, his wealth, his position, Asher could only think of one reason that the marquis would allow the colonel to freely pilfer his pocket: blackmail.

Yet that was an incredible thought—what the devil, Asher wondered, could his stepfather have discovered that would hold Ormsby hostage? Except for murder, he couldn't think of anything that would have brought the marquis to his knees. Not that he didn't believe Ormsby capable of murder—he did—but rather thought that if Ormsby *did* murder someone he'd take great pains to ensure that the deed was never connected to him. And how would his stepfather have learned of it—and, as important, gotten his hands on that proof? John must be mistaken.

The idea of blackmail occurred to John also and, his gaze fixed on Asher's face, he asked uneasily, "You don't think the old fellow is blackmailing the marquis, do you?"

Asher grimaced. "With what? It's certainly a possibility, but

I can't, at the moment, think of anything your father could have discovered that would make Ormsby dance to the tune of the colonel's piping. And nothing short of murder would be serious enough to give the marquis pause. Perhaps you misread the situation?"

John shrugged. "I might have, but there was something. . . ." He shook his head. "I'm sorry, I shouldn't have mentioned it." He paused, then said forcefully, "I know that I am not clever like you or that I haven't traveled all over the world. . . ." He shot Asher a hard look. "I'm aware that I've lived most of my life at Apple Hill and that I'm little more than a country bumpkin, but I ain't a fool and dash it all—I know that there is something peculiar going on between father and Ormsby!"

Asher regarded him for a long moment. "Then that is good enough for me." He smiled faintly. "And anyone who makes the mistake of dismissing you as a fool or dares to call you a country bumpkin will have me to answer to."

"I'm old enough to fight my own battles," John muttered. "I don't need you to stand up for me."

"My dear fellow," exclaimed Asher, his brows raised, "you misunderstand the situation." At variance with the dancing gleam in his eyes and in his haughtiest voice, he drawled, "If someone speaks ill of you, it reflects badly on *me* and I would have no choice but to take action."

John laughed. "Oh, put that way . . ."

Asher was thoughtful as he rode away from the meeting with his brother. He trusted John's instincts and if John sensed that there was something amiss, then it was entirely likely that something was indeed amiss between Ormsby and the colonel.

It has to be a murder, Asher finally decided. A by-blow, even by a lady of high station, would cause scandal, but nothing the marquis couldn't rise above. Seduction of an innocent? Again scandalous, and parents would warn their daughters against him, but in the end only the highest sticklers would look at Ormsby askance. The *ton* was very forgiving of man with Ormsby's title and wealth. Cheating at the gaming table? He paused in his thoughts. Now *that* could cause some very serious problems for the marquis. If it could be proven and became public, Ormsby would be shunned and no man of honor would ever gamble with him—or allow him to cross his threshold.

Asher considered the gambling angle for several minutes. Of all the crimes to be laid at Ormsby's door and one that the colonel could have discovered, cheating seemed the most likely, yet . . . What sort of proof could his stepfather have discovered? Usually a cheater was unmasked in the act of cheating and to bring proof days or weeks later would be impossible. And the act would have had to occur where several people could attest to it. With no witnesses, his stepfather could claim that Ormsby had cheated him during one of their private, late night gambling sessions until a blue dog blushed and no one would pay him any heed. Regretfully, he put that idea aside.

No. It had to be murder. But whose? And when? For a moment, his thoughts drifted back to the gossip his grandmother had passed on to him just the other night. According to her, several prominent people in the area suspected that Ormsby had had a hand in his brother's death . . . that he had murdered him, just as Cain had Abel. Knowing Ormsby, Asher would put nothing past him, but assuming Ormsby *had* murdered his brother in order to inherit the title, what sort of proof could the colonel have laid his hands on? Asher didn't think Ormsby was fool enough to sit down and write a confession that decades later found its way into the colonel's possession.

It had to be something more recent and, he decided, sensational. Ormsby's hand in the death of a mere nobody could be explained away or ignored—unfortunately, when dealing with someone of Ormsby's stripe, the *ton* was able to overlook the most appalling activities. To be named as a murderer would certainly cause Ormsby trouble, but money and the aid of powerful friends could make it all go away. Whispers would linger, but it would not cause Ormsby any lasting harm. If the person murdered was someone of consequence, however . . . Hmmm. Ormsby, no matter how wealthy and titled, wouldn't be able to escape unscathed from something like that. He frowned. At the moment he couldn't recall any particular death of a member of the *ton* that would provide fruitful ground for blackmail. Wondering if he was chasing shadows, Asher pushed aside thoughts of murder and blackmail and rode to his next destination.

Having left his gloves with Hudson and been shown into Kirkwood's library to await the arrival of Mr. Kirkwood, Asher stared at the couch where he'd made love to Juliana last night with decided fondness. Imagining her lush body reclining against the soft cushions caused a certain part of his anatomy to rouse. Tearing his gaze away from the innocent-looking sofa, he took a quick turn around the room, cursing the unruly member that in his formfitting pantaloons clearly revealed where his thoughts were wandering.

By the time Mr. Kirkwood arrived a few minutes later, Asher had himself well in hand, as it were, and was able to greet Juliana's father normally. The two men exchanged polite pleasantries and Asher wasn't surprised to see that the man who met him this morning was vastly different than the anxious host he had seen the night of the dinner party. Mr. Kirkwood moved and looked like a man newly invigorated and Asher didn't doubt that Juliana had given him the letters, or that they had been destroyed with her father's knowledge. He hoped the latter—he didn't want to have to steal the bloody things again.

Mr. Kirkwood seated himself in a comfortable chair, thankfully from Asher's point of view, at the far side of the large room, and out of direct sight of the scene of last night's wild lovemaking. The glance Mr. Kirkwood gave him was politely curious as he said, "Your note this morning said that you wished to see me?"

"I appreciate your being able to see me on such short notice," Asher replied, standing before Juliana's father. "I'm leaving for London in the morning and I wanted to speak to you before I left." He hesitated a moment before saying, "I realize that since she is of age and a woman of independent means that I am not required to ask your permission, but I would very much like to have your approval to court your eldest daughter, Mrs. Greeley. I mean to marry her by special license just as soon as it can be arranged."

Chapter 13

To his credit Mr. Kirkwood did not look particularly astounded by Asher's declaration. In fact, several things immediately became clear in his mind. Despite his preoccupation with the Ormsby matter, Mr. Kirkwood was not an unobservant man and it had not escaped his attention that when Mrs. Manley had come to call that, while she had been visiting Thalia, Juliana had been wandering through the gardens with Asher. Nor had it escaped his attention that when faced with Ormsby's descent upon them for dinner, that one of the people his daughter had relied upon to distill a dangerous situation had been, again, Asher Cordell. Looking at the elegantly attired young man before him, Mr. Kirkwood noted the stubborn cast to his jaw, the air of tough ruthlessness and determination that radiated from him—not a man he'd want to cross. But it also occurred to him that in difficult, even dangerous situations, Asher Cordell was precisely the type of man he would want at his side . . . and he was suddenly certain that he was staring at the person who had placed Thalia's letters in Juliana's hands. And now, the same young man who had rescued Thalia, the whole family in fact, from the ugly quagmire that threatened to drown them, wanted to marry his daughter? By heaven! Even if Asher hadn't already been a neighbor and the grandson of a dear friend and exactly the sort of man Kirkwood wished for his eldest daughter to marry, after what Asher had done for them, he'd joyfully surrender his daughter's hand to him. Because of him, the meeting he would have this afternoon in his study with Ormsby was going to be extremely different than it would have been only hours ago. He owed this man an enormous debt and if Asher wanted to marry Juliana, who was he to gainsay him?

Mr. Kirkwood's gaze dropped from Asher's lean face. Asher's part in the return of Thalia's letters was apparently to remain a secret. . . . He sighed, wondering when life had become so complicated, but if Asher and Juliana wanted to keep Asher's part in their return secret, as it appeared they did, then he was willing to pretend ignorance.

Aware that he needed to say something, Mr. Kirkwood asked, "Er, have you discussed this with Juliana?"

"Yes, I have, but I'll confess that after first accepting me, she took a pet and withdrew her acceptance." Asher grinned. "I intend to hold her to the acceptance."

Mr. Kirkwood stared at him in awe. This was a formidable young man, indeed. "You do realize," he warned, "that I have no control over her whatsoever? It will be up to you to change her mind."

A glint in his eye, Asher nodded. "So I have your permission?"

Mr. Kirkwood leaned back in his chair and smiled. "Your grandmother and I have been friends for a long time; I knew and admired your mother. From what I know you appear to be a man of substance, a landowner whose people speak well of him, and your devotion to your siblings is much admired. My dear boy, I would be most happy and honored to welcome you into my family."

"Thank you," Asher replied, absurdly flattered with Mr. Kirkwood's answer. He hadn't expected any objections to his suit and even if Juliana's father withheld his approval, it wouldn't have made any difference: it was Juliana he had to convince to marry him. Feeling more was required of him, he murmured, "I shall be a good and loving husband to her."

A hint of a smile around that hard mouth, he murmured, "Ah, I think it would be best for all concerned and the furtherance of my suit if we kept this conversation to ourselves, don't you?"

Mr. Kirkwood blinked. "Oh, my, yes!" he breathed.

London in July was hot and unpleasant, and walking up the steps to the set of rooms he kept on Fitzroy Square, Asher was hopeful that he could be on his way back to Kent within twenty-four hours. Upon his arrival in the capital city very late Monday night, though tired from the punishing ride, he wasted little time in determining that Roxbury was still in residence and that the duke was attending a dinner with several friends from the Horse Guards on Wednesday evening. Tuesday morning he called upon the local bishop and less than a day after arriving in the city, a special license rested in his vest pocket.

He whiled away the intervening time, visiting with his boot maker, his tailor, but mostly verifying his information about Roxbury's plans and even a quick reconnoiter of the duke's residence. Returning to his rooms late Wednesday afternoon, Asher sat down and wrote a note to the duke. Just before midnight, having first made certain that the duke kept his dinner engagement, he slipped into the impressive Roxbury town house and, following the same route he'd taken less than a year earlier, Asher entered the duke's library. Finding his way in the pitch black of the room, pleased with his memory and glad the furniture had not been rearranged, he approached the desk at the far side of the room. Running his hands across the smooth surface of the desk, he determined that the surface was clear and not cluttered with other papers. Withdrawing the letters and his note, he placed them in the center of the desk. Grinning, he took out the black silk mask he'd worn last year and dropped it on top of the letters. Roxbury would know precisely who had left the letters for him—even without the note.

As silently and unobserved as Asher had entered, he departed. He was careful, though, and didn't come out of the shadows until he was well away from the duke's neighborhood. Pleased with the night's work, he whistled a little ditty as he made his way to his rooms.

In the generous sitting-cum-dining room that adjoined his bedroom, Asher shrugged out of his jacket and poured himself some brandy from one of the various crystal decanters lined up on the oak sideboard. The light from the candles in a pair of silver-plated candelabram danced around the room, and seated in an overstuffed black leather chair, a snifter of brandy in his hand, he contemplated Roxbury's reaction when he discovered the letters. A devilish grin lit his face.

Asher had considered personally handing the letters to Roxbury but had decided it was unnecessary and that there was too much risk and planning involved. He'd confronted the old duke once and escaped unscathed, but he hadn't been keen to do it again. Roxbury might have taken precautions against unexpected late night visitors since last year . . . although tonight's excursion proved that he hadn't, but Asher had been disinclined to push his luck—especially when he didn't have to. And then there was the timing of the whole thing; if he wanted to hand them to Roxbury, he'd have had to choose a time Roxbury would be at home—and in the library—and he simply hadn't wanted to waste the effort and time in planning it all out. Much easier to deliver the letters and disappear into the darkness.

Even with the majority of the *ton* having deserted the city, the constant racket of London traffic permeated the walls of his rooms. Listening to the shouts of the drivers, the faint clop of the horses' hooves, the clink of harnesses and the rattle of wheels rolling over the cobblestone streets, he found himself longing for the quiet of Fox Hollow.

Sipping his brandy, he admitted that his eagerness to return home was due to the knowledge that Juliana was there and that before too long she would be his bride—whether she knew it or not. He was looking forward to making Juliana his wife and he didn't doubt that she would *be* his wife and that he'd win that stubborn heart of hers and make her love him as he loved her.

Asher sat up as if someone had just dumped a bucket of ice down his back. Damn it to hell! He was in love with her. Moodily, he stared at his boots. Marriage had always been something he'd planned to do, but he'd always assumed when the time was right, he'd simply look around, select a pleasing, acceptable young woman and settle down to domestic companionship. Not for him the high passion and delirious heights and desperate lows that love brought, thank you very much! With his mother's example before him, he hadn't planned on losing his heart and falling in love, but it appeared that was exactly what he had done. He snorted. Being in love was *not* part of his plan for the future.

A frown on his face, he sipped his brandy. But would it be so bad? Yes, he answered himself with a grimace—particularly if Juliana didn't love him. He suspected that she did, but it wasn't a sure thing. And how could he compel the woman he loved to marry him, if she didn't love him? What sort of a cad would that make him? A cad little better than Ormsby, he decided, irritated.

Until now his pursuit of Juliana, if one could call it that, had been halfhearted and not much more than an amusing game he had every intention of winning, but love . . . Love changed everything and he wasn't happy about it. More than just respect and affection was involved. . . . Devil take it all! His heart, his deepest emotions were in jeopardy now and he was conscious of a feeling of vulnerability he had never before experienced. Juliana had the power to *hurt* him and he wasn't best pleased to realize that his future happiness lay in the hands of another person.

So what was he going to do about it? A slow smile curved his lips. With his heart hanging in the balance, her pursuit was no longer merely a game and he was, he decided, hunting the delectable Mrs. Greeley in earnest now. His smile became a grin. And he was a very, *very* good hunter.

Juliana didn't learn of Asher's visit with her father on that Sunday morning until minutes before Ormsby was due to arrive at Kirkwood. She understood the necessity for her father to speak to the marquis alone and she applauded his determination to face their tormentor by himself. But while she was confident, with the letters destroyed, that Mr. Kirkwood was perfectly capable of dealing with Ormsby, curiosity and her protective instincts wouldn't allow her to retire to some other part of the house and meekly await the outcome of their meeting.

Consequently, as the time approached for Ormsby to arrive, she was in a small room across the hall from her father's study, fiddling with several bouquets of intoxicatingly scented lilies that would be placed around the house. She'd deliberately left the door ajar knowing she'd be able to hear anyone walking down the hall in this direction and she could also discreetly keep an eye on the door to the study.

Flora, the young housemaid, was with her, watching as Juliana created the charming arrangements before periodically bearing off the finished product to the various rooms in the main living areas. Flora's return from one such errand coincided with the marquis's arrival.

Just as Flora stepped back into the room Juliana heard the voices of Hudson and the marquis coming down the hall as they walked toward her father's study. Their voices were very clear as they approached and, standing next to Juliana, Flora exclaimed, "My goodness, but we have had company today! Here his lordship has come to call on the master this afternoon, and this morning, Mr. Cordell was closeted with him in the library."

Juliana stiffened, hardly aware of Ormsby being shown into her father's study. Asher had been here? This morning? To see her father? A sense of foreboding bloomed within her.

Surely, Asher wouldn't . . . Her eyes narrowed. Oh, yes, he would! That devil!

With admirable restraint, Juliana said airily, "Really? It must have been very early."

Flora shook head. "Not when Mr. Cordell came to call. But Hudson said that you could have knocked him over with a feather when one of the servants from Fox Hollow was here pounding on the door before eight o'clock with a message for the master."

Juliana's heart sank, but she forced a smile. "Well, I'm sure that there was reason for it," she muttered.

Flora nodded. "Most likely something to do with Mrs. Manley." Losing interest in the subject, Flora glanced at a big bouquet of pink and white lilies, deep green wispy fern wands framing the heavy blossoms, and said, "Shall I place this one on the table in the hallway?"

"Yes, that would be perfect."

Left alone, Juliana stared blankly at the wall in front of her. Asher had been to see her father! She bit her lip. His visit might not have anything to do with her . . . or with what happened between them last night, but if his desire to see her father this morning had been to do with Mrs. Manley, her father would have mentioned it. Not that her father told her everything, but there had been plenty of moments today for him to mention Asher's visit, yet he had said nothing. Not a word. Which was odd. Out of character. But if the visit involved her . . . She frowned. Now that she thought about it, there had been a pleased air about her father all day and she'd caught him looking at her with an indulgent gleam in his eyes from time to time, and then there had been that odd, little smile. . . . She'd put his manner down to the return of Thalia's letters, but now she wondered.

Uneasily, she considered what she knew. Her father had been silent about Asher's visit this morning and Asher had never once indicated that he intended to call upon her father, at any time, let alone this morning. It was possible that there was an innocent reason behind Asher's visit and her father's reticence, but she didn't think so. Only one explanation fit perfectly—they were *scheming* against her.

A glitter in her fine eyes, she paced around the small room. Asher had asked her to marry him and she had accepted him . . . and then she had retracted her acceptance—somewhat forcefully, she confessed with a half-contrite smile, remembering the sound of her hand slapping his cheek. The question was, had Asher accepted her retraction? Knowing him, she suspected not, and that made his visit to her father this morning suspicious. He was trying, she guessed, to out-maneuver her.

She had not been a party to the meeting between her father and Asher, but if she was inclined to wager, it was better than even odds that Asher had tried to cut the ground beneath her feet and had offered for her. She smiled tightly. Her father probably fell on his neck with delight, but it didn't matter if her father approved of the match or not—she was of age, a widow with control of her fortune, and no one, not even her father could compel her to marry Asher Cordell.

If Asher had offered for her and her father had given his approval to the match, it would explain everything. Scowling, she took an agitated turn around the small room as she examined her thoughts. If Asher had requested her father's blessings and he had acquiesced, it explained everything, even that soft, fond expression on her father's face. It would also explain why he had made no mention of Asher's visit.

Torn between laughter and fury, Juliana shook her head. Did Asher really think that her father could coerce her into marriage?

The sudden boom of the door to her father's study slamming shut and the sound of rapidly retreating footsteps wiped all speculation about Asher from her mind and she ran over to the door and peeked down the hall. Ormsby was striding toward the front door and the set of his head and ramrod stiffness of his back and shoulders indicated that the marquis was *not* happy.

Hudson met the marquis halfway through the entry hall, but before the butler could reach the door, Ormsby brushed past him and snarled, "Get out of my way, you oaf! I can show myself out."

The front door was flung open and Ormsby charged outside.

Following behind Ormsby as he had stalked down the hall, Juliana observed the scene between the marquis and the butler. She also saw the small, satisfied smile that flickered across Hudson's face as Ormsby stamped out of the house. Gently, Hudson shut the front door Ormsby had left open in his haste to leave the house. Turning away and finding Juliana watching him, the smile still lurking on his lips, he murmured, "I fear the marquis has received some unpleasant news."

Her own smile beamed into being. "Why, yes, I believe that you are right. I don't believe that the marquis will be coming to call very much in the future."

"Which is just as it should be," Hudson said, and disappeared into the nether regions of the house. Walking toward her father's study, Juliana's expression was thoughtful. Had the servants known of Ormsby's threats? She nodded slowly. They might not have known the exact details, but they had to have guessed that something was in the wind. She smiled. And that it wasn't anymore.

She tapped lightly on the door to her father's study and at his command, entered the room. His hands clasped behind his back, Mr. Kirkwood was standing and staring out one of the windows that overlooked a section of the garden when she walked into the room.

"Ah, did everything go as you hoped?" she asked softly. Mr. Kirkwood swung around to face her and the huge smile that creased his face brought forth her own.

Walking back to his cherrywood desk, almost grinning, Mr. Kirkwood said, "I am sorry to admit it and it isn't Christian of me, but by Jove! I enjoyed telling that treacherous blackguard precisely what I thought of him and his tactics. How dare he try to blackmail an innocent child like Thalia into marrying him!" A glint in his eyes, he muttered, "It was a pleasure to tell him precisely what I thought of his methods—and him! Enjoyed even more tossing his threats back into his face and ordering him from the house—and I promised him if he ever stepped foot on the place or ever approached one of my daughters again, that I'd take a horsewhip to him. Told him I knew about his little spy, too—and that I would be sending him packing within the hour." His voice full of satisfaction, he continued, "He couldn't believe it at first, but when I stood firm it dawned on him that something had gone seriously awry with his plans and that he had no power over us." He smiled warmly at Juliana. "Thanks to you we will have no more troubles with Ormsby."

One of the servants must have told Thalia that Ormsby had left the house because she came into the study just in time to hear Mr. Kirkwood's last statement and, rushing up to her father, she cried, "Oh, Papa, is the nightmare really over? Is Ormsby truly out of our lives? I no longer have to fear him?"

Mr. Kirkwood enfolded his youngest daughter next to him. "Indeed, yes." His eyes sparkling, he added, "I told him that I'd take a horsewhip to him if he dared to show his face near one of you or stepped foot on Kirkwood again." A hardness that hadn't been there before entered his face. "And by heaven, I would!"

Nothing would do but that Mr. Kirkwood relate the encounter word by word for Thalia and when he finished speaking, her face was glowing and the joy of her smile was nearly tangible. "I cannot believe that it is finally over. That we are free from that horrid man."

A slight frown on her forehead, Juliana looked at her father. "Do you think that he might try to hurt us in some other way?"

Mr. Kirkwood shrugged. "I have no idea. Until this happened I had never seen this side of Ormsby and I would never have believed that he would act in such a disreputable manner." He sighed. "I can't think of any way that he can harm us now, but I would warn both of you to be on your guard against him." He gave Thalia a long look. "Particularly you, my dear. You must be careful."

Thalia shuddered. "I never want to see him again, let alone speak with him. He is a monster."

Aware of how easily her sister could work herself up, Juliana smiled and said quickly, "Since our troubles with the marquis appear to be behind us and you are on the mend, I think we should begin thinking about the house party we had to postpone."

Instantly diverted, Thalia clapped her hands together in delight. "Oh, yes! I cannot wait to see Piers again." A faint blush stained her cheeks and she shot a shy look at her father. "And Papa can now announce my engagement to him."

Mr. Kirkwood lightly pinched her cheek. "Will marriage to Piers make you happy?" he asked, a hint of smile curving his mouth.

"Oh, Papa, I wish it above all things," Thalia breathed with shining eyes.

Looking across at Juliana, he said, "Well, then, I believe that we have a house party to plan and an engagement to announce." His eyes twinkling, he murmured, "I predict that it is going to be a busy, exciting summer for all of us."

His words were innocent enough, but Juliana detected an undertone in his voice that heightened her suspicions. Knowing her father and his abhorrence of discord, if Asher had asked for his approval of the match and he'd given it, it would do her little good to confront him with what she suspected. She half smiled. Poor father. Cornered, he'd mumble and stammer and deny everything.

"How soon can we have the house party?" Thalia asked, breaking into Juliana's thoughts.

Pushing aside the vexing problem of Asher's visit this morning, Juliana smiled at her younger sister. "I shall see to it that the invitations are sent out tomorrow." She ran a critical eye over Thalia's pale features. "While you are on the mend, I believe that it will be several days yet before you have recovered your bloom, so I think it best if the guests do not start arriving until a week from Thursday—that will also give us time to prepare for their influx."

"Why, that's over ten days away. Surely, we could have it sooner," Thalia protested.

Juliana put her arm around Thalia's shoulder and hugged her. "Indeed, it is," she said, smiling fondly at her sister, "but, poppet, we cannot have your husband-to-be arriving and finding you looking pasty faced and haggard, now can we?"

Thalia's hands flew to her cheeks and her beautiful blue eyes widened. "Oh, indeed, not!"

Ormsby rode away from Kirkwood in a white-hot rage, hardly able to think of anything beyond making Kirkwood regret those insulting words. His lips in an angry narrow line, eyes narrowed, he stared blindly ahead, not even seeing the few vehicles and horses that passed him. How dare Kirkwood speak to him in such a manner! How dare that country bumpkin order him from his house as if he was a thieving servant! How dare he! He was Ormsby! No one spoke to him that way. No one. Scarlet flooded his cheeks. And no one, he thought viciously, denied him what he wanted.

Long before she had burst onto the scene in London and become the darling of the *ton,* as he had watched her bloom from a pretty child into a stunning beauty, he had determined that Thalia Kirkwood would make him a worthy bride. Her family, while not of the first stare, was respectable, and with his wealth, her dowry meant nothing to him, but her loveliness . . . her loveliness was without parallel. He had laid his plans accordingly and begun a stealthy courtship of the innocent beauty right under her father's nose.

When the Kirkwoods had removed to London for the season, he had been supremely pleased with Thalia's conquest of the city and the *ton* and he had savored the moment he would sweep aside all the young fools clustered around her and claim the exalted beauty as his bride. Oh, the envy and jealousy that would burn in the breasts of her spurned suitors when she accepted the hand of the powerful Lord Ormsby. He had spent many an enjoyable hour imagining that moment. What he had never imagined was that Thalia would fancy herself in love with that cub, Caswell, and spurn him or that her father would allow her to follow her heart. It never occurred to him that she would turn her back on the vast Ormsby fortune or that she would prefer a mere earl to a marquis. She had wounded his vanity and his consequence and his determination to marry her had only intensified.

He would have preferred not to use the letters to get his way, but Thalia's featherbrained insistence that she loved Caswell and would only marry the young earl had left him no choice. He'd been confident that the threat of blackmail would turn the tide in his favor and until today his threat had seemed to be working. But something had changed. . . . A prickle of unease slid through his fury. He could only think of one thing that could have changed, only one thing that would have given Kirkwood the courage to speak to him in such a manner. With sudden urgency, he whipped his horse into a breakneck gallop.

Arriving at Ormsby Place, the marquis threw the reins of his lathered horse to the waiting footman and strode into the house. Brushing past his butler, he made straightaway for his study. Entering it, he shut the door behind him and glanced around the handsome room. Nothing seemed out of place. Crossing to the Gainsborough, he considered the painting and the area around it for several moments. Again nothing seemed to have been moved or changed. Lifting down the painting, he opened the safe, his body freezing the moment he realized that the oilcloth-wrapped packet was gone.

Struggling against the rage that choked him, Ormsby made himself check the contents of the safe, his racing heartbeat slowing when he found the Ormsby diamonds and the other jewels; only the letters were missing. With a curse, he slammed the door to the safe shut and threw himself down in a chair. Looking at the intricate pattern of the Turkey rug on the walnut parquet floor, he grappled with the knowledge that an exceedingly clever thief had invaded his home. He wasn't surprised that the letters were gone; he suspected as much the moment Kirkwood had as good as thrown him from the house. Thalia's weren't the only letters lifted from the safe, though, and that widened the pool of suspects for the theft.

His face harsh with concentration, he dismissed the letters from the erring wives—the scandal they would face should the letters become public would be unpleasant, but not so unpleasant that they would have dared to hire someone to steal them. Now Lord . . . and Colonel . . . For them, if the letters became public, it could very well bring them utter ruin—if they escaped the gallows. It was possible that one of them had been desperate enough to break his power over them and had hired someone to steal the letters.

He frowned. The thief had been after only one thing—the letters. Whoever had opened the safe and taken the letters had left behind a fortune in jewels and no common thief would have done so. No. The thief had been after only the letters. And had been astute enough to ferret out the location of the safe and able to open it without difficulty. His gaze swept the room again. The intruder had left no sign of his invasion and Ormsby wondered—if not for the interview with Kirkwood today—how long it would have taken him to discover the theft.

His eyes narrowed. Which begged the question: when had the theft taken place? Based on today's interview with Kirkwood, he was convinced that it had to have occurred very recently—once the letters had been returned to Kirkwood, Thalia's father would have acted immediately, but it hadn't been until today that Kirkwood had confronted him. So the theft had to have happened, he realized, after that bloody awful dinner at Kirkwood's on Friday evening but before Sunday morning when he had received Kirkwood's summons. If the theft had been accomplished prior to dinner on Friday evening, the meeting with Kirkwood would have taken place that very night. If it had been done while he was dining at Kirkwood's Friday night, the request for his presence would have arrived on Saturday morning, but it hadn't. . . .

Ormsby stood up and took a turn around the room, thinking hard. Last night he had dined at Apple Hill. His mouth thinned. It had been very late when he had returned. The logical time for the theft to have occurred was while he had been occupied with that fool Denning. Satisfied he knew the timing of the theft, he next considered the identity of the person who had had the most to gain by the theft and who was the likeliest person to have set the thief on him.

Again, he dismissed the adulterous wives. They were silly women easily manipulated. But his two treasonously-inclined-gentlemen, they were another kettle of fish. Either one of them could have risked the robbery. He frowned, staring down at his boots. They'd been in his pocket for years. Why would either one of them strike now? No. It wasn't one of them. Which left Kirkwood . . .

Ormsby nodded to himself. Of course. Kirkwood was the culprit. That Kirkwood had had the gumption to hire a thief to steal the letters surprised him. He would never have expected it of him, but that eldest daughter of his . . .

The knock on the door to his study brought his head up, and he barked, "Yes? What is it?"

"Er, my lord, Colonel Denning has come to call," replied his butler, Baker, through the door.

Ormsby cursed and his hand clenched into a fist. The last thing he wanted at the moment was Denning's company. But aware he had no choice, he snapped, "Bring him here and prepare some refreshments."

The sight of Denning's smiling face did not lessen Ormsby's foul mood, but he forced a cordial expression and greeted the other man. Once they were seated and Baker had served them some hock and left the room, Ormsby asked, "And what can I do for you?"

Denning leaned back in his chair and murmured, "I find the country boring. I thought perhaps that you would be up for a hand or two of piquet to while away the hours."

"Last night's winnings weren't enough for you?" Ormsby asked sourly.

Denning regarded his glass of hock. "Well, you know there is a piece of land I'm thinking of buying to add to the Apple Hill holdings." He looked over his glass at Ormsby. "And you know how very expensive land can be."

Ormsby ground his teeth together. "And if I decide not to play?"

Denning smiled gently. "Oh, then I think I shall have to have a long conversation with my stepson. I think he would find what I have to say most illuminating, don't you?"

Chapter 14

Ormsby took a long swallow of his wine. Denning had him strangling in his coils for the moment, but it wouldn't, Ormsby thought savagely, stay that way. He *would* get his own back sooner or later. Calmed by the realization that this was only a momentary bit of unpleasantness, he forced a smile, albeit without humor. His pale blue eyes cold and hard, he said, "I find that a game or two of cards with an old acquaintance is precisely the way I wish to spend a quiet Sunday afternoon in the country."

Having enjoyed another spectacular run of luck at the marquis's expense, it was nearing two o'clock in the morning when Denning rose from the table and rode home. Once Denning had ridden away, Ormsby's polite mask fell and, his face dark with fury, he stormed up the stairs to his room filled with impotent rage.

In his palatial rooms, he stripped off his clothes and, leaving them in a trail behind him on the floor, sought out his bed. Lying in the huge silk-draped bed, he tried to focus on the problems before him, but half drunk, exhausted from the congenial facade he'd worn all evening, he fell into a restless sleep.

Waking the next morning, his head clear but aching, after bathing and dressing, Ormsby walked slowly down the grand staircase. Ordering Baker to prepare him a tray of some mead and smoked ham, cheese and bread to be delivered to his study, he continued on down the hall.

While he waited for his breakfast to arrive, Ormsby paced back and forth across the Turkey rug, his thoughts on the situation, not only the one with Denning, but also the theft of the letters. Even when he had been smiling and losing to Denning, his mind had been on the theft but befuddled with alcohol, he hadn't been able to fully concentrate. But this morning he was able to put together some interesting facts.

Cordell's sudden affinity with the Kirkwoods had not escaped Ormsby's notice. After all, until yesterday he'd had a spy in the Kirkwood stables and Willie had dutifully reported that first visit to Thalia by Asher and Mrs. Manley. Ormsby might have dismissed it as simply a neighborly call, but Cordell and Manley had also been at that humiliating dinner at the Kirkwoods. Again, it could have been a coincidence; he knew that Mrs. Manley and Kirkwood were longtime friends, but there had been something in the way Mrs. Greeley had looked at Cordell when she thought herself unobserved that made him wonder about her true feelings for Cordell.

The rap on the door was no surprise since he was expecting Baker with his breakfast, but Baker's news did cause his eyebrows to raise.

"Dockery wants to see me right away?" he asked, wondering what the devil his head stableman wanted at this hour. His breath caught. Of course. Willie!

Baker bowed. "Yes, milord. He is presently waiting in the kitchen."

"Bring him to me."

Dockery came into the study a few minutes later, his cap in his hands. Dipping his head, he muttered, "Sorry to bother you this early, my lord, but Willie came home from Kirkwood last night." Under Ormsby's icy stare, Dockery cleared his throat and said nervously, "He didn't do anything wrong. He was minding his own business and first thing he knows,

Mr. Kirkwood comes down to the stables and orders him gone."

"Yes. Yes. I know that—now tell me something I don't know," Ormsby snapped.

Wetting his lips, Dockery said, "Well, Willie did have something interesting to say about the day before he was fired. Willie said that early yesterday morning a servant from Fox Hollow was at Kirkwood delivering a message from Mr. Cordell and that Mr. Cordell himself came to call and had a private meeting with Mr. Kirkwood a few hours later. Willie don't know what the meeting was about, but later on he overheard Hudson gossiping with the housekeeper about Mr. Cordell's unexpected visit and that Mr. Kirkwood had mentioned that Mr. Cordell was leaving for Lunnon this morning."

Several things coalesced in Ormsby's mind. *Asher Cordell!* White lines of fury appeared around his mouth and, nearly choking on rage, he barely got out, "Why wasn't I informed of this last night?"

"Begging your pardon, my lord, but you had company last night." Dockery swallowed, frightened of the expression on his master's face. "I didn't want to interrupt. It didn't seem important."

"Not important?" Ormsby screamed at him. "I'll decide, you idiot, what is or isn't important." His face purple with temper, he snarled, "Get out of my sight."

Alone in his study, the worst of his rage under control, Ormsby walked over to the French doors that overlooked the manicured expanse of oaks and lawn. There were many reasons Cordell could have called upon Kirkwood yesterday morning, but in view of his own mortifying meeting later in the day with Kirkwood, he could think of only one reason for Cordell's presence in the Kirkwood household on Sunday. . . . That hell born whelp had been returning Thalia's letters to her father, letters he had stolen from *him!*

He stared blindly at the charming scene in front of him.

Cordell's trip to London today only confirmed his suspicions of the identity of the thief who had invaded his home, stolen from him and been the cause of him having to endure a humiliating tongue-lashing from Kirkwood. Asher Cordell, he thought savagely, was becoming a very big problem and he knew just the solution. . . .

His business in London taken care of, eager to return to the pursuit of Juliana, Asher set out for home at first light Wednesday morning. It was a long hard day in the saddle and he stopped only long enough to change horses and for a quick meal of cheese and bread and ale at the various posting inns along the road before heading out again. The need to see Juliana, to hold her in his arms and kiss that tempting mouth was a siren's call that gave him no rest.

Only paying half attention to the road, his thoughts on Juliana and all the decadent things he would like to do to her at the first opportunity, he was still several miles from Fox Hollow when he became aware of a rider behind him. It was a public road and it wouldn't be out of the ordinary that someone else would be on the road, but there was something about the rider that aroused his suspicions. Dusk was falling and as the minutes passed and the light lessened, Asher realized that whoever was behind him was hanging back, deliberately keeping pace with his own mount.

Expecting some sort of move, Asher wasn't so very surprised when another horseman appeared on the road ahead of him. He smiled grimly. If he had been planning a trap this was exactly how he would have played it out. A blue scarf covering the lower half of his face, the newcomer positioned his horse across the road and, pointing a pistol at Asher's breast, he cried out, "Stand and deliver!"

Asher pulled his horse to a stop, his eyes on the horseman in front of him, but his ears were pricked for the sound of the rider behind him. A moment later, the second horseman came trotting up and halted his horse beside Asher's mount.

"Well, well, what have we here?" drawled the rider next to Asher. Asher glanced at him, noting the burly build and the black scarf concealing the lower half of his face. He also noted the strong odor of gin floating in the air between them.

"As fine a gentry cove as these glimms have seen in many a day," said blue scarf, urging his horse nearer.

Asher remained still, calculating the odds of being accosted by not one but two highwaymen on a sparsely traveled country road. The odds that this was a simple robbery were zero, so it was unlikely this would end well for him . . . unless he could change the odds.

He considered the man with the pistol. If, as he suspected, they'd been hired to kill him, why not shoot him and get it over with? The road never carried much traffic at this time of the evening, even less than would normally be found during the day, but every minute that passed increased the possibility that someone might come upon them. So why wait? There was no point to it unless, he thought slowly, they wanted something from him before they killed him?

Blue scarf approached and sidled his horse next to Asher's. Trapped between the two men, Asher glanced from left to right, wondering how to play this scene out. His pistols were in the greatcoat strapped to the back of his horse; a knife was in his boot and a smaller one rested snugly in the sleeve of his coat in the special sheath his tailor had sewn for him. The pistols were useless at the moment, but the knives . . .

Still appraising the situation, Asher asked, "What do you want?"

"What do we want?" demanded black scarf on his left. "Why, anything that we take a fancy to!"

Both men laughed and though he was half prepared for it, the vicious blow from blue scarf nearly knocked him from the saddle, the pistol butt striking his cheek. Reeling sideways, Asher fought to stay on his horse, but blue scarf followed up with another, more powerful clout and he tumbled to the ground.

Dazed, Asher fought to clear his head but black scarf jumped down from his horse and kicked him in the head. The world went dark.

He had to have lost consciousness for only a few minutes, but when his senses returned, Asher found himself in a small copse slumped against a tree with his wrists tied behind him. Feeling as if his head would explode, he bit back a groan and feigning unconsciousness, through slitted eyes, took in the situation.

There was very little light left, but he could still discern shapes and shadows. All three horses were tied to some beech saplings directly across from him and standing in front of them were his two attackers. They hadn't realized that he was conscious and were speaking freely.

"I dunno about this, killing a gentry cove," one man said to the other. From his voice, Asher determined that it was black scarf, the fading light making it hard to see colors. "It's was one thing to beat up that young lordling in Lunnon awhiles back," black scarf continued, "but I ain't so keen on bloody murder. What's to stop us from just taking his blunt and be gone?"

"The nob says that we was to kill him. Dead." Blue scarf hesitated. "Said that first we was to mill him down and then get them letters. After we get them letters we're to kill him— the nob didn't care how. Said not to hide the body. He wants it found."

Asher closed his eyes. The nob could only be Ormsby. While his mind gnawed on that bone, the fingers of one hand were cautiously edging up the sleeve of his coat on his opposite side. Touching the cold steel of the small knife hidden there, he almost smiled, but aware that his best chance of survival was to keep his captors thinking he was still unconscious, he kept his expression blank and his body motionless.

With the knife in his hand, it took only seconds to cut through the ropes that bound his wrists together. His hands free, he considered his next move. The knife he held was small and he wondered if he could reach the larger, more effective blade in his boot before they noticed he was awake.

His eyes mere slits, he stared across the small area that separated him from them. Both men were looking at each other, involved in their conversation, not paying any heed to him. . . .

"I still don't like it. Don't like doing the dirty work for a cove not man enough to do it himself," muttered black scarf.

"I ain't saying I'm dancing a jig myself," admitted blue scarf. "We ain't done a murder before, but he's promised us a rum cod for the killing."

"A purse of gold ain't going to matter if we get snapt. Why should we risk a date with the nubbing cheat? I say we nab his prancer and blunt and leave him here. When he wakes we'll be far way."

Absorbed in their exchange, neither man noticed Asher's stealthy movements. His head hurt fiercely and he worried that any swift action would make him dizzy—which could determine the success or failure of his escape. Moving slowly, he reached for his boot and his fingers just closed around the knife hidden there, when one of the men shouted, "The cove's awake! Get him!"

Both men rushed Asher and, gritting his teeth against the pounding in his head, he bounded to his feet, meeting their attack. In the near darkness neither man had been aware that their once helpless victim was now armed and it was only when Asher's knife slashed black scarf's arm to the bone and blue scarf was stabbed in the shoulder that they retreated. Asher followed after them, intent upon blue scarf. He pegged blue scarf for the leader; blue scarf had been the man who had held a pistol on him and he wanted blue scarf eliminated—not dead, just out of the fight.

Asher closed with blue scarf and, using the rounded end of the handle of his knife, struck him solidly on the temple. Blue scarf moaned and crumpled to the ground. Bending over the fallen man, Asher snatched up the pistol from his waistband.

Pistol in hand, quick as a cat, Asher spun around and

leaped toward black scarf. Black scarf, clutching his bleeding
arm and backtracking as fast as he could, cried out, "Let us
go! We've no quarrel with you."

Almost swaying on his feet from his swimming head, Asher
said, "That's not what I heard while I was lying on the ground
over there. I seem to remember that the word 'murder' was
mentioned."

Black scarf gulped. "It's true—the nob hired us to kill you,
but we wasn't set on it. We ain't easy with doing murder."

Privately Asher agreed, though he was just as happy to no
longer be at their mercy. After searching black scarf and finding no other weapon on him other than a blade much like the
one he carried, he stepped away from the man. He glanced from
the man in front of him to the man on the ground and back
again. Startling black scarf, he reached out and jerked down
the scarf that hid his face. There was still just enough light to
make out his features and Asher stared long enough to mem-
orize them.

Keeping an eye on him, Asher walked back to the other
man and yanked down the blue scarf. He hadn't expected to
recognize either one of the men and he hadn't; they were
strangers to him. Both men were nondescript, black scarf's
features younger and heavier and blue scarf's older and thin-
ner; a scar, probably from a knife fight, angled down across
the latter's cheek. He'd remember both men, but there was
no reason for him to kill them. Thanks to overhearing their
conversation, there was no reason to question them—he
knew precisely who had hired them and why.

That Ormsby wanted him dead and would hire this inept
pair to kill him was curious. He was to be murdered because
he'd stolen some letters from Ormsby's safe? Asher found it
hard to believe—and he would believe a great deal of Ormsby.
But perhaps the simplest explanation was the best; Ormsby
had had enough of him. Asher half grinned. He'd certainly
had enough of Ormsby.

Motioning with the pistol to the fallen man, who was

groggily attempting to sit up, he said to black scarf, "Help him to his feet and mount your horses."

When the men were astride their horses, he said with quiet menace, "I'll give you fair warning. . . . If our paths should cross again, I'll kill you."

The men disappeared into the darkness and Asher walked to his own horse and, ignoring the waves of dizziness washing over him, swung into the saddle. Though the men seemed cowed and were unarmed, he was alert for an ambush as he urged his horse in the direction the men had taken. A few minutes later, his horse stepped out of the small stand of woodland and onto the road.

It was full dark by now and more by instinct than anything else Asher rode slowly home. Eventually leaving the public road behind, as he traveled down the driveway toward Fox Hollow, the glimmer of the candlelight from the house pierced the darkness and he sighed with relief. Home had never looked so inviting.

Juliana was thinking similar thoughts that evening as she and Mrs. Rivers enjoyed a cup of tea in the charming sitting room at Rosevale. With Thalia on the mend and the problems with Ormsby resolved, she had sought to escape to her own home for a few days before returning to Kirkwood to begin overseeing the preparations for the house party. Mr. Kirkwood and Thalia had protested, but Juliana held firm. She needed to be among her own things.

She, and her maid, Abby, had returned home to Rosevale on Tuesday morning and since then had been happily rediscovering the pleasures to be found in dearly familiar surroundings. Her housekeeper and cook, Mrs. Lawrence, and the rest of the small staff had cheerfully welcomed them home as if they had been gone to India instead of just down the road.

"Oh, my dear," Mrs. Rivers cried, her faded blue eyes filling with tears as she had hurried forward to meet Juliana. "I have missed you so! It is so wonderful that you have returned to us, if only for a few days."

Embracing the smaller, frailer woman, Juliana replied warmly, "And I, you! It seems as if I have been gone an age. Have you been very lonely? Have Mrs. Lawrence and the others been taking good care of you?"

Mrs. Rivers blushed with pleasure at Juliana's expression of concern. Recalling some of the places she had worked as a nursemaid over her lifetime, Mrs. Rivers was inordinately glad that she had had the good fortune to have been hired by Mrs. Kirkwood over twenty-five years ago. When the family no longer needed her services, to her profound gratification, Mr. Kirkwood had offered her a small stipend and a home in one of the tiny cottages on the Kirkwood estate.

After Juliana had purchased Rosevale, she had asked her old nursemaid to come live with her as her companion. Mrs. Rivers hadn't had to think twice about it and had instantly accepted the new position with her dear Juliana. In the time since, both women had been quite pleased with the bargain they had made.

Mrs. Lawrence followed by Sarah Penny, the housemaid, and Webster Arnett, the footman, had trailed behind Mrs. Rivers out across the flagstone terrace. A huge smile on her face, Mrs. Lawrence said, "It is good to have you back home, Madame. Mrs. Rivers has been fretting since you've been gone and picking at her food—no matter what I fix to tempt her appetite."

"Well, we can't have that, now can we," said Juliana with a fond glance at Mrs. Rivers. "You know that it is never wise to upset the cook."

Mrs. Rivers shook her head shyly, smiled and kept her small, wrinkled hand firmly in Juliana's.

Juliana's staff was small. In addition to her own maid, Abby, and the others, she employed Mrs. Lawrence's husband as gardener and stable man. Mr. Lawrence was helped in his various chores by his oldest son, twenty-three-year-old James.

The other servant was Anne Boone, Sarah's aunt, and she helped where needed but also acted as Mrs. Rivers's maid—much to the old lady's flustered pleasure.

Even though her every comfort had been seen to at her former home, Juliana thoroughly enjoyed sleeping in her own bed in her own bedroom. Kirkwood was far grander, larger than Rosevale, but the half-timbered, hip-roofed house with the profusion of roses surrounding it and from which it had taken its name suited her just fine. With five generous bedrooms it was big enough that she could invite friends to stay if she wished and the sitting, drawing and dining rooms, though not remarkable, were more than adequate for her needs. There was a pleasant room just beyond the morning room that she had claimed as her office and where she discussed menus with Mrs. Lawrence, paid her bills and oversaw the running of her small household.

That Wednesday evening as she sat in the green and cream sitting room sipping tea, she was already, if not dreading, not looking forward to returning to Kirkwood on Monday.

She half smiled. Before she had returned to Rosevale she had seen that the invitations had been sent out for the house party and had left several lists for her father, Thalia, Hudson and Cook of things that needed be done in her absence. While she might not have full confidence in her father and Thalia's competence, she knew that Hudson and Cook would see that all was as it should be.

During these fleeting days at Rosevale Asher had not been far from her mind. Wandering the paths of the herb garden, the scent of chives, mint, thyme and marjoram wafting in the warm summer air, she agonized over the choices before her.

Glumly she admitted that she wasn't so determined to keep her independence and remain at Rosevale that she would whistle away a life with the man she loved. But when she thought of trading her small, loyal staff and Mrs. Rivers and the tranquil life she had made for herself for an unknown, uncertain future as Asher's wife, aware that as her husband he would rule her life, a knot formed in her chest. Did she love him enough, trust him enough to place her future and that of those around her in his complete control?

Looking across the small room at Mrs. Rivers contentedly enjoying her tea, she wondered how Asher would feel about a bride who arrived with her old nursemaid and a half dozen or so servants in tow. What would his staff think? Her lips twitched. Would there be domestic wars?

Juliana slept badly that night; even her dreams were conflicted, swinging from joy to anxiety. During the day it was little different. Thoughts of Asher kept constantly popping into her head and she'd stop in the middle of some task and drop her concentration as the image of losing herself in his arms clouded her mind. Then she'd look around and remember that once she married him, everything she owned became his, that he would and could rule her life. . . .

Exhausted from the conflict raging within her breast, she escaped to the garden to try to make some sense of her emotions. Seated in the gazebo well away from the house, her gaze on the small stream that trickled nearby, she realized that all her indecision came down to one elemental thing—did she love him enough to risk her future happiness?

Asher had had a busy morning. Upon arising, he'd ridden directly to his grandmother's to assure her that he had returned in time to meet Mrs. Sherbrook and Lord Thorne. A welcome surprise awaited him.

Joining his grandmother for breakfast Thursday morning, he was informed that Mrs. Sherbrook had fallen and sprained her ankle and that her trip to Burnham had been postponed by several days. Mrs. Sherbrook's note explaining the reason for the delay had been delivered only yesterday.

Asher tried to look unhappy by the news. "Are you very disappointed?" he asked his grandmother.

She shook her head. "No. I am just grateful that it was not worse—a broken ankle would have put paid to the trip for this year." She shot him a sly glance. "And I'm sure that with the delay that you will be able to keep your calendar clear for me."

"Of course," he murmured.

Escaping from his grandmother, anticipation thrumming in his veins, he'd ridden to Kirkwood only to find that Juliana had escaped to Rosevale.

Muttering under his breath at the waste of time, after a brief conversation with Mr. Kirkwood, he rode impatiently to Rosevale. The near brush with death on Wednesday evening had honed both his desire and his determination to claim Juliana as his bride and, hardly aware of what he was doing, he swung out of the saddle and strode to the door of Juliana's house.

Mrs. Lawrence answered his knock on the door. She was a local and even before he spoke knew immediately the identity of the tall, handsome man inquiring after her mistress. He flashed a stunning smile in her direction and murmured, "If you don't mind, I would prefer to announce myself. Where is she?"

Mrs. Lawrence studied him for a second and then, a knowing gleam in her eyes, she told him where to find Juliana.

Lost in thought, staring off into space, Juliana jumped when Asher strolled into the rose- and morning-glory-covered gazebo.

"Oh! You startled me," she exclaimed, rising to her feet from the filigreed iron chair in which she had been sitting. Suddenly shy, remembering how they had parted, she stammered, "D-d-did you e-e-enjoy your trip to London?"

Asher's breath caught at the sight of her looking utterly adorable in a confection of pale yellow muslin and lace and her dark hair fashioned into a knot at the back of her head. Her full breasts strained against the soft fabric and, remembering the weight and taste of those silky globes, he forgot everything but how much he wanted her. All the passion he'd kept tightly leashed sprang free and in one step he was in front of her.

"Enjoy London?" he said thickly. "Never as much as I'm going to enjoy *this.*" And he dragged her into his arms.

Juliana shuddered as those strong hands closed around her and when his mouth captured hers, she never thought to repulse him. He kissed her deeply, hungrily, his tongue taking immediate possession of her mouth. Flattened against him, his lips and tongue mated with hers, fire curled up from between her legs and her nipples stiffened. Oh, God, she thought wildly, I do love him so.

Her head fell back under the onslaught of his mouth and her fingers clutched his shoulders to keep upright. Blind desire bound her in his embrace and nothing in the world existed except Asher and the magic he forged between them. Greedily she drank in the scent and taste of him, her body clamoring to be taken by his.

Asher hadn't meant to fall upon her like a ravening wolf, but he couldn't control himself. Even before he touched her, at just the first sight of that lush, feminine body, heat and passion erupted through him and there was only the primitive demand to take his woman burning in his brain. Gripped by a fierce hunger to know again the drugging pleasures of her body, his trembling hands roamed everywhere, caressing her breasts, cupping her buttocks and gently probing between her legs.

Juliana never thought to deny him. It was as if their first joining had unleashed a demanding wanton creature within her and she wanted him desperately, wanted his hands upon her, wanted his thick length driving into her as she had never wanted anything else in her life. Even when he backed her up to one wall of the gazebo and pushed up the skirts to her gown, she didn't call a halt to his blunt advances.

He kissed her as if he was starving and her mouth provided his only sustenance; her hunger matched his, her tongue sliding along his, urging and demanding at the same time. His swollen member bulged at the front of his breeches and he wedged his knees between her legs, widening her stance. Her muslin skirts bunched up between them, he stroked through the tight curls at the junction of her thighs and his fingers found her. She melted onto his delving fingers and he groaned when he found her damp and hot and ready for him.

Juliana shivered under Asher's kisses and caresses and, her back supported by the wall of the gazebo, her hands slipped from his shoulders, traveling down his broad chest to his waist and lower. Finding the opening in his breeches, she freed the solid, swollen length of him. The hard rod of flesh was warm and heavy in her hands and she nearly purred as she ran her fingers over its width and length.

Asher tore his mouth from hers and, his dark blue eyes glittering fiercely, he said, "Christ! My brain is on fire. You have bewitched me."

Her eyes glazed with desire, her face flushed, Juliana nodded dazedly. "No less than you have me," she managed.

He growled something under his breath, and he shifted slightly, his hand cupping her buttocks, lifting her, positioning her. "Your legs," he groaned. "Wrap them around me."

She did and with one heavy stroke, he plunged into her. She was hot and tight and he drove into her, his heart beating so hard he thought it would burst, his blood licking like fire in his veins. With her mouth on his, her body clenched around him, he gave himself over to the urgent pursuit of the mindless pleasure that beckoned him with every deep thrust.

Pinioned against the gazebo wall, her mouth plundered by him, Juliana hung on for dear life. The sensation of his rigid member sliding rapidly in and out of her body was so sweetly, explicitly carnal that she moaned with pleasure. She twisted in his embrace, wanting, seeking, *needing* that glorious pinnacle she knew she would find with him. A second later, her body quaked around him and she choked back a cry as waves of ecstasy rolled through her.

The sudden clasping of her body around him and the small gasp she could not suppress was Asher's undoing. With one last, frantic stroke he sought to prolong the honeyed madness, but his body would have none of it and his seed exploded from him. His spine arched, his hands clutched her to him and he tumbled into oblivion.

They remained locked together, their bodies gently rocking against each other, but the world gradually returned and Asher groaned softly when his spent member slipped from her. His lips gentle on hers now, he muttered, "I fear that if I could, I would remain buried within you all my days."

Small shocks of pleasure still running through her, Juliana's legs loosened their grip around him and her feet slid down to the floor, the skirts of her gown freed from between them, following the same path. Her bones felt as if they were made of sun-melted honey and she was grateful for the support of the gazebo at her back. If not for the wall of the gazebo and Asher's hard body in front of her, his hands on her waist, she was certain she'd have fallen to the ground.

Her lips rosy and swollen, her gaze blurred, she stared dazedly around her. The creek burbled in the background; the scent of roses filled the air and sunlight danced over the interior of the gazebo through the holes in the latticework walls. Reality trickling into her brain, she staggered away from him and sat down heavily in the chair she had abandoned such a short while ago.

Asher had hastily rearranged himself and, standing before her, he demanded, "*Now* will you marry me?"

Chapter 15

The sensual haze surrounding her vanished and Juliana's gaze narrowed. Asher Cordell was undoubtedly the most unfeeling, insufferable coxcomb it had ever been her misfortune to meet! With great relish she said, "Not if you were the last man on earth."

Asher burst out laughing and, sinking down on one knee before her, he murmured, "I deserved that, but won't you please reconsider?" His amusement gone, his eyes very dark and blue, he took one of her hands in his and said, "I very much want to marry you. I cannot promise you that I will always please you but, Juliana, as best that I can, I will damn well try."

It was so unfair of him, she thought bitterly, to cut the ground beneath her feet this way. And did he have to look quite so appealing as he knelt before her, his pristine cravat only slightly mussed after their wild coupling, his morning coat of Spanish blue intensifying the hue of his eyes, the rich darkness of his hair and olive skin.

She glanced away from him, unable to meet those intent eyes. Her gaze wandered over the tranquil scene before her, but a flush bloomed in her cheeks when she accidentally glanced at the wall of the gazebo where she had just allowed him, no, encouraged him to take her like a harlot in an alley.

Her hands covered her cheeks and she squirmed in horror

and shame. What was wrong with her? That wanton creature wasn't her! She glared at Asher. It was all *his* fault! He did something to her, bewitched her, and made her act as no self-respecting, decent widow ever would. And she liked it. A lot.

"If I marry you," she began carefully, "what will happen to Rosevale and my servants?"

Taken aback, he blinked. Trust Juliana, he thought amused, to be thinking of practical measures at a time like this. Recovering quickly, he shrugged and said, "Juliana, I don't give a damn about your house, or your servants or your fortune . . . all I care about is whether you will become my wife or not."

Her eyes searched his. "Asher, I . . ."

His grip on her hand tightened. "Can you deny what is between us? Can you deny that I only have to touch you and you go up in flames in my arms? I certainly cannot deny that you are the only woman I have ever wanted to be my wife, nor that I only have to see you to want you more than I've ever wanted anything in my life. I catch sight of you and all I can think of is how much I want you, how sweet and giving you are in my arms."

His words touched her and she nearly tossed caution to the winds and gave him the answer he wanted, the answer she wanted to give him. She took a deep breath. "I want to marry you," she admitted softly, "but until my husband died, I never had the freedom to make my own choices. . . . My entire life had been arranged around my father and then my husband's wishes." She half smiled. "Do not pity me or think that I was abused or that I was unhappy, I wasn't . . . but I wasn't entirely happy either." She looked away. "After my husband died and I put my grief behind me, I discovered that I very much liked ordering my life as I saw fit, making my own decisions. My father objected to my buying Rosevale, he wanted me to return to Kirkwood, but I no longer had to obey him—I could buy my own home, if I wanted to, and I did. It was a heady experience. During the past few years I've learned that with no husband or father to answer to, for the first time in my life, I only have to consider my needs and I have liked it very much." Her troubled gaze swung back to him and she murmured, "Once we marry, Rosevale, my servants, my independence will no longer be mine—everything I own will be under your command."

He studied her for a long moment, thinking about what she had said. He supposed he should be outraged by her reservations. The law and custom would indeed put everything she owned under his control, but with his mother's example before him, he didn't dismiss Juliana's fears out of hand.

When his mother married Denning there had been no lands or large fortune involved, but even if she had been an heiress, except for perhaps a widow's jointure, his stepfather would have been able to use any lands or money she brought to the marriage as he saw fit. Asher's mouth thinned. And Denning would have gambled every penny of it away. He supposed he should be insulted, if not affronted by Juliana's reservations, but having watched his mother struggle to keep the family afloat while Denning gambled and drank away the funds that would have made his mother's life so much more comfortable and easier, Juliana had his sympathy.

Rising to his feet, he sat down in the chair next to hers. Keeping her hands in his, he said quietly, "I am not asking for your hand because I wish to gain control of either your property, your servants or your fortune. I am asking you to marry me because I cannot imagine a life without you." He frowned. "We can resolve part of the problem by putting Rosevale and as much of your fortune as you like in trust for your exclusive use. I would naturally settle a generous amount of pin money on you." He half smiled. "As for the rest . . . Juliana, do you seriously believe that I would deny you the comfort and company of your own servants? I may be high-handed at times, I cannot pretend otherwise, I may even enrage you at times, but you must believe that I would never mistreat you or be deliberately cruel."

Shaken, she stared at him. She could not think of any other

man who would so calmly accept her position. "You really would put Rosevale in trust for me?" she asked carefully.

"Yes, I really would." His eyes darkened. "I would do just about anything to have you as my wife." A whimsical expression crossed his face. "How much more must I grovel? Won't you give me the answer I want? Won't you trust me enough to know that I will always care for you?"

Did she trust him? Her gaze moved slowly over his handsome face. She loved him. How could she love him and yet not trust him? Didn't they go hand in hand? He had made huge concessions, concessions that would have disgusted or enraged a lesser man, and he had done it generously and with little hesitation. Did she honestly believe that Asher would suddenly turn into an ogre? Of course not!

"You must think me very silly or a grasping harpy," she muttered, her eyes dropping to where their hands lay locked together between them.

He smiled at her down-bent head. "I think you are infuriating, stubborn and absolutely adorable. Now will you marry me?"

She flashed him a shy look and half laughing, half crying, she said huskily, "Yes. Yes, I will."

Asher gave a great shout and dragged her from her chair onto his lap. Raining kisses across her flushed features, he murmured, "I will make you happy—I swear it!"

Except for the drone of the bees in the background and the soft murmurings between lovers, it was quiet in the gazebo for a very long time.

"But where will we live?" Juliana asked when their minds turned to practical things.

With Juliana settled comfortably in his lap, her head resting against his shoulder, he said, "It doesn't matter, but I think that since Fox Hollow is the larger of the two houses that it might be the better place." She looked up at him and he added hastily, "But I shall leave that choice up to you."

She smiled at him. "You are probably right."

"And don't forget," he added reluctantly, "that eventually I will inherit Burnham and we will live there one day—hopefully that date will be far in the future."

Juliana nodded somberly.

They discussed the mundane matter of the mingling of their staffs, both agreeing that it shouldn't be a problem. Brow raised, she questioned him, "And you truly will not mind Mrs. Rivers living with us?"

"Provided she is not constantly underfoot," he said with a frankly carnal grin, "and I am able to make love to my beautiful wife whenever I want, I will have no objections to her presence."

A flutter went through Juliana at the idea of the two of them locked in passionate lovemaking in Asher's bed. She glanced around the gazebo and a faint smile curved her lips. Or anywhere else he wanted to make love to her . . .

Asher cupped her breasts and bent down and nipped her ear. "How soon can we marry?"

She felt him stirring beneath her and her own body responded, heat and desire simmering deep in her belly. She wiggled in his lap, reveling in the sensation of rubbing against that growing hardness under her bottom.

"Stop that!" Asher said in a strangled tone.

Juliana smiled mysteriously. Rubbing her bottom suggestively against him, she asked, "Why?"

"Because if you don't," he growled, "I am afraid that I shall have to show you how much more ungentlemanly I can behave."

It was an intriguing possibility, but aware that a servant or anyone could come across them at any time and not willing to risk discovery a second time, Juliana stood up and shook out her skirts. "Do you think your grandmother will be pleased?"

He nodded. "Delighted. In fact, I suspect that she will

think that it was all her doing." He looked over at Juliana, his head cocked to one side. "Shall we tell her?"

"Today?"

"Why not? We can ride over together and tell her the news and then ride to Kirkwood and tell your father."

"Who won't be so very surprised, will he?" she asked with a challenging gleam in her eyes.

He grinned. "No, not very." Without the least trace of regret on his face, he said, "You know that I already asked him for your hand, don't you?"

"I suspected as much." She shook a finger at him. "And it was very underhanded of you."

He rose to his feet. "But necessary—I intended to marry you and wasn't about to let you hide behind your father."

"As if I would," she said, incensed.

"So how soon can we marry?" he asked again, pulling her into his arms and kissing her nose. "I have a special license in my pocket."

She leaned back in his arms. "Were you so certain of me?"

He shook his head. "No. Determined. And once I had the answer I wanted, I had no intention of waiting weeks or even months to claim you as my wife." He dragged her close and, nibbling on her ear, muttered, "Besides, I would like my heir to be born in wedlock and if we delay our marriage, since I seem unable to keep my hands off you, I can almost guarantee that he wouldn't be."

Juliana gasped. Not once had she contemplated children. And I should have, she realized, astonished. While she and her first husband had never had children, it didn't mean that the same would hold true with Asher. Why, I could be pregnant right now, she thought giddily. Asher's child could be growing within her womb right this very minute!

Honesty compelled her to say, "I could be, uh, barren. . . . I never conceived with my first husband."

"It doesn't matter—if we remain childless, between us we

have several siblings who can be named as heirs." He kissed her deeply. "In the meantime, I shall take great pleasure in working very hard to cut them out of any inheritance they might expect in the future. So when shall we marry?"

Events were happening too fast for Juliana. She had barely accepted that she was to marry Asher and now he wanted a date set for the wedding? It was too soon, she thought distractedly. She had so many demands on her time and none of them had anything to do with her getting married anytime soon. The house party at Kirkwood sprang to her mind and the looming announcement of Thalia's engagement to Lord Caswell and the planning of the grand wedding that engagement would entail. It occurred to her that if she and Asher tarried too long that their own marriage plans could be pushed back for months. By rights, Thalia's betrothal and wedding, delayed only because of Ormsby, should come first, but if I am pregnant . . . Juliana bit her lip. She loved Asher and wanted to marry him and being pregnant would only add to her joy. There was no *real* reason for them to delay becoming man and wife as soon as possible, except . . . She sighed. The last thing she wanted to do was steal Thalia's thunder. Announcing her own engagement prior to Thalia's wasn't what she would have liked and certainly a sudden marriage was going to cause even more of a flurry of talk and gossip. . . . But if she and Asher waited until Thalia's engagement to Lord Caswell was made public, it was likely that their own wedding would be delayed. Asher's special license suddenly became very appealing.

Why should they wait? With the special license, she thought, half giddy, they could be married within days. Before the house party. Before Thalia's engagement. Before Thalia's wedding to Caswell. If she and Asher married soon, Juliana mused, hopefully the firestorm over their sudden marriage would be eclipsed by the announcement of Thalia's engagement. Her marriage to Asher might be a nine-day's wonder, but the moment Thalia and Caswell's betrothal was announced no one would pay them any heed—everyone's attention would be on Thalia and Caswell—as it should be.

"Let us tell the family first that we intend to marry and then we shall see about setting a date," she temporized.

He pulled her into his arms. His lips brushing against hers, he said huskily, "Very well, but, Juliana, be warned—I'll not wait long."

Mrs. Manley and Mr. Kirkwood were ecstatic when Asher and Juliana came to call and told them of their engagement. Only Thalia was shocked by the news her sister was to marry Mr. Cordell, but, a sweet smile curving her mouth, she had embraced her sister and exclaimed, "Oh, Juliana, how wonderful for you! Papa and I had so hoped that you would marry again." She beamed at Asher. "And to think it is to the grandson of Papa's friend, Mrs. Manley. I do, indeed, wish you both very happy." A puzzled expression crossed her lovely features. Looking from first Asher and then to Juliana, she said, "It is rather sudden though, isn't it? I don't recall there ever being any hint, any sign of . . . of a growing attachment between you."

Her cheeks slightly flushed, Juliana said hastily, "Asher and I have always had great affection for each other and during your illness and his visits here with his grandmother, we discovered that our feelings were deeper than we realized."

Thalia's face cleared. "Oh, that explains it." She smiled impishly. "It is a good thing, is it not, that I came down with measles? Otherwise you might never have discovered your true feelings for each other."

With Mr. Kirkwood and Mrs. Manley's encouragement, an engagement party was hastily arranged for that evening at Rosevale. As Juliana hurried about the house seeing that all was in readiness, she was reminded of that last dreadful dinner party she had overseen at Kirkwood. How full of anxiety she had been. How fearful of what the night might bring.

How very different this gathering would be, she thought joyfully. It might be hastily arranged, and many of the same guests would be attending. But Mrs. Rivers, who was beside herself with excitement, once her fears of her place in the new household had been eased, and Thalia, released at last from the sick room, would be in attendance tonight, along with the addition of Asher's stepfather and brother. A small blot crossed her horizon. And, she thought grimly, Ormsby would be nowhere in sight. This party, she reminded herself, was being held at Rosevale and it was her servants, with the help of some of the staff from Fox Hollow, who were scurrying about seeing that all was in readiness.

To Juliana's relief, Mrs. Lawrence and Mrs. Hannum, after sizing up each other, had amicably divided the chores between them. With Mrs. Lawrence, assisted by Sarah Penny and Mrs. Hannum's granddaughter, Nancy Liggett, bustling about in the kitchen, Mrs. Hannum and her daughter, Margaret, were overseeing some of the Kirkwood servants who had been pressed into service to see that the house was in readiness for tonight's dinner. Hannum appointed himself butler at Rosevale for the evening and was cheerfully terrorizing Juliana's footman, Webster, into seeing that the crystal gleamed and the china glowed.

If the Birrel family and the Denning men thought it strange to receive such a sudden and unexpected invitation to dine at Mrs. Greeley's this evening, it was not apparent when they arrived. Mrs. Manley had come early as had Mr. Kirkwood and Thalia. Thalia was still a trifle pale, but she was a breathtaking vision in a cream muslin gown with an overskirt of glittering blue gauze.

Dinner was a lighthearted affair. The food was superb; the service exemplary, although speculative glances followed Hannum and Webster as they moved about the long, linen-covered table serving the guests. More than once Juliana saw one of the guests look from her to Asher and then eye Hannum and Webster.

At the end of the meal, when Mr. Kirkwood finally rose from the table and announced the engagement, no one was very surprised. Several toasts were drunk to Asher and Juliana's health, and eventually leaving the gentlemen to their port and wine, Juliana ushered the other ladies into the green and cream sitting room.

As she fended off excited questions from the ladies, Juliana wondered if Asher was running the same gauntlet with the gentlemen. He was.

"Well, you're a sly one, I must say," murmured the colonel as he sipped his port. "You've breathed not a word that you were thinking of marriage, much less that you had already decided upon the lady you wished to marry."

Asher shrugged, his long fingers idly turning the snifter of brandy before him. "You forget that Juliana and I have known each other from childhood." And taking a leaf from Juliana's book, he said, "It wasn't until Thalia was taken ill and we spent some time together that we realized our, er, deepest feelings."

John looked at him, an unholy gleam of amusement glittering in his eyes. "Wait until Robert and the girls learn of this! Martha and Elizabeth will be over the moon and tax you unmercifully for every detail of your courtship. And Robert! Oh, how he will crow that you are now firmly under the cat's paw."

Mr. Birrel chuckled. "Having siblings can be a blessing, but there are times one wishes they were not *quite* so interested in one's private affairs." He raised his glass in another toast. "But you are to be congratulated. Mrs. Greeley is a most worthy young woman and I wish you happy. Let us drink to your long and happy life together."

Mr. Kirkwood beamed. "I have cherished the wish that Juliana would marry again and I had hoped that it would be someone who would not take her far away from me. I could not be more pleased with the match than if I had arranged it myself."

"So when do you plan to wed?" asked the colonel, his gaze on his port.

Asher saw no point in prevaricating. "While in London I procured a special license. If I have my way, we'll be married before the week is out."

"That soon?" exclaimed Mr. Kirkwood, startled.

"I would remind you that at the end of next week," Asher said, "your home will be inundated with guests for the house party and sometime during that event, it is most likely that Thalia's engagement to Caswell will be announced. The last thing that Juliana and I wish to do is take away from the occasion by announcing our engagement at the same time. It should be Thalia's moment and she shouldn't have to share it with Juliana."

"Well, yes, I see your point, but surely you realize that your sudden marriage will, no doubt, cause the very thing you wish to avoid," protested Mr. Kirkwood.

Asher shook his head. "Juliana and I have discussed it and we feel that if we are already married when the guests begin to arrive, while it will be exciting fodder for the moment, the instant Thalia's engagement is made public, no one will pay Juliana and I any heed. Everyone will be much more interested in Thalia and Caswell—Juliana and I will simply be a passing diversion."

Mr. Kirkwood looked thoughtful. "Yes. Yes. Your argument is a valid one. But to marry so suddenly . . . Won't Juliana want to plan a big wedding? Women seem to love all the pomp and fripperies associated with their marriage."

Asher grinned. "Which is one of the reasons I'm in favor of our marriage taking place as soon as possible. Juliana has been married before and she has told me that she has no desire for a huge, gala affair. She's indicated that whenever we marry, she'd prefer that it be a simple affair, perhaps held here at Rosevale with only our family in attendance. If I had my way, we'd marry tonight."

The others looked astounded.

"Tonight?" croaked Mr. Kirkwood, nearly choking on his wine.

Asher smiled. "If I had my way. Juliana prefers to wait until Sunday."

"Sunday? But what about Martha and Elizabeth?" asked John with a frown. "Of course, Robert can't be here, he's God knows where on the continent with Wellesley. But do you think there is enough time for either one of the girls to receive the news of your impending nuptials and arrive here in time to see you married on Sunday?"

Asher tossed off the last of his brandy. "I sent letters to both of them this afternoon and gave my servants directions to ride through the night. By my calculations they should both receive the news tomorrow morning." He grinned. "And if they truly wish to see me married, my sisters will arrive at Apple Hill sometime Saturday afternoon."

John laughed. "Oh, they'll be here! It would take an act of God to prevent them seeing you step into the parson's mousetrap."

From across the table the colonel regarded Asher pensively. "This is a major step you're taking, my boy. A wife usually means children. . . ." An odd expression in his eyes, he said almost to himself, "This time next year you could be the proud father of a son, an heir. . . ." He took a long swallow of his port. "Heirs tend to make a man look at things differently. One thinks more of the future and what one will leave behind for one's children."

Asher kept his face blank, but inwardly the razor edge of the old rage sliced through his belly. The fate of his own children had never troubled Denning in the past, Asher thought bitterly, so why was the old devil concerned about *his* heirs?

By the time the gentlemen joined the ladies, Juliana had imparted the same information that Asher had given the men; she and Asher were planning on being married on Sunday at Rosevale. Naturally, there were exclamations of surprise and amazement, though not, she noticed, from Mrs. Manley, but when she explained the house party and the public announcement of Thalia's engagement, Mrs. Birrel nodded her head.

"Perhaps that would be for the best," she agreed. Smiling at Thalia, she said, "You are very fortunate in your sister—there are not many sisters, even ones that have been married before, who would be willing to give up a big wedding in order for their younger sister to be the cynosure of all eyes."

"Oh, I know," Thalia said fervently, thoughts of Juliana's miraculous recovery of those never-to-be-sufficiently-regretted letters flitting across her mind. "I am the most fortunate of females to have such a loving sister."

By the time the guests left that evening, all had been settled. Vicar Birrel would marry Juliana and Asher on Sunday afternoon at Rosevale.

Asher's two younger sisters, Martha Beckley and Lady Elizabeth Claxton, accompanied by their indulgent husbands, arrived as Asher had assumed they would—breathless, excited and scolding—late on Saturday afternoon. Both young women—Martha, twenty-one, and Elizabeth, just turned twenty in February—having known Juliana since they were children, were thrilled with his choice of a bride. He and Juliana had been invited to a gala family dinner that evening at Apple Hill, but it was only as he, Juliana and Mrs. Manley prepared to leave that his sisters managed a stolen moment alone with him to express their approval. While his grandmother and Juliana were deep in conversation with the colonel and John as they all strolled toward Asher's waiting carriage for the trip home, his sisters, one on either side of him, drew him apart from the others.

"Do you know," confided Martha, her striking green eyes so like her mother's alight with pleasure, "that Liza and I always thought that it would be the most romantic thing in the world if your choice should fall upon dear Juliana?"

"Yes," murmured blue-eyed Elizabeth from his other side, "we so hoped that you would chose someone *nice* and we could not think of anyone nicer than Juliana."

He grinned—something he seemed to do frequently these past few days. "So I take it that you both approve of my choice?"

Martha laughed and pinched his arm. "As if you would care whether we did or not."

"Indeed," said Elizabeth with a giggle, "I can just imagine the expression on your face if either one of us dared to say a word against your intended bride." She reached up and kissed Asher's cheek. "Oh, Asher, I do so hope you will be happy." Passionately, she added, "You are the best brother in the world and you *deserve* to be happy." When he glanced at her quizzically, she said, "If not for you, I know I would not be married to my beloved Claxton."

"Nor I to Beckley," chimed in Martha. "You may have allowed Papa to have all the glory, but we know that it was *you* who made certain we had dowries of sufficient size to follow our hearts." She kissed his other cheek. "Thank you."

Embarrassed and deeply touched, for once Asher's ready tongue deserted him. With two pairs of twinkling eyes locked on his face, he knew he had to say something and, clearing his throat, he muttered, "Ah, I may have helped the colonel a trifle."

His sisters gave him knowing looks and Martha said as they joined the others, "Of course you did. Just as you helped a trifle with securing Apple Hill for John and added a trifle to the purchase price of Robert's commission." She smiled a smile so reminiscent of his mother that his breath caught. "You think you are so sly . . . but be warned—we are all onto you."

Nonplussed, Asher had never been so glad for a conversation to end as this one did when they finally caught up with the others.

* * *

Juliana and Asher's wedding in the gardens at Rosevale on Sunday afternoon went as smoothly and serenely as any affair planned for months instead of mere days. The July afternoon was warm, the air perfumed with the scent of roses, lilies and heliotrope and the lazy drone of bees provided a soft concert in the background. The wedding was small; except for Mrs. Rivers, the vicar and Mrs. Birrel and their two daughters, only family was there to see Asher take Juliana as his bride.

Standing under the hastily erected arch festooned with greenery and hothouse white lilies, Asher looked tall and impressive as he waited for his bride to approach. In his form-fitting coat of dark blue with brass buttons and buff pantaloons, he was the epitome of manly grace, the whiteness of his cravat and shirt intensifying his dark, handsome features. Juliana wore a periwinkle gown, a small cornet of yellow roses crowned her dusky curls and a veil of delicate Mechlin lace cascaded down her back; she carried a bouquet of yellow roses.

Catching sight of her as she slowly walked toward him on her father's arm, Asher knew that if he hadn't already loved her, that he would have fallen heedlessly in love with her at that very moment.

The look in Asher's eye when Mr. Kirkwood placed her hand in Asher's made Juliana's very toes curl with anticipation of their life together. There was such heat, such passion—and dare she believe it?—love in the depths of those cobalt blue eyes that her heart turned over in her breast and she was suddenly very glad that she had allowed him to rush her to the altar.

The ceremony was simple and in a matter of minutes, Juliana and Asher were married. Listening to Asher's firm voice as he repeated his vows, she knew unequivocally that she had made the right decision. She loved him. More importantly, she trusted him.

The remainder of the afternoon passed in a blur. She knew

that they had been engulfed in a warm wave of good wishes; she had been kissed and hugged more times than she could ever remember and had smiled so much, the muscles in her face ached. It didn't matter—she couldn't stop smiling. The combined staffs of Fox Hollow and Rosevale had moved about the small group, offering all manner of delectable fare concocted by Mrs. Lawrence and the others.

Eventually, followed by the laughter and joyous shouts of the others, she and Asher departed for a charming cottage overlooking a small lake on the far edge of the Burnham estate to begin their married life together.

"I insist," said Mrs. Manley when she had first broached the idea to Asher. "It will be perfect for the two of you to spend your first night together." She looked away, a dreamy expression in her eyes. "Your grandfather and I spent our first night together there. I like to think that he would approve." She seemed to shake herself and then said calmly, "It is private—Hannum and his wife can see to your needs and on Monday or Tuesday you can return to either Fox Hollow or Rosevale and determine where you will live."

Asher saw no fault with her reasoning and Juliana was agreeable. Dusk was falling when Asher pulled his horses to a stop in front of the one storied, half-timbered house. Hannum and his wife had gone on ahead to prepare for their arrival, and through the falling darkness, the candlelight spilling out from the mullioned windows beckoned and charmed. The cottage was nestled next to the lake, which was edged with willows and water lilies, the water glinting under the silver glow of the rising moon.

"Oh, Asher," exclaimed Juliana as he swung her out of the curricle and carried her toward the front door, "it is perfect."

He stopped and, allowing her feet to touch the ground, swept her into a crushing embrace. "No," he said huskily against her lips, "*you* are perfect. For me."

Chapter 16

Beyond the passionate nights spent in her husband's arms, Juliana remembered little of the first days of her marriage to Asher. After the night spent at the lake cottage at Burnham, they returned to Rosevale late Monday afternoon and immediately began combining the two households.

Even with all the joy that was now hers, Juliana thought that leaving Rosevale behind would be painful, but she found it not to be so. Bustling about, selecting the items to be packed, she discovered the task to be exhilarating. She smiled, aware that much of her exhilaration had a great deal to do with her very new, very exciting husband and less to do with the actual removal from her former home.

What to do with Rosevale presented a problem, but Tuesday morning while she and Asher were overseeing the last of the packing of her favorite items from the house, the colonel strolled in with an astonishing offer. He wanted to buy Rosevale!

Asher stared at him narrowed eyed. "Why?"

Denning smiled benignly. "I was thinking of adding some acreage to Apple Hill, but then I thought of Robert. Right now he's Cavalry mad, but eventually he'll have a wife, a family and need a place of his own." He glanced around the elegant wainscoted room in which they stood. "I think Rosevale would be an excellent place for him, don't you? It's a charming house and has some land to go with it—and it is not far from Apple Hill and Fox Hollow."

Asher shrugged and glanced at Juliana. "It is your choice to make."

Juliana hesitated a moment, her thoughts jostling together. Sell Rosevale? Her first reaction was a resounding no! But when she thought of Asher's youngest half brother living here one day with a family of his own, she realized that it would be the perfect solution. Smiling at the colonel, she said, "I will drive a hard bargain, sir, but if you really want to buy Rosevale, I am willing to sell it to you."

The colonel named a price and Juliana agreed. That same afternoon at a solicitor's office in the nearby village, she signed the papers that would transfer Rosevale into Denning's name. Again, she thought it would be a wrench, but she was ruefully aware that these days she viewed the sale of her home as just one more obstacle to be cleared from her path.

While Juliana chatted with the solicitor inside the office for a few moments longer, Asher, standing outside waiting for her, regarded his stepfather. "Not to be rude, but where did you get the money?" he asked bluntly. "You were able to pay Juliana's price in full."

"Ah, I've been very, very lucky of late with the cards. Rosevale will make a nice investment and a home for Robert."

"So, you're taking your winnings and buying the house for Robert?"

"Why not? He's my son and I'm able to provide for him." Denning sighed and muttered, "I know you think I don't give a damn about my children but I do. The opportunity presented itself and I took advantage of it."

"And the house is just for Robert?" Asher pushed.

Denning smiled. "Well, yes, but I intend to live there in the meantime. John needs his privacy, he doesn't need his old father hanging around his neck."

"*John* needs his privacy?" Asher asked incredulously, wondering precisely what game his stepfather was playing. He'd grant that Denning loved his children, but he'd never worried about their welfare before now. And there was no denying that for Juliana events had fallen almost miraculously in place—Denning conveniently having money and eager to buy Rosevale, but Asher was suspicious.

Denning waved a hand. "Well, of course, I need some privacy, too." He wiggled his eyebrows. "There's an attractive little widow I've had my eye on and perhaps I'd like to entertain her . . . without your brother hovering." When Asher remained unmoved, he said somewhat testily, "If you must know, John disapproves of my gaming nearly as much as you do and having my own place will take me away from his scowls and lectures."

Since that sounded a bit more like the truth, Asher thought maybe that was the real reason behind his stepfather's sudden yearning for privacy.

Smiling once more, Denning said, "And since your wife generously allowed me to buy many of the things she won't need at Fox Hollow, most likely I shall be able to move in to the place within a day or two. I know that John will lend me a few servants until I hire my own and Woodall can have my things packed in no time. Why, this time tomorrow I could be living in Rosevale."

"Some urgency to your move?" Asher asked.

"No. No. You should know, I'm not one to let the grass grow under my feet."

Juliana, escorted by the solicitor, came up just then and after a moment of polite conversation, bidding them all goodbye, Denning mounted his horse. Frowning, Asher watched him disappear in the distance, but Juliana touched him on the arm and he forgot about his stepfather, and what he might be up to. After helping Juliana into the curricle, he jumped in on the other side and, picking up the reins, set the horses into motion.

Once the village was left behind and the horses moved

smoothly into a high-stepping trot, Asher asked, "Are you sorry?"

She grinned at him. "I thought I would be, but your stepfather paid me a good price for everything and I like the idea of Robert living there one day. It's as if it is still owned by the family." Thoughtfully, she added, "It is a little strange, though, isn't it, that your stepfather intends to start living there himself. I thought he was perfectly happy at Apple Hill. You don't think that he and John have had a falling out, do you?"

"No," he said. "But I'll wager there's more to his sudden desire for privacy than he's telling us."

Juliana puzzled over that for a while, but soon gave it up. It was a glorious day and she had more compelling things to consider . . . such as seducing her handsome husband the first moment they were alone at Fox Hollow.

Fox Hollow proved to be charming and she and Mrs. Rivers and the staff from Rosevale with a minimum of upheaval settled comfortably into the sprawling, onetime farmhouse. Presently, Juliana shared Asher's big bedroom and sitting room, but the prospect of adding on an entirely new wing to the house, which would give them much needed additional space, was already being discussed.

Longing for the time when the house party at Kirkwood and the announcement of Thalia's engagement was no longer lurking at the back of her thoughts, Juliana was grateful that her father had hired Mrs. Starling to lessen her involvement in her father's household. Mrs. Starling was a widowed lady of some fifty years, who had acted as a governess-cum-companion from time to time for both Juliana and Thalia and was now living at Kirkwood. Mrs. Starling's nature was calm and kind and she was not a lady easily ruffled. With Juliana embarking on marriage, Mrs. Starling was exactly what Thalia needed at this time and she would also prove to be a much-needed female chaperone once the house party was underway—which didn't mean that Thalia didn't still rely heavily on Juliana's advice.

Receiving an appeal from her sister that Wednesday morning, Juliana sighed and prepared to ride to Kirkwood. Putting aside Thalia's missive, she went in search of Asher. She found him standing in the entry hall, frowning. "Is something wrong?" she asked.

Asher shook his head. "No, nothing is wrong. My grandmother's friend, Mrs. Barbara Sherbrook, and her nephew, Lord Thorne, have arrived at Burnham ahead of schedule. Grandmother would like me to ride over and meet them." He grinned lopsidedly. "She apologizes very sweetly for the intrusion, but hopes that I can tear myself from my bride to spare her a few minutes."

"Oh, that'll be fine. I have to go to Kirkwood this morning anyway." Juliana smiled. "I remember her speaking of Mrs. Sherbrook often when I was younger and I always hoped to meet her one day."

"Well, you'll get your chance," he said dryly. "Grandmother has invited us to dine tomorrow night at Burnham." He looked ruefully at her. "This wasn't how I envisioned the first week of our marriage," he muttered, his eyes caressing her and making her heart pound. "I want to spend time *alone* with my bride, not dance to the tune of everyone else's piping. Dinner at Burnham tomorrow night. Then Kirkwood . . ."

They'd known that their sudden wedding would put paid to any hope of them stealing away for a few weeks of privacy, but neither had realized how very little time they would have to themselves. Even the sale of Rosevale, while fortunate, had eaten into their time, and no less than Asher did Juliana long for the day that they please only themselves.

Regretfully, she bid him good-bye and rode to Kirkwood. Her father in his usual absentminded way, beyond smiling vaguely at his youngest daughter, had more or less left the arrangements for the house party in Thalia's inexperienced hands and disappeared into his library. Ably assisted by Hudson and Mrs. Starling, Thalia seemed to be handling the pressure—except for the note to her sister for some last minute advice.

Her visit didn't take long and the crisis wasn't any crisis; Thalia just needed reassurance. Preparing to return home shortly, she gave Thalia a hug and said, "You are doing just fine and my help is really unnecessary. Stop fretting, my dear, over the smallest detail. You will look lovely in your new gown. Don't worry about the lack of lobster for Saturday evening's meal—no one will notice it missing with all the other delicacies Cook is preparing. And having an informal dinner in the gardens Friday evening is a splendid idea."

Thalia blushed prettily. "Oh, thank you! I know I am being a ninny with all my constant worries, but I so want everything to be just perfect."

"And it will be," Juliana said firmly, eager to return to Asher. With only a small pang of guilt and a great deal of relief, Juliana mounted her horse, waved good-bye to Thalia and departed for Fox Hollow.

Being introduced to Mrs. Sherbrook and Lord Thorne the next night at Burnham, Juliana decided that Mrs. Sherbrook was just the sort of friend one would expect Mrs. Manley to have. Mrs. Sherbrook's nephew, Lord Thorne, a commanding, dark-complexioned gentleman with a military bearing and an easy manner, was equally charming and amusing.

They had finished dinner and the three ladies were seated in the rose and cream sitting room partaking of tea, while Asher and Lord Thorne presumably entertained themselves in the dining room with a glass or two of brandy or wine before joining them. Apollo, having accompanied Dudley into the room with the tea tray, was now happily snuggled next to Mrs. Manley on the rose satin sofa. A pair of French doors thrown wide to allow a cooling night breeze to drift inside, also allowed the exotic scent from the peonies, jasmine and roses that edged the small terrace at the side of the house to perfume the air.

"Our fathers had long been friends," Mrs. Sherbrook was saying, her striking green eyes bright and friendly. "But I didn't really get to know Anne until she came with her parents to attend a house party at Wyndham Hall." She looked over at Mrs. Manley. "I was fifteen at the time and felt very grown up being allowed to a few of the less formal events planned by my parents. It was my first venture into society and I was nervous mingling with all the titled people that had been invited, but Anne was kind to me and took me under her wing."

Mrs. Manley smiled across at her friend, her fingers absently caressing one of Apollo's silky ears. "Which was very easy to do—you were a taking young thing. All big eyes and glossy locks." Mrs. Manley chuckled. "Oh, but do you remember that simpering, awful girl, Patricia, Pricilla . . . ?"

Juliana listened with only half an ear as the two ladies reminisced, her thoughts drifting to Asher. She had loved him for a long time, even if she hadn't acknowledged it, and to be his wife was the culmination of every secret dream, every secret wish she'd ever had. But as her life with him progressed, she'd begun to have, not second thoughts or regrets, never that, but she wondered if she hadn't allowed herself to be rushed into marriage. By giving in to Asher's demands that they marry *now*, she'd foregone the pleasures of courtship, the delightful never-to-come-again moments leading up to his declaration of love and their marriage. And just you never mind, she thought ruefully, that she'd have ruthlessly quashed any idea of postponing her marriage to Asher.

She'd be the first to admit that everything had happened with unseemly haste, but she'd been hurled willy-nilly into circumstances she'd never thought to encounter and she admitted, had probably not always acted as wisely as she should have. There had never been time for her to question the decisions she'd made . . . or to consider the state of her husband's feelings for her. She knew the state of her own heart, but what of his?

Juliana was certain that he had affection for her, but had it been affection or a sense of honor that had really prompted his desire to marry her? It had not escaped her notice—in fact, she was beginning to become more and more aware of it with each passing hour—that he had never said that he loved her. Not once. Not even in the throes of the wildest passion. So did he? Even though she brushed it aside, the lowering notion would not go away, that after that frantic coupling in her father's library, he had felt *obligated* to offer for her. Or equally depressing, it occurred to her, that he had simply reached an age to marry and she was conveniently at hand and suited his needs. Some marriages were based on less. Was hers?

The entrance of the two gentlemen brought Juliana back to the present with a start and Apollo woke and leaped to his feet and began to bark. Laughing, Mrs. Manley shushed the puppy and said to Asher, "You see what a wonderful little watch dog he is turning into?"

Asher laughed. "Watch dog? I think lapdog is more like it."

"Well, yes, that, too," Mrs. Manley admitted shamelessly as she resettled Apollo by her side. Apollo stared suspiciously at the two men for a second longer, but then put his nose between his paws and dozed, lulled by Mrs. Manley's gentle strokes.

Amusement curving his mouth, Asher walked to Juliana's side and propped one hip on the padded arm of her chair. An arm resting possessively along the top of the tall, channel-back chair in which she sat, he glanced down at his bride and said, "Jack and I decided that we had left the three of you alone long enough. Did you enjoy your gossip?"

Juliana wrinkled her nose at him. "Contrary to what you gentlemen may think, we ladies have other things to discuss besides gossip."

Asher laughed. "Well, you may aspire to a loftier plane but I enjoyed hearing all the latest *on dits* from London." He rubbed his jaw. "Of course, it was far more interesting hearing of his exploits when he was in the military." He looked at his grandmother. "He even crossed paths with Robert. Said he had the makings of a fine officer."

Juliana looked at Lord Thorne where he had taken a seat near Mrs. Sherbrook's. "Oh, that's right. I forgot. You did mention that you were in the Cavalry, I think, before you inherited your title."

Jack nodded. "Yes, I was. I sold out over a year ago."

There was a note in his voice that made Juliana ask, "Do you miss it?"

"There's not much I wouldn't be willing to give up to be with Wellesley on the continent fighting Boney right now, I can tell you," Lord Thorne admitted.

"Which is absolute nonsense!" remarked his aunt. Shaking a finger at him, she said, "You are the head of your family and you have responsibilities that have first call on your time these days. You cannot go traipsing all over the world, risking life and limb and ignoring your estates."

"Yes, Aunt Barbara, you are perfectly correct and I am a careless jackanapes for thinking differently," Jack said meekly, the dancing light in his green eyes at variance with his words.

Barbara snorted, not taken in by his meek answer at all. "What is there about the male sex that they are always happiest when in the midst of some hazardous enterprise? Even my son, Marcus, who is normally the most reliable and cool-headed individual I know, was involved in something dangerous last year." She shot Lord Thorne a challenging look. "And you'll never convince me otherwise."

Lord Thorne appeared uncomfortable and murmured, "Ah, I think you are mistaken."

"Oh? And what about that dreadful smuggler who was murdered right in front of the stables at Sherbrook Hall? What about that? Are you going to tell me that there isn't more to the story than just a tragic mishap?"

"What would you have him say?" Asher asked sharply. "Would you be happier if your son told you that a murderous rogue had been lurking about with Lord knows what terrible intentions? Would that make you feel better? Safer?"

Realizing everyone was staring at him, Asher forced a smiled and continued softly, "Perhaps, your son was merely trying to protect you. Perhaps, he didn't wish you to be fearful and so made light of the event."

Mrs. Sherbrook paused, nodded thoughtfully and the conversation drifted onto general topics, in particular the coming house party at Kirkwood and Jack's departure tomorrow for Thornewood, his country estate, leaving Mrs. Sherbrook to enjoy an extended visit with Mrs. Manley.

Laughing, Mrs. Sherbrook indicated the silver-headed cane she used to walk with leaning against the sofa. "I was just miserable when I fell and hurt my ankle, but now I think of it as a stroke of good luck. With everyone insisting upon coddling me, there was no reason for my visit with my friend to be as fleeting as originally planned. I may have to hobble around, but that doesn't prevent me from thoroughly enjoying myself."

"How long will you be staying?" Juliana asked, smiling.

"Oh, probably not more than a week, although that depends upon when my son, Marcus, can wrest himself away from his wife's side." Glowing she added, "They are expecting my first grandchild soon."

Mrs. Manley glanced at Juliana and, a twinkle in her eyes, she murmured, "Well, I certainly hope that I shall soon hear that I have a grandchild in the offing."

Juliana blushed and looked down at her hands. It was possible, she thought giddily, that even now a child was growing within her. She wouldn't know for a week or two yet, but, oh, she dearly hoped so.

Eventually, Asher and Juliana prepared to leave. When Mrs. Manley and Mrs. Sherbrook started to rise to accompany them to the front of the house, Asher gently dissuaded them. "There is no need," he told them. "I know my way out and you two look very comfortable where you are."

Asher brushed a kiss across her forehead and she touched

him on the cheek. The movement woke Apollo and, finding someone bending over Mrs. Manley, he charged to his feet and broke into frenzied barking.

Straightening, Asher smiled and shook his head. "Ungrateful cur! You owe your comfortable life to me and that is the thanks I get?"

"He is very protective, isn't he?" Mrs. Manley said proudly as she sought to convince Apollo that Asher meant her no harm.

Laughing, Asher and Juliana took their leave of the others and walked out of the room. A moment later, they were in the curricle and driving away from Burnham.

Asher and Juliana talked idly about the evening they'd just spent, but the conversation turned soon enough to the house party at Kirkwood and the arrival of the guests on Friday.

"Thalia can hardly wait for Piers to arrive," Juliana said with a laugh. "You'd think that it was months since she last laid eyes on him, instead of mere weeks."

"You wouldn't pine if I was gone for weeks?"

She dimpled and pinched his arm. "I don't know that I'd *pine* precisely," she teased, "but I'm certain that I would miss you . . . somewhat."

He took his eyes off the horses and looked at her. A distinctly carnal twist to his lips, he murmured, "I think I shall punish you for that . . . when we are home and abed."

Juliana's nipples instantly peaked and there was a delicious flutter low in her belly. To distract herself, she said hastily, "At least Thalia is back in her usual looks and by now I'm sure that all trace of Piers's bruises will have faded."

Asher looked at her again. "Bruises? What are you talking about?"

She made a face. "With everything that has been going on, I'd completely forgotten about the terrible beating Piers suffered just before we left London." When Asher's brow lifted, she added, "A pair of footpads set upon him. They robbed him and thrashed him soundly in the bargain. His poor face! Though he dismissed it aside as nothing, I know it must have been most painful—he looked frightful. It was because of that, well, the bruises, that he did not escort us to the Ormsby ball that night."

"I see," Asher said slowly, recalling vividly his own altercation with a pair of footpads hardly a week ago. He hadn't forgotten the incident, nor that Ormsby had been behind the attack. . . . His lips twitched. He'd had other things on his mind the past few days, in particular the enchanting darling sitting beside him, but Juliana's words reminded him, as if he needed reminding, he thought grimly, his grin fading, that Ormsby had hired someone to kill him. Not beat him, but kill him . . . Thinking about those moments he'd lain on the ground listening to his captors talk, he frowned. Hadn't they mentioned beating up a member of the peerage in London for the nob? Something about a young lordling? And not very long ago?

His jaw tightened and Asher stared ahead, barely aware of the jingle of the harness and the thud of the hooves of his horses on the road as the curricle rolled swiftly through the night. Lord Caswell, the suitor favored and loved by Thalia, had suffered a terrible beating by a pair of men in London around a month ago. . . . What was the likelihood, he wondered sourly, that Lord Caswell's beating and his own near murder had been the acts of two separate pairs of men? Each pair hired by a "nob"?

Connecting the two events wasn't so far-fetched—he'd heard the two men talking about their beating of a gentleman in London at the right time for it to be Caswell. Setting a pair of thugs on the winning rival for Thalia's hand was just the sort of underhanded trick Ormsby would pull. And hiring them to murder him because he'd stolen Thalia's letters . . . and the other letters wasn't such a stretch of imagination.

"What are you scowling about?" Juliana asked, jerking him from his thoughts.

"The house party," he replied mendaciously. "I wish the bloody thing was behind us."

She nestled her head against his shoulder. "Only a few more days and we can hide away from the world."

"I sincerely hope you are right, but don't forget— Mrs. Sherbrook's son, Marcus, will be coming to pick her up and grandmother will insist we come and meet him." Another joy I have to look forward to, Asher mused wryly. Meeting Jack and Mrs. Sherbrook had presented no real problem, except taking up time he would have preferred to spend alone with his bride, but Marcus . . .

"Oh, pooh, that shouldn't be such an ordeal," said Juliana airily. "I'm sure that Marcus Sherbrook will prove to be every bit as charming as Lord Thorne."

Asher cocked a brow. "You think Lord Thorne charming, do you?"

She smiled demurely. "Yes, but not quite as charming as my husband."

"And when we arrive home, I shall show you just how *very* charming I can be," he murmured huskily, explicit promise in his gaze.

He wasn't, Juliana decided, as he pulled her into his arms the moment the door to their bedroom shut behind them, the least bit charming. What he was, she thought dreamily, when he ruthlessly stripped her gown from her body and tossed her naked onto their bed, was irresistible. His clothes joined hers on the floor and he slid next to her on the bed, his body warm and muscular against hers.

The light from the filling moon shone through the windows and glided over them with a silvery glow. Propping himself up by one elbow, Asher gazed down into her face. "Do you know," he said huskily, "that I have been waiting all evening to have you thus—naked and in my arms?"

She smiled mistily up at him, her arms closing around his neck. His mouth came down on hers hungry and searching, his tongue a fiery blade, seeking and finding an answering hunger from her. Sighing her pleasure, she arched up when

his fingers found her breasts and began to knead and toy
with the warm, heavy globes.

Her hands began their own exploration, sliding down his
back to hard buttocks and upward again, reveling in the play
of muscles as her fingers traveled slowly over him. Intoxicating heat spilled through her veins and sweet tension curled
and coiled in her loins when her lower body grazed his, her
breath catching as she felt the size of his bulging staff between them.

Groaning at the teasing brush of her body against his, his
head dropped and he scraped his teeth against her nipples,
smiling fiercely when she shuddered and her fingers slid into
his hair and urged his mouth closer. Pleasing both of them,
with teeth and tongue he lavished great attention on those
hard little nubs of flesh, Juliana's soft, excited murmurs exciting him.

She was silk and fire in his arms, her body, long and lush
and for him, perfectly fashioned. He ached for her; ached for
that moment when their bodies were one, when he discovered again that powerful pleasure he had found only with
her. His wife. His lover. Her generous response to his kisses
and caresses sent his head spinning, his heart pounding, and
unleashed a primeval passion.

Clasping her hips, he held her still as his lips and tongue
slid slowly down her body, across the flat belly down to the
nest of curls at the junction of her thighs. She moaned and
stiffened when he buried his head between her legs and his
lips caressed and brushed against the satiny heart of her hidden beneath the sable thatch.

"Oh, Asher," she cried, gripped by feverish agitation, "I
don't think . . ."

Asher's head lifted and looking up at her, he said thickly,
"Then don't think, my sweet. Just feel." He bent his head
and spreading her, pressed a blunt, deeply intimate kiss upon
the delicate flesh he had exposed.

Feelings, wild, nakedly carnal feelings she had never experienced shot through her at the first thrust of his tongue between her legs, and she gasped. It was wicked and wanton, what he was doing to her, yet she was powerless to stop him. Each flick of his tongue took her higher and higher and pleasure, pleasure never dreamed of streamed through her. Never stopping the rhythmic exploration of his tongue, he slowly pushed in one and then two fingers deep inside her and Juliana was swamped by waves of erotic sensation.

The blood thudding in his ears, his member swollen and tight, Asher fought against the goading demands of his own body. Her scent, the hot, musky taste of her and the shifting of her body, the muffled sounds of pleasure she gave, were driving him mad and his fingers plunged quicker, deeper within her.

Helplessly, Juliana's grip tightened on his hair and her hips rose up to meet his marauding mouth, reaching, begging for relief from the ever-tightening coil of increasingly urgent demands of her body. Stretched taut, she teetered at the velvet edge and then with a soft, astonished shriek she tumbled over.

With savage satisfaction, Asher felt her release and, pressing one last, lingering kiss into the sable curls, he slowly slid upward. Lying beside her, in the moonlight, he stared down into her face.

Her eyes were wide and dilated, her expression one of dazed wonder. Gently, he brushed a lock of dark hair away from her face. She blinked and, turning her head, looked at him. She swallowed. "I never . . ." Words failed her. How could she explain the exquisite sensations that had racked her body, small tremors still quaking through her?

Asher smiled. "But you will again, because I don't think I can deny myself that particular pleasure."

Her eyes got very big. "Oh." Her hand trailed down his body, stopping when she reached that upstanding, impudent member between them. "You didn't . . ."

"No, I didn't, but I intend to," he said roughly, his mouth coming down on hers.

To her great delight and no little surprise, the touch of his lips on hers, the caress of his downward-seeking hand, stirred her senses once more and this time, this time when he slid between her thighs and buried himself within her, they found that sweet oblivion together.

Chapter 17

The alfresco dinner held in the gardens at Kirkwood Friday night garnered many flattering comments and the announcement Sunday evening by Mr. Kirkwood of the engagement of his youngest daughter to the Earl of Caswell was met with happy acclaim—although no surprise. The announcement had been expected for weeks and only the Kirkwoods knew precisely why it had been delayed.

Watching Piers and Thalia as they stood in the middle of the small, flower-bestrewn ballroom at the rear of the house, Juliana thought that they made a beautiful couple. Caswell's dark handsomeness was a perfect foil for Thalia's blond loveliness and there were many misty eyed sighs from the ladies present at the romantic picture they made. The tender way Piers bent his head toward Thalia and the glow that illuminated Thalia's face when she looked at him left no one in doubt that this was indeed a love match.

The house was overflowing with guests on Sunday night, not only those staying at the house, but everyone of consequence in the neighborhood including Mrs. Manley and her dear friend, Mrs. Sherbrook, who had been invited for the lavish buffet that had preceded the announcement. There was of course, one notable exception: the Marquis of Ormsby was nowhere to be seen in the throng of the elegant crowd.

Squire Ripley, glancing around the room shortly after the engagement was announced, commented to the circle around him, "Odd not to see Ormsby here."

The circle included Asher, John, the colonel and the vicar, and for a moment Asher's and the vicar's eyes met. The vicar didn't know the full story, but he had been present at the unpleasant scene between Ormsby and Asher at the Kirkwood home and drew his own conclusions. He'd also noted the cavalier way in which the marquis had treated Mr. Kirkwood that same evening, so Ormsby's absence didn't surprise him.

Staring down into his crystal cup of champagne punch, Asher replied to the squire's comment by saying, "I believe that he cried off—he'd made other plans out of the area for tonight and they could not be changed."

"Ah, that explains," said Ripley, nodding his head.

Colonel Denning bent a penetrating look at Asher. He didn't know what was going on, but he knew that Ormsby wasn't out of the area—and that the marquis had *not* been invited to Kirkwood for tonight's announcement—or to any of the festivities associated with the house party. Ormsby had nearly snapped his head off only last night, when Denning had made mention of attending the Kirkwood affair, and because he was meeting with Ormsby later tonight at Rosevale for deep play, he knew damn well that the marquis was *not* out of the area.

Denning had been surprised that Ormsby wasn't here tonight, but since he wasn't a man who exhibited much interest in his fellow man—except as it pertained to himself—he brushed it from his mind. But now that he thought of it, it was queer. Ormsby was the leading landowner in the area and with his title and wealth there was no denying he was a man of great consequence. That Kirkwood had snubbed him was most interesting.

His gaze narrowed and he studied Asher's face. He'd wager a handful of yellow boys that his stepson knew exactly why

Ormsby wasn't here tonight. . . . But was the reason for Ormsby's absence tonight, he wondered, something he could use to his advantage?

Maneuvering a private moment with Asher, Denning said, "You know, the squire was right, it *is* odd, damned odd that Ormsby isn't here tonight."

Asher shrugged. "But not the end of the world—despite Ormsby's opinion of his worth."

Denning chuckled. "You've never liked the man, have you?"

"Since he's an arrogant bastard, who believes the world is his for the taking, he makes it hard," Asher said, sending his stepfather a smile that was all teeth and no amusement. Under his breath, he muttered, "You, however, seem to get along with him well enough. John says that you and Ormsby have been thick as thieves since you moved to Rosevale—gambling."

It was Denning's turn to shrug. "Just a friendly game or two of cards to break the boredom of the country."

"See that it stays that way," Asher said bluntly, "and that your gaming doesn't cause John any trouble."

"Don't you mean you?" Denning asked dryly.

Asher nodded. "All right, then, me. I'm not pulling you from the River Tick again. Ever."

Denning took a drink of his punch. "You worry too much, my boy," he said, putting down his empty cup on a nearby table. "Where Ormsby is concerned Lady Luck sits on my shoulder."

"For how long?"

Denning smiled. "Oh, for as long as I want."

Asher smothered a curse. His stepfather had to be blackmailing Ormsby. It was the only thing that could account for Denning's certainty that he would always win against Ormsby. And with the memory of the two London bullies vivid in his mind, Asher knew first-hand that twisting Ormsby's tail could be dangerous.

Attempting to turn the conversation back to Ormsby's absence, Denning murmured, "Can't get over the fact that Ormsby isn't here tonight. I thought that he and Kirkwood were friends. Close friends at that." When Asher remained silent, he went on, "Seems to me that Ormsby wouldn't have missed an opportunity to wish his friend's daughter good wishes on snaring one of the most eligible males in the country."

Asher looked bored. "Who knows what Ormsby is thinking? Or cares, for that matter."

Realizing he wasn't going to get anything out of his stepson, Denning gave up. Clapping Asher on the shoulder, he said, "It's been a most pleasant evening, but I think I shall bid my host and the engaged couple good night and toddle on home."

"For another hand of cards with Ormsby?" Asher asked grimly.

Denning smiled and wagged a finger at Asher. "I'm a big boy, Asher, and while you might act nursemaid to your brothers and sisters, you do not have to look out for me. Besides, Ormsby and I understand each other."

Giving his stepfather a hard look, Asher said, "I do not know what game you are playing, sir, but I would warn you to be careful. Ormsby is not always a gentleman."

"You worry too much. I can take care of myself." He winked at Asher. "I might even be able to do you a good turn while I am about it."

Asher's brows snapped together. "What the devil do you mean by that?"

Denning chuckled. "Ah, that would be telling." And leaving Asher to scowl after him, he strolled away, his peg leg tapping on the polished oak floor.

Juliana and Asher dutifully attended all the various festivities associated with the house party up to this point, but now that the engagement was official and the house party well underway and running smoothly, after tonight, they intended to retreat from the social scene for a few months. Except for meeting Marcus Sherbrook when he came to Burnham to escort his mother to Sherbrook Hall, they were both determined to be "not at home" to just about everyone.

Feeling he had spent more than enough time involved in Thalia's affairs, Asher cast a look around for his wife. Spying Juliana standing and talking to his grandmother and Mrs. Sherbrook where the two older ladies were seated on a tapestry settee on the far side of the room, with long strides he crossed the distance that separated them.

Juliana smiled at him when he came up and they exchanged a look. "I believe," she said, "that my husband is ready to leave."

Mrs. Manley nodded, knowing amusement in her gaze. "Yes, he has been very good about all of the fuss surrounding Thalia's engagement, hasn't he?"

Asher grinned. "More than you know. More than you know." Taking Juliana's hand and placing it on his arm, he looked at his grandmother and said, "I assume that your coachman will see you home safely?"

Mrs. Manley snorted. "You know, my dear, before you returned to the area, I somehow managed to arrange things to suit myself, but to answer your question, yes, Wiggins will be here with the carriage when I need him. And young Pelton will accompany him, so we two old ladies are well provided for. Now run along," she smiled impishly, "as you are longing to do."

Laughing, Asher bent forward and kissed her cheek. "Thank you. I shall do just that."

Their good-byes said to his grandmother and Mrs. Sherbrook, they went in search of Mr. Kirkwood and bid him good night. Seeing that Thalia and Piers were still the center of attention, they decided to forego saying good-bye to the couple. Five minutes later, like children escaping the schoolroom, they scampered out the doors, down the steps and to the place where Asher's curricle and horses stood tied.

Asher tossed Juliana up into the vehicle, untied the horses, climbed in on the other side and set the horses off at a brisk clip.

Kirkwood disappearing in the distance behind them, Asher breathed a sigh of contentment. Slanting a glance down at Juliana where she sat beside him, he murmured, "Now aren't you glad that I rushed you to the altar? If not, we'd have been languishing on the sidelines watching enviously and longing for the moment our own engagement could be announced." He grinned. "Not to mention sleeping in our own cold and lonely beds. Instead, we are on our way home where I intend to thoroughly ravish you the moment we reach the bedroom." His gaze slid over her, lingering on the soft swell of her breasts above the lace-trimmed bodice of her spotted muslin gown. "Or perhaps, I shall just pull over to a shadowy spot in the trees and satisfy my manly lusts at the first opportunity."

Juliana rested her head against his shoulder and giggled. "Stop sounding like a character out of a gothic novel." She peeped up at him. "But yes, I am most happy that our marriage is behind us. I would have been dreadfully unhappy to have had to remain at Kirkwood and watch you drive away."

"I wouldn't have driven far," he said. "Just far enough away to hide the horses and then I'd be climbing into your bedroom window." He pressed a kiss on her mouth. "You, my sweet, are addictive."

His words warmed her, but she wondered again about the depth of feelings for her. Did he love her? Or simply enjoy her? Her head against his shoulder, she sighed. Was she being too greedy? Wanting too much?

Asher heard her sigh and, looking down at the top of her head, frowned. "What is it?" he asked.

Juliana half straightened and said, "Nothing." Then added reluctantly, "I suppose it is just that Thalia and Piers look so in love. . . ."

"And that's a bad thing?"

"No. No. It is just that . . ." She sighed again, wishing she was brave enough to just come out and ask him how he felt about her. Instead, she said, "Thalia looked lovely tonight, didn't she?"

Asher shrugged. "Yes, but I've always thought you were the real beauty of the family."

Juliana's head whipped in his direction. "Really?" she asked in a breathless voice, delight coursing through her.

"Of course," he said in a tone that indicated only a simpleton would have thought any different.

He thought she was prettier than Thalia! But that didn't mean, she reminded herself, that he loved her. Trying again, she said, "Don't you think it's wonderful that Thalia is able to marry the man she loves? And Piers's devotion to her is so apparent that everyone commented on it." She sighed. "It was so very romantic."

Asher was puzzled by Juliana's preoccupation with the state of emotion between Thalia and Piers, but he was not a stupid man and it only took him a second to realize what was behind her sighs and uncharacteristic interest. He smiled. Of course. While he knew he loved Juliana, he had never told her so and *that,* he decided, needed to be changed. Abruptly pulling his horses to a stop in the middle of the road, he looked down at her, the moonlight playing over his face. Gently, he said, "I do love you, you know."

Juliana gasped and stared wide-eyed up at him, her heart thumping madly in her breast. "D-d-do you? You n-n-never said so," she stammered shyly.

He smiled tenderly at her. "You have been in my heart for so long that I cannot tell you when I first fell, madly, wildly in love with you, but I am now and forever yours. Never doubt it."

Feeling as if she had just been given the stars and heaven, too, Juliana simply looked at him, her lips half parted, her face glowing.

"I knew for certain in London," Asher murmured, his eyes

caressing her bemused features. "That time away from you made me realize that I could not imagine a life without you." He kissed her, his warm lips lingering a long moment, the horses snorting and rocking the curricle at the delay.

"Oh, Asher," she breathed. "I love you, too!"

"I know," he said calmly. He shook his head, a tender smile on his mouth. "And you are a little goose if you didn't know long ago how helplessly in love I was with you. Aren't you women supposed to have instinct about that sort of thing?" His attention on his horses once more, he urged them to the trot and asked dryly, "Did you really think I risked life and limb to regain Thalia's letters for you out of the goodness of my heart? And that I dragooned my grandmother to visit your sister in the sick room because I was a model of nobility?" He snorted. "If I hadn't been over the moon about you even then, I'd simply have made a polite demur and ridden away without a thought." His eyes on her face again, he said huskily, "I love you, Juliana. Now and forever."

Heedless of their surroundings, she flung her arms around his neck and kissed him. "And I love you—more than you deserve—you wretchedly arrogant man."

Laughing, with no little maneuvering between the horses and the confines of the curricle and his wife's wiggling body, Asher pulled her into his lap. Keeping his horses under control with one hand, with the other, he settled Juliana comfortably across his thighs.

Cradled next to his chest, one of his strong arms holding her close, Juliana rained soft, little kisses across his jaw and chin, her fingers tangling in his hair. "I thought I was happy before, but now . . ." She beamed up at him. "Oh, Asher, isn't it marvelous we love each other?"

His head dipped and he kissed her long and deep. When he raised his head, his breathing was ragged and uneven. "Marvelous," he said in a strangled tone, painfully aware of his rigid member pushing insistently into her bottom. "And now,

if I don't get us home right away, I very much fear that anyone traveling along this road a few minutes from now will be
shocked. Extremely shocked."

About the same time that Asher and Juliana were revealing
what was in their hearts, Denning and Ormsby were sitting
in a pleasant room at the side of the house that Ormsby had
designated as his study. It was a good space; oak wainscoting
gave it character and the French doors that opened onto a secluded courtyard allowed for the discreet arrival and departure of certain, ah, ladies.

Denning brought several items from Apple Hill with him
and they were currently scattered about the room—a baize-
covered table for gaming, a half dozen well-worn, but exceedingly comfortable chairs, an older oak sideboard and
Asher's mother's desk. Juliana had left behind a large mahogany bookcase and Denning had it already filled with his
favorite books from Apple Hill. On the sideboard there was
a pewter tray containing four crystal decanters and some
glasses and snifters; mismatched silver candelabras were at
either end of the sideboard. A platter holding some fruit and
bread and cheese along with a small paring knife sat near one
of the candelabras. Two blue-striped satin sofas flanked the
French doors.

The two men were seated at the table, cards spread out in
front of them, and snifters of brandy nearby. They'd already
played one hand of piquet with Denning winning easily.

Ormsby was sprawled in the chair across from Denning, a
sullen, moody expression on his handsomely jaded features.
He'd arrived half foxed and in the time since he had been at
Rosevale he had continued to drink heavily.

Picking up the cards fanned out in front of him, Denning
riffled through them, his gaze on Ormsby. "Incidentally, I
meant to thank you for recommending that Will Dockery.
My groom tells me that the young man is settling in nicely
and knows his way around horses."

Ormsby grunted, his sullen expression not changing.

Denning sighed and murmured, "You seem out of sorts this evening. Not feeling quite the thing, old fellow?" he probed delicately.

Ormsby shot him an ugly look. "And what do you care? Your only concern is that I continue to lose and fill your pockets when you feel the need to jingle some coins."

Denning shrugged and pushed the cards away. Ruefully, he admitted, "You know I thought I would enjoy always winning, but I find I miss the thrill of never quite knowing the outcome of the hand I'd been dealt. Our little arrangement takes some of the excitement out of the game, don't you agree?"

"Are you complaining?" Ormsby growled.

"Oh, no. It is just that always winning is not quite the pleasure that I thought it would be."

"Does this mean that we can stop this little facade? Have you 'won' enough to satisfy you?" The marquis looked around the room with its almost shabby furnishings and his lip lifted contemptuously. "Although I can't see that you've spent much in here."

Denning smiled. "I like the familiar about me." His gaze rested on Jane's desk. "I treasure several of these items. You might say that they represent my good fortune."

Having noted the direction of Denning's gaze, a speculative glint leaped in Ormsby's eyes, and he asked, "That little desk has brought you good fortune?"

"Oh, no, not that little desk," Denning said lightly, "but many of the other things—such as this fine table before us. I've won many a hand sitting right here."

"But have you won enough?" Ormsby demanded in a grating voice, his eyes hard on Denning.

Denning sighed and looked down at the cards on the table. "Yes, I've won enough." He hesitated, then admitted slowly, "I thought the money would be enough, but I find, unfortunately, that I have a conscience where my stepson is concerned."

Ormsby stiffened and something dangerous leaped to his eyes. "I hope," he said carefully, "that you are not about to do something very, very stupid."

Tugging on his ear, Denning said, "I don't know. I have to think about it. He's married now. Means it's likely that this time next year there might be an offspring. Seems to me you might want to think about that and what you're going to do about it . . . or what I might be forced to do."

Ormsby moved with the speed of a striking snake and lunged across the table, his hands encircling Denning's throat. The table crashing to the floor, the two men struggled together, Denning's chair toppling backward from the force of Ormsby's attack.

They fell to the floor, Denning desperately trying to break Ormsby's lethal grip around his throat. His hands clamped around Ormsby's wrists, he fought to free himself . . . and for breath. Struggling against the crushing strength of Ormsby's hands, Denning rolled across the floor, slamming loudly into the bottom of the oak sideboard, the crystal decanters rattling together from the impact.

As the seconds passed, unable to draw in air, spots danced in front of his eyes and Denning knew a thrill of fear. Good God! Ormsby was killing him! A knock on the door and his manservant's voice, saying, "Master, is all well? I heard a noise," brought the fight to an instant finish.

Ormsby's hands fell from Denning's throat and, flinging himself away, Ormsby pushed up off the floor and staggered over to his chair. It took Denning a few moments longer to recover, but he managed to lever himself upright and, gasping for air, he stumbled to the door.

He took a second to straighten his cravat and, opening the door, he said somewhat breathlessly, "Nothing to worry about. The marquis, er, fell. Everything is fine."

The manservant, Denning's former batman, Beckham, who had been with him for decades, was well used to the ways of gentlemen and nodded sagely. Most likely cup-shot, the pair of them. "Very well. I shall just be down the hall should you need me."

Shutting the door behind him, Denning walked back across the room and, righting the table, he surveyed his attacker. Aware that strong emotions fueled by drink could cause even the meekest man to react violently and having been involved in his share of savage drunken brawls, Denning took a more lenient view of Ormsby's attempt to throttle him than someone else might have. It would be a long while, though, before he forgot the sensation of the marquis's fingers around his neck and it occurred to him that Ormsby might be far more dangerous than he had realized.

Deciding to make light of the situation, he straightened his chair and said, "That wasn't very wise of you." At Ormsby's curled lip, he added, "My servants all know that you are here and if they were to find me strangled to death, suspicion would fall upon one person and one person only. You."

"Do you want an apology?" Ormsby snarled. "Fine! I apologize. I lost my head." Jerking to his feet, he half walked, half tottered toward the door. His hand on the knob, he swung around to look at Denning. "We struck a bargain, you and I. I've kept my side of it. Threaten to break your part again and I'll kill you," he spat. Turning away, he flung out of the door and disappeared.

Alone in the room, the cards scattered across the floor, one of the snifters in shards from the fall from the table, Denning sat down heavily and considered the situation. He rubbed his chin. Ormsby's words didn't frighten him, but the memory of the other man's rage sent a warning chill down his spine. Only a fool, he reminded himself, ignores a death threat. . . .

Thoughtfully, he rose to his feet and, his peg leg thumping faintly across the maroon carpet on the floor, he made his way to his wife's small desk. He riffled through it until he found pen and paper and then, seated again at the table where he and Ormsby had so recently played piquet, he began to write. When he was done, he had covered two pages with his large, looping scrawl. He reread what he had written, nodded to himself several times and then signed his name and the date with a flourish.

As he waited for the ink to dry, he returned to his wife's desk and slid out the long drawer at the top in the middle. Setting aside the drawer, he reached deep into the cavity created by the removal of the drawer. He fumbled a bit, cursed under his breath, but his seeking fingers found precisely what he was after.

Smiling, a small bundle of papers in his hands, he replaced the drawer and, taking the papers he had retrieved, he returned once more to the table and the letter he had just written. He folded his letter around the papers he had taken from the desk and considered his next step.

His first thought was to return the packet of papers along with his letter to the original hiding place; after all, they had remained safely hidden for thirty years or more. But some instinct warned him that it might be wise to find another place. He hadn't forgotten the look in Ormsby's eyes when he had made the mistake, and he admitted it had been a mistake, of bringing attention to Jane's desk. He also didn't put it past Ormsby to break into the house and see if the desk did hold any secrets.

No, the desk wouldn't do. He had to find someplace else to hide this little packet until he could ride to London and place it safely in the hands of his solicitor.

Looking around the room, his gaze fell upon the mahogany bookcase. Walking over to it, he opened one of the glass doors and stared at the array of leather-bound books. Perhaps? His fingers ran randomly over the green, gold and scarlet bindings, stopping when he came to a hefty book containing all of Thomas Chaucer's works. He smiled. Perfect.

Removing the book, he picked up the small paring knife from the platter of food and carefully cut out a place just big enough to hold the packet. The packet, with his letter wrapped around it, fitted tightly in its new hiding place. Shutting the book, he examined his work and smiled in satisfaction. Outwardly there was no sign of the alteration he'd made. When closed, the book looked the same as any other book on his shelves. Wedging the book back into the case, he shut the door.

He stared at the bookcase for several minutes. Not the best, but it was unlikely that a thief, even a thief like Ormsby, would think to paw through the books. Satisfied with his night's work, still smiling, he walked over to the sideboard and poured himself another brandy.

Sitting down on one of the blue-striped sofas, he sipped his brandy thinking about the evening. Would Ormsby really have strangled him right there in his own home? He didn't believe so, but he was damned grateful Beckham had heard the table fall and had knocked on the door.

Denning had known that he was playing a dangerous game, but until this evening, he hadn't feared Ormsby. Of course, he admitted wryly, it hadn't been wise to threaten the man with exposure either or to imply that he would go back on the bargain they had made. What had he expected him to do? Clap him jovially on the back? He made a face, aware that he'd made a mistake tonight. What repercussions it might have, he couldn't guess.

His eyes slid to the bookcase. He should have taken the packet to his solicitor when he first discovered it because should something happen to him, the last thing he wanted was for them to remain hidden for another thirty or more years. Or for Ormsby to find them and destroy all the evidence.

Finishing his brandy, Denning rose to his feet and, walking to the sideboard, poured another one. Standing there, he stared down into the amber depths as if looking for answers there. None came to him.

He was a selfish bastard, he concluded wearily as he walked to one of the sofas and sat down. If it had been left to him, he'd have beggared his family and thrown them penniless in the street—all because he'd always been chasing after the next hand, the next turn of the card. And Jane? What of her? He winced. His obsession with all games of chance had caused her great anguish and hardship. Thank God for Asher. Denning didn't know precisely how his stepson had managed to lay his hands on the impressive sums of money Asher had lavished on his siblings and his grandmother over the years but he suspected he was better off *not* knowing. The boy had the devil's own luck at cards, but no one, and he should know, was *that* lucky. By whatever means it had been done, Asher had saved them all, he admitted, not only Apple Hill and his siblings, but himself included. And I thank him, Denning thought in bitter shame, by feathering my own pocket. . . .

Which brought him back to Ormsby. How dangerous was the marquis? Dangerous enough to plot murder?

Galloping through the night toward Ormsby Place, the marquis was doing exactly that: plotting murder. Once he had gained control of the naked fury that was whipping through him, he realized that the manservant's interruption had been fortuitous. If not for that interruption, he'd have made the mistake of killing Denning then and there, which would have been pleasurable but exceedingly foolish—the moment the body was found, suspicion would have landed on him.

More than suspicion, he thought grimly, as he rode through the wide gates of Ormsby Place. Denning's servants had known he was there and even if he had managed to escape undetected from the house and the body wasn't discovered until morning, without question he would be the prime suspect for the murder. And since it was likely the body would have been found tonight when one of the servants came into the room during a final round of the house, snuffing candles and the like, Ormsby wouldn't have wagered a farthing on his escaping the hangman's noose.

The worst of his temper had abated by the time he threw the reins of his horse at the yawning stable boy who waited near the grand steps to the house. His thoughts cooler, although no less deadly, he stalked to his study.

Shutting the door behind him, he prowled around the shadowy room, one small candle on the mantel of the fireplace the only light. His gaze wandered to the Gainsborough landscape and a new flash of fury roared through him.

He had no proof, but he was certain that he had been violated by that blasted Asher Cordell. For that alone, he thought viciously, the man deserved to die. His hand closed into a white-knuckled fist. Those incompetent cretins! If they'd done their job, Asher would be dead and moldering in the grave.

He stopped his pacing, thinking hard. Asher was a problem. Denning was a problem. If he eliminated Denning, the drain on his purse would end immediately. But Denning's death might not be the resolution he needed and might actually precipitate discovery of the very thing he wanted destroyed. However, if he killed Asher . . . His lips twitched in a feral snarl. Asher Cordell was the root of every misfortune that had befallen him of late. By God! He'd have liked Cordell's neck in his hands tonight. . . . But Denning would suspect and he wasn't about to hand Denning another weapon to use against him.

His jaw clenched. So which one did he kill? Denning? Or Asher? Or both?

Chapter 18

With their most immediate social obligations out of the way, Asher and Juliana were finally able to indulge themselves—which they did. There were lazy mornings spent abed and leisurely afternoon rides down green, dappled lanes. Warm summer evenings were spent wandering around the grounds adjacent to Fox Hollow discussing the plans for the expansion of the house and the changes to the gardens they had in mind—and passionate kisses and embraces in secluded nooks. And the nights? The nights were filled with sweet lovemaking and the joyous knowledge that each time they came together, they loved and were loved in return.

The outside world did not intrude until the first of August when a note from Mrs. Manley arrived. Juliana and Asher had been seated in the garden, enjoying a late morning cup of tea when Hannum appeared with the note. Isabel Sherbrook had unexpectedly given birth, a girl, and Mrs. Sherbrook was in a fret to return home to dote upon her first grandchild. Understandably, Marcus was reluctant to desert his wife and newborn daughter, but already this morning, Mrs. Manley had dragooned John into agreeing to escort Mrs. Sherbrook home. They were invited to a farewell dinner for Mrs. Sherbrook tonight.

Having made himself aware of the contents, Asher smiled

and handed the note to Juliana. "Mrs. Sherbrook's grand-child has arrived. A girl."

Juliana's eyes lit up and she clapped her hands together. "Oh, how wonderful! She must be so excited."

"Well, that's not everything. . . ." He sighed theatrically. "I knew it could not last," he murmured. "It seems that my grandmother has decided we've had enough time alone to-gether and requires our presence at Burnham tonight."

Juliana snatched the note from his hand and read it. "You may sulk all you want, but I shall be quite happy to see Mrs. Sherbrook and wish her well before she leaves." Her eyes dancing, she added, "And as for us being alone, with a house full of servants and Mrs. Rivers hovering about, I would not say that we have been alone precisely."

Asher grinned. "I suppose I should have said, as alone as it is possible without having to do everything for ourselves." Lightly, he added, "Your Mrs. Rivers is to be commended—she has been most discreet. Except for breakfast and dinner we rarely see the woman."

"Yes, and she has been enjoying herself immensely running the household and directing the servants while I have been . . . distracted," Juliana said with a demure expression. "She is having such a fine time bustling about that I fear I may have a tyrant on my hands when I start overseeing things myself."

"I doubt that. Your Mrs. Rivers is a nice old tabby and she is devoted to you. I can't see her cutting up rough over any-thing you wanted to do. I like her."

"I thought you might—especially since she thinks that you are little less than a god come to earth," Juliana teased.

"Hmmm, I'll just have to make certain," Asher said with a grin, "that I do nothing to shatter her illusions, won't I?"

The arrival of Mrs. Manley's invitation was timely. Asher and Juliana had both known that they could not hide away forever and had already begun to take up the reins of a normal routine. Juliana was meeting with Mrs. Lawrence and Mrs. Hannum that very afternoon and with Mrs. Rivers's help planned to draw up a list of everybody's needs and to complete the organization of her household.

While Asher had been content for the time being to settle down to the life of a man of leisure, he knew he would soon grow bored leaving everything in the hands of servants, his bailiff and his man of business in London. He was not, he realized, a man with indolent inclinations. With Juliana busy seeing to household affairs this afternoon, he'd decided that it was time for him to actually start taking a hand in the future course of his holdings and arranged for a meeting with his bailiff, Wetherly.

In addition to some orchards, Asher owned several farms that were planted in pasture and grazed cattle and some sheep, and during the discussion with Wetherly it was apparent that there was no cohesive plan when it came to the type or the breeding of the cattle. Each farmer followed his own desires and having seen some of the herds, Asher thought they could be improved upon. He smiled remembering his theft of Ormsby's best bull decades ago. Perhaps that had been the start of his interest in cattle? Who knew, but once the idea took hold, he couldn't quite put it from him. When he mentioned the notion of an improved breeding program, Wetherly greeted it with flattering enthusiasm.

"Oh, I say, sir, that would be marvelous!" Wetherly shook his head. "I have long thought that the beef stock on your farms could be vastly improved upon."

Asher frowned at him. "Well, why the devil didn't you say anything?"

Wetherly looked uncomfortable. Clearing his throat, he muttered, "Um, I assumed you were happy with the income generated and saw no reason to change anything." Warily, he added, "It will be costly to replace the stock currently on some of the farms with better bred animals."

"In the beginning," Asher said impatiently, "but eventually there will be a good return on the money spent now." He sent Wetherly a long look. Carefully, he said, "I don't employ you to merely see that things continue as they are, I employ you to help me insure that my farms and lands produce only the highest quality—whether it is livestock or food. I don't intend to settle for mediocre. Is that understood?"

Wetherly nodded eagerly. "Indeed, sir, it is!"

After Wetherly vacated his office, Asher put his feet up on his desk and stared into space. The news that Mrs. Sherbrook was leaving Burnham without Asher being forced to meet her son, Marcus, lifted a nagging worry from the back of his mind. Knowing he wasn't going to face the man whose wife he had kidnapped last year put his grandmother's invitation in a whole different light. He might, he decided, actually enjoy himself. Especially, when Mrs. Sherbrook drove away.

He was, he admitted with a slow smile, happier than he had ever been in his life. Juliana had been the elemental part of his life that had been missing and with her at his side, everything else just fell into perfect place. He was looking forward to the coming years, Juliana sitting beside him, a quiver full of offspring gamboling at their feet. I shall grow very fat, he thought contentedly, and turn into one of those red-faced old men, always blustering about and telling tales of "why when I was a boy. . . ."

But there was one very large, very black and ominous cloud on his golden horizon. Ormsby.

His cheerful mood vanished and with a sigh Asher considered Ormsby. He'd known that sooner or later he would have to deal with the marquis and he was uneasily aware that he had allowed Juliana and his marriage to distract him from the problem Ormsby represented. It wasn't only that Ormsby and Denning had some sort of unholy alliance, but the fact that Ormsby had gone so far as to hire a pair of London bullies to kill him changed the entire dynamics of the situation. I've been hiding my head in the sand these past few weeks, he admitted grimly.

While it was true that Juliana had taken up most of his thoughts, from time to time the situation with Ormsby and how he was to resolve it had drifted through his mind but for the first time ever, Asher wasn't quite certain of his next step. He wasn't afraid of risks: God knew he'd taken more than his share over the years. But things had changed. With the Ormsby dilemma bubbling like a noxious tar pit at the edge of his garden, he wouldn't be the anonymous stranger slipping in here and there, doing what had to be done and then disappearing, leaving no trace behind.

He grimaced. If Ormsby lived anywhere else in the British Isles, except practically right at his front door, he'd have known what to do, known what steps he needed to take, and he wouldn't have been left with this unsettling feeling that his hands were tied. Ormsby was too close to home, too close to everyone he loved. Whatever ultimately happened between himself and Ormsby, it *must* not be allowed to impact the very people he had always fought to protect. He scowled. He was no longer only his grandmother's grandson, his siblings' half brother, he was Juliana's husband. He could not live with himself if any act of his brought disaster upon her.

His face tightened. But he had to do something about Ormsby. He could no more allow Ormsby to roam about freely than he could allow a viper in his bed. If only, he thought savagely, the bloody man wasn't right at my doorstep.

Content in his life, in love with his wife, Asher would have put away any further plans to tweak Ormsby's ego by the theft of the Ormsby diamonds, long and dearly held though the notion of stealing the diamonds was. But the marquis's hiring of the two thugs to murder him had changed everything and Asher's plans no longer merely considered how to tie a knot in Ormsby's tail. . . . I'm going to have to kill the bastard, he concluded dispassionately. And in a way that will not bring ruin and shame to my family. A duel? he wondered. Though duels were against the law, they were fought all the time, but killing a peer of the realm would most likely insure that he would be transported or would live a life on the run on the continent . . . or hang. None of which appealed to him.

His mouth twisted. It was going to have to be plain old-fashioned murder, he admitted tiredly. And soon.

A few miles away at Rosevale, Denning was also thinking about Ormsby, but his thoughts didn't include murder. Since Ormsby had stormed out of the room over a week ago, Denning had heard nothing from or of him. Of course, he'd been quite content that this was so; it gave him a chance to consider his options.

Denning had convinced himself that the tussle between himself and Ormsby had been perfectly normal. It had been, he told himself repeatedly, merely the sort of thing that often happened between high-spirited gentlemen; when fueled by drink, tempers flared. It had been pure folly, he told himself, to think a man of Ormsby's stature would have murdered him. And he didn't blame the man—he *had* threatened him.

Which brought Denning to the reason for the discourse in the first place. Seated in his study that Tuesday evening, he stared at the mahogany bookcase, his eyes settling on the book that held his letter and the packet taken from Jane's desk. It wasn't beyond the realm of possibility that Ormsby would hire someone to break into the house and search for the evidence. Or even do so himself. Once the packet fell into Ormsby's hands, Denning knew the marquis would destroy it, and with the proof gone . . . My little arrangement would end, he thought glumly.

The right thing, the honorable thing, he knew, would be to place the packet in Asher's possession and let him deal with it, but the notion of giving up his control over Ormsby was a powerful argument against that idea. He grimaced. It was sad but true that he *liked* having the marquis dancing to the tune of his piping. He liked knowing that he could tap into the vast Ormsby fortune at will . . . as long as he didn't get too greedy.

And it wasn't, he reminded himself virtuously, as if he'd *never* let Asher know about the contents of the packet. He would . . . just not right now.

While his initial thought had been to ride up to London with his letter and the packet and place the whole thing safely in the hands of his solicitor, as the days passed, he procrastinated. What was the hurry? he asked himself. The ugly incident with Ormsby had been an aberration. He didn't really believe that his life had been in danger, did he? It was ridiculous. He had nothing to fear from the marquis and there was no need for him to hotfoot it to London. Besides, he was enjoying himself in his new home.

This time of year London was hot and thin of convivial company, he reminded himself. Oh, he could probably find a few friends at the Horse Guards for a friendly game of cards, but by now even the least member of the *ton* had deserted the city for the country. In September, the start of the "little season" would be much better.

Yet for all his procrastination and whitewashing of those moments when Ormsby's fingers had closed around his throat, choking him, Denning couldn't quite shake the feeling that Ormsby was, perhaps, much more dangerous than he wanted to believe. The thought of Ormsby stealing the packet had also taken strong hold of his mind, making him rethink his decision.

Ormsby could have no idea where he had placed the packet; he could have concealed it anywhere within the house. Remembering Ormsby's lingering gaze on Jane's desk, Denning got up and walked to the bookcase. Even if Ormsby tore Jane's desk apart he'd not find what he searched for, but if he didn't find it there, logic said, he'd start casting about for another hiding place. Would an intruder look further in this room or assume the evidence was in another part of the house? The packet was hidden but was it hidden well enough to escape the probing eyes of a thief?

Growing increasingly uneasy with his hiding place, Denning opened the bookcase and took out Chaucer's works. Holding the book in his hands, he shook his head. He'd have to find a better place.

With the book in hand he left the study and walked slowly up the stairs to his bedroom. Opening the drawer of the marble-topped table next to his bed, he gently placed the book inside. It was unlikely a thief could steal it with him sleeping only inches away, so tonight was taken care of. But the daylight hours presented another problem—he could hardly walk around with the book in his hand all day. For a day or two, he could keep the book nearby, but after that . . .

He sighed. Convenient or not, he was going to have to go to London. He would send Beckham off to London tomorrow at first light with his luggage and a letter to his solicitor warning of his impending arrival: he would follow at a more leisurely pace on Thursday and meet with him Friday afternoon.

It was only after his plans were clear in his head that he admitted that he would be relieved once the evidence was no longer in his hands . . . and he warned Ormsby that upon his death, his solicitor had orders to open the packet immediately. Ormsby wouldn't dare touch him then. He smiled. In fact Ormsby would take great care that he stayed hearty and hale, because if he didn't . . .

With Will Dockery planted amongst the servants at Rosevale, Ormsby learned of Denning's planned trip to London within hours of Beckham's departure the next morning. His expression thoughtful, he tossed a coin at Dockery and sent him back to Rosevale.

Wandering through the much-remarked-upon flower gardens planted by a mother he could hardly remember, Ormsby smiled to himself. It had taxed his patience beyond bearing to simply go to earth and wait, but he'd always known that sooner or later Denning would give himself away. And his patience had paid off. The colonel was about to fall into his hands like a ripe plum.

More than once since that black day Denning had revealed what he had found, Ormsby had been aware that there was really only one way to solve his problem. If Asher Cordell was no longer alive . . . He grimaced. Killing Asher would give him great satisfaction, but Denning was, he had finally decided, his most pressing concern. In time, he would kill that cocky bastard Asher, too, but first there was Denning. . . .

From the beginning Ormsby had faced two problems. Killing Denning and gaining possession of those damning papers. With his blackmailer gone and the proof destroyed, all his worries would disappear like dandelion fluff blown on a spring breeze. An ugly gleam entered his eyes. He regretted little he'd ever done in his life and he bitterly, most bitterly regretted that he had not strangled Jane Manley decades ago.

With an effort he tore his thoughts away from matters beyond his control and focused on the situation before him. Killing Denning would be simple, but laying his hands on Jane's letters and the rest of it, would not be quite so easy. Denning could have hidden the evidence anywhere and with Denning dead and having no idea where or when the proof of his treachery might resurface, Ormsby decided sourly, would be like standing in front of a canon for the rest of his life waiting for the fuse to be lit.

His hand clenched into a fist. He didn't intend to spend his remaining days always wondering when someone *else* might find proof that would prove very, *very* unpleasant for him. Right from the beginning he'd considered breaking in to first, Apple Hill, and then latterly Rosevale and searching for the papers, but he'd known, without having a clue where Denning kept them, that sort of endeavor would fail—and put the wind up Denning. And so he had endured the white-hot rage, the clawing humiliation, and suffered the colonel's blackmail.

Some of the tension eased from his body. But that, he reminded himself, smiling again, was all at end. This time of year, Denning's trip to London could have only one purpose: to take Jane's papers to a safer place. Ormsby nearly laughed aloud. By the time the sun set Thursday evening, his troubles would be over. He was certain he'd have no trouble laying his hands on that damnable, *damnable* evidence that Denning had so inconveniently discovered. Familiar with his quarry, Ormsby knew that Denning wouldn't trust the papers to anyone else—he'd have them with him. And this time, the marquis would handle the situation himself. . . .

Ormsby was correct: Denning did have the packet with him. Still hidden in the Chaucer book, it was now neatly packed in a small black leather valise that sat on the floor of the gig near his foot.

Not in any hurry, Denning pulled away midmorning on Thursday, his smart black and scarlet vehicle drawn by a frisky gray stallion he'd purchased only a few weeks previously. Jingo was known to be hot at hand. The vicar and the squire both had warned him about the stallion's personality, but confident in his skills and preferring a spirited animal to one of a calmer temperament, Denning was looking forward to testing the gray's mettle.

Bowling along under the green canopy of oak, beech and ash trees that lined the country lane, the colonel was anticipating a pleasant, uneventful journey. He knew of a comfortable inn several miles this side of London and planned to stay the night there before traveling on to the city in the morning. The inn employed a plump little serving maid who had proven inventive and accommodating in the past and he saw no reason why she would prove less so tonight.

He was grinning, delighting in Jingo's fluid, ground-covering trot—and the gray's attempts to get the bit between his teeth, when some six miles later they swept around a curve and came upon a lone rider. Denning's hands tightened fractionally on the reins, intending to temper in some of Jingo's enthusiasm as they approached the newcomer on the narrow lane.

The gray took strong exception to Denning's pull on the reins. The stallion's pace obediently slackened, but he tossed his head and fought against the bit, half rearing and generally making his displeasure known.

Concentrating on his horse, Denning paid little attention to the approaching rider and it was only when the horseman came abreast of the gig that he felt that first quiver of unease. There was something . . . the black, broad-brimmed hat pulled so low that it half obscured the man's face? The heavy, dark, concealing cloak worn on a warm summer day?

When the newcomer brought his horse next to the gig, despite the attempts of disguise, Denning recognized him. Ormsby. A thrill of fright snaked through him and heedless of Jingo's antics, he dropped one of the reins and fumbled for the small pistol he carried in his vest beneath his elegant bottle green jacket.

"Don't be a fool!" hissed Ormsby, leveling his own pistol at him. "I mean you no harm . . . but we have to talk."

The sight of a pistol aimed at his breast stilled Denning's movements for the moment. "You're the fool," Denning snapped, "if you think that I believe that! You're pointing a bloody pistol at me."

"Only to gain your cooperation," Ormsby said, casting a quick look around to assure himself that the road remained empty. It was market day and while most of the farmers were already at the village with their goods at this hour, there was always a stray or two that ambled in late.

"And that you'll not have," Denning replied, his fingers inching toward his pistol. "Now move away."

It was a standoff. Denning wasn't budging and Ormsby wasn't prepared to shoot him in such a public setting, though he did plan to murder him . . . once he had Denning in the small, secluded glen just a scant distance through the trees that edged the lane. For a long, tense moment they stared at each other.

With only one rein controlling him, Jingo's agitated behavior worsened, his hooves beating out an impatient tattoo on the road, his head constantly whipping against the remaining rein: he was ripe for disaster. The gig rocked back and forth from the stallion's violent movements and Denning knew it was only a matter of minutes before the gray ditched him.

A faint high-pitched sound drifted toward the two men from beyond the curve in the road behind Denning and as the noise grew in intensity, Ormsby glanced uncertainly in that direction. A second later he realized what he was hearing: pigs.

The cacophony of squeals and grunts became louder, filling the air, and a half dozen or so big red pigs ambled into view. Ormsby cursed under his breath. Just what he needed, a bloody farmer driving his pigs to market.

The instant Ormsby's gaze left him, Denning's fingers closed round his pistol and in one swift action, dragged it free of his jacket. Ormsby caught the movement from the corner of his eye and swung his attention back to Denning, just as Denning got off a quick shot.

Ormsby's reaction was instinctive; he fired back. Denning's bullet missed, but Ormsby's did not. The remaining rein fell from Denning's hand and he groaned, clutching his chest as a horrifying blotch of blood bloomed across his white linen shirt and buff waistcoat.

The first of the pigs were only a few feet behind the gig and more were spilling around the curve, followed by a pair of farmers, when the shots were exchanged. The squealing, grunting pigs and the pistol fire were too much for Jingo and the stallion bolted, lunging forward and galloping down the road as if chased by a pack of wolves, the reins slapping in the air behind him.

Ormsby spared a harassed glance at the disappearing gig and, cursing virulently, he stuffed his pistol into the waist of his breeches, swung his horse around and plunged into the forest. Desperate to put distance between himself and the site of the shooting, Ormsby spurred his horse to a reckless pace and they careened through the forest. A mile from the road, he remembered the hat and cloak and with fumbling fingers tore off the hat and sent it flying. The cloak followed, falling in a black heap on the forest floor near a huge old oak.

His heart banging frantically in his chest, he fought to catch his breath as his horse dodged through the woods. Truly frightened for the first time in his whole spoiled life, Ormsby was light-headed, terrified that he might have been recognized. Had the pig farmers seen his features clear enough to identify him? Was word already flying through the neighborhood that the Marquis of Ormsby had shot Colonel Denning down in cold blood? Would he find himself a hunted man? Good God, how had things gone so very, very wrong?

But by the time he came out of the forest several minutes later a scant half mile from Ormsby Place, he had himself better under control. That first debilitating flare of fright had passed and he had regained command of his thoughts.

Only mere seconds had passed, he reminded himself, before he had disappeared into the forest. The pig farmers had been some distance away; the most they would have seen as he had left the road was a fleeting glimpse of a horse and rider. The black hat and cloak had effectively hidden his features and covered his build and clothing. He'd been riding a plain bay gelding of no distinction, chosen this morning for precisely that reason.

Feeling more assured with every passing moment, he was able to hand over his horse to the stable boy without an outward sign of the turmoil that roiled in his gut. Reaching the house, he told his butler that he was not at home and disappeared into his study.

Despite the hour he poured himself a snifter of brandy, cursing again when he noticed his fingers trembling. Forsaking the swirling of the amber liquor in the crystal snifter and the enjoyment of the heady scent, he gulped down a big draught of the brandy.

As the pleasant burn from his throat to his chest ebbed, he took a deep breath and looked around with pride at the handsome room. He had nothing to worry about. He was Ormsby. Why would anyone connect him with something as unsavory as common murder on a country lane? Besides, who would believe a pair of ignorant farmers over the powerful Marquis of Ormsby? The notion was nonsensical!

The brandy warming his belly, his sense of well-being increasing, a flush of satisfaction rose within him. At least that troublesome Denning was taken care of. He'd not have to worry about him any longer. But Denning, he reminded himself sickly, had been only one of his problems. . . .

An icy shaft slid down his spine. Denning was dead, but Jane's papers were still out there. Somewhere.

Jingo traveled nearly four miles before he came across any other traffic on the road. Having dropped back to an erratic canter from his initial breakneck gallop, the sweat-flecked stallion slowed to a walk as he approached a cart traveling toward him.

Mrs. Birrel was driving the dark green cart home, having just come from the marketplace. The vicarage stable boy, Perkin, had accompanied her to carry any items she might buy and was sitting beside her in the cart. It was he who recognized Jingo.

"That's the colonel's new horse!" he cried as Jingo walked aimlessly down the road.

Further inspection revealed the trailing reins and almost as one, their eyes swung to the occupant of the gig. During the wild ride, Denning had fallen over onto his side; one arm was hanging down, his hand resting limply on the small black valise on the floor of the gig.

"Oh, my goodness! Catch that animal before he runs away!" commanded Mrs. Birrel as she jerked her own horse, a nice, quiet little chestnut mare, to an abrupt halt.

Perkin scrambled from the cart and cautiously approached the horse, but there was nothing to fear now; Jingo had left his fidgets behind him some time ago. The gray stood quietly as Perkin walked up to him and carefully captured the bridle. A moment later Perkin had the reins in his hands, Jingo standing docilely beside him.

Mrs. Birrel alighted from the cart, tied the mare to a small tree at the side of the road and hurried to the gig. That something was terribly wrong was obvious from Denning's position, but expecting he had suffered a stroke or such, after receiving no response to the calling of his name and admonishing Perkin to hold the gray firmly, she lifted her skirts and gingerly clambered aboard the gig.

With gentle hands she pulled Denning upright, gasping at the sight of his blood-soaked shirt and waistcoat. Her eyes huge, she looked at Perkin, who was peering interestedly around Jingo.

"Move the gig from the road and tie the horse to a tree," she ordered calmly, despite her trepidation. The colonel's face was pale and he lay still and heavy in the gig beside her. Mrs. Birrel feared that he was dead and from the amount of blood that stained his clothes, she knew immediately that there was foul play afoot.

Perkin positioned the gig off to the side of the road and securely tied Jingo to an oak sapling. Mrs. Birrel was considering her move when the sound of an approaching vehicle came to her ear.

Mrs. Birrel looked behind her and to her relief she recognized the driver of the small chaise drawn by a pair of bays trotting down the road. It was the squire accompanied by his wife.

Even before Mrs. Birrel called to him, the squire realized that something was amiss. Stopping his horses abreast of where Denning's gig stood at the side of the road, Ripley called out, "Is there trouble, Mrs. Birrel? May we help you?"

"Oh, Squire! Thank heavens you are here," Mrs. Birrel cried in great agitation. "It is Colonel Denning—I fear someone has murdered him!"

"Upon my soul! Never say so," exclaimed the squire, shocked.

There was a flurry of activity. Driving the Birrel cart, Perkin was sent to the village to find the surgeon and return with him posthaste. The squire parked his vehicle near the side of the road in front of Denning's gig and he and his wife quickly dismounted from the chaise. Hurrying back to the gig, they were able to see for themselves the amount of blood covering Denning's chest. The three exchanged shaken glances.

A muffled sound from the seeming corpse startled them and to everyone's horrified astonishment, Denning's eyes flew open. "Ash . . . er. You . . . must," he mumbled weakly. He shuddered, took a labored breath and began again, "Asher must . . ." Denning's eyes closed, his breathing seemed to stop, but then with an agonizing effort, he forced his eyes open once more and said thinly, "Saucer boo . . . poem."

Mrs. Birrel tried to hush him, saying urgently, "Save your strength. The surgeon is on his way here."

His gaze fixed pleadingly on Mrs. Birrel's, he paid her no heed and gasped, "I wronged . . . him. Or . . . by . . ." He gathered his fading senses and, fighting for breath, he said, "Tell Asher. Tell Asher . . ." He could not go on and his eyes fluttered shut.

A minute passed, then two, and suddenly his eyes opened one last time. "Tell him!" he cried, and breathed his last.

There was a moment of stunned silence and then Mrs. Birrel leaned over and very gently placed her fingers on his wrist. She looked at the squire and said, "He is dead. Murdered."

Chapter 19

The news that Colonel Denning had been murdered on a quiet country lane, and that his murderer had been seen by two local farmers, scorched like wildfire through the area. From the highest to the lowest, the colonel's shocking death was the topic of conversation wherever people gathered, in their homes, in the fields and in every tavern and inn in the neighborhood. No one could stop talking about it.

A member of the gentry murdered in broad daylight on a public road! Shot! There'd been nothing like this in the area for decades—except when wealthy landowner Mr. Lockheed's sister ruined herself twenty years ago by falling in love with and running away with a local smuggler. Oh, how the tongues had wagged then, but everyone agreed that a runaway match, no matter how shocking, didn't compare to the colonel's murder. Even Vincent Beverley's tragic death over thirty years previously was dragged out and gossiped over once again. Of course, young Beverley's death had been only mildly suspicious while Denning's death had been cold-blooded *murder!*

Because of the events surrounding his demise, Colonel Denning's funeral attracted a far larger crowd than it would have under normal circumstances. His face tense and grim, aware of the looks and the whispered comments of the avid onlookers as his stepfather was laid to rest in the village cemetery, Asher growled under his breath to Juliana, "Have they nothing better to do? Than gawk and stare?"

She calmed the growing rage she felt within him by laying a hand on his arm and murmuring, "They mean no harm. Your stepfather was a popular man in the neighborhood. People liked his bluff manner. Many would be here even if he had not been murdered."

He took a deep breath and nodded, tamping back the helpless fury that seared through him. His gaze swept over the anguished faces of his brother and his two sisters standing across the grave from him and the feeling of helplessness and fury only increased. For as long as he could remember he had protected them, but their grief, their loss was something he could do nothing about and it only added to his feeling of impotent rage. Though they'd sent notification to Robert, fighting God knew where on the continent, they'd known that even if he was granted leave, highly unlikely, he would be unable to be with them, and Asher suffered for him, too, having to bear this terrible pain alone. Losing their father, so suddenly, so violently, had been a horrid jolt for the entire family. And moodily Asher admitted that for all his faults, in his fashion, Denning had loved his children. They would all miss him, his jovial presence and his easy affection.

To his surprise, Asher found that he, too, mourned the passing of a man he had been so certain that he despised. He may have resented Denning, may have harbored ill will against the man for the pain and despair he had carelessly inflicted upon Asher's mother and his lack of concern over the future of his children, but even in Asher's blackest moments, he had never wished the man dead. Changed. Different. More responsible, yes. But never dead. And never murdered.

Denning's death hit him hard, devastated him, and as the days passed, he understood for the first time that underneath all of his resentment and contempt for the man, he'd loved him in his own fashion. Aware that Denning had also loved his children in his own fashion, his lips twisted. Perhaps there was little difference between himself and his stepfather, after all.

The funeral behind them, the family faced the reading of the will. Denning's will had been simple and, drafted just a few days after he had purchased Rosevale, held few surprises. As John and Asher had known, Rosevale was to go to Robert. Never having much more than two coins to rub together, with his daughters comfortably settled and John established at Apple Hill, Asher always able to fend for himself, Denning had stipulated that the remainder of his belongings were to be divided amongst his children and his stepson. Asher had been touched that Denning had seen to it that Jane's desk had been specifically designated as going to his stepson. There was one surprise: an addition to the will signed and witnessed the day before Denning died, left his small library to Asher. Being no great reader, Asher was puzzled by the bequest, but he shrugged it away. He'd never understood his stepfather in life, why should he in death?

Martha and Elizabeth along with their husbands stayed at Apple Hill with John for a few more days after the reading of the will. Along with Asher and Juliana, they helped go through Denning's belongings and generally consoled each other. On a Monday morning some eleven days after the colonel's murder, Denning's two daughters tearfully departed for their homes with their husbands. Asher, with Juliana, Mrs. Manley and John standing beside him in the driveway at Apple Hill, watched them ride away in the big traveling coach with mixed feelings. He was relieved that he would no longer be faced with sad faces, tears and woeful questions . . . questions without any answers about Denning's death, but there was a part of him that ached to see them go.

When the coach disappeared around the bend and there was only a cloud of dust to indicate its passing, the four of them slowly walked back into the house. There was not much conversation between them as they wandered into the front parlor of the house and each one drifted to either a chair or the horsehair sofa covered in rich brown and fawn figured velvet.

Her face tired and drawn, Mrs. Manley summed up everyone's feeling. "I am certainly glad," she said in her forthright manner, "that horrible ordeal is behind us and we can begin to move forward now."

"I cannot believe that he is gone," John said huskily, his gaze dull and wounded. "I keep thinking I'll hear his horse and he will come striding through the door, with some quip or story to relate."

Mrs. Manley nodded. "I felt that way when your mother left us. I kept thinking I'd hear her voice or her laugh and she'd walk into the room eager to tell me some prank one of you children had pulled . . . or how clever you had been." Her expression kind, she said, "I know that it isn't much comfort now, but just as it did after your mother died, the pain does gradually fade and there will be a time that you can think of him without this terrible empty ache in your heart. You'll always miss him, just as we all still miss your mother, but time really does heal the wound."

"Will you be all right?" Asher asked, searching his brother's face.

John flashed him a crooked smile. "May I remind you, though I know you think differently, that I am a grown man and that I don't need my big brother to coddle me?" At Asher's wry smile, he added, "I shall be fine. I do think, however, that once I have assured myself that the farms can survive without me for a few weeks, I might go to Brighton and watch the antics of Prinny for a while."

Asher nodded, thinking that it would be good for John to be away from Apple Hill—and the avid looks and rampant gossip.

At present it was the general opinion of officialdom and the neighborhood at large that a stranger, perhaps a passing highwayman, had killed the poor old colonel. The region had its share of miscreants, but everyone was convinced that no one local could have done such a wicked deed.

During the time following his stepfather's murder, to the exclusion of just about everything else but his wife, Asher had been deeply involved with consoling the family and all the usual arrangements and business connected with the death of a loved one. But with the departure of his sisters, he felt he could now turn his full attention to the task of avenging his stepfather's death.

The minute Asher learned of his stepfather's murder, he'd *known* as if he'd seen it happen that Ormsby had murdered Denning. He wasn't leaping to conclusions either. From everything he knew about the relationship between Denning and Ormsby, it was an inescapable conclusion that Denning had been blackmailing Ormsby. Being the victim of blackmail, Asher reasoned, gave Ormsby a powerful motive to want Denning dead. And from his own experience with the London thugs, he knew that Ormsby was capable of murder. With a bone-deep certainty he was convinced that Ormsby had killed Denning, and if he'd needed another prod to kill Ormsby, which he didn't, Ormsby's murder of his stepfather definitely gave it to him.

Bitterly aware that it would never occur to anyone else to consider that the Marquis of Ormsby would have had a hand in anything so sordid as murder, he hadn't been surprised that Ormsby's name had never arisen in connection with the colonel's death. Which bothered him not a bit—he had his own plans for the marquis and he had no more qualms about killing him than he did a rat in a grain bin.

Ormsby had been noticeably absent from all the various functions arranged in connection with Denning's death, and Asher had noted it. Guilty conscience? Asher doubted it. But the thought of a guilty conscience pricked his own conscience and he decided that it was time he made some overdue visits.

The squire and his family and the Birrels attended all of the functions connected with Denning's death and expressed their condolences. But to Asher's mystification, the squire and Mrs. Birrel both sent him private notes, requesting that he call on them, but busy with everything else, Asher hadn't yet gotten around to it. With family duties taken care of, he rode over to the squire's house that afternoon.

His face somber, Squire Ripley said heavily, "You need to talk to Mrs. Birrel. She was actually in the gig with him when he died. He spoke to her. I couldn't make any of it out . . . except that he wanted you told something. He kept repeating, tell Asher. But talk to Mrs. Birrel." He shook his head. "This is a terrible thing to have happened. You know that you and your family have our deepest sympathies. Anything we can do for you, say the word."

This was the first he'd learned that Denning had still been alive when Mrs. Birrel and the squire found him. His curiosity aroused, Asher swung into the saddle and rode directly to the vicarage. Shown in to the comfortable sitting room at the front of the vicarage, Mrs. Birrel greeted him warmly, saying, "Oh, my dear boy! I am sorry for your loss. Such a tragedy."

Brushing aside her sympathy, he said, "I am sorry that I could not come sooner. You wanted to speak privately with me?"

She nodded. "I should have simply told you when we came to call just after your stepfather's murder, but I hesitated to burden you with what I'm afraid is utter nonsense at such a painful time."

"Tell me what he said," Asher said quietly.

"Saucerboo poem?" Asher repeated incredulously, when Mrs. Birrel repeated the colonel's dying words to him. "What the devil is that supposed to mean?"

"I don't know, dear," Mrs. Birrel said unhappily, "but he was most insistent that you be told. 'Tell Asher.' Those were his final words." She frowned. "He also said that he wronged you—at least, I believe that's what he meant." She looked miserable. "I don't think that he was in his right mind because the rest of it was just fragments and I'm sorry to say that with the shock of it all, I don't remember exactly what he said. I know he muttered something like 'or' or 'by' but the one thing that is very vivid in my mind is that he most desperately wanted you to know something." She blushed faintly. "The vicar and I discussed it and we saw no need to tell the constable. It was just nonsense."

"You're right," Asher muttered, "it is nonsense." He questioned her at length, but beyond the fact that Denning wanted him to know something and it had to do, she thought, with whatever "saucerboo poem" referred to, he learned little. Eventually, he thanked her and rode away. None of it made sense, but he puzzled over the colonel's strange words, racking his brain to find some clue in "saucerboo poem."

Neither John, Juliana or Mrs. Manley could deduce anything from Denning's dying utterances either and the consensus was that he had been out of his mind and that the words meant nothing. The colonel's last words were just one more element in the mystery surrounding his death.

On Tuesday, without his sisters' calming influence and irritated by the lack of progress, John suggested that they hire a Bow Street Runner from London. It took all of Asher's tact and delicate persuasion to guide John away from such an idea. Committed to killing Ormsby himself, the last thing Asher needed was to be stumbling over a Runner.

Unknowingly Mrs. Birrel had given him damning evidence that Ormsby killed his stepfather. At first he dismissed as gibberish what she had related, but lying in the bed the previous night, going over the conversation with Mrs. Birrel for perhaps the hundredth time, the words "or" and "by" leaped out at him. All that was missing, he thought savagely, was the "ms" from the middle. Add "ms" between "or" and "by" and you had *Ormsby*. A fierce exultation rose up within him. I have you now, you murdering bastard, he swore to himself, and I'm coming for you.

Asher's diplomatic steering away from John's notion of a Bow Street Runner did not go unnoticed by either his grandmother or his wife and both women studied him intently. Juliana knew that he was grappling with some inner torment; she was constantly aware of a preoccupied air about him— an air that only disappeared, she admitted with flushed cheeks, when he made love to her. Since his stepfather's murder, she had the feeling that while he listened and talked and *appeared* to be paying attention to events around him, that his mind was elsewhere. At first, she'd assumed it was merely grief and shock that weighed on him, but lately there was something about him, something about the inimical gleam she sometimes glimpsed in his eyes that made her increasingly uneasy.

No less than Juliana was Mrs. Manley anxious about Asher's state of mind. His grandmother knew him best of anyone alive and she was perhaps the only one who suspected that there was a deeper, darker side to her eldest grandson. Upon occasion, in particular when he had returned from one of his long absences, she had detected an aura of violence about him, an icy glitter in his eyes that transformed him into someone she didn't recognize, a hard-faced stranger who frightened her. . . . And then in a split second, as if recalling himself, all sign of that dangerous stranger would be gone and her oh so charming scamp of a grandson would be laughing down at her, his gaze warm and affectionate. Worriedly, she studied his face. That dangerous stranger was peering out of his eyes too often of late for her liking and she was afraid for him.

On Thursday afternoon Mrs. Manley came to share a light meal with Asher and Juliana. The invitation had come from Juliana with the intriguing notation that she wanted to speak privately with her. The moment Mrs. Manley had arrived, Juliana had glanced over her shoulder and, seeing no sign of her husband, whisked her away to the small room at the side of the old farmhouse that was her temporary office.

Shutting the door behind her, she looked at Mrs. Manley. An uneasy smile on her pretty mouth, Juliana said, "I know you think that I'm acting mysteriously, but I wanted a word with you before Asher arrives—he's been looking at cattle this morning with Wetherly—and he's due back at any moment."

Mrs. Manley took a seat in one of only two chairs in the whitewashed room and asked, "Is there something wrong? Asher?"

Juliana's smile fled and, her face the picture of anxiety, she nodded. "I do not know what is wrong with him, but something is. He is so . . . absentminded. . . . No, that's not it. It's as if he's here, but not here. I thought at first that it was his stepfather's death, but with every passing day, instead of abating, his odd mood seems to be getting worse." Baldly, she said, "He frightens me. There is a remoteness, a wall that I cannot seem to breach and I don't know what to do about it." She bit her lip and glanced down at the wide-planked oak floor. "Yesterday a note from Wetherly arrived and I carried it to Asher's office. He must have been lost in thought and he didn't hear me enter the room. I think I startled him." Juliana swallowed and her eyes met Mrs. Manley's. "He was standing, looking out the window, but when I spoke his name, he whirled around and the look he gave me. . . ." She sank down onto the chair opposite Mrs. Manley's, her hands twisting in her lap. "It was as if I faced a stranger. His expression was so cold, so hard, so, so *violent*—as if he could commit murder, that I actually stepped backward and screamed." A flush stained her cheeks. "Of course, he laughed at my reaction, kissing me and smiling at me in that charming way he has and telling me it was my imagination. Oh, but Mrs. Manley, it was *not* my imagination!"

Mrs. Manley sighed. "No, it probably wasn't. I've been worried myself lately about him."

"You, too!" exclaimed Juliana, feeling the knot of anxiety that had been lodged in her chest loosening. Instantly, she no longer felt alone—or that she was going mad, imagining things. "I do not know what to do," she admitted. "Ever since his stepfather died, he has been preoccupied and when I press him or try to talk to him about it, he simply smiles, changes the subject and pushes me aside."

"What do you want me to do?" inquired Mrs. Manley helplessly. "You are the center of his world now. If you cannot get him to tell you what is bothering him, what do you think that I can do?"

Looking glum, Juliana shook her head. "I don't know. . . . I guess I was hoping that you could give me a hint how to banish the terrible well of blackness I sense within him."

A rap on the door startled both ladies and, leaping to her feet, Juliana rushed to open it.

"Ah, here you are," said Asher. "Hannum told me that my grandmother had arrived and I wondered where the pair of you had vanished."

He dropped a kiss on his wife's cheek and walked over to his grandmother and bowed gallantly over her hand, pressing a kiss on her fingers. Straightening, a teasing gleam in his dark blue eyes, he glanced from one woman to the other. "I am indeed a lucky man—I have two beautiful ladies to grace my table this afternoon."

Not by one word or one look, did Asher betray anything but real pleasure in the company of his wife and grandmother during the entire afternoon. He talked easily about the cattle and his plans to improve the herds of the farmers who leased his lands, sent his compliments to the kitchen for the tasty repast before him, expressed interest in Apollo's preference for Mrs. Manley's silk slippers and inquired warmly into his wife's day. Anyone observing him would have decided that the concerns of his wife and grandmother were pure folly.

But Asher was very aware that his actions were causing the two most important people in his life great distress. And that had to stop, he thought grimly, replying to some question asked by his grandmother. Unfortunately, he knew too well that the only way it was going to stop was when Ormsby was dead.

Balancing on a tightrope, Asher struggled to keep his murderous emotions well in hand, keeping that dark, violent side of himself buried deep and showing only the loving and affectionate husband and grandson. Until today, he assumed he was doing a good job of it, but it appeared not. Though they tried to hide it, it was obvious that both his wife and his grandmother were deeply worried about him. He sighed. There was only one way to end this torture and, looking from one woman to the other, he decided that the marquis had just run out of time.

John arrived just as they were finishing the light meal. He was carrying a book in one hand. After greetings were exchanged, declining offers of refreshment, John handed the book to Asher and took a seat next to Mrs. Manley.

John said, "I plan to leave for Brighton tomorrow and I was going through some more of father's things this afternoon when I came across the book." He swallowed. "It was in the valise he had with him when he was killed." He forced a smile. "Since he left you his library, I thought it only fair to give it to you."

It was a hefty volume and, picking it up, Asher glanced at the spine. Reading the name, he stiffened. Saucerboo poem. Chaucer. Book. Poems.

He set the book down and stared at it as if it was a snake. His stepfather's dying words could only have been referring to this book. And something in this book—in one of the poems?—Denning thought was vital for him to know. But was it something Asher wanted to know? For a moment a morbid fear swept through him. Had Denning discovered the source of his money? What he had done to keep the family safe? What if inside this innocent-looking volume there lay proof of his other life? Proof that would destroy everything he had worked for?

He glanced around the table and found that everyone was looking at him. He made his lips stretch into a semblance of a smile. "Ah, thank you, John. I shall add it to the library. Perhaps, I might even read it someday, although poetry would not be my first choice."

"What book is it, my dear?" asked Mrs. Manley, who was watching him closely.

Wishing his grandmother was not quite so clever, reluctantly, he muttered, "Chaucer's complete works."

His grandmother looked puzzled and then she gasped. Just as Asher had, she put it altogether. Excitedly, she said, "*That* was what he was trying to say before he died. Saucerboo poem." When Juliana and John stared at her astonished, she explained, "Chaucer's book of poems."

Juliana's eyes widened. "Of course! And he was taking it to London with him." Smiling at her husband, she said, "Perhaps he has underlined some words for you. Look through it."

"By Jove! She's right," exclaimed John, leaning forward excitedly.

Asher knew there was no escaping his fate. His heart beating raggedly in his chest, gingerly, he placed the book in front of him and flipped it open. He hadn't known what to expect but the small packet lying snugly in the hole cut into the middle of the book didn't help his laboring heart any.

"Oh, my word!" breathed his grandmother. "There *is* something inside it."

Asher sat frozen, staring at the small packet as if he faced death itself. How? he wondered dully. How had Denning gotten proof? He'd been so careful. So bloody careful, and it appeared all for naught.

"Open it," urged Juliana, who had come to sit beside him. "Let us see what it was he felt was so important to you."

With trembling fingers Asher plucked the packet from its hiding place. The first thing he found was Denning's letter that was wrapped around the main part of the packet. He quickly scanned it, his heart almost literally stopping when he realized that what he held had nothing to do with his nefarious deeds. He had to read the letter twice before he understood the full import of it. Then a third time to make certain he hadn't misunderstood what he read.

Wordlessly he handed the letter to Juliana. "Read it aloud."

Hardly aware of Juliana's soft voice reading Denning's letter aloud, with dazed eyes he stared at the small packet, recognizing his mother's fine script. Reverently, he unfolded the old papers, startled to find a heavy gold ring adorned with the Ormsby crest folded in the middle of the creased pages. Holding the ring in his hand, he scanned the papers, his chest feeling as if girded by steel bands as he realized the significance of the ring and the papers he held.

Light-headed, he set the ring gently in the middle of the table.

Mrs. Manley cried out, recognizing it immediately. "The Ormsby ring! It was stolen from Vincent Beverley the night he died." She looked from Asher to the ring. "But how? How did it end up in Denning's possession?" She looked horrified. "Never say that *Denning* killed him?"

Asher shook his head. "No. Ormsby killed him. Mother saw him do it. She took the ring to prove it."

"Your mother had the ring all this time?" Mrs. Manley asked, astonished.

"Yes. She hid it and these papers in that little desk of hers. Going through the desk after it had been brought down from the attic, Denning found everything." Wearily, he added, "And that's what he used to blackmail Ormsby. Mother's letter relates what she saw that night . . . the night Ormsby killed his brother."

"Good God!" John swore softly. "No wonder father was so certain he'd never lose anytime he played with Ormsby. It was all a sham to extort money from Ormsby." He looked at Asher, his face tightening. "And it gives Ormsby a powerful reason to want him dead."

"It does indeed," Asher said lightly. "But it doesn't prove

he killed your father. Only that he had a compelling reason to kill him."

"We must turn this over to the constable at once!" John declared fiercely. "Ormsby must be brought before the law and be made to pay for what he has done."

Asher scratched his jaw. "Ah, yes, there is that, but it appears that murder isn't the only crime to be laid at Ormsby's door."

John frowned. "What do you mean?"

"Mother's letter explains everything. But this," Asher said as he slid a piece of paper toward John, "proves that an usurper has paraded before us as the Marquis of Ormsby all these years."

Everyone looked at him as if he had gone insane. Asher smiled grimly. "Beverley obtained a special license in London and those, my dear ones, are the marriage lines between Jane Manley and Vincent Beverley, dated July 12, 1775, performed in a small hamlet in Surrey. They were married almost exactly nine months before my birth in April, which means that Ormsby isn't Ormsby. I am."

Chapter 20

There was a thunderstruck silence as the other three stared at him with mouths agape. Mrs. Manley recovered first. Torn between shock and gratification, she murmured, "Those scheming little wretches! I should have known something was afoot when Jane begged to visit her friend Elizabeth in Surrey. Previously, she'd never cared much for the young lady, but that summer nothing would do but she visit Elizabeth. I never suspected, not even for a moment, that there was something between she and Vincent." Shaking her head, she said, "They hid it very well. In fact, I thought they disliked each other. There was never *any* hint that they had more than a passing acquaintance with each other. Even that last week after she came home from visiting Elizabeth—even then she hid everything from me."

"But why?" asked Juliana. "I would have thought you would have been pleased for her to marry the heir to a marquis."

"I would have been, but Vincent's father would have never countenanced the match. His heir married to the granddaughter of a lowly baronet? A lowly baronet whose title was defunct? That aside, he'd have been aghast at Vincent marrying a young lady with little fortune or even great beauty to recommend her. He'd never have allowed that to happen. Oh, no, he had his sights set much higher. I remem-

ber there was quite a bit of gossip at the time that he was angling for a union with the daughter of the Duke of Hazeltine.
From all accounts, Lady Anne was a beautiful young lady
with a large fortune, but was also known to be haughty and
possessed of a viper's tongue." She looked thoughtful. "That's
probably what pushed them into acting—they were afraid
the marquis would act without Vincent's consent and he'd
find himself shackled to a woman he didn't love."

Asher nodded, holding up one of the pages where Jane had
written out the whole story. "That's what mother wrote. They
felt they had no choice but to marry in secret." He glanced
sympathetically at his grandmother. "She regretted not telling
you, but they were too fearful that if *anyone* learned that
they had fallen in love and planned to marry, Vincent's father
would get wind of it and put a stop to it."

"And he would have!" Mrs. Manley said viciously. "He
was a horrid, horrid, *horrid* man."

"I don't understand," John complained. "If they were
married, why didn't they tell anyone?"

"Because," Mrs. Manley muttered, "Vincent may have been
brave enough to secretly marry my daughter, but he was terrified of facing his father with what he had done." She
looked at Asher. "Am I right?"

Asher sighed and, across the table, handed her several
pages covered with Jane's handwriting. "Yes. They were married almost three weeks before Vincent was murdered and,
afraid to live openly together, they met clandestinely several
times." He half smiled. "Obviously, I am the result of one of
those meetings."

"But how did she get the ring? She saw the murder? Why
didn't she say something at the time? Why keep quiet about
it?" Juliana demanded, sitting beside Mrs. Manley.

"Because she was afraid," said Mrs. Manley, looking up
from the pages she held in her hands. At Juliana's blank expression, she sighed. "You would have had to have known
the second Marquis. He was a big, violent man with a leg-

endary temper. Few people crossed him, finding it easier . . . and safer simply to let him have his way. Which only made the problem worse by increasing his belief that he could and should always have his way. Bertram was little better. And poor Vincent was bullied by both of them."

When Juliana still didn't look convinced, Asher found himself defending his parents, saying, "Remember that they were young and frightened by what they had done. Mother was only eighteen. Vincent had just turned twenty-one in July. In fact he married mother only two weeks after he reached his majority. They carefully planned the whole sequence of events, but what comes through in her letter is that while they were determined to be married, they were also absolutely terrified of his father."

"And they were wise to be so," Mrs. Manley stated unhappily. I was there the night Vincent's father nearly beat a footman to death because he was displeased with the service, before the other gentlemen pulled him off and prevented him from killing the unfortunate man. There were other incidents. . . . He took a whip to one of his stable boys and left the boy scarred for life. Vincent may have reached his majority but he was still under the iron fist of his father." Her face grew hard. "Once his father learned of the marriage he might have put a good face on it, but if he couldn't have found a way around it, I wouldn't have wagered Jane living to see her first child born or to celebrate the first anniversary of her marriage."

"Oh, he wouldn't have!" Juliana protested.

"Wouldn't he have?" Asher asked with a lifted brow. He pointed to Jane's letter. "With her own eyes Mother saw Bertram kill his older brother. From what Grandmother has said, violent things happened to people that cross the Beverleys. Do you think the father would have caviled at murdering an inconvenient daughter-in-law?"

"But if the marriage was still a secret, why was Vincent killed?" demanded John.

Asher looked away, his mother's words seared across his brain. She had written so vividly of that fateful night that it was almost as if he was there, seeing it himself through Jane's eyes as he relayed the story to the others. . . .

They met at the old gatehouse, not far from the main gateway that led to Ormsby Place just as daylight was fading. His young face determined, Vincent said, "I know you think we should just tell him, but knowing my father, I believe it would be better if I prepared him first. I shall tell him tonight that I mean to marry you—but not that we have already married. I want to give him time to get used to the idea."

"Oh, Vincent, why not just tell him? We are married! I may already be with child. We cannot delay. You must tell him we are married!" Jane urged.

Bleakly, he stared down into her beloved face. "You don't know him. He flies into vicious rages. . . ." He swallowed. "Just telling him that I want to marry you is going to gain me a beating." Helplessly he tried to explain. "If I tell him that we are already married, he may very well kill me—or you. I know him intimately—you do not. Believe me, beloved, this is the best way."

"You don't have to face him alone," Jane argued. "Let me come with you. We can confront him together." And when Vincent paled and shook his head vehemently, she added, "Very well then, we don't have to face him. My mother will stand by us. We can send him a note telling him of our marriage. And if he strips everything from you—it doesn't matter—my mother will provide for us." Seeing his resistance, she pushed on urgently. "He will not live forever, my love, and he can only hold you in penury during his lifetime. You are his heir, Vincent. Someday the title and everything that goes with it will be yours."

But Vincent remained firm. "No. It is bad enough that we married in secret and have been sneaking around like we've done something wrong in order to see each other. It cannot go on. As you yourself said—you could be with child. We must let the world know that we are man and wife—even if our union infuriates my father. This is something I must do if I am ever to call myself a man." He smiled crookedly at her. *"What sort of man will not face danger for the woman he loves?"*

It was only after he left that Jane realized he had left behind his crop. He was only minutes ahead of her and thinking to catch him, she took a shortcut through the woods. Swiftly, she guided her horse through the forest until she was just ten feet from the main road. In the falling twilight, hearing loud, angry voices ahead of her, she halted her horse and peered forward. Though she was concealed in the forest, she could see Vincent and Bertram on the road in front of her. She had missed the first part of the argument, but it was clear that Vincent had told Bertram that he planned to marry her.

"You're mad if you think that father will allow you to disgrace our name and allow you to marry that little nobody," Bertram snarled.

"She is not a little nobody," Vincent said coldly. "And father cannot stop me. I mean to have her as my wife."

"By God! I always knew you were a fool! You can marry as high as you choose and you chose her? If you want her that badly, set her up as your mistress, but don't marry the chit."

"May I remind you," Vincent said icily, "that you are talking about the woman I love?"

"Oh, save me from mawkish sentiment!" Bertram snapped. "For God's sake think what you are doing! She has nothing to offer—no fortune, no great titled family. . . ." Bertram laughed. "Of course, if she was a great beauty, Father might be willing to overlook her lack of fortune and pedigree, but while she's a pretty little thing, she'll never be the toast of London." Arrogantly, he boasted, "When I marry, I don't intend for my wife to be some country mouse. Whether she has *fortune or title, my wife's beauty will be celebrated through-out all of England!"*

"Congratulations," Vincent drawled, and goaded by Bertram's dismissal of Jane, he added, "Yours may be the toast of London but mine will be the Marchioness of Ormsby!"

Bertram cursed and launched himself off his horse at Vincent. Both men fell to the ground. Quick as a cat, Bertram twisted Vincent face down in the dirt and straddled him, his hands clamping on either side of Vincent's head. Shocked by the suddenness and viciousness of Bertram's assault, Jane stared, frozen. But almost instantly fury replaced her shock and her heels dug into her horse's flank. Even as her horse started forward, Vincent gave an odd cry, followed by a sudden, ominous silence. Instinctively, her hands tightened on the reins, halting her horse. Less than six feet away, in horror she watched as Bertram stood up over Vincent's unmoving form. Bertram stared down at Vincent's body for a moment, then brushed himself off and, after a quick, furtive look up and down the road, never sparing a glance to the wooded area where Jane remained still as a stone, he mounted his horse and rode off.

His voice thick, Asher finished, "She went to him once Bertram was gone, but he was dead. Bertram broke his neck." He glanced over at the pages his grandmother had laid down on the table while he was speaking. "I think she must have been half mad with grief and terror and even she admits she doesn't know what she was thinking at the time. She had just seen her husband murdered before her very eyes. But one thing was very clear to her: no one would believe her if she named Bertram as Vincent's killer and so she did the only thing she could at the time, she took Vincent's ring and wrote down everything she saw and heard that night." He smiled crookedly, unaware of how much he looked like his dead father in that moment. "She suspected she was pregnant, and if she had any lucid thoughts at all that night, it was that she had to protect her unborn baby. She writes that one day her son would avenge his father." A bittersweet expression flickered across his face. "From the beginning she was certain I would be a boy." Soberly, he added, "She planned for the day she could tell me the truth and I could take my rightful place, but she was determined to say nothing until I was a grown man. The last thing she wanted was for her child to become a pawn of the Beverleys. She admits she lived in terror that they would find out who I really was and that my grandfather and then later my uncle would swoop down and tear me away from her." His eyes cold, he ended, "Which would most likely be followed by the news of my unexpected demise."

Heavily, Mrs. Manley said, "But she died before she could tell you any of it. . . ."

"Yes," John said miserably, "and she hid the evidence where my father found it after all these years and used it to blackmail Ormsby."

Mrs. Manley leaned forward and said urgently, "Do not judge your father, John. He *was* taking the proof to London and you must believe that he would have done the right thing in the end."

Asher nodded, his face kind as he looked at his half brother. "You bear no blame for what Denning did. And grandmother is right: in the end, he would have done the right thing—he even says so in his letter."

"Perhaps . . . it is just so . . . incredible—all of it." John sighed. "But at least we now know the truth."

"But not all of it," Asher muttered. Fixing a grim look on his grandmother, he said, "Isn't there something you'd like to add? Something you've known all along?"

Their eyes locked. "Was it such a terrible crime?" she asked quietly. "Who did it hurt?"

"What are you talking about?" John demanded with a frown, glancing from his grandmother to Asher.

"That there never was a Lieutenant Cordell," Asher said bluntly.

Juliana's eyes widened and John stared.

Mrs. Manley sighed and looked away. "Well, actually there was a Lieutenant Cordell and everything you ever heard about him was perfectly true . . . except for the fact that your mother married him. We made that up." Her eyes came back to Asher. "I couldn't think of anything else to do." Her gaze dropped and, looking every one of her seventy-five years, she said sadly, "I couldn't believe it. My sweet, respectable daughter. Pregnant and unmarried and no husband in sight and she stubbornly refused to name the father." Her expression thoughtful, she continued, "She'd always been such a biddable child and while she had been popular amongst the young gentlemen in the neighborhood, it never crossed my mind that there had been anything between her and Vincent—or that they planned a secret marriage. I realize now that their very avoidance of each other was a definite sign that something was going on between them." She half smiled and glanced at Juliana. "I racked my brains trying to figure out who the father of her child was—I even wondered briefly if your father wasn't the culprit. There had been a time when he paid her a great deal of attention. But then your mother swam into his orbit and his heart was lost."

"Well, thank goodness for that!" Juliana said. Interjecting a light note, she glanced impishly at Asher. "I would not like you as a brother at all." Her gaze went back to Mrs. Manley. "But what did you do," she asked, "once she told you she was pregnant?"

Mrs. Manley gave a shamed little laugh. "I'm embarrassed to admit that I berated her like the commonest fishwife! I was furious and for the only time in my life, I threw a most unseemly fit. And then I calmed down and thought about the best way to protect her and the child. The only solution was to find her a husband—not a real one." She shrugged. "She would not name the father and she was equally adamant that she would not countenance a hastily arranged marriage with some impecunious gentlemen who, for a price, was willing to overlook his bride's expanding belly. And since she would not identify the father, my hands were tied." She sighed. "We argued—horrible, hurtful arguments. But eventually I agreed with her that the less people who knew the truth, the less likely any story we put forth would unravel. A fictitious husband was the only solution." A faraway look in her eyes, she went on, "Once that was decided, I immediately packed us off to East Riding, to Hornsea, a small village on the coast. I deliberately picked a place where we didn't know a soul in the area and I rented us a secluded property not far from Hornsea. I felt that hidden away there she could have the baby in secret. And then I set about finding a husband to give her child a name . . . and respectability."

"How did you find Cordell?" Asher asked.

Her fingers gently caressing Jane's letter, Mrs. Manley answered, "I don't remember exactly how I learned about him, but we had not been in East Riding more than a few days, when on a trip to the village, I heard his name and learned of his recent death. Some discreet inquiries gave me all I needed to know about the poor young man. He had been gone for years and was the last of his family. The Cordells had been a member of the gentry, a respectable family but with no lands or fortune or estate to complicate things." She took a deep breath. "Having chosen Cordell, I wrote right away to several friends and neighbors that Jane, after a whirlwind courtship, had married a lieutenant in the Navy and that I intended to remain in Cornwall with her until her husband returned from sea. Later I wrote that Jane was thrilled to find she was with child and then later that my poor daughter had been widowed." She smiled. "When Asher arrived, only Jane and I knew that he was full term and not the seven months' child we claimed." She made a face. "If anyone had bothered to check dates or places or had looked for proof that a marriage had actually taken place, our little charade would have come tumbling down around our ears. But there was no reason for anyone to question the story we put forth . . . and we never set foot in East Riding again."

"You took a risk," Asher said slowly.

"I didn't have a choice! I wasn't about to have my daughter branded a harlot and a slut—or have my grandson labeled a bastard," Mrs. Manley said fiercely. "What we did hurt no one."

Across the table from him, Juliana reached for one of his hands. Softly, she said, "She's right, you know."

His lips twisted. "Do you know, I suspected that there was something smoky about mother's marriage to Cordell? And I was fairly certain that I was illegitimate."

His grandmother nodded. "I worried that you might. You always were an astute child."

Looking stunned, John said, "I can hardly take it all in. *You* are the Marquis of Ormsby! And Ormsby . . ." His gaze flew to Asher and apologetically, he said, "I'm sorry I cannot think of him as anything else."

"I think it will take time for all of us to become accustomed to the changes," Asher murmured, not certain how he felt about becoming Lord Ormsby himself—and all that it entailed. He glanced around the pleasant garden, the sturdy farmhouse that was his home and thought of the grandeur of Ormsby Place and for a moment he knew precisely how Juliana had felt about leaving Rosevale.

"But what are we to do now?" John asked, interrupting Asher's thoughts. "We have not only uncovered evidence that Ormsby murdered his brother . . . your father, but he murdered my father as well. We may not have an eyewitness to my father's murder, but from everything we have before us, including my father's own letter, there is no question of Ormsby's guilt in both deaths." John ran an agitated hand through his thick hair. "And there's the title . . . you are the rightful heir to the title and all that goes with it."

Asher nodded thoughtfully. "Establishing my right to the title will have to be placed before the courts in London, but as for Ormsby . . ." Something moved behind his eyes that made his wife and grandmother look anxiously at each other.

Oblivious to the undercurrents, John said, "Well, I think we should tell the squire and the vicar and the constable right away. This matter has been kept secret long enough." His mouth tightened and he said harshly, "There is good reason to move swiftly—if my father had spoken out, he would still be alive today. Ormsby knows that the evidence exists and until his perfidious acts become known, Asher you are in danger." John's hand clenched into a fist. "Before he can harm anyone else, I want that scoundrel punished. It's time, nay past time, that he was held up for all to see as the reprehensible murderer he is. Let us ride right now, before another moment is lost, to the squire's and tell him everything."

John's words pulled Asher from the cold, dark place where he had retreated. Forcing himself to concentrate on the matter at hand, Asher agreed. "Yes," he said. "That sounds like an excellent start." A hard smile curled his lips. "It is indeed time for . . . my uncle to reap what he has sown."

The two men arose and prepared to leave. Mrs. Manley and Juliana exchanged a helpless glance and, fearful of what Asher might do when left to his own devices, Juliana leaped to her feet and cried, "Wait!"

Both men looked at her. Her jaw set determinedly, her eyes fixed on Asher, Juliana demanded, "I want to know what you intend to do to Ormsby."

Asher smiled innocently. "Why, nothing at all."

"Don't lie to me!" Juliana fairly shouted. "You have been acting strange ever since your stepfather was murdered." She looked to Mrs. Manley, seeking support.

Wearily, Mrs. Manley said, "Juliana and I have discussed your manner of late—we are convinced that you are planning revenge against Ormsby."

The shake of his head didn't surprise them—they expected

him to deny it. And his calm, "I had been planning to murder him," confirmed every fear they held. "But those plans were made," he added softly, "when I thought that Denning's murder was the only one to lay at his door. . . ." An odd expression crossed his face. "Now I discover that he also murdered my father," he said quietly, "and that has changed my mind about killing him."

Confused, Juliana sank to her chair. "What do mean? I would think that your father's murder would have made your desire to kill him even stronger."

"I cannot believe my ears!" John declared, clearly taken aback. "You were planning on killing Ormsby?"

Asher nodded. "Yes, I did indeed plan to kill him." Casually, he confessed, "In fact, I'd planned to do it tonight. Shoot the bastard right between the eyes."

"But you're not, er, planning to do that now?" John inquired with fascinated horror.

"No. Killing him is too easy."

His grandmother studied him with narrowed eyes. "But you're not going to simply let matters take their course, are you?"

"Oh, but I am," Asher answered without hesitation, almost as surprised as everyone else by that decision.

At Mrs. Manley's and Juliana's disbelieving expressions, he said, "He is going to die anyway—whether by my hand or hanged at Newgate for the murder of Denning, as well as that of my father. I find the notion of him swinging from the scaffold at Newgate before a jeering crowd very, *very* appealing."

"And you will be satisfied with that?" Mrs. Manley asked, skepticism apparent in her voice and her face.

Asher took a deep breath. "Would I prefer to be the one who ends his life? Yes, I would, but I want you to stop and consider as I have the man we know as the Marquis of Ormsby. Consider the great wealth at his fingertips, his colossal pride and his vaulted position amongst the *ton*. He possesses all of those things simply because he is the Marquis of Ormsby." A tiger's lethal smile crossed his face. "Now think of him with all of that stripped away. Picture him standing before all those lofty members of the *ton* . . . with each and every one of them knowing him for the murderer and usurper he is. . . ." The cobalt blue eyes bright and hard, he added, "Shorn of everything that ever meant anything to him, he will be humiliated and shamed before the world." He leaned forward, his expression intent. "Think about it—everything he ever wanted, everything that ever mattered to him vanished. All of it, the title, his position in society, the wealth he coveted long before he killed my father, all will have been stripped from his grasping hands and given to . . . me." The tiger's smile widened. "Yes, I could kill him and his life would end in an instant, but contemplate what happens if I hold my hand. . . . If I forsake the quick pleasure of killing him, the rest of his days, right up until the moment he is hanged, will be tormenting hour after hour of shame and disgrace. Former friends and acquaintances will look at him with scorn and contempt, he will become a creature held in aversion and viewed with revulsion by everyone."

A hushed silence fell when Asher stopped speaking, his spellbound listeners seeing vividly in their own minds, the fitting and ignominious fate Bertram would suffer for his crimes—if Asher did not kill him. And slowly, one by one, they began to nod.

Asher straightened and took a deep breath. "And now," he said with remarkable coolness, "I think that John and I should call upon the squire."

It was late when Asher returned to Fox Hollow, but he wasn't surprised to see either the lights of the house gleaming through the darkness or his grandmother sitting on a russet and green sofa beside Juliana in the front parlor. They looked, he thought, as tired and drained as he felt.

Smiling faintly at the pair of them, he said, "Brace yourself for the devilish firestorm that is about to break over our heads."

Taking a heavy overstuffed chair across from them, he said, "The vicar was visiting when we arrived at the squire's, and so Birrel was there when John and I showed Ripley the ring and mother's letter and Denning's as well." Asher made a face. "There was an unholy uproar when they realized what they were reading and nothing would do but that the constable and oh, Christ, a half dozen other people"—he glanced at Juliana—"including your father and Caswell be sent for and told the truth." He ran his hand wearily over his face. "John and I plan to ride to London tomorrow and lay the evidence before the courts. As for the other—even as I sit here before you, accompanied by the squire and a few other gentlemen, the constable is on his way to arrest Bertram for the murder of Denning and my father." His jaw clenched. "Bertram's descent into hell has begun."

The moment Baker announced to Ormsby that the constable and the squire and several gentlemen were standing in his entryway demanding to see him, he'd known the reason for their unexpected visit. Carefully he put down the book he'd been reading in his study and, his face expressionless, he said, "Show them in."

The days since he'd killed Denning had slid by uneventfully for Ormsby. When he'd first returned from shooting Denning, he'd considered running, packing his bags and taking what gold and valuables he could lay his hands on before anyone knew what he was about. Despite the war, he knew he could make it to the continent and once there disappear into the tumultuous upheaval Napoleon had created in Europe. Who knew? He might even prosper.

But in the end, even though he was signing his death warrant, he could not bring himself to leave behind all the glory that was Ormsby Place. He was Ormsby and by God, he would die Ormsby!

He'd expected the constable's visit several days ago, but as time had passed, the faintest flicker of hope had bloomed in his breast. Jane's damning letter had remained hidden, a secret for thirty years. What was to say that Denning hadn't hidden it and the ring somewhere where they wouldn't be found for another thirty years? It was obvious that there had been nothing on Denning to incriminate him, else the constable would have appeared at Ormsby Place within hours of Denning's death. Only Jane's letter or something from Denning connected him to the murders and unless they were discovered, he had no fear of being exposed. As time passed, he wondered if it was possible that he had been incredibly lucky and had gotten away with murder a second time. The news that the constable was here told him that his luck had just run out. . . .

Getting up from where he had been sitting, he walked over to the massive gilt and walnut desk and sat down behind it. He looked around the elegant room, pride washing through him. Ruin faced him, but he had no regrets. No, he had no regrets, he thought ruthlessly, and if he had a second chance, he'd kill Vincent again in an instant. . . . His lips tightened. And find that bitch, Jane, and strangle her.

I should have, he realized bitterly, killed Asher instead of going after Denning. Denning would have guessed who killed his stepson, but money would have kept him quiet . . . at least for a while. With Asher dead and Denning kept in check for the moment, he'd have had time to find the letter and the ring. Once those were in his possession, Denning would die and he would be safe. But no, I killed the wrong man first, he thought, angry and disgusted with himself. And now I have to pay for that mistake. An ugly expression contorted his face. And Vincent's brat will reap the rewards. Like acid that knowledge ate at him. If only I could have killed Asher, he thought venomously, and made certain that *he* never lived long enough to dare call himself the Marquis of Ormsby. . . .

Hearing the sounds of approaching footsteps, Bertram

stiffened. Time had run out and he opened the middle drawer of the desk. His gaze ran lovingly over the superb silver en-graved dueling pistol lying there.

Baker tapped on the door, and picking up the pistol, Ormsby said calmly, "Come in."

Epilogue

"I don't have to go with her to Sherbrook Hall, you know," Asher said casually to Juliana one hot August morning almost a year to the day that Bertram had killed himself. "John could act as her escort. It doesn't have to be me." When Juliana looked unimpressed, he added almost desperately, "I don't think I should leave you and Vincent alone."

Almost as one, Juliana and Asher looked down at the sleeping infant lying in her arms. Ignoring the actions of most ladies of her station, Juliana had eschewed a wet nurse and had just finished nursing Vincent herself. Her son, she was convinced, was undoubtedly the most beautiful baby in all of England and Asher heartily agreed.

At nearly three months of age, Vincent, named for his paternal grandfather, was clearly Asher's son. He had inherited his father's black hair and olive skin and though the color of his eyes was not yet definite, odds were they'd be the same cobalt blue of Asher's. Vincent had been a big baby at birth and it was obvious he would grow into a tall man, his height coming from both parents. There were some hints of Juliana in her son's features; something about the shape of the face and the nose reminded Asher besottedly of his wife.

Every time Asher looked down at that small body, a wave of love so fierce and powerful swept through him that he almost trembled from the force of it. His eyes slid to Juliana's face and he felt that same elemental emotion flood through him. His wife. His son.

They were in their grand suite of rooms at Ormsby Place and though they had lived in the magnificent mansion since the previous fall, Asher still wasn't certain that he didn't prefer Fox Hollow. Wasn't so certain that becoming the Marquis of Ormsby was quite the wonderful thing everyone thought it was.

When Juliana only cocked a brow at his complaints about escorting his grandmother to Sherbrook Hall, he muttered, "I don't know why grandmother has to go visit Mrs. Sherbrook this summer. She just saw her last year. It's bloody inconvenient, I can tell you, to be away from you and the baby right now."

Juliana laughed at him. "Darling, your son and heir will not miss you for the few days you will be gone."

"And you? Will you miss me?" he asked thickly, thinking she was even more desirable since the arrival of their child, her curves more lush and pronounced. And just to his liking, he thought as his gaze skimmed over her tall, voluptuous form, the low cut bodice of her pale yellow gown giving him an enticing glimpse of those soft, heavy globes he had kissed and fondled last night.

Heat and need simmered through him and for the briefest second he was almost jealous of Vincent's position against her breast. Then his son blinked open sleepy eyes, burped, stuck a pudgy fist into his mouth and promptly fell back asleep. Asher and Juliana exchanged proud looks—just as if Vincent had done something remarkable.

There was a tap on the door and at Juliana's, "Yes?" Mrs. Rivers opened the door and peeked around the frame. At Juliana's welcoming smile she walked the remainder of the way into the room.

"I see our little man is asleep," she said, her eyes resting on Vincent's small body. "Shall I take him to the nursery now?"

No one doted on Vincent more than Juliana's old nursemaid—except perhaps his grandmother, Mrs. Manley, and though Mrs. Rivers was not officially his nursemaid, Juliana had hired a younger, well-qualified woman for the job— Mrs. Rivers spent a great deal of time in the nursery. She never passed up the chance to get her hands on Vincent and this morning was no exception.

Juliana pressed a kiss to her son's pink cheek and handed the sleeping infant to Mrs. Rivers.

When they were alone again, a glint in his eye, Asher said, "I believe we were discussing whether or not you would miss me while I am gone this week. . . ."

Juliana stood up and wound her arms around his neck. Brushing his lips with her own, she murmured, "I will, indeed, my love, and long every day for your return."

His arms tightened around her and he said thickly, "You do know that I love you more than anything on this earth, don't you?"

She smiled softly. "And I, you." But when he would have taken their embrace a step further, she wiggled from his grasp. Laughing at him, she escaped his advance, and said, "But no matter how much I shall miss you, you *are* going to escort your grandmother to Sherbrook Hall tomorrow and you will just have to meet Mrs. Sherbrook's son and daughter-in-law, after all."

Asher scowled.

Her eyes dancing, she said, "Oh, Asher, it is only for a few days and you know how much your grandmother enjoys introducing you as her grandson, the Marquis of Ormsby."

A rueful smile curved his lips. It was true. Of all of them, his grandmother took the most delight in his changed circumstances and never tired of calling him by his title, Lord Ormsby.

Once the news of Jane and Vincent's marriage and all the rest of it became public, the "devilish firestorm" that Asher predicted had indeed exploded over them. In drawing rooms, taverns and coffeehouses all across England, only the continuing war with Napoleon took precedence over the astonishing developments that had taken place at Ormsby Place and the revelation of Asher's true identity.

The first few months had been the worst, but Asher wondered morosely if the time would ever come when he or Juliana could walk into a room full of people and wouldn't immediately become the cynosure of all eyes—and the subject of every whispered conversation. Probably not.

It was a peculiar position for him. He had never hungered after a title of any sort, had never yearned for great wealth—only enough to keep his family secure and comfortable—and now he had both. Not just any title, but that of a marquis. And not just any fortune, but the vast wealth of the Ormsby estates. And all the responsibilities that went with it. . . . Sometimes he woke up at night terrified by the thought of all the people that were dependent upon him, all those people whose livelihoods depended upon his whims and decisions. . . . But then he'd remind himself that he'd kept his family safe and he'd damn well do the same for the Ormsby people. At least this time, he'd think as he fell back to sleep, a smile curving his lips, I won't have to steal the money to bring everyone safely to shore.

His position secure, his wife at his side and his healthy son sleeping soundly in the nursery, Asher was a happy man—except for the fact that his grandmother had badgered him into escorting her to Sherbrook Hall.

Did he really think that Marcus or Isabel would identify him as the man who had kidnapped her and stolen a vital memo from the safe at Sherbrook Hall two years ago? No, but simply on principle, he wasn't easy about it either and he'd be bloody well glad when the trip was behind him.

Despite all his reservations, the trip and his overnight stay at Sherbrook Hall went well. The elder Mrs. Sherbrook was every bit as charming as he remembered; Sherbrook Hall itself a comfortable and elegant home, and Marcus and Isabel

Sherbrook were exceedingly gracious hosts. Isabel was expecting another child in October and looked very much like a plump little pouter pigeon in her high-waisted muslin gown when they were introduced.

In those first tense moments when he met Marcus and Isabel he was half prepared for Isabel to shrink back and exclaim, *"You!"* But that didn't happen and he settled down to enjoy his grandmother's friends. He spent a few enjoyable hours with Marcus inspecting some of the foals that had been born that spring and expressed an interest in purchasing one or two when they were weaned. He even enjoyed the antics of Marcus and Isabel's year-old daughter, Emma, as the adults sat in a shady part of the garden and chatted that afternoon. Emma had learned to walk only the previous month and, watching her toddling here and there, Asher wondered if Vincent would be walking at the same age.

For reasons that escaped him, Emma took a liking to him and gazed up at him with adoring, big golden brown eyes she'd inherited from her mother. Instead of the fire-bright hair of her mother, a mop of inky black curls covered her head and kept tumbling over her forehead. Asher couldn't help tweaking one particularly impudent curl when she leaned confidingly against his leg and ogled him. Her nursemaid came to carry her away and she cried and clung to Asher's lower leg, refusing to let go. Smiling, he gently removed her little fingers and murmured, "Yes, yes, I know it's a tragedy, poppet, and I apologize, but I'm afraid you'll have to let go. It is my leg and I am afraid I am rather fond of it."

At his words, Isabel started and looked at him. His tone and his words stirred some memory, but she could not call it to mind. She shrugged and dismissed the incident, but still it nagged at her and several times during dinner she found herself listening intently to his voice, trying to pin down that elusive memory.

Asher was aware of her sudden interest in him, but he could not think of what he had done to disturb the polite tenor of the visit. One of the reasons he made it a point never to return to a scene of any of his previous, uh, escapades, was to avoid the remote possibility of being unmasked. Isabel had not seen his face, but he had spoken to her, he thought warily. Had his voice triggered a memory? Christ! He hoped not. Catching her eye on him once again, he reminded himself that it was impossible that she would connect the Marquis of Ormsby with the man who had abducted her two years ago. Tomorrow, and his departure, he decided uneasily, could not come soon enough.

Naturally, the topic of his dramatic inheritance of the title came up during the visit. It was after dinner when they were scattered around the charming rose and cream front parlor, the gentlemen enjoying brandy, the ladies teas. Putting down her delicate china cup, the elder Mrs. Sherbrook said, "It is so odd to think that when I met you last year, you were just plain Mr. Cordell and now you are the Marquis of Ormsby! It is a very good thing that your uncle killed himself and you and your family didn't have to have the whole sordid tale dragged before the magistrates."

Asher shrugged. He still had mixed feelings about Bertram's cowardly escape from public humiliation, but in the main, and with the passage of time, he tended to side with Mrs. Sherbrook's opinion. Sometimes, guilt struck him that he had not avenged his father, but it was difficult, he admitted, to harbor vengeful thoughts about a dead man—especially when his death, in some respects, righted a terrible wrong. Would he have preferred to see Bertram shamed? Probably, but these days, content in his life with a wife he adored and son who was the center of his universe, he found it difficult to dwell on what he could not change. He was a happy man, and a happy man had no business brooding over vermin like Bertram.

"I agree with my mother-in-law and think it a very good thing that horrid man killed himself," Isabel said firmly. Her eyes kind as they rested on Asher, she added, "It is a wonder that he didn't murder you, too."

"I have little doubt that he would have put a dagger in my liver if he'd had the chance," Asher replied, "but fortunately I managed not to oblige him."

Isabel's eyes narrowed. Now where had she heard the phrase or something similar? The idea that she had met Lord Ormsby previously crossed her mind. But when? Where? It was a puzzlement.

She said as much to Marcus that night in her bedroom. Seated at her dressing table, her glorious red gold hair spilling down her back, she spun around on the green satin stool and looked at him where he lounged against one of the bedposts watching her.

"I have the most uncanny feeling that I have met him before. Is that possible?" Thinking that being pregnant agreed with his wife, even if she complained of looking like a sow ready for market, Marcus wasn't interested in Lord Ormsby, but he followed her lead, and said, "Well, certainly not as Lord Ormsby. He only came into the title recently. I don't recall ever meeting him when he was Mr. Cordell."

"I know, but it is very strange. . . ." Her eyes narrowed and she gasped as a memory popped into her mind. She'd never forgotten a moment of that terrifying time when she had been abducted and held captive two years ago and she finally realized why there was something familiar about Lord Ormsby.

"What is it?" Marcus asked, his gray eyes alert.

Isabel laughed. "I am so silly! My 'gentleman' called me 'poppet' once during my captivity and said something about liking his liver and not wanting me to put a dagger in it. When Lord Ormsby called Emma 'poppet' this afternoon and tonight said something similar about his liver, *that's* why I thought he sounded familiar." She half flushed. "How embarrassing! To even consider for a moment any connection between my abductor and Lord Ormsby is the height of folly. I feel a perfect fool."

Marcus smiled and, walking over to her, pulled her up

from her seat. "Do you know, I am tired of talking about Lord Ormsby. I would much rather go to bed with my wife."

She beamed at him and, brushing her lips against his, said, "And I would much rather have you make love to me. . . ."

With the prospect of his departure looming large, Asher was relaxed the next morning as he prepared to leave for Ormsby. His grandmother was comfortably ensconced in her suite of rooms; he'd been a dutiful grandson and been affable to her friends and now he was eager to return to his wife and son.

He had taken his leave of his hosts, kissed his grandmother good-bye and was on the point of escaping when Marcus exclaimed, "By Jupiter! I've forgotten to give you those copies of the pedigrees I had my secretary write up last night on those two fillies you're interested in. Come along to my study and I can give them to you now before you leave."

While Marcus looked for the papers on his desk, Asher glanced around the room and, seeing a vibrant portrait of Isabel hanging on the wall, he said absently, "I see that you have removed the Stubbs."

Finding the papers he sought, Marcus looked up and said, "Yes, since the Stubbs was of her horse, Tempest, Isabel wanted it in her office." He grinned. "But in exchange for giving it up, I insisted she sit for Lawrence." Handing Asher the pedigrees, he said, "I find I much prefer looking at my wife's lovely face than that of her horse."

Asher laughed and, taking the papers from him, he placed them inside his jacket. Together the two men walked to the front of the house and a few moments later, Asher drove away. Sherbrook Hall and the events that had taken place there receded from his mind. His thoughts were on his wife and the Ormsby diamonds he had once thought to steal. The Ormsby diamonds that one could claim had brought him and Juliana together. He grinned. Upon his return home, he had a mind to see Juliana wear the Ormsby diamonds . . . and nothing else. . . .

* * *

Back in his study, Marcus went to the portrait of Isabel and moved it aside to place the original of pedigrees inside the safe behind the portrait. He was in the process of replacing Isabel's portrait when he suddenly stiffened. Forcing himself to complete the task, he stepped away from the portrait.

Frowning, Marcus stared at the gilt-edged portrait of his wife, not really seeing it. Isabel's portrait had been hanging here for the last year and a half. And before that the portrait of Tempest. So how did a man he had never met before, a man Marcus was certain had never stepped foot inside of Sherbrook Hall before, know that Tempest's picture had once hung here?

Isabel's laughing confession of last night flashed through his mind. There was, Marcus realized wryly, one explanation for Isabel's sensation of familiarity and Ormsby knowing of the change of portraits. He winced. He'd be the first to admit that it was an outlandish explanation, at that! But it held together. Isabel's gentleman, the same who had called her "poppet," had been inside this very room two years ago—the audacious fellow had had to move Tempest's portrait to get to the safe hidden behind it and what lay inside. . . . Marcus took a deep breath and shook his head. Now he was the one being silly. The Marquis of Ormsby, Isabel's gentleman, the brazen thief who had stolen the memo and given it to Roxbury, one and the same? *Preposterous!*